CHAOS IN THE BLINK OF AN EYE

PART NINE:
YAHWEH'S REMNANT

AWARD-WINNING
END TIMES SERIES BY
PATRICK HIGGINS

CHAOS IN THE BLINK OF AN EYE:
PART NINE – YAHWEH'S REMNANT
COPYRIGHT © 2024 PATRICK HIGGINS

All rights reserved under International and Pan-American copyright conventions. No part of this book may be reproduced, stored in a retrieval system, or transmitted in any form, electronic, mechanical, or other means, now known or hereafter, without written permission of the author. Address all inquiries to the author.
All scripture quotations are taken from the Holy Bible, New International Version (NIV)
© 1973, 1978, 1984 by International Bible Society.

Library of Congress
Cataloging in Publication Data
Paperback ISBN: 9798990727205

Published by
www.ForHisGloryProductionCompany.com

Publisher's note: This is a work of fiction. All names, characters, organizations, and incidents portrayed in this novel are the product of the author's imagination or are used fictitiously. Any resemblance to actual persons, living or dead, or events is entirely coincidental.

Manufactured in the United States of America.

Once completed, there will be 10 installments. Look for the ninth installment of the series to be available for pre-release in September 2023.

Prologue...

"After this I looked, and I saw in heaven the temple—that is, the tabernacle of the covenant law—and it was opened. Out of the temple came the seven angels with the seven plagues.

"They were dressed in clean, shining linen and wore golden sashes around their chests. Then one of the four living creatures gave to the seven angels seven golden bowls filled with the wrath of God, who lives for ever and ever.

"And the temple was filled with smoke from the glory of God and from his power, and no one could enter the temple until the seven plagues of the seven angels were completed.'" (Revelation 15:5-8).

PATRICK HIGGINS
Main Characters:

Brian Mulrooney – late 30s –Mulrooney was at Michigan Stadium with his childhood friend, Justin Schroeder, to watch the Ohio State-Michigan football game, when Schroeder suddenly disappeared along with thousands of others.

Tamika Moseley – 30 – Head nurse at safe house number one, who lost her two sons, Jamal and Dante, and mother, Ruth Ferguson, on the day of the Rapture.

Charles Calloway – mid 40's – Calloway was inside Tamika Moseley's cab when his colleague, Richard Figueroa, suddenly vanished while sitting in the back seat next to him. It didn't take long for Calloway to piece things together and realize it was the Rapture of the Church, and that he had been left behind.

Clayton Holmes and Travis Hartings – Co-founders the *End Times Salvation Movement*.

Tom Dunleavey – 65 – Former Catholic priest who tried consoling Brian Mulrooney the day after the disappearances. After both men had similar dreams for three straight nights, it ultimately led to Tom's leaving the Catholic church.

Dick and Sarah Mulrooney – Married for more than 30 years, the solid relationship they always had was showing small cracks in the dam, after their son Brian converted to Christianity and distanced himself from the Catholic church.

Doctor Lee Kim – Lead IT man for the website www.LASRglobal.org, and all other *End Times Salvation Movement* IT operations.

Jacquelyn Swindell Mulrooney – early 30s – Lost her husband at Michigan Stadium when he was killed by an object that fell from the sky, after a plane collided with a Goodyear blimp hovering above the stadium. Swindell also lost the child in her womb at that time.

Jefferson Danforth – 60 - Former President of the United States of America. His first wife, Melissa, was killed on board Air Force One when it was blown out of the sky. Jefferson later remarried his former White House chef, Amy Wong. Both are living in hiding at safe house number one in Chadds Ford, Pennsylvania.

Salvador Romanero – 33 – As the world mourned the loss of more than a billion people—either by death or disappearance—Satan raised up the young lawyer from Spain as his main agent in human form. No one knew it yet, but the young phenom was about to take the world completely by storm and become the unchallenged leader of the world…

Doctor Meera Singh – early 50s – *ETSM* Doctor at safe house number one, in Chadds Ford, Pennsylvania.

Joaquim Guzman – 16 – Married to Leticia, who was the first -to give birth at safe house number one, when she was only 12. Joaquim accepted the child as his own when he married Leticia. His parents were taken in the Rapture while working at the Kennett Square farm before it was turned into a safe house.

Julio and Marta Gonzalez – Julio (34) and Marta (32) were the parents of Leticia Guzman. Julio had owned a successful construction business in Providence, Rhode Island, before relocating to safe house number one with his family. He was one of two construction foremen on site.

Tony Pearsall – (39) – Construction worker from Nevada. He was one of the first to be invited to safe house number one and as a construction foreman.

Hana Patel – Late 20s – The first woman to give birth, post Rapture. Her husband Yogesh died after humiliating Salvador Romanero in a jam-packed arena in Dubai, with the whole world watching. He was later killed in the Philippines for his faith. Hana recently came to faith in Christ and is living in hiding with her daughter Cristiana.

Yasamin Dabiri – Late 20s – When the parents of the fourth child to be born, post Rapture, were killed for not naming their son, "Salvador", Yasamin was ultimately granted full custody of the boy.

Benjamin Shapiro – (68) – Benjamin was Salvador Romanero's personal physician, before his spiritual conversion.

1

CHADDS FORD PENNSYLVANIA

TOM DUNLEAVEY BLINKED HIS eyes a few times, grimaced in pain, then coughed into his right hand. The center of his chest ached like he'd had another mild heart attack.

Even with his limited knowledge of Heaven, he knew enough to know he wasn't there now. For one thing, it was pitch dark. Darkness and pain were two things he knew he would never encounter in Paradise.

And because of what Christ did for him on the cross, Dunleavey knew he wasn't in hell, praise be to God.

That meant he was still in the fallout shelter buried beneath safe house number one. The force from the blast that struck the property had apparently knocked him out. As for how long he was unconscious, the former Catholic priest didn't know. All he knew was that he was amazed that he had survived the blast, even if just barely.

What woke Tom wasn't the pain racking his body. It was the voice of Yahweh's third angelic messenger flying high above, making his final bold proclamation, at least publicly.

Said he, "If anyone worships the beast and his image and receives a mark on his forehead or upon his hand, they, too, will drink the wine of God's fury, which has been poured full strength into the cup of his wrath. They will be tormented with burning sulfur in the presence of the holy angels and of the Lamb.

"And the smoke of their torment will rise for ever and ever. There will be no rest day or night for those who worship the beast and its image, or for anyone who receives the mark of its name."

Because the fallout shelter was virtually soundproof, the sound of the bomb being dropped on them was mostly muffled, until just before it made impact. But Tom heard every ear-splitting word of the angel's warning, loud and clear, as if the angel was down there with him. It was remarkable.

He wondered if Brian was still alive. If he was, he, too, would have no doubt heard the Voice. *One way to find out...*

Tom turned on the small LED flashlight he brought underground with him. He pointed it at the glass partition on the hatch a few feet above his face. Not surprisingly, it was covered with dirt.

But he didn't need this visual to remind him that much of the foundation had shifted. Before losing consciousness, his pod had shifted too. He thought for certain that the earth would swallow him whole.

That was the last thing he remembered. Now that he was alert, it very much felt like the foundation of his body had shifted as well, like it had been jarred apart. He felt woozy and lightheaded. His body still trembled, and his ears still throbbed unlike any other time in his life.

Dunleavey placed the small flashlight in his mouth and gripped it with his teeth, then slowly opened the pod using both hands. He was surprised he had the strength to do it, with his on and off chest pains.

To make matters even worse, his right hip felt like it had been thrown out of place, so it took even longer to climb out of the pod.

He took the flashlight out of his mouth and aimed it at Brian's pod. The light exposed a blizzard of dust in the air. Before the strike, their pods were level. It looked as if Brian's pod had also shifted at a 25-degree angle, tilting away from Tom's pod. But at least it was still intact.

Four of the twelve pods were badly damaged. They lay on the dirt-covered floor, which had seeped in through several holes in the walls, that were breached shortly after impact.

Tom held on to the wall with his free hand, taking very small steps, so he wouldn't slip and fall on what he feared was a dislocated hip.

If the vibrant pulse did this kind of damage 30 feet beneath the earth's surface, he didn't need to venture aboveground to be convinced that Salvador Romanero had succeeded in destroying the property.

Tom silently thanked God for allowing his brothers and sisters in Christ to evacuate the property beforehand. Had they not, they all would have been killed.

"Brian? Are you still alive?" Not getting a reply from his friend, he trudged ever so gingerly through several inches of dirt, with a severe limp. Each step was a new lesson in pain. It stabbed at the center of his chest. The thick dust in the air made it difficult for him to breathe.

It took a while, but he finally managed to pry open Brian's pod. He asked again, "Brian, are you still alive?" Tom heard faint grunting.

Mulrooney was also awakened by the Voice. He briefly opened his eyes before closing them again. It hurt too much to keep them open. The bright flashlight piercing the darkness only made it worse.

He coughed a few times, then spoke in hushed tones, in case officials were above ground using ground penetrating radar listening for signs of dissident life. "Yes, but I'm not sure for how much longer. It feels like I have triple pneumonia now, if there was such a thing. It's like my lungs have collapsed in on me. How about you?"

Relief flooded Tom's soul just hearing Brian's voice. The last thing he wanted was to go through this alone. "What can I say? Guess I feel like anyone surviving a bomb being dropped on him would feel. My body's still pulsating. My right hip feels dislocated, and I'm sure I had another mild heart attack. I honestly don't know how I was able to climb out of my pod."

Through heavy wheezing, Mulrooney said, "Wish there was something I could do for you, brother, but I can barely raise my hands. Ever since my bed shifted, my right lung's been killing me. I'm even weaker now than I was before Charles carried me here. I've never felt this way before. How long have we been down here?"

Tom shrugged his shoulders. "Your guess is as good as mine." He shone the flashlight on the half-full intravenous bag. "I'm no doctor, but if your IV drip lasts for six hours, like Meera said, that would mean we've been down here for three hours, unless it stopped dripping. But since it's battery-operated, I don't think it malfunctioned."

The dust quickly invaded Brian's pod. He became short of breath. He coughed loudly a few times without bothering to cover his mouth. He didn't have the strength to. "Do you see my inhaler? I remember clutching it in my left hand just before impact. That's all I remember…"

Tom searched the floor of Brian's pod with the flashlight. Locating his inhaler, he stretched his left arm as far as it would go, thankful that it was just enough, and snatched it up.

He dusted it off with his sweatshirt, put it in Brian's mouth, then waited for him to take a deep inhale before pressing on it. In his weakened condition, Tom knew his friend didn't have the strength to do it himself.

Brian nodded his thanks to Tom, without opening his eyes. "What do we do now?"

Tom shrugged in the darkness. "We wait to be rescued. What other choice do we have?"

Brian coughed loudly again, sending spittle in all directions. "I'm not sure I'll still be alive when they arrive."

Tom gulped back fear. "Hang in there, brother. They'll come for us as soon as they can. They won't leave us behind…" It took every ounce of strength Dunleavey possessed to try to sound optimistic. But he, too, felt like he was dying.

"I'll try," Brian said, through more heavy wheezing, "but I'm not thrilled about waiting in a darkened safety shelter, for however long it will take, with no one here to care for us. The sensation of feeling like I'm being buried alive, is so much worse than the physical pain I feel."

Tom became terrified by Brian's comment. He could almost feel the darkened walls closing in on him. A shiver ran through him. "I wish you hadn't just said that…"

Brian replied, "Sorry, brother, but I feel like I'm dying."

Another strong dose of panic swelled through Tom, as thoughts of being trapped underground alone ate away on his insides.

He tried opening the escape hatch, but since so much of the earth had shifted from the impact, even if he was at full strength, he still wouldn't be able to push it open. Then again, there was nothing above ground Tom wanted to see. Their beloved safe house was no doubt in tatters. "Just do your best to hang in there a little longer, brother."

"I'll try," Brian said, with another prolonged cough.

Tom replaced Brian's half-full intravenous bag with a full one, in case he couldn't check on him for a while. He shone the light at a table that had food and water on it. The pain he felt from reaching over to grab a bottle of water and a pack of peanut butter crackers for his friend was excruciating. But he muffled his grunts for Brian's sake.

With his hands still shaking, it took a while before Tom was able to remove a cracker from the pack. "Eat this, Brian."

"I don't feel like eating, brother. I'm too weak…"

Tom persisted. "Please try. I'll feed you." He put it in Brian's mouth. He chewed it several times before he could swallow.

Tom tried feeding him another cracker. Brian said softly, weakly, "Maybe later. For now, can you read the end of Revelation to me?"

Tom had offered the last rites to many dying Catholics over the years. Now that they were standing on the precipice of eternity, was this his way of saying goodbye? It very much sounded like a dying man's last wish.

He plucked Brian's Bible off the floor, opened it to Revelation 20, and read the last three chapters of the Holy Bible to his brother in Christ.

When Dunleavey was finished, he said, "It may not appear that way to us now, but that's what we have to look forward to! Soon, we'll never suffer again." Tom said, trying to muster the courage to say it with conviction, not sure if he had succeeded or not.

"Amen." Brian coughed loudly again. The thick dust in the air was more than his lungs could bear. Finally, he said, "Thank You, Jesus, for dying for a sinner like me…"

It was faint, but Tom heard him clearly. "Amen." Dunleavey felt another sharp pain in his chest. "I need to lie down again. I'll check on you later if I can…"

Brian tried smiling in reply, but even that hurt too much. "I love you, brother. How can I ever repay you for what you did for me? I couldn't imagine being trapped down here alone."

Tom looked around in the darkness. "If our roles were reversed, you would have done the same for me, right?"

Brian nodded yes. There were no tears this time. Whatever tears they had left in their bruised and damaged bodies were shed in Brian's bedroom, before they were taken to this place. They had both fought the Good fight. They were resigned to the fact that this very well might be the end for them.

Before closing Brian's pod, Tom checked to make sure his asthma inhaler was still in his right hand. He gently attached the nasal cannula in Brian's nostrils and turned on the portable oxygen concentrator, to hopefully stabilize his erratic breathing. "I'll leave these crackers and water beside you; in case you feel like eating them later."

"Thanks, brother…"

"Rest now, Brian. Either I'll see you again in Kennett Square, or in Heaven, whichever comes first.'"

Brian whispered a soft, "Amen…"

At that, Tom closed his hatch to prevent more dust from filling Brian's pod. Even he was having difficulty breathing at this point.

Brian pulled the blanket all the way up to his neck. He started having one of those life-flashing-before-his-eyes moments. He wondered who he would see when he opened his eyes again, Jacquelyn or Justin Schroeder.

It had only been a few hours—as far as he could tell anyway—yet he already missed his wife so much. She was the best thing that ever happened to him. But even if they were rescued, as much as he wanted more time with Jacquelyn, and with everyone else, he didn't feel he had the strength to be of service to anyone.

If this was his graduation day, at least he would finally be free of his pain and suffering. *Thy will be done, Lord…*

Tom grabbed a few packs of peanut butter crackers and a half dozen bottles of water for himself, then slowly made his way back to his pod.

With his free hand, he leaned on three still-standing pods along the way for balance. He shrieked in agony every step of the way from the pain in his hip. He was also wheezing from the unhealthy amount of dust he had inhaled on the walk to and from Brian's pod.

Before closing the hatch, he sat on his curved bed, and tried eating a few crackers, but it hurt too much to swallow. He closed his pod with one hand, and covered his heart with his other hand, as if trying to prevent it from popping out of his chest.

Tom didn't feel that he would have the strength to open the hatch again, if it ever came to that. And with no way of opening the main safe shelter door, the only thing he could do at this point would be to check on Brian, when he could, and wait for his friends to come to their rescue.

He would also pray that he and Brian wouldn't be overcome with claustrophobia before help arrived. "Lord, if this will be our final resting place, please spare us the sensation of feeling like we're being buried alive."

He laid back on his pod and attached the nasal cannula to his nostrils and turned on the portable oxygen concentrator, to hopefully help stop the wheezing. If the oxygen ran out before help arrived, and he went Home to be with the Lord, that would be even better.

"Now I know how Jim Simonton felt before he died..."

Tom was referring to his best friend in the *End Times Salvation Movement*, before Pastor Simonton was killed. It happened when their safe house in the Upper Peninsula of Michigan was targeted and destroyed, as a target practice of sorts before the global quake.

No one had helped Tom grow in the scriptures more than he did. "Looks like I'll be seeing you again soon, brother..."

2

NEW BABYLON – THE FOLLOWING DAY

FIVE MINUTES BEFORE THE Pope went live, billions of mobile devices pinged and vibrated, planetwide, alerting users that he was about to give his daily address.

The global push alert took complete control of each smartphone, interrupting everything his followers were doing, leaving all mark takers with no choice but to listen. Even volume control would be monitored by global community officials. So, if anyone silenced their phones before the Pope was finished speaking, the owner of that phone would be investigated.

Now that the Pope was back in New Babylon, one of his daily rituals would be to read, then expound on, the only recognized source of truth for humankind, from start to finish, throughout the year.

The video was enabled, allowing his scores of listeners a limited view of his religious palace, which, in many ways, was superior to his residence at the Vatican, before it came crumbling down in the global quake.

"Greetings global citizens!" the Pope declared, wearing the same futuristic clerical robe he wore before the first failed peace treaty signing with Israel. "Before we begin our first reading in the New World Book of Life, I'd like to update you on the global bombing campaign that took place twenty-four hours ago.

"I'm proud to report that the hundreds of thousands of enemy camps that were marked with a seal, and targeted, were all destroyed. This includes all subterranean locations. I'm sure many who were hiding underground felt we might never find them, that they had somehow outsmarted us.

The Pope smirked. "They were wrong. Whatever hope they clung to was dashed, when they felt the full brunt of two-ton laser guided, bunker buster missiles being dropped on them, from fifty-thousand feet above the earth's surface. These bombs effortlessly penetrated the ground, destroying all enemy bunkers, including those situated more than a hundred feet beneath the earth's surface."

The expression on his face turned somber, with a trace of anger. "All in all, it was a successful campaign. Unfortunately, all dissidents at some of the targeted locations managed to escape beforehand, including all children. Either someone tipped them off in advance, or it was a complete dereliction of duty on behalf of the guards sent to those locations yesterday. All were executed."

The Pope took a moment to let his words settle in their minds, then went on, "Even as I speak, the hunt continues for our precious children who were taken to these combatant hideouts against their will. We must rescue them before their impressionable minds become even more corrupted by the enemy!

"For those of you who have dissident family members living in hiding, and you want to know if they're still among the living, including children and teenagers, kindly forward any images and recordings you may have to any location administering the mark.

"If they haven't already been, they will be added to the international database, then linked to the billions of microfliers blanketing the skies above, patrolling the planet. Naturally, if they are still alive, you'll receive a thousand-dollar credit for aiding in their capture, once they have been located.

"Without getting into too much detail, let me just say that the microfliers are the smallest-ever human-made flying structures known to man. Some of them are roughly the size of a grain of rice. All are GPS guided with pinhead-sized cameras and microphones, to record and even livestream as directed, making them the perfect spying tool!

"Needless to say, they have been an invaluable resource for us. You may not be able to see these miniature drones, but I assure you they're up there! Millions of dissidents have already been captured by them. But fear not, if you are an upstanding citizen in the global community, you have nothing to worry about."

The Pope paused for a moment, then grew somber again. "Many of you living close to the destroyed targets have suffered property damage. Some homes were destroyed beyond repair. Some of you have even lost friends and loved ones, by way of collateral damage. All were upright citizens. Please accept my heartfelt condolences.

"As promised, all damaged and destroyed homes will be repaired or rebuilt at no cost to you. And all burial expenses will be paid for by us, plus a predetermined amount will be given to the next of kin, for the pain and suffering this has caused you. I know this can never bring back your cherished loved ones. My hope is that you'll spend it in their honor. May their souls find peace in the loving arms of our lord and savior."

It was bizarre hearing him talking so clinically about the deaths of followers who were all killed at his hands. He very much sounded like a wartime politician, not a religious leader. His words sounded scripted and disingenuous. He didn't mention that hundreds of thousands of mark takers had died from heart attacks due to the bombing campaign.

He went on, "Due to an overwhelming demand for citizens wanting to receive the mark at the New Temple, in Jerusalem, we've decided to extend the free global internet deadline another six months. But until you receive the mark, your Wi-Fi signal will be nowhere near as strong as it is for those who have already received it.

"As an added extension of grace, even if you haven't yet taken the mark, free travel, hotel, and food vouchers will be made available to anyone wishing to travel to Israel for that purpose. These digital vouchers will be honored on all modes of transportation, whether you choose to travel by plane, train, boat, or by bus.

"Naturally, all seats will be available on a first-come first-serve basis. Upon landing at Ben Gurion International Airport, all air travelers will be taken to the New Temple in Jerusalem by ground transportation, at no cost to you. If you travel to Israel by sea, you will be met in Tel Aviv, then driven to the New Temple.

"Upon receiving the mark, all finances that were temporarily frozen on your now-expired global monetary cards, will be transferred into your global accounts. Once that happens, my hope is that you'll help reinvigorate the economy in Israel, by eating in restaurants, going to coffeehouses, visiting museums, and so forth.

"More importantly, it will give you all the chance to worship the dazzling statue of our most high lord and savior at the New Temple. If you haven't seen it up close and personal, you're missing out!

"For all who aspire to make this pilgrimage, you must wait until after we are finished with our reading before looking to obtain seats to the Holy Land. No business will be conducted anywhere on the planet during any of our daily readings.

"For those of you not wishing to go to Jerusalem, tolls will remain suspended on all toll roads in your area, until the new deadline expires. But you must always carry your mobile devices, so you can display the digital code confirming your identity whenever you are out in public.

"Anyone caught attempting to travel without a digital voucher will be dealt with swiftly. Make no mistake, this will be the last Wi-Fi extension that will ever be offered. It won't happen again."

The Pope folded his hands on the desk before him. "Despite the many setbacks we've faced, at the hands of the God of Israel, the economy is starting to show signs of growth. Hundreds of billions of dollars in payments have already been dispersed into your global accounts, for helping us find Christian dissidents. This opportunity has been extremely profitable for so many of you.

"Another surefire sign that the global economy is growing is that multitudes of citizens on every continent are relocating to New Babylon. You should see it! No other city in all human history can compare to it! It's so majestic in scope, to gaze upon it makes Dubai, before the Rapture, look merely like one of its neighborhoods.

"While Jerusalem will always be the spiritual city, New Babylon will remain the global city of commerce, and the business model for the rest of the world to follow. This is what all cities will look like within the next five to ten years! Only on a much smaller scale.

"Even after the city was destroyed in the global quake, our most high lord and savior masterfully rebuilt it from the ground up, and in record time. He also cleansed and sterilized it from the plague of frogs that the God of Israel had sent there a while back.

"It truly is the perfect place to live! It's with that in mind that I wish to announce that everyone flying to Israel, to receive the mark and pay homage to the statue, will also be flown to New Babylon, to take a four-hour bus tour of the city, before you head back to your home countries.

"Needless to say, trillions of dollars will be needed to accomplish our lofty goal in reconstructing the world to look like New Babylon. Up until now, the billions of dollars that have already been dispersed, have been tax free to all receivers.

"Naturally, this isn't sustainable. It's with that in mind that I wish to announce that, from this day forward, a flat tax of thirty-three-point-three-three percent will come straight off the top on all future earnings.

"So, what this means is, for every thousand dollars you receive for capturing dissidents, or from any other mode of income you earn, six hundred and sixty six dollars will be dispersed into your global accounts.

"A nice round number, don't you think? But the good news is, with all transactions now being documented on a purchase-by-purchase basis, I'm happy to report that none of you will ever have to file taxes again."

The Pope paused to let his words settle in the minds of his listeners. "Finally, I hereby declare that from this point forward, Salvador

Romanero will no longer be addressed as 'miracle maker', but as 'most high lord and savior' or 'Supreme See'. As for me, I will now be referred to as the new 'miracle maker' and 'Holy See'. So, make sure you adjust your vocabularies accordingly.

"Let us pray, 'Oh Lucifer, creator of the universe and everything in it, as we gather to read your word, please receive our dedication as a form of worship to you. We eagerly await the day when you make plain to us your power and majesty. May we all be blessed in your name.'

"Now, if you will open your bibles, we can begin." The Pope declared, "In the beginning..."

After reading the 31 verses in chapter one, he expounded on only one verse, verse 26, "'Then God said, 'Let us make mankind in our image, in our likeness, so that they may rule over the fish in the sea and the birds in the sky, over the livestock and all the wild animals, and over all the creatures that move along the ground.'"

A glow formed on his face, as He explained to the billions listening, "The 'us' in the text refers to Lucifer the creator, Salvador Romanero as the Christ, and me as the Holy Prophet."

At that, the reading came to a close.

WHAT THE POPE DIDN'T say about the New World Book of Life, was that it was nothing more than a condensed version of the Roman Catholic Bible. Much of it was merely copying sections of the Old and New Testament, then modernizing them, with Romanero being inserted in Christ's place, and with the Pope being the king's prophet and healer.

Only the creation parts of Genesis, the book of Psalms and Proverbs, and the prophetic parts of the Old Testament were added. There wasn't a trace of Jewish or Church history in it. Genealogies were also scrubbed.

Not only were the four gospels rewritten, but all applicable references formerly made about Christ Jesus now centered solely on the Supreme See himself, Salvador Romanero.

All scriptures regarding the Holy Spirit now pointed to the Holy See, the Pope. All scriptures regarding Yahweh now pointed to Satan, also known as Lucifer. And all verses which pointed to Satan as being evil, were now aimed directly at Israel's God.

Parts of the Book of Revelation were also sprinkled in, to help readers better determine the future, including the Supreme See's death, and his resurrection at the hands of the Holy See, as the world watched, before the

Supreme See declared himself to be god, which started the exodus of Jews leaving their beloved Israel.

It was written so simply that children could easily understand it, which was entirely the point.

With all things "Jesus" having already been removed from their young minds and hearts, and subsequently replaced by him, without having access to any other references to challenge this new bible, all children exposed to it would have no choice but to accept it as truth...

What the Pope didn't say about the six-month Wi-Fi extension, was that it was partly being done in the hopes of detaining Christian dissidents who escaped the global bombing campaign. If they tried reaching out to family members to let them know they were still alive, they would be linked to their IP addresses and apprehended.

The diabolical duo identified in the Bible as the Antichrist and False Prophet, were eager to tie up all loose ends with the Christians who had managed to escape, so they could commence their assault on the Jews.

Another unspoken reason for the extension was that the flu was spreading globally. Since many who had already ingested the chip were also complaining about flu symptoms themselves, it wasn't good for business.

But the biggest reason for the six-month extension was that many recipients of the mark were starting to complain about painful sores appearing on their bodies. The first complaint was recorded a few hours after the global dissident bombing campaign had ended.

Within hours, hospitals were flooded with patients, all complaining about the very same thing. The fact that only mark takers had these sores on their bodies couldn't be brushed aside as coincidental. If word ever got out, it would be the worst kind of publicity they could ever want.

Instead of warning the public that it could happen to them as a possible side effect, or even as an allergic reaction, hospital workers were ordered to keep a lid on it until they had a better understanding of what was happening.

What made it so difficult was that doctors and nurses also had these harmful sores on their bodies. Even so, they were prohibited from discussing it with anyone, until they found a way to bring it under control.

Hopefully soon. Until then, the important thing for now was that everyone received the mark...

3

THE INSTANT THE POPE was finished reading for the day, millions were frantic trying to secure their seats online to the Holy Land. They prayed to Lucifer, asking him to open this door for them, so they could receive the mark, and worship the statue of their beloved lord and savior.

Had it not been for this free offer, the majority now hoping to secure seats wouldn't have bothered wasting their time. Most citizens on the planet had already lost everything among the constant chaos rocking the world, including all their savings.

In that light, upon receiving the mark, there would be nothing to transfer over from their global monetary cards.

Without the food and hotel vouchers also being offered, even if they were fortunate to reserve seats for travel, most wouldn't be able to take the trip. They were grateful for what would be a much-needed vacation.

A big part of stabilizing the economy was jumpstarting the floundering transportation industry. That could only happen by filling seats on airplanes, trains, buses, and boats, and filling hotel rooms and tables at restaurants that had been mostly empty since the Rapture.

Workers in these industries were thrilled to finally have jobs to go back to. They couldn't wait to put the extreme recession conditions they felt trapped in for far too long behind them. Hopefully for good!

With signs of steady growth all around them, business owners in other industries were eager to see the prosperity impact them as well. They were grateful that all indicators were pointing in that direction.

Everyone was thrilled that their two leaders were working so hard to stabilize the global economy. But with trillions of dollars in past debts wiped out in this final reset of sorts, including all bankruptcies, and with a healthy global tax base soon to be filling their invisible global coffers, it wouldn't have taken a genius to fix it.

While most mark takers weren't thrilled that 33.33% would come straight off the top, on all future earnings, the thought of no longer filing tax returns appealed to them.

All in all, they were encouraged by the Pope's address, even if it was riddled with lies. The first lie he told was by saying all compliant citizens in the global community didn't have to be concerned about the blizzard of microfliers hovering above.

In truth, everyone was being surveilled around the clock. With all transactions being controlled by the two global leaders, credit scores were nowhere near as important as they were in the past. It all came down to social scoring.

This sort of system had been used in many countries before the Rapture. But since governments didn't have total control back then, they tried ensnaring their citizens by scoring them on what purchases were made, what books they read, who they followed on social media, what chat rooms they entered, who they voted for, and so on.

All those things combined determined an individual's social credit score, which was adjusted in real time. Just like private credit scores, social scores could go up or down, depending on an individual's actions and behavior on any given day, whether good or bad.

In this new global scoring system, social credit scores were assigned based on an individual's behavior, loyalty, dedication, and obedience to both the Supreme See and the Holy See.

With the Word of God and all things "Jesus" having been banned for quite some time, the two global leaders weren't concerned about what their followers read or what purchases they made.

But what would lower their social scores in this draconian society, could be something as innocuous as lowering the volume when the Pope was speaking or turning off their mobile devices. When that happened, the owner of that phone would have their social score lowered.

Those with high social credit scores had their job profiles boosted, thus increasing their chances of finding higher paying jobs in the new global economy. They also received discounts on utility bills, faster internet speeds, better interest rates at banks, and on and on.

Those with low social scores had higher utility bills, slower internet speeds, higher interest rates at banks, plus they were banned from the best schools and universities that were slowly but surely reopening.

Salvador Romanero loved being the unanimous leader of the world. He loved having absolute power. But what he wanted more than anything else was to be worshiped.

With millions taking the mark every day, there was a growing group of mark takers who wanted the benefit of the mark and the chip, but they didn't want to bow down to the statue, or address Romanero as the "Supreme See", or the Pope as the "Holy See".

To him, it was the most grievous sin any mark taker could ever commit. All mark takers not bowing down to him would receive the lowest social scores and would require stricter monitoring.

This group of mark takers who were previously dubbed as the "still on the fencers" were now being categorized as their "secular followers".

Tragically for them, whether they ultimately bowed down in worship to Salvador Romanero or not, by simply taking the mark, they were still on the same eternally condemned side as the figure they refused to worship.

All individuals securing seats to Israel over the next six months, would all have their social credit scores boosted, for their willingness to bow down to his likeness in worship. This would place them on the religious side, making this free vacation fully deserved.

Another lie the Pope had told was by calling the microfliers the perfect spying tool. That designation was reserved for the mark of the Beast. There wasn't a place on the planet their followers could go to avoid detection. The microfliers were certainly helpful, but even without them, the mark allowed them to always know where their followers were.

About the only thing it couldn't monitor was their dreams.

The next lie he told was that all children living in dissident hideouts had been taken there against their will. Nothing could be farther from the truth; they all went voluntarily.

The next lie he told was by promising that all cities would look like New Babylon within five to ten years! The Word of God was explicit that no city would be left standing a little more than three years from now, including New Babylon.

Five years from now, Christ will have already returned, and His Millennial Kingdom would already be firmly established…

MEGAN MCCALLISTER LISTENED TO the Pope's speech. Unlike most other mark takers, she wasn't comforted in the least by what she had heard. She first became aware of the massive bombing campaign, after receiving a text message 36 hours ago, warning about what would soon happen in her area.

The message stated that their location was situated close enough to the bombing target to possibly feel the ground shaking upon impact, but they were far enough away that they wouldn't have to worry about property damage.

Her wife, Rachel Stein, was also notified on that day.

A few minutes later, they both felt the ground shaking all around them. Their son, Zachary felt it too.

When the living room sofa stopped shaking, and the three of them were safe, Megan's next thought was about the $6K she stood to receive, for helping local authorities identify Christian dissidents.

What started the ball rolling in this regard was when two officers came to their apartment, to administer the mark to Megan and Rachel. Before proceeding, they asked the married couple to listen to a recording of what authorities believed was Dick Mulrooney's voice.

After positively confirming it was him, Megan then gave the names of five other dissidents she believed Dick was staying with—his wife, Sarah, his son, Brian, Brian's wife, Jacquelyn Mulrooney, Tamika Moseley, and Charles Calloway.

The two officers were mindful of the five of them. They did Megan a huge favor by assuring her that when they were captured, she would receive credit for all six dissidents, which would amount to $6K in her global account. At that, they both received the mark…

With the promise of those funds pending, for the first time in many months, Megan was able to look Rachel in the eye, knowing she would soon be contributing financially again. From that day forward, she thoroughly enjoyed spending time with her wife and son, Zachary.

Now that 36 hours had passed since the bombing, Megan no longer felt joyful. If the six dissidents were killed in the strike, why hadn't her global account been credited yet? She was told the funds would be available to her immediately, but she still hadn't received them.

Were they among the group the Pope had said escaped from their targeted locations? If so, did that mean she would have to wait until they were found again?

Megan had a foreboding that she would never receive what was promised to her. What angered her the most was that local authorities knew where they lived all along. Why couldn't they have arrested them before the global bombing campaign commenced? Had they only done that, Megan would already have the $6K in her account.

And what about the millions of dissidents the Pope said were captured by those microfliers? Had those commissions been promised to others, only to be taken off the table, like she felt had just happened to her? Wasn't Salvador Romanero supposed to be her savior?

Megan felt deceived by the one person she thought would never hurt her. If this was the new utopia her hero kept promising to his followers, she no longer wanted anything to do with it.

She was tired of waiting and hoping and trusting, all for nothing. She was only in her mid-30s, but the constant worrying had turned her hair almost completely gray. A severe depression once again set in. She saw no reason to keep living this crazy life.

Before going to bed for the night, Rachel said to Megan, "Why don't we go to Israel? Ever since we came to Pennsylvania, we haven't done a single thing. I'm sick and tired of being stuck indoors, always fearing for my life. It will be good for us to get away. Let's do it."

"If you feel like registering us, go ahead," Megan said, halfheartedly, "I'm not in the mood to go online."

Rachel kissed her wife hard on the lips. "I'll take care of it!"

Apparently, the Pope's offer had filled her with a new burst of excitement. It took a while, but Rachel finally succeeded in reserving three seats on a future flight to Israel.

She explained to her wife, "It's done! But since we already have the mark, we were placed on a waiting list and may have to wait five months before seats become available to us. But at least it's free, right?"

Megan replied, "Good job, honey." She didn't have the heart to share the many morbid thoughts running through her mind with her.

Rachel kissed Megan on the forehead. "Good night, my love."

Megan wasn't about to ruin her mood. "I'll be in in a while." With the last bit of wind sucked out of her sails, the only way she could see out of this mess was to follow in her younger sister Renate's footsteps and take her life too.

With a spirit of despair, helplessness and hopelessness choking the very life out of her, Megan sent a text message to her father: *Sorry to make you go through it again, Dad, but I don't know where else to turn or what else to do. I feel completely ruined. The only way I see out of it is by ending it all. At least I'll get to see Mom and Renate again.*

I don't have the heart to leave a farewell text message to Rachel. Can you please tell her for me? I hope she can forgive me. Hope you can too. All my love, Megan...

Megan went into the bedroom to check on her wife and Zachary one last time. She kissed them both on the forehead, then retreated to the kitchen. She opened the half-full bleach container, then added enough

Drano to do the trick. She sat on a chair, and shoved a plastic funnel down her throat as far as it would go.

The instant she tilted her head back, her cell phone started ringing. Megan knew it was her father. She ignored it, blinked away a few tears, closed her eyes, then poured so much of the liquid into the funnel that it spilled over onto her face, burning her eyes and nostrils, before trickling down the front of her neck.

Even if she had second thoughts, and tried pulling the funnel out of her mouth, it was jammed so far down her throat that it wouldn't have mattered. The damage was already done.

Megan fell hard to the kitchen floor with a loud thump, as the deadly concoction devoured her insides, inch by inch.

After calling his daughter three times, and getting no answer, Dylan McCallister called Rachel next.

The ringing of the phone woke her. She answered it quickly so it wouldn't wake Zachary. "Hello?"

"Rachel, it's Dylan McCallister. Can you please check on Megan for me?" The panic in his voice was alarming.

"Is everything okay, Mister McCallister?"

"I don't think so. Megan just texted me. It sounded like a suicide message. Is she with you now?"

Rachel glanced over at Megan's side of the bed. She panicked. "Hmm, no she isn't..." She raced out of the bedroom. She found her wife lying on the kitchen floor, her body convulsing, eyes rolled up, her mouth foaming.

Rachel screamed into the phone. "Oh, no, she drank bleach!"

Dylan shouted in a panic, "Call 9-1-1!"

By the time first responders arrived on the scene, Megan was already dead.

Rachel watched her wife's lifeless body being rolled away on a gurney, and thought to herself, *the chip may potentially cure cancer, but it certainly can't protect from suicide...*

Rachel was too numb to shed tears now. Suddenly left to raise her son alone, she, too, was on the brink of destruction...

She texted Megan's father. *She's gone. The paramedics just left with her body. I'm so sorry. I'll inform my parents in the morning that I'm coming home to Michigan. I'm done with Pennsylvania.*

I'll let you know when I'm back. I know you still haven't seen your grandson. When I feel up to it, let's make it happen. But it may be a while. I'm completely wrecked...

As it turned out, Megan McCallister got her wish to go to the same place as her mother and her kid sister, Renate. Only there would be no communication between them, no comforting one another, only eternal torment...

4

THREE DAYS AFTER THE GLOBAL BOMBING

TO SAY THAT THE Kennett Square safe house was filled to the brim with newcomers, would be putting it mildly. Three days ago, 500 residents had called it their home. Within 72 hours, that number had swollen to more than 4,000 souls living on the property.

Prior to the Rapture, Kennett Square, Pennsylvania was known as the "Mushroom Capital of the World". The rich soil on which billions of mushrooms had been grown, over several decades, now had thousands of Christian dissidents living 60-feet beneath the surface.

Despite the many preparations that had already been made, in anticipation of receiving many more believers, when Salvador Romanero moved the strike date up, it left those in charge with one less week to get organized. All surviving *ETSM* safe houses were faced with similar circumstances.

What made it so difficult at this particular location was that there wasn't a back entrance for newcomers to sneak in through, like at most others safe houses. All vehicles coming and going went through the main barn, which was the only building still standing on the property.

From there, the only way to access the subterranean shelter was by climbing down three separate 20-foot aluminum ladders, then walking through a tunnel that easily stretched a hundred yards, before ultimately reaching the steel door which led to the main gathering room.

With only one way in or out, up or down rather, it took a while to shuffle everyone underground in so little time.

Newborns and infants were lowered down the ladders in padded baskets. Grown-ups with special needs, those who were handicapped, or bedridden before being transported to Kennett Square, were lowered down either on the backs of other residents, or on hard plastic rescue beds. This presented quite a challenge for their handlers.

Seventy of the new residents were Messianic Jews, sent there by Jakob. When Romanero desecrated the New Temple, and declared himself to be God, it caused Jews to flee Israel by the thousands.

Suddenly, Yahweh's 144,000 sealed servants, to whom Jakob belonged, were being invited to speak in synagogues the world over.

As Jakob shared the soul-saving Gospel of Yeshua HaMashiach in local synagogues, what had sounded so utterly ridiculous to some of them all their lives, now made perfect sense to them.

So much so, that they left most of their belongings behind and relocated to Kennett Square. All were mildly shocked to see Benjamin Shapiro residing there. He felt a special kinship with his Jewish brothers and sisters, knowing they were all part of Yahweh's remnant.

When the Kennett Square farm officially became an *ETSM* property, more than three years ago, they were granted full access to the metal earth worms that Jefferson Danforth had designated for their organization, when he was still President.

They took full advantage of that equipment by digging twelve subterranean holes, all of which were the equivalent of two football fields. All were set apart from their present living space.

When the holes were dug, they brought the automatic bricklaying machine down to fortify all walls and ceilings, as workers connected the twelve massive size holes with corridors. Since there wasn't much other construction needed at that time, when the large equipment was shipped elsewhere, most of the workers left to help fortify those other locations.

Some of them were later destroyed in the global quake a little more than two years ago. The Kennett Square safe house also suffered substantial damage to the property. They also suffered many casualties—120 of the 300 residents living there perished in the global quake.

More than half of the livestock, chickens, fish and crops also fell victim that day. And more than half of the glass Mason jars storing the goods they had worked so hard to preserve, at the outset, were shattered.

On top of that, much of their farming equipment, and many of the aquatic fish tanks they were using to farm tilapia and catfish were destroyed. The main silo storing wheat and grain also collapsed to the ground. Thankfully, much of it was recovered and moved underground.

If there was one benefit that resulted from the quake, it marked the day that the Kennett Square safe house stopped producing food and dairy for the unconverted.

The farm owners, Eli and Susanna Yoder, had filed numerous property and equipment claims, already knowing their insurance provider wouldn't recompensate them for their many losses. How could they pay their claims, when the company had filed for bankruptcy?

Married for more than 30 years, their children and grandchildren were all in Heaven. All were taken in the Rapture.

The reason the former Mennonites wanted to put it on the record was once the mark of the Beast was administered, and the economy steadily improved, with no funds to rebuild or replace damaged and destroyed farm equipment, local government officials wouldn't expect them to resume producing crops and dairy for the main public.

They took it one step further by tearing down all buildings which had stood for nearly a century, to hopefully remove all suspicion that they would ever produce food again.

Only the main barn was left. But it hadn't been maintained since the global quake. For all intents and purposes, the Yoders were insolvent.

But unbeknownst to the Powers that Be, 60 feet beneath the surface, thousands of Christians were still being fed each day.

Julio Gonzalez Sr., Tony Pearsall, and Shamus Harmon were placed in charge of various construction projects. After all, the three men were integral in reconstructing safe house number one.

Harmon hailed from Boston. His family of eight was reduced to five on the day of the Rapture, when he lost a son, two daughters, and four grandchildren. All were in the construction business.

After slowly piecing things together in his mind, Shamus repented of his sinful lifestyle, then turned to Christ with all his heart and mind. His wife, daughter, and his two sons, who were also left behind, repented a few days later, before ultimately becoming Chadds Ford residents.

Julio Gonzalez moved his family from Providence, Rhode Island, to safe house number one, when his teenage daughter was pregnant with her first child. Leticia gave birth to his grandson, Julio Jr., a few months later. Not too long after that, his wife, Marta, gave birth to his daughter, Ruth.

And with Leticia soon to give birth again, the Gonzalez family would essentially double since moving underground.

Whereas Tony Pearsall relocated from New Mexico to Chadds Ford alone, Gonzalez and Harmon both felt blessed to have their wives and children with them. They were two of only a handful of "complete families" residing at safe house number one.

After taking a little time to scout the location to get a lay of the land, the first decision they made was to designate five of the twelve vacant areas as sleeping areas. Each would have military cot-style beds placed inside. Men were assigned to one area. Women were assigned to another.

With 70 percent of the inhabitants being children and toddlers, they would occupy three areas. There were some exceptions. A handful of fathers had left their unbelieving wives, taking their children with them. Those toddlers would remain with their fathers for the time being.

Until they had time to get better organized, even married couples were being separated for the time being.

The biggest problem they faced was that some of the corridors leading to those areas had partially collapsed in the global quake. They needed to be refortified. But with so many people now living on the property, they had no choice but to risk it. Their present living space could barely house 500 residents, let alone 4,000!

Gonzalez, Pearsall, Harmon, and their crew of 20, spent the past three days reinforcing all corridors leading to all twelve holes. They frequently exchanged, "What are you gonna do," glances at each other, knowing all their hard work would soon be destroyed again.

There wasn't a chance they could make this residence resemble anything close to what Chadds Ford residents had grown accustomed to. But at least they were being productive, instead of sitting around sulking over their plight like everyone else.

It had only been three days, and they still had a long way to go, but significant progress was being made all throughout the property.

Another group was placed in charge of setting up fish tanks and the hydroponics equipment that were brought in from Chadds Ford.

A group of four men from another destroyed safe house out near Harrisburg, were busy creating fire escape exits, which would also serve as escape routes, at each of the twelve areas, if the need ever arose.

The seven remaining spaces would be used as another hospital, a school for children and teenagers, a play area for the kids, and as an exercise area for the adults. One area would be used as a church and worship area.

One area would be used as a giant bathroom. It was still being filled with 200 porta potty toilets. The other hundred were being placed all throughout the subterranean space, according to need.

And lastly, one space would be used as a quarantine area.

The bathroom and quarantine areas would occupy the locations which were the farthest away from the main gathering area.

Once all twelve subterranean locations were functional, much of the space that they were presently occupying would be converted to a common living space. One section would be for married couples wanting a little privacy. Another one would be for parents with newborns.

This way, they wouldn't wake the rest of the married couples trying to sleep every time their child woke up crying for milk.

Only three areas of the present living space would remain intact. One was the kitchen. Since the proper exhaust units were already intact, it would remain where it was.

The second area was the underground farm, which housed cows and chickens for meat and dairy. It was also used for farming fish and growing crops hydroponically.

The third area was where they kept all storage. It was filled with the many essential items that Benjamin Shapiro had sent to them—including 5,000 military-style beds, 300 porta potty toilets, 100,000 asthma inhalers, and millions of face masks to this location alone.

With thousands of people now sharing this dingy hiding place, the face masks and inhalers would be desperately needed in the coming months. The rest of the space was filled with items transported from other safe houses. Since safe house number one was the closest *ETSM* location to Kennett Square, most of the things came from there, including many pints of blood, medicines, fish tanks, hydroponics equipment, and power generators.

Aside from diapers, bottles, toys, books, and clothing, and what little medicines they still had with them, displaced residents from other now-destroyed safe houses couldn't bring much else with them. They were too far away, and they only had so much space in their vehicles.

For most newcomers, being drearily connected in this dungeonlike location, like one big slab of outdated subterranean living space, represented a time warp on steroids to them.

They were already shell shocked and discombobulated, having barely escaped before their former safe houses were obliterated. Would they ever see the sky above in the next three years?

They feared the answer to this question was no. In that light, how could they not be depressed? This would take some getting used to.

As Jakob kept preaching in synagogues, no one in Kennett Square knew for certain how many more Jewish believers would be sent their way. They still had a thousand extra beds available for newcomers.

If they needed more underground space to accommodate thousands more, as time marched on, they could expand out in all directions, but it would have to be done the old-fashioned way, with shovels.

The fact that they were living beneath rich farmland was a blessing. With no pipes or electrical wires deterring them, just like the first time they started digging, a surveyor wouldn't be needed this time.

The Yoders had assured all newcomers that there would be enough grain and other necessities to last them until Christ returned. But if the next round of God's judgments did significant damage to their subterranean hideout, all could be lost...

BUT GOD'S CHILDREN WEREN'T the only ones living in subterranean dwelling spaces. More than a half billion unsaved individuals also retreated as far as they could go underground, before the global dissident bombing campaign commenced.

A large percentage of them were global community staffers and the world's elite. The wealthier among them lived in mansions, that were equipped with swimming pools, spas, full-sized gyms, and even bowling alleys and movie theaters. You name it, they had it!

They all heard the third angelic messenger making his final blood-curdling proclamation to humanity. The fact that they were 100 feet beneath the earth's surface mattered not. Up until two days ago, everyone heard the Voice with absolute precision.

When they didn't hear anything from them over the past 48 hours, they all sighed relief. Apparently, the judgments that the three angels kept warning about must not have applied to them.

The fact that they actually believed they had outsmarted the One who had sent them, was yet another proof of their spiritual blindness.

With the global flu quickly gripping the planet, most subterranean dwellers were determined to remain where they were, until things got better above ground, and the global flu was alleviated.

What made this easier for them was that the many essentials they needed were being delivered to their subterranean residences, by hazmat suit wearing individuals, just in case.

The delivery charges were quite steep, but the wealthy could still afford it, as could those on Romanero's and the Pope's staffs.

But even underground, the proof that they hadn't outwitted God, was when those painful sores started appearing on their bodies.

It started after the bombing campaign concluded. Even the wealthiest of the wealthy couldn't prevent it from happening...

5

PACIFIC OCEAN – DAY 4

DONALD JOHNSON, SERGEI IVANOV, and Analyn Tibayan were sailing southeast on Sergei's 30-foot motorized sailboat.

As much as Ivanov would have preferred to sail due east to California, then hitchhike cross country to Pennsylvania, something he always liked to do in his hippie days, there wasn't a chance that it would happen.

For one thing, the vast majority of the Golden State was no longer inhabitable. What wasn't destroyed in the global quake was wiped out in the tsunami, following the first meteor strike to rock the planet.

Even if California was still intact, and they could find a place to dock the boat, as Christian dissidents without the mark, they wouldn't last 10 minutes without being spotted by someone, or something, namely the microfliers always hovering above.

Since they didn't have the proper documentation to pass through the Panama Canal—namely the mark on their right hands or foreheads—which would have cut their trip in half, they were left with no other choice but to sail all the way down to the southernmost tip of South America, before ultimately heading north toward the United States.

Even barring God's impending bowl judgments, which would soon pummel the planet, Sergei didn't expect to arrive in New York for at least six months. Without God's providence leading the way, it would be a doomed voyage.

During daylight hours, Donald taught Bible prophecy to Sergei and Analyn. Though he seriously doubted there were many microfliers out patrolling the oceans of the world, he spoke very softly, just in case.

When Johnson first boarded Sergei's boat in Singapore, his reading glasses fell out of his shirt pocket. The right lens was badly scratched when he accidentally stepped on it. It made reading the Bible difficult in daylight hours, and impossible at night.

Now that the sun had just set, like they had done the past two nights, Sergei and Analyn took turns reading the Word aloud, so Donald could listen. In a frugal attempt to conserve the few remaining batteries they had on board, they only used one battery-operated lantern at night.

It was difficult even for the two of them to see the words on the pages, as they read Zechariah this night, from start to finish.

When they finished reading and praying, Analyn thought back to their study of Revelation earlier in the day. As a newcomer to the faith, most of what she had heard frightened her, like it did for most, after being exposed to it for the first time.

Despite the trauma of seeing her daughter, Juliana, being ripped out of her arms and swept away by the tsunami waves, along with her parents, this was the safest she had felt ever since that horrific moment took place. She asked Donald, "Ninong, have the bowl judgments begun?"

Donald was stretched out on the couch. This was infinitely better than being stuck in a container on a massive cargo ship, for seven weeks, like he was on the voyage from Jacksonville, Florida, to Singapore, with no windows to look out of, and no one to talk to.

But with the second and third bowl judgments looming, it was impossible to relax just knowing they were potentially in harm's way.

"Since the first bowl judgment will result in painful sores on the bodies of all who take the mark, now that we're isolated from the rest of society, it's impossible to say for sure.

"When we were in Manila, I didn't see anyone with them. Then again, I wasn't looking. I just wanted to find you and get back to the boat as quickly as possible. Did you see anyone with them?"

"No, I only saw the mark."

Donald scratched the lower part of his back. "Since we haven't heard from the flying angels in a few days, perhaps their aerial ministries have ended. If so, this may be the time for all mark takers to have those festering sores covering their bodies."

Sergei asked, "What about those who aren't saved, but who have yet to take it?"

Donald explained, "Scripture's clear it's intended only for those who have taken the mark. Perhaps it's God's final visual warning to the unconverted. I can almost hear Jesus shouting at them, 'Take the mark, and suffer the consequences.' With so many unexplainable things happening in the world, it should be easy for the eye for the unconverted to connect the dots, but even that won't stop them from taking it."

Sadness covered Donald's face. Having led so many souls astray, in his many years spreading Mormonism, including Analyn's late parents, he hated to think of anyone going to hell. "They will be too concerned with the here and now, and with feeding their families, then with the eternal destination of their souls. Even so, they'll take it willingly, so they'll all be without excuse."

Analyn sensed his sadness. A few short weeks ago, she was bound and determined to take the mark. She saw no other way out. Then God sent these two beautiful men to the Philippines to rescue her soul from destruction.

She had already suffered through the sting mark era. Had she taken the mark, chances were good that she would now be dealing with those festering sores on her body. She glanced up at the darkened ceiling, and uttered a soft, grateful, "Thank You," skyward to her Maker.

Donald rolled onto his side to face them. "It should go without saying that I'm much more concerned about the next bowl judgment..."

Neither Sergei nor Analyn needed Donald to expound on it. They both knew when the second angel poured out his bowl on the sea, it would turn into blood, and every living thing in the sea would die. The fact that they were out in the open waters didn't bode well for them.

Sergei constantly monitored the waves during daylight hours, knowing they wouldn't remain calm once the second bowl judgment was released. He was already bracing for it. "Another meteor?"

Donald replied, "That would be my guess. But since the Word says all living things in the seas would die, we must assume multiple meteors will be required this time, not to mention more global volcanic eruptions. One thing is certain, we'll know soon enough."

Sergei asked, "What about nuclear weapons?"

"I've thought about that. But since these are God's judgments, my guess is that He will use His creations to carry it all out. Man can take credit for inventing nuclear weaponry, but what we can't take credit for are hundreds of meteors falling out of the sky, or for volcanic eruptions.

"Bottom line: God doesn't need man's help to carry out His judgments. But chances are good that nuclear weapons will be used at some point, perhaps at the battle of Armageddon, which will involve millions of men and women. But I don't think they'll be used with the bowl judgments."

"If it will be multiple meteors," said Sergei, having already been through it once, "I don't want to be within five hundred miles of impact."

"A thousand miles even!" said Donald, shaking his head, knowing it was wishful thinking at best.

Ivanov gulped hard in the darkness, then brushed off a shiver. He still had nightmares about the first meteor strike. When it happened, a wealthy Thai couple had chartered his sailboat and hired him to be their captain, from Bangkok to Singapore.

When the tsunami waves came racing toward them, mere moments after the meteor struck the Pacific Ocean, they were close enough to feel its impact to the point of nearly capsizing on several occasions.

Thankfully, they were far enough away to be spared their lives.

In an ironic twist of fate—at least Sergei thought it was fate back then—the tsunami destroyed his apartment building in Bangkok, but not his sailboat. It became his new residence that day.

He wondered if the Thai couple were still alive. If so, did they take the mark? Were they saved? If they were, they would be reunited on the other side on the day of God's choosing. If not...

Sergei pushed that morbid thought out of his mind. "All we can do is prepare for what's still to come and pray for God's supernatural protection. Since we don't know when it will happen, we haven't a moment to waste."

Analyn gulped fearfully. "How can we prepare for it?"

Sergei answered the question, "Well, now that we're forced to take the long way to America, the bottled water may only last us for half the trip."

"So, what will we do?"

"Come daybreak, we'll fill all empty fuel barrels with sea water and let them soak in bleach for three days, to remove all faint traces of fuel from the steel barrels. After that, we'll dump them and refill them again with more seawater, for desalinization purposes."

In the past, Sergei would never have attempted to dump polluted water into the ocean. Even if he had been saved before the Rapture, it would have never even been a passing thought.

When it came to the world's oceans, he was a true environmentalist. He often volunteered his time to do his part to help keep them clean.

Now convinced the planet on which he lived really was disposable, and that God would soon make all things new, dumping it into the ocean was suddenly no big deal to him.

Donald was familiar with the desalinization process, but he wasn't quite sure how the process worked.

Sergei explained in layman's terms so they both could understand, "Essentially, desalination removes the salt from seawater using semipermeable membranes that allow the water to pass, but not the salt. These membranes are made of ultra-thin polyamide, which sometimes can be contaminated with bacteria. That's why the water must be treated."

Analyn asked Sergei, "Does it taste different than fresh water?"

Sergei nodded. "It's slightly different, because some of the minerals are removed during the desalination process. But it's not bad. I drank it many times. Did you know before the Rapture, there were more than twenty thousand desalinization plants in the world?"

Analyn and Donald both nodded no.

"Most countries in the Middle East depended on desalinated water for their daily consumption. For example, ninety percent of the drinking water in Kuwait came from desalinization plants. In the United Arab Emirates (UAE), nearly half the drinking water came from the ocean. Israel got thirty percent of its water that way, as did most island nations, Bahamas, Malta, and the Maldives to name a few."

Donald asked, "How about the U.S.?"

"Less than three percent. I'm sure it's much higher than that now. I'm sure most countries are desalinizing water now. After all, more than seventy percent of the earth was covered by water. This equates to twenty-four million cubic miles of this precious resource covering the globe. I'm sure countries are still fighting wars over it."

Sergei grimaced. "Soon it will be worthless for human consumption. Which is why we need to act quickly. Anything we have that holds liquid must be filled with seawater, even our empty water bottles. Desalinized water will be used for cooking and drinking only.

"The rest will be used for washing clothing, and for cleaning the boat. We can still bathe in the ocean for now. Soon we will no longer have that option. Let's just hope that my portable desalinization system lasts until we get to the States. I think I'm down to three replacement filters."

"What happens if we run out of filters?" asked Donald.

"I have a backup solar distiller that I have never used. We may have to use it at some point." Sergei looked at his dirty fingernails. "Another problem we have is fuel. We're running low, which means we'll need to keep relying on the wind to power us. But having our sails up during daylight hours will make it easier to be spotted by the enemy."

Analyn was frightened by what she saw in their eyes. She changed the direction of the conversation. "Ninong?"

"Yes, Analyn?"

"Can you tell us about the place we're going to?" This was a question she wanted to ask many times, but she wanted to wait until she knew for certain they were safely out of the Philippines. With Manila Bay three days behind them, and no land to be seen in any direction, she felt now would be the appropriate time to ask the question.

Up until now, Donald had tried his hardest to bottle up his thoughts and emotions about the Chadds Ford safe house, in case he never made it back there. Mindful of what would soon come, as sure as his salvation, in fact, it needed to remain that way for now. "Eager as I am to tell you all about safe house number one, let's wait and see if we survive the second bowl judgment. If we do, I'll tell you all about it. Fair enough?"

Analyn shivered at his words. "Okay, Ninong…"

6

JEFFERSON DANFORTH WAS STRETCHED out on a cot, in the subterranean living area, in Kennett Square, Pennsylvania. His eyes were closed, but he wasn't sleeping. How could he possibly sleep with all the commotion?

Grateful as he was to have survived the bombing—or was he?—with the constant flurry of activity going on all around him, to allow for the sudden rush of new inhabitants, it was a wonder the former President of the United States could sleep at all, let alone think.

So much had happened to him since his days living at the White House. As it was, this was his fourth safe house, and his third subterranean shelter, since Air Force One exploded in midair on that horrific day. He was supposed to be on the plane with his first wife, Melissa, when it crashed to the ground in a great ball of fire, essentially bringing his Presidency to an end.

The first two locations were similar in that both had offered him plenty of living space, including personal sleeping quarters, personal offices, and his own showers and toilets.

In the brief time he had spent at the first underground location, situated 50 miles west of Washington D.C., he was too emotional and too shell shocked to think straight about his sudden living conditions.

It was a dreadful time in his life, as he tried to come to grips with being a widower, being stripped of all power, and trying to adjust to living a subterranean existence at the same time.

He couldn't even go back to 1600 Pennsylvania Avenue to collect his personal belongings! What made it even worse was that he didn't have his family by his side to comfort him in his time of mourning and great loss.

Jefferson was also battling intense guilt knowing the bomb on board the plane was intended for him, not his first wife, Melissa. Yet she was the one who paid dearly for it with her own life, not him. Even more tragic, he was ever mindful of her eternal whereabouts.

It wasn't a cause for rejoicing.

And how did he honor Melissa's memory for essentially dying in his place, at least physically? By marrying Amy!

When Jefferson was transferred to the second subterranean hiding place, in Coeur d'Alene Idaho, he had access to the same technology he had at the Virginia location, situated 50 miles west of Washington D.C. But since he was sharing it with only a handful of people, it became a lonely place for him at times. Extremely lonely, as thoughts of his former life, namely the loss of his family, constantly invaded his brain.

That is, until he eventually fell in love with and married Amy Wong.

When the couple were relocated to safe house number one, it was like receiving manna from Heaven. Although they wore hoodies and ski masks whenever they left their cabin, at least they got to breathe fresh air through their nostrils and see the sky above them again. It had proven to be therapeutic for the Danforths.

Safe house number one was the place where Jefferson had found his smile again. By then, he had plenty of time to mourn the loss of his first wife. Being surrounded by fellow believers gave him the strength each day to carry on. He came to love that place just as much as Amy had. And seeing her so happy added to the overall contentment he felt.

Another thing he liked about Chadds Ford was that there was no protocol in place. Even though he was no longer President, since his fellow inhabitants in Idaho were all part of his previous administration, a protocol of sorts still existed between them.

But not in Chadds Ford. The Danforths were treated as equals to everyone else, never above them, just as they had both wanted. They never wanted to leave that wonderful place...

Now they were underground again sharing this crammed parcel of land with thousands of other believers. The way it was sectioned off so evenly, Jefferson felt like a sardine trapped in a can with thousands of other sardines. It was overwhelming to say the least.

Of the four hiding places, this one, by far, offered the greatest contrast to the massive mansion that had once stood so proudly on 1600 Pennsylvania Avenue, for more than two centuries, before it was destroyed in the global quake. The way the White House had collapsed to the ground, instantly killing former President Lois Cipriano and her wife, as they slept in bed, was sort of like a microcosm of his life now.

The old, unconverted Jefferson Danforth might have said something along the lines like, "Serves her right! She was never the rightful President anyway!" But now that he was a believer, that way of thinking was exchanged with a sadness in his heart knowing she would spend an eternity separated from God, in the worst place imaginable.

If ever there was an exact opposite of his prior living conditions as President of the United States, this place would surely hit the mark. It was so outside the realm of what his former life had been, which would explain the depression he felt. Being "temporarily" separated from his wife only made it worse for him.

Then again, the constant pressures that came with being the most powerful man on the planet, paled in comparison to the daily pressures common citizens had to cope with since the Rapture. He never felt this level of ongoing stress as President.

If there was one thing for which Jefferson was thankful, it's that the first two subterranean locations had allowed him to gradually prepare both mentally and psychologically for this major downgrade of sorts.

In truth, he didn't miss the many material things he recently had full access to at those other locations. But what he did miss was having his own personal sleeping quarters and bathroom. He would never have that kind of privacy again.

Had he been taken to this place first, he would have been fit to be tied by now, not to mention severely claustrophobic.

Jefferson couldn't remember a time in his adult life when he had so much free time on his hands to think. Whenever he could think clearly in this chaotic setting, his mind was usually focused on two things.

The first was on the glorious world to come. Clearly, there was nothing good to look forward to on this fallen planet. Each new tragedy caused him to long to be with his Savior even more.

The second thing on his mind, person rather, was Daniel Sullivan. Jefferson couldn't help but wonder if his former secret service agent had survived the latest mayhem to rock the planet.

If he was still alive, had there been any progress made in locating Tyler Stephenson? If so, was his former brother-in-law really a believer like Jefferson kept seeing in recurring dreams?

Even more importantly, had he found Jefferson's two children who had survived the Rapture, William and Janelle? His daughter Erica, son-in-law Ronald Whittingham, his granddaughter Rebecca, and the couple's unborn child, were all taken in the Rapture.

As of yet, since he no longer received daily briefings, like he had as President, all Danforth could do was wait and see. And keep praying that Sullivan had successfully located them, and the end result of their hopeful reunion would be the salvation of their souls.

That is, if they were still alive...

With his soul eternally secure in the loving arms of his Savior, the only other thing that gave Jefferson the slightest motivation to still want to be alive on this planet—aside from caring for Amy, and the rest of his brothers and sisters—were the souls of his two remaining children.

Other than that, with an eternity in Paradise awaiting him, what other reason could there be?

But if Tyler wasn't a believer, his hopes would be dashed...

Jacquelyn Mulrooney entered the men's section of the subterranean area, with baby Sarah on her left hip. Spotting Jefferson, she held up the SAT phone with her free right hand, signifying that he had a phone call.

Danforth sat up on the cot he was lying on. He couldn't remember seeing Jacquelyn looking so distraught. The poor woman looked as if she no longer had a pulse. He wanted to ask how she was holding up, but there was no need to. She looked like she was a breath away from coming apart at the seams. The not knowing if her husband was dead or still alive kept gnawing away at her. Not being able to mourn in private only made things worse.

"It's Daniel Sullivan," she said softly, sadly, unable to hold his stare.

Jefferson's heart rate quickened. On the one hand, he was thankful that his former secret service agent was still alive. He was also terrified. He took the phone from Jacquelyn. "Praise God, you're still alive!"

"Wish I could say the same about everyone else residing at you know where," Sullivan answered, referring to the subterranean safe house in Coeur d'Alene, Idaho.

Jefferson knew he was referring to his former National Security Adviser, Nelson Casanieves, his former Chief of Staff, Aaron Gillespie, his former military Joint Chief of Staff, William Messersmith, and Secret Service Agent Anthony Galiano. But he knew not to ask specific questions over the phone.

When the Danforths were relocated to Pennsylvania, the four men remained behind in Idaho, so they could make full use of the advanced technologies they had access to, which they used to patch into the global system, the facial recognition app, and many other top-secret government files.

Had it not been for those technologies, the *ETSM* would have never known that 500 of their locations had been targeted for destruction, which ultimately led to the majority of their properties being wiped out. The code name for the initial campaign was the "Montpelier Project".

They also wouldn't have known that Romanero had strategically moved the strike date up one week. Had they not had access to this crucial information, many more lives surely would have been lost...

Jefferson glanced up at Jacquelyn and baby Sarah, then asked his former secret service agent, "Do you have any other news for me?"

"I do…"

Jefferson wasn't sure what to make of his tone of voice. He brushed off a shiver, then braced himself. "Did you find him?" He knew not to mention Tyler Stephenson by name, just in case.

"Yes."

Jefferson sat as straight up on the cot as he could, using his free arm behind him to stabilize himself. His heart rate accelerated. "Is he with you now?"

Sullivan motioned for Tyler to answer the question for him. "Yes, I am!" This was the first time either man had spoken in more than 800 miles. They knew how much of a risk they were taking.

"Praise God!" Even among the mayhem, Jefferson's joy knew no bounds. He removed his reading glasses and massaged the bridge of his nose. He breathed warm air onto his glasses to fog them, then cleaned them using the bottom of his shirt. "And my kids?"

Agent Sullivan interjected, "Sir, I think it would be wise to refrain from asking any more questions until we arrive at your location. Then we can all speak freely."

Danforth silently chided himself for his carelessness. "Do you know where I am?" The last time they had communicated, he was still at safe house number one.

Sullivan answered, "I do. If everything goes well, expect to see us soon." At that, the call ended.

Jefferson practically jumped off the cot. He took a deep breath, tempered his excitement, and handed the phone back to Jacquelyn. "Amy and I are here for you no matter what." He almost said, "Hey there's still hope, right?" but he thought better of it.

Jacquelyn's lower lip quivered. The pain in her eyes was too much to bear. She spotted Charles Calloway in the men's area. She gave him the satellite phone where all messages were sent. "I can't be in charge of it now…"

"I understand." The faraway gaze on her face told Charles everything he needed to know. She was still consumed by grief and, therefore, incapable of performing even the simplest of tasks.

When she headed for the corridor connecting to the women's side, Charles said to Jefferson, "Poor woman. I struggle to find the right words to say to her."

"Same here," said Jefferson. After a lengthy pause, he said, "I do have good news to share. Sullivan found my brother-in-law. They're on their way here now."

"Wow! That is good news! What about your kids?"

"Still not sure. I didn't ask questions on the phone. The conversation was brief. Guess we'll know soon enough. But since Tyler's on his way here, that must mean he's a believer, like I saw in my dream."

"Amen!"

Sadness covered Jefferson's face. "I also received bad news. Sullivan told me the safe house in Idaho was destroyed. I lost four good friends who were former members of my administration, Nelson Casanieves, Aaron Gillespie, William Messersmith, and Secret Service Agent Anthony Galiano."

"Sorry for your loss. But at least we know where they are now, right?"

Danforth nodded. "Changing topics, how's the honeymoon going?" Charles and Meera were wed a few minutes after they arrived in Kennett Square. Vishnu and Yasamin Uddin were also wed at that time. The two couples had asked Jefferson to officiate their weddings.

"Hmm, let's see, well, ever since you married us, I haven't really seen my wife. She's even busier here than she was in Chadds Ford. When we do see each other, she's too exhausted to enjoy my company. Besides, even if she had free time, where can we go for privacy?"

"I know what you mean."

"Don't get me wrong, I knew what I signed up for. But we can't even sleep in the same bed, let alone hold each other at night. That's one of the reasons we decided to get married in the first place. So, I'd have to say it isn't off to a good start by any stretch of the imagination..."

Jefferson regretted his mock stab at humor. "I'm sure you'll get to spend quality time together before too long. Give it time..."

Calloway rubbed his scalp with his right hand, using all five fingers. "I'm doing my best. It hasn't even been a week, but I already feel trapped in this dungeon. Man, how I miss safe house number one."

"That makes two of us!" Jefferson glanced around to make sure Dick Mulrooney wasn't within ear shot. "Speaking of Chadds Ford, do you think Brian and Tom survived?"

Charles grimaced. "All I can say is, I was five miles away when the bomb struck the property. The van shook so violently, it felt like another violent earthquake. How much worse was it for the two of them? If they did survive, they should have enough food, water, meds and oxygen to hold them over until we can get to them."

Jefferson knew Charles was still bothered for leaving Brian and Tom behind, as he escaped to safety. "I hope someone checks on them soon."

"Me too." Charles closed his eyes and took a deep breath. "Just waiting for the all clear to be given. We need to be sure no one will be there waiting for us."

Jefferson nodded in agreement. "Has anyone heard from Clayton or Travis yet?"

Calloway shook his head. "Not a word. Nothing from Lee, either."

"It's unusual. They always make it a point to contact us." Jefferson took a deep breath and exhaled. "Think they're still alive?"

Calloway shrugged. "Guess we'll know soon enough…"

Jefferson said, "I need to find Titus, and inform him that Daniel and my brother-in-law are on their way here."

"Think I'll head over to the hospital, to see if Meera has time for lunch with me."

"Now that you're in control of the phone, if you hear anything, let me know…"

"You know I will…"

At that, they parted company…

7

EVEN THOUGH DANIEL SULLIVAN and Tyler Stephenson were less than an hour away from the Kennett Square safe house, it still took them three hours to get there.

Sullivan's training had taught him to always be on the highest alert when protecting his subjects. Tyler wasn't POTUS, and Sullivan was no longer a secret service agent, but he was still determined to protect his brother in Christ to the best of his ability, as if Tyler was President.

Sullivan was mindful that the supernatural covering God had provided, when relocating children from one location to the next was now gone. Since the two of them were adults, he couldn't comprehend how they had travelled this far without being detected by the billions of microfliers blanketing the atmosphere above, looking for people like them.

He knew they were up there. The counter measure technology in his car kept pinging, alerting them of possible danger.

What he didn't know was if the technology had successfully confused, jammed, or blocked them from uncovering their identities.

With so many of them up there, all it would take would be for one of them to escape their counter measures, and it would be all over for them. In short, one mistake could be deadly…

The darkness did nothing to stop them from being out in full force. Sullivan knew all it would take would be for one of them to succeed in capturing their voices, and it would mean the end for them.

Their images wouldn't be necessary. They were as effective at nighttime as they were in the daytime.

Now that they had just made a huge mistake, by breaking the strict code of silence they had maintained all the way from Wisconsin to Pennsylvania, Daniel was wondering why they were still alive…

When the vehicle pulled behind the service station, Titus and Shamus Harmon were already there waiting for them. Sullivan and Stephenson hurried into the back of the solar-powered 4-wheeler, and they left at once for the safe house situated a few miles away.

They arrived at the Kennett Square safe house a few minutes later. When Tyler first laid eyes on Jefferson, his first observation was how unpresidential his brother-in-law looked. It almost required a double take. His hair was brittle now, with wispy gray strands that seemed to be suffering from static cling. And it looked like he hadn't shaved in a few days.

For someone who was blessed at birth with good looks, the contrast couldn't be brushed aside. Then again, everyone looked older now.

Tyler was still trying to let it sink in that his brother-in-law was still alive, and they had been reunited after all this time. He gripped Jefferson's shoulders with both hands, to make sure he really was standing before him. "So glad you're still alive."

"I thought this day would never come," said Jefferson.

Tyler replied, "That makes two of us. Then again, how could I, when I didn't even know you were alive? When Air Force One was blown out of the sky, I thought for sure that you and my sister were dead. Then I started having dreams that you were still alive and living in hiding as a Christian."

This would be Jefferson's first time sharing that harrowing experience with a family member. It was just another surreal moment in a world so full of them. He didn't know where to begin. He had tried so hard to keep these traumatic memories buried as deeply as they would go into the furthest depths of his mind, with moderate success.

But now that Daniel had located his brother-in-law, they were once again forced to the forefront. "Sorry for keeping you in the dark all this time. Believe me when I say, I wish it had been me instead of your sister. I was already a believer at the time. I seriously doubt Melissa was…"

Just hearing those words caused a new wave of deep emotion to well up within Tyler. "Not a day passes when I don't think about what happened at Camp David on the day of the disappearances. I can still remember how excited I was when the chopper landed a few minutes before the Ohio State-Michigan game. The selfies I took! It was the coolest experience of my life. I felt so important that day."

He grimaced. "I felt anything but important on the short flight back, after the Rapture. Everything's changed so drastically since that day. I came close to committing suicide after the plane crash. I saw no point in living. This went on for many months."

Jefferson nodded at his brother-in-law empathetically. "When did you get saved, Tyler?"

"When the locusts invaded the planet, I repented of my sins and trusted in Christ for my salvation. Suddenly, I stopped being stung by them. That's when God put it on my heart to reach out to William and Janelle and explain to them why they were being stung by them and I wasn't. But I was too afraid to tell them, for fear of being incarcerated."

Tyler lowered his head sadly. "Even though I knew God was shielding me from them, I was still too afraid to leave the house, let alone travel to Georgetown to meet with them. It got to where I dreaded turning on my cell phone. Spineless, I know."

"I understand," Jefferson said. "Look how long it took for me to finally reach out to you. But it was for your overall protection."

Just talking about it caused guilt to swell throughout him. Tyler shook his head in shame. "It wasn't until I saw that prison guard from Europe boldly sharing his faith in Christ on my phone screen, that I finally grew a backbone. Talk about doing a one-eighty!"

"Hans Greinhold inspired multitudes of Christians who were living in hiding. Just goes to show that no one is beyond God's salvation."

Tyler nodded at his brother-in-law. "That was when I started looking for ways to contact William and Janelle. If that man was willing to be beheaded for his faith, it was time for me to do the same. Believe me when I say, Daniel was answered prayer."

Jefferson asked, "How are my children?"

"It's been a while since I last saw them. What I can say is they haven't been the same since Air Force One went down. It's been a steady stream of psychiatrists ever since. It only got worse for William when Christine was killed in the global quake. It was the last straw for him. He had a complete meltdown after that."

Jefferson gulped back a large dose of remorse. It had been more than three years since he last saw his children. And he had no idea that his daughter in law had died. "I pray every day that William and Janelle will both come to faith in Christ."

Tyler sighed softly. "You and me both…" He paused a moment to catch his breath, then asked, "When did you get saved, Jefferson?"

"Soon before Melissa's death. She wasn't happy about it. Nor was she happy when I invited the two founders of this organization to the White House, when they were just getting started. She told me later that night that they gave her the creeps."

Tyler took a deep breath through his nose and exhaled. "Yeah, she told me about their visit and how strangely you were acting, but she never mentioned anything about you having a spiritual conversion."

Jefferson wasn't surprised hearing this. "What upset your sister even more than that, was when I left her at Joint Base Andrews to fly to Colorado with one of my body doubles."

Tyler asked, "Can I ask why you did that?"

Jefferson had a faraway look in his eyes. "I still thought America could be saved back then."

"You and me both, sir," said Sullivan, shaking his head sadly.

Jefferson frowned. "I wanted to remain in the D.C. area and put a counter government in place. Had I known it would be the last time we would ever see each other, I would have never let her get on that plane."

Tyler twisted his lips from one side of his mouth to the other. "It isn't your fault..."

"It sure feels like it at times." Jefferson paused a moment to collect himself. "As many celebrated our deaths, I remained underground so no one would spot me out in public. The thought at that time was that Everett would be President, and I would help him run things behind the scenes. That plan didn't last long."

After the in-laws shared a lengthy emotional embrace, Jefferson asked Agent Sullivan, "Where did you find him?"

"Wisconsin, sir." Try as he might, Sullivan couldn't stop addressing Jefferson that way.

Jefferson asked Daniel, "Are you sure the Coeur d'Alene location was destroyed?"

Daniel took a few swigs from his water bottle. "Most definitely, sir."

"How can you be so sure?"

"I was halfway through the state of Montana, when I suddenly felt compelled to travel back to Idaho, in case it was bombed. I wanted to be there to help them escape if they somehow managed to survive. I couldn't just leave them behind."

"That's so like you, Daniel," said Jefferson, gratefully.

Sullivan shrugged, then looked down at his feet. "When I was five miles away from the safe house, I saw the faint plumes of smoke rising in the air, and I knew it had been targeted."

Jefferson asked, "Could it be possible that Casanieves, Gillespie, Messersmith, and Galiano escaped at the last minute?"

Daniel explained, "Let me put it this way, sir, when I arrived, law enforcement was already there, circling the property looking for signs of life. Had they somehow found a way to escape, they wouldn't have gotten too far. So, I'd have to say, 'no' to your question.

"Since we weren't sure if that property was on Romanero's strike list, they seemed resigned to remain there and ride it out. Then again, it's not like they had other options."

Jefferson saw sadness creeping onto Sullivan's face. "It's not your fault, Daniel. Besides, they're with Jesus now. Let's just hope the bomb silenced them, and not Romanero's goons."

Sullivan nodded grimly. "Since they were connected to you, I can only imagine what the enemy would have subjected them to before ultimately killing them."

Jefferson tried blinking his terrifying remark away. "They were good men and faithful servants to this country. We can rest assured knowing we'll see them again soon, in a couple of years, anyway."

"Amen to that," Sullivan answered. "Had you not asked me to locate Tyler, chances are good I'd also be dead, because I probably would have remained in Idaho with them. So, in a way, the favor you asked of me saved my life."

Danforth waved him off. "You've done more for me over the past four years than I ever did for you." He paused a moment to collect himself before asking, "Did anyone spot you there?"

"No. I made a U-turn and got out of there before they did. I still find it amazing how God's judgments always seem to give us clear advantages over our enemies…"

Jefferson was confused. "What do you mean, Daniel?"

"With our fuel supplies depleted, and with no access to any charging stations, I had no choice but to drive one of our solar-powered cars. Up until just recently, solar power was all but useless to us. Even when the sun did shine, the skies were so hazy and so full of smoke that it took forever to charge our car batteries even halfway.

"Now that the sun is shining more these days—it was sunny on all but one day of the trip—we have plenty of solar electricity to draw upon. I never had to deal with a dead battery. It's a blessing."

Jefferson stared at Daniel Sullivan. For the first time since the former secret serviceman became part of his detail team, more than a decade ago, he hugged him and clung to him very tightly, like he would a close friend. "Once again, Daniel, you've risked your life for me. I can't thank you enough."

Sullivan said, "Just glad we made it here in one piece. Those microfliers are something else! My senses were always on the highest alert because of them. I'm delirious from being on the road so long. And I'm mildly shocked that we actually made it here without being detected by one of them, especially after we spoke on the phone."

Tyler watched the emotional exchange between them. Just hearing his brother-in-law practically wailing on Daniel's shoulders forced a new round of raw emotion to well up inside him.

When Stephenson last saw the two of them at Camp David, it was strictly professional, which made this endearing moment between them look so out of the ordinary. The only thing that remained the same was that Daneil still addressed him as "Sir".

Sullivan, on the other hand, had noticed a gradual softening in his former boss over the past three years, so he wasn't overly shocked by it. But this was the most emotional he had ever seen him.

The embrace felt a little awkward. But, having just endured a grueling cross-country trip, as a wanted fugitive, and seeing plumes of smoke rising in the air, from many locations that used to house his brothers and sisters in Christ, it was badly needed.

Jefferson released his grip, cleared his throat, then said to Tyler, "There's something else you need to know..."

Tyler braced himself. "What is it?"

Jefferson slumped. "Romanero knows I'm alive. I believe he's known for quite some time. He also knows where I was staying before we were transferred to this place."

"Yeah, Daniel told me before we left Wisconsin." Tyler grunted. "Which explains the enhanced surveillance on me and your children."

Sullivan massaged his throbbing scalp, then added, "The only reason none of you were ever questioned was that they were convinced you had no idea Jefferson was still alive.

"Had you known, and you tried contacting him, Romanero would have been alerted, and nothing good would have followed it. Now that he knows everyone escaped from the other safe house, I'm sure he'd want nothing more than to catch you all in the act."

Jefferson nodded in agreement. "Like I said, the lack of contact was for your own protection. I'm just glad you're hearing it from me instead of from the wrong news sources."

Jefferson shot Sullivan an uneasy glance. "Did you tell Tyler about my present situation?"

Sullivan shook his head no. "Until our phone conversation with you, we drove in silence, for obvious reasons."

Jefferson let his eyes settle on his former brother-in-law. He looked anguished. "I want you to know I've since remarried."

Tyler blinked hard a few times to let his words register. He had half expected to hear him say he had cancer or something along those lines, like his daughter-in-law, Christine. "I see. Do I know her?"

Jefferson momentarily glanced away from Tyler, before their eyes connected again. This wasn't going to be easy. "Do you remember my former White House chef, Amy Wong?"

Tyler flinched, then nodded that he did. Even though his sister was dead, he felt hurt hearing this, betrayed even. But, in this strange, new world, anything seemed possible. He lowered his head. "Well then, I guess congratulations are in order. How long have you been married?"

"Going on two years now." Jefferson sensed what Tyler was thinking. His tone of voice had sounded too awkward. He held out his hands, palms out, his eyes begging for understanding. "For the record, there never was anything between me and Amy in all my days as President. You know how much I loved your sister. I was always faithful to her.

"Never in a million years did I think I'd ever remarry, let alone be in another relationship with anyone. It was the farthest thing from my mind. But since our final destinations are at the opposite ends of the eternal spectrum, I had to gradually remove Melissa from my heart and mind, if I wanted to maintain my sanity. I hope you can understand this..."

Tyler tipped his eyes up at him. "I do..." His tone of voice was full of empathy.

Jefferson nodded his thanks to him. "When I was relocated to another subterranean hiding place with a few members of my administration, Amy also accompanied us. Daniel stayed there too, when he wasn't snooping around in D.C., looking for anything he could find to give us an advantage.

"As the days kept passing, I felt lonelier and lonelier in Idaho. But being in a relationship with her was the last thing on my mind. Hers too. But I didn't want to be alone in these crazy times."

Tyler asked, "Does this mean we're no longer in-laws?"

"Of course, not. You will always be family to me. Now that we're believers, it makes us even more related than I ever was to your sister." Realizing his comment was distasteful, he backpedaled, "Let's just pray that my children get saved before it's too late."

"Amen to that. Is Amy here?"

Jefferson answered, "Yes, she is. Would you like to see her?"

Tyler paused a moment to absorb what he had just been told, then nodded yes. "But first, I'd like to take a nap."

Daniel yawned into his fist again. "I heard that. I can't even think straight. Just glad to be off the road."

Jefferson said, "If there's one thing that we have plenty of, at least for now, it's beds to sleep on. Follow me."

Within ten minutes, even among the constant noise, both men were out cold...

8

CEDAR RAPIDS, IOWA

JACK NELSON SAT AT the dining room table with his wife, Vicky, and their two children, Liam and Laura.

When he returned from Pennsylvania, 24 hours ago, his family wasn't surprised to see him walking through the front door 30 pounds lighter, and with his tail between his legs.

After being detained in the Keystone State, for more than a month, and being interrogated daily for his possible role in Benjamin Shapiro's escape, Nelson was placed on leave from the job he loved so much and felt honored to have.

His two colleagues, Russell and Umberto, weren't detained, but they were also relieved of their duties pending a full investigation.

During this time, Nelson was prohibited from communicating with his family. When he was finally released from custody, the two agents who escorted him back to Iowa were ordered not to let him out of their sight. He couldn't even access his phone until he was free of their custody, which turned out to be his front doorstep.

Aside from being physically and emotionally drained, Nelson also brought the flu bug back with him, that had quickly infected millions of humans on the planet. It started attacking his body before he was released from custody. By the time he got on the plane at Philadelphia International Airport, it had taken control of his body.

Jack's 19-year-old son, Liam, and 16-year-old daughter, Laura, showered him with hugs, hoping to cheer him up. He tried warning them not to touch him, that he wasn't feeling well, but it happened so fast.

Eager as they were to hear what had transpired in Pennsylvania, Jack felt worse as the hours passed. It would have to wait. For now, he needed rest.

Vicky had already scheduled an appointment for the family to receive the mark before Jack returned home. That appointment was for tomorrow morning.

As Jack slept, Vicky pulled the last package of chicken breasts out of the freezer, that she was saving until her husband returned home. Once it defrosted, she would prepare chicken noodle soup for dinner.

After receiving the mark in the morning, they would go food shopping and stock up on anything they could.

When the soup was ready, she woke her husband and told him to join them for supper.

Liam and Laura were starting to feel the flu symptoms. Hugging their father had turned out to be a big mistake. They were fading fast.

Vicky asked Jack, "Tell us what happened in Pennsylvania?"

Jack blew his nose into a tissue, then explained to his family, "There isn't much to tell, really. Everything was going smoothly until a woman came to deliver food to Doctor Shapiro. He invited her inside. When she left a few moments later, emptyhanded, the facemask wearing woman innocently waved to us and went on her way."

Jack dipped his spoon into the bowl and filled it with soup. He blew on it three times, before putting it in his mouth. It was the first thing he had eaten in 36 hours.

After repeating the process again, he went on, "Everything seemed perfectly normal until Doctor Shapiro came outside a minute later, holding a cell phone that she had left on his kitchen table.

"I offered to chase her down and give it back to her, but Doctor Shapiro was insistent that he do it himself. When he pulled out of the garage in his Mercedes SUV, to go in search of her, even then, nothing had seemed out of the ordinary.

"How could we possibly know he was leaving his house for the last time? After an hour had passed, and he still hadn't returned, I became concerned for his personal safety. I didn't know if he was in an accident, if he had been kidnapped or even killed on my watch."

Jack put another spoonful of soup in his mouth and swallowed. "I alerted Russell and Umberto to stand guard, as I went inside the house, and discovered a GPS locator in a plastic baggie, floating in a bowl of lukewarm water on the kitchen table, that was removed from Doctor Shapiro's arm."

Seeing the shocked expressions on their faces, he added, "I haven't told you the weirdest part yet. Ready for this? Instead of finding food in the delivery bag, there was a copy of *The Way* inside..."

The shocked expressions on their faces were taken to the next level. They were all mindful of that dangerous book that kept circulating the planet illegally, brainwashing so many, and destroying so many families in the process.

Liam asked, "So, what did you do?"

Jack coughed into his left fist. "I showed it to Russell and Umberto, then ordered them to search the upstairs for more possible clues. When they came back downstairs, I doused the book in lighter fluid and set it ablaze in the outdoor fireplace."

Liam nodded at his father. "Good move."

Jack hoped his son couldn't see the deception he felt for not being entirely truthful with them. "Yeah, well, not everyone thought that way, son. Two supervisors questioned us for hours on end. Even after facing stiff scrutiny from our superiors, our stories remained unchanged. What was there to tell? The only identifying feature was that the delivery woman was Asian. Other than that, we knew nothing else."

Jack blew his nose again and put another spoonful of soup in his mouth. "Since I was the one who made the odd discoveries, I faced the stiffest questioning. The female supervisor asked me how long she remained inside Doctor Shapiro's house. When I told her it wasn't for very long, she snapped at me saying, 'Apparently, it was long enough to remove the GPS locator from his arm!'

"She then asked me why I burned the book, instead of putting it into evidence. I told her I couldn't bear to look at it for even one second, let alone hold it in my hands. Since it was illegal anyway, I thought it would be in everyone's best interest to destroy it."

Vicky said, "I probably would have done the same thing."

"Can you believe that woman slapped me in the face?"

Vicky gasped, hearing this. Laura too.

"Yeah, she hit me so hard, blood trickled out of my nose." Jack grunted more to himself than to his family. "She then berated me by saying it wasn't my call to make, that she was apparently part of Shapiro's escape plan, and now they couldn't extract her fingerprints from the book hoping to identify her! There's more than just one Asian woman on the planet, Agent Nelson!" she said, sarcastically.

"I'm sure she was worried about what would happen once Romanero became aware of it. In the past, a blown assignment like this may have ended in a reprimand at best, and a job termination at worst. Now it could potentially lead to a loss of life."

Jack had a faraway look on his face. Clearly, he was still trying to come to grips with his tumultuous ordeal. "The three of us were then taken to an FBI headquarters that's now being used for global purposes. Since

Russell and Umberto had nothing to do with destroying evidence, they were ultimately let go. Not gonna lie, I was fearful for my life."

Vicky was incredulous. She was offended that another woman had assaulted her husband. "I understand all that. Still, it gave her no right to slap you. How dare she!"

Jack nodded in agreement. "Especially since the delivery woman was wearing gloves and a facemask. Not even the top experts on the planet could have possibly identified her with the naked eye!"

Laura asked her father, "So, what happened next?"

"You know the rest. Before I was taken into custody, the three of us were relieved of our duties, pending a full investigation. Just hope I'll still have my job once they make their final conclusions…"

Vicky was terrified at the prospect that he might not have a job to go back to. They couldn't survive without it. She would be even more terrified had she known the full story about what really happened in Pennsylvania.

What Jack didn't tell his family was that Dr. Shapiro had left the book there for him, and him alone, as evidenced by the personal inscription he found handwritten inside. Nelson was more frightened by this discovery than he was with finding the GPS locator in the bowl of water.

He also refrained from telling them when Russell and Umberto raced up the stairs, he tucked the book in his coat, raced outside, and placed it in his briefcase in the trunk of his government-issued vehicle. There wasn't a chance that it would be ever logged in as evidence.

When he returned, he plucked a similarly sized paperback book from Dr. Shapiro's library, then motioned for his two partners to watch, as he set it ablaze in the backyard of his house.

As the three men watched the book being burned to a crisp, Nelson hoped no one would be able to forensically identify it later.

On the way to Philly International, Nelson kept looking for opportunities to get rid of the book. He concluded that his best chance would be to deposit it in a trash can at the airport.

He never got that opportunity. The two men who had escorted him there never left his side. They even followed him into the bathroom.

Jack Nelson went from having a stellar 28-year career with the FBI, which led to his being chosen to protect the world's most renowned physician, to feeling like a criminal, just like that.

Before boarding his private flight back to the Midwest, Nelson was petrified that the men escorting him back to Iowa would search through his briefcase once they were on the plane. If they found the book inside, he would be taken into custody upon landing in Cedar Rapids, to face even more stiff questioning from his superiors. Or worse.

When the plane touched down in Iowa, the agents assigned to him escorted him home, leaving him no other choice but to bring the book into his house, then set it ablaze for real in his living room fireplace when everyone was sleeping, without ever telling them. He couldn't wait to no longer have it in his possession.

Liam and Laura kept coughing and sneezing all throughout dinner. They felt worse as the minutes passed. "I'm going back to bed."

"Me too," said Laura.

"Leave the dishes in the sink," said Vicky. "I'll wash them later. Take more Nyquil." It was the only thing they had left in the medicine cabinet. Until they took the mark, they couldn't obtain more of it.

Jack said to his wife, "The way I feel, I'm not going anywhere tomorrow. I feel worse now than I did before my nap." He was all in favor of taking the mark. But not until he felt better.

Vicky grimaced. "Let's play it by ear. If you're not feeling better in the morning, I'll reschedule. Don't forget to take more Nyquil."

"I won't." Jack coughed into his fist. "Think I'll sleep in the spare bedroom tonight, so you don't catch it too."

"My throat's already a little scratchy. But I'll be fine." Vicky kissed Jack's left hand. "Night night, Jack. Feel better soon. I love you."

"Love you back..." Jack slowly ascended the steps leading to the spare bedroom. His plan was to stay in bed until Vicky went to sleep, then go back downstairs and finally dispose of the book without her knowing about it.

Seeing her husband still looking crestfallen forced more angst to surface within her. "Everything will be fine," she told herself, under her breath.

Vicky knew something was bothering her husband. Whatever it was, it went beyond the depression he felt, from being placed on leave from his job. She had no idea that the global flu wasn't the only thing Jack had brought back to Iowa with him...

9

ONE WEEK AFTER THE GLOBAL BOMBING

TITUS SHOOK SHAMUS HARMON on his cot. When he rolled over, Titus said softly, "It's time." Harmon nodded that he understood.

Titus then woke Joaquim Guzman and David Wilcox, who were sleeping a few beds away from Shamus. It was just after 4 a.m.

Wilcox was the man that God had used to drive Hana Patel, Yasamin Dabiri-Uddin, their two children, and Vishnu Uddin from Jacksonville, Florida to safe house number one. He felt certain that the safe house he had occupied for three years, in the Sunshine State, was also destroyed.

Whether or not it had been, Kennett Square was now his home.

The three men got dressed then joined Titus in the dining area. Tony Pearsall and Julio Gonzalez were already there having breakfast, with a crew of 12 men. After eating, they would resume retrofitting the corridors leading to the other areas that hadn't yet been used.

They were happy to have a double portion of their daily food rations, which consisted of each having a large bowl of hot wheat and grain cereal, and two slices of wheat bread with homemade strawberry marmalade. It had very quickly become a favorite for most newcomers.

More than half of what they had canned at the outset was lost in the global quake. It needed to be used sparingly. Even so, they would take two loaves of fresh-baked bread with them, and a jar of marmalade.

Julio said to Shamus, "You'll do anything to get out of work!"

Harmon laughed at his coworker's joke, then replied, "We'll probably work harder than the rest of you today!"

"You may be right," said Julio, putting a spoonful of hot cereal in his mouth. He swallowed, then added, "Godspeed out there…"

"Eat up," said Titus, after blessing the food. "We're going to need all our strength."

For Joaquim Guzman, this was a coming home of sorts. Before the Rapture, the young man was a farmhand/IT technician living in Kennett Square with his parents, before it ever became a safe house, until they were taken in the Rapture. He remained in Kennett Square until he made a food delivery in Chadds Ford one day, and he met a very pregnant Leticia Gonzalez for the first time. After they were married, Joaquim remained there with her. Now, here he was in Kennett Square again.

He asked Titus, "Do you think Brian and Tom survived?"

Titus twisted his lips from one side to the other. "Guess we'll find out soon enough. It all depends on where the bomb struck. Since we don't know where the bullseye was, a slight difference of just a few inches above the property, could easily equate to several feet post impact."

Titus took a large bite of wheat bread covered in marmalade. He didn't wait to swallow the food in his mouth before adding, "Another concern I have is that the fallout shelter was only buried thirty feet beneath the surface, instead of the required one hundred feet. You heard what the Pope said. Many shelters that were buried that deep were destroyed."

Shamus Harmon didn't need to be reminded of this. He was one of the men who dug the hole and buried the 12-person fallout shelter that day. When Romanero moved the date up, they simply didn't have enough time to dig any deeper. He knew it was highly susceptible to most GPS guided, bunker buster bombs.

The only comforting thought was that the shelter in which his two friends were trapped was far enough off the property, several feet beyond where they buried their trash. Titus was right. It all came down to where the bomb struck the surface. If Brian and Tom somehow survived, at least they wouldn't have to dig too deeply to reach them.

"Good morning," said Lila Choharjo, joining them in the dining area. Her somber tone of voice was indicative of the dreary conditions at this place. The free spirit inside her felt trapped. The corners of her lips that usually pointed upward, as if she was always smiling no longer did that. She looked sad now, dreadfully sad.

Titus nodded at her, then explained to the others, "I've asked Lila to join us, in case either of them survived the impact, and they need medical attention."

"Unless Romanero's goons found them first!" Joaquim gulped fearfully at the thought.

Titus rubbed his chin. "Thanks to Daniel Sullivan, we know Romanero's troops are no longer standing guard there. But since he knows we escaped, I'm sure he has plenty of microfliers stationed there looking for us."

David Wilcox asked, "Anything else we need to know?"

"Yeah. Despite Ingrid's strongest protests that she's about to pop, and I should stay with her in case it happens today," said Titus, referring to his expectant wife, "I've decided to join you…"

"Pop?" Lila knew what Titus meant, but she decided to ask him anyway.

Even to this day, no one knew Titus' last name. Raised in a life of crime, mafioso style, once he got saved, he chose not to disclose his surname to anyone. It would be too painful. Since there were no marriage certificates to be registered with the state, among *ETSM* residents, Titus and Ingrid it was. "Sorry," he said. "Give birth. Better?"

Lila put a spoonful of hot cereal in her mouth. "Much!"

"Anyway," remarked Titus, "Ingrid keeps telling me she doesn't want to end up like Jacquelyn, only pregnant. I hate having so much free time on my hands, with nothing to do but sit around and wait. It's only been a week, but I'm already starting to go crazy…"

After everyone had filled their bellies with enough food to eat, the five of them left the subterranean hideout for the automobile repair shop, a few miles away, to get the solar-powered car that Daniel Sullivan had parked there, when he arrived the other day with Tyler Stephenson.

They couldn't risk driving it anywhere near where safe house number one had once stood. It would be too risky.

They crossed over Brandywine Creek on U.S. 1 and parked their vehicle behind a vacant building that used to be the Brandywine Conservatory. From there, they waited for daybreak to cover the vehicle with the camouflage tarp that they had brought with them.

When Titus gave the signal, Lila retrieved the First Aid kit from the back seat, Joaquim fetched the bag full of bread and orange-honey marmalade, and the five of them set out on foot, for the final three miles north. Mindful of the bounties on their heads, not to mention the microfliers hovering above, they did their best to walk just behind the leafless tree line fronting U.S. 1, with their heads always down.

When there was no thick brush to hide behind, or when they came to a cross section along the way, and they were forced to come out of hiding, their hope was that they wouldn't be seen by common citizens searching for them with their smart phones.

They all heard the False Prophet assure his listeners that they would receive a thousand-dollar credit for aiding in their capture. Even if it meant killing them, that was permissible. Now that they were out in public, it sounded even more frightening to them.

When they reached Chadds Ford, Joaquim led the way. Having traversed them numerous times on his 4-wheeler, no one knew these woods and backwoods better than the teen. They had no intention of going anywhere near U.S. 202.

When they had what was left of the safe house in sight, they saw faint plumes of smoke still rising in the air.

They fully expected to see the mass destruction, but it was even worse than they had imagined. Most of the buildings that were outside the circumference of the crater were gone, or they were left partially standing.

Two years ago, the global quake did significant damage to their beloved safe house. There was nothing left of it now.

Titus silently concluded that there wasn't a chance that Brian or Tom could have survived what hit them.

They surveyed the location in complete silence, using binoculars, looking for any possible traps. They knew not to expect enemy guards, not alive anyway. But they didn't even see dead bodies.

What they didn't know was that the 100 soldiers who stormed safe house number one to rescue the children, before it was bombed, had retreated to a military command center that was set up five miles southeast of Chadds Ford, in the parking lot of what used to be a popular shopping center.

Their hope of being hailed as heroes for their bravery never came to fruition. Each had been loyal to the cause, even proudly taking the mark. In the end, it mattered not. All 100 of them were killed, including the commanding officer.

After waiting 30 minutes, and not seeing any law enforcement or spy cameras, Titus decided it was time to get a move on. They raced off to where the fallout shelter was buried. If there were enemy microfliers patrolling the area, like aerial sentries, like the False Prophet had warned about in his address, they couldn't see them.

They kept their heads down just in case...

Harmon was grateful that the shovels he had buried a foot below the surface, a few feet away, were still there. Another thing he was grateful for was, even though the edge of the crater was roughly 10 yards away from the fallout shelter, it was still close enough that it loosened much of the dirt covering it in the process.

This would probably save them an hour of digging, at least that much. "Guess we'll soon find out if it really could withstand a twenty-kiloton nuclear blast, as advertised," Harmon said softly.

Had it been buried at the suggested 100 feet beneath the surface, instead of just 30, it would have taken all day for five people to dig that far using shovels only.

Even so, it still took nearly two hours of rigorous picking away at the earth, then shoveling what they had loosened to the side, before Joaquim's shovel finally struck the bomb shelter. "If you can hear me, brothers," he yelled, "hang in there a few minutes more."

"They can't hear you," Harmon said. "The fallout shelter's virtually soundproof. But if there are microfliers up there," he said, pointing skyward, "they can!"

"Sorry," said Joaquim sheepishly. He raised his shovel to bang on it.

Titus stopped him this time. "If they're still alive and they think we're the enemy, Tom might have another heart attack if you do that."

The first thing Shamus noticed was that the fallout shelter was slightly dislodged. It took another 30 minutes before he was able to open the hatch from the outside.

Titus turned on his flashlight and pointed it down into the shelter. He saw the many damaged pods, and footprints in the dirt going in both directions. They appeared to be the same size prints.

Joaquim was the first to lower himself down inside the hole.

"Be careful. We don't know how sturdy the shelter is…"

When Joaquim reached the bottom, the others quickly joined him.

Shamus opened Brian's pod. He took one whiff and wished he hadn't. The smell of death hit him square in the face. He gagged and nearly vomited.

Lila made sure her facemask was tightly secured, then checked his pulse. There wasn't one. Brian's face was blue, his eyes were closed, and he was unresponsive to her commands. She shone her flashlight over his lifeless body. There was no need to check under his clothing to confirm that decay had already set in. One whiff was enough.

She was taken aback at how thin her deceased friend was. She noticed the needle in his left arm, and the empty intravenous bag hanging a foot or so above his bed. She expected to see those things. But what she didn't expect to see was the half-used IV bag on the floor next to his pod. Even more shocking was the open pack of peanut butter crackers on the floor next to it, with one cracker missing.

Lila scratched her head in befuddlement. *What in the world?*

"Oh, man!" shouted David Wilcox, opening Tom's pod.

Lila was already rattled; his voice made her jump. She shone her flashlight over at him. What she saw on David's face told the story.

She readjusted her facemask then slowly trudged toward Tom's pod, already knowing what to expect. Had he still been alive, he would have grunted or pounded on the inside of his pod before David opened it, hoping to capture their attention. But there hadn't been a peep from over there.

Lila pointed her flashlight at Tom's face. He, too, lay motionless, lifeless. Even with a face mask on, the pungent odor of death and urine quickly invaded the fallout shelter, like an unrelenting mold or fungus. But the smell of death was far worse than those two things combined. It nearly knocked her over.

Lila pinched her nose over the face mask, silently wishing she had a hazmat suit on instead. Spotting a few empty wrappers and water bottles on the floor, next to Tom, she quickly deduced that both men had survived the attack. For how long, she didn't know.

All she knew was that they couldn't have consumed those things before the bomb destroyed safe house number one. There wouldn't have been enough time to. Even if there was, she seriously doubted they would have been hungry before the strike. And who changed Brian's intravenous bag? Weakened as he was, it couldn't have been him. There wasn't a chance it would have been empty before the strike.

She pointed the flashlight at the floor and saw the footprints that weren't covered by their own tracks. She quickly concluded that they were Tom's. Did her two brothers in Christ die while waiting for someone to rescue them? Had they starved themselves to death?

Lila couldn't help but think that had she only been able to come sooner to care for them, they might still be alive now.

First, it was the pulse-pounding journey from Kennett Square to Chadds Ford, with scores of microfliers hovering above looking for them. Then, to see the safe house she had come to love blown to smithereens, all she could do was shake her head sadly.

After many years of living as a lesbian Hollywood actress, and losing her daughter in the Rapture, she repented of that sinful lifestyle, and was ultimately sent to Chadds Ford.

This was where Lila had grown ever so close to her Maker. She had come to love safe house number one even more than her glamorous house in the Hollywood Hills. Now it was gone.

This was the final straw. Lila lost it. Tears streamed down her cheeks one after the next.

She took a few moments to collect herself, then glanced back at her four still-alive brothers in the faith. "In the end," she opined, speaking through her face mask, "the double pneumonia plus the lack of nutrition was too much for Brian's body to absorb. And the added stress and anguish caused by the blast, probably caused Tom's heart to eventually beat for the last time."

Joaquim looked deflated. He loved Brian and Tom like family. "What should we do with their bodies?"

With as much empathy in his voice as Harmon could muster, he answered, "We can't take them back to Kennett Square with us…"

"The least we can do is give them a proper burial." Joaquim's voice trembled with every word.

Shamus glanced over at Lila. She shrugged. His eyes volleyed back to the bravest teenager he had ever known. Still, he was a teenager. Then again, this was too much for anyone to absorb, let alone digest, regardless of age.

Harmon placed a hand on Joaquim's shoulder. "Sure, kid, if it means that much to you, we'll bury them before we leave."

Joaquim wiped dust-filled tears from his eyes. "Thanks."

It took a while for the four men to hoist their two deceased brothers' bodies to the surface, but they somehow managed. The stench coming off them was overpowering.

As Lila kept a steady eye on their surroundings, Shamus, David, and Joaquim got busy digging two holes in the ground, as quickly as they could, hoping they weren't being watched and recorded from above.

Titus went back down into the fallout shelter. He filled three duffel bags full of whatever food, water and medicines that weren't used, to bring back to Kennett Square with them.

That is, if they ever made it back. Part of him silently wished they wouldn't. As much as he wanted to take the dozen portable oxygen tanks with him, their car was parked too far away to carry them that far.

Titus returned to the surface, to find Joaquim holding his breath and hoisting Brian's lifeless body onto his right shoulder, then gently placing him into one of the holes. Shamus did the same with Tom's body.

With the bodies of their two fallen brothers now in their final resting places, they covered them with some of the loose earth they had removed earlier.

At that, Shamus said a brief prayer, and they left at once on foot, hoping the car would still be there when they arrived back at the old Brandywine Conservatory.

Lila asked, "I think it would be best if we don't mention anything about the empty cracker wrappers and open bottles of water to Jacquelyn or to Brian's parents."

"Agreed," said Shamus, on behalf of everyone else. "I just hope the car's still there when we get there. I don't think I have the stamina to walk all the way back to Kennett Square, if it was stolen or towed away."

David Wilcox replied, "I heard that!"

All five were emotionally drained and bone tired.

The greatest sadness Lila felt now was knowing it would be up to her to confirm Jacquelyn's worst fears, that her husband had indeed perished.

What really ate away at her was that the guards were killed on the same day the safe house was bombed. Had they only known, they could have gone back much sooner to rescue them, but they didn't.

Would Brian and Tom still be alive if they did? The very thought forced even more tears from Lila's eyes.

When they saw the road sign advertising the once-historic Brandywine Battlefield, half a mile north from where the car was parked, they breathed a collective sigh of relief. They reached what used to be the Brandywine Conservatory, a few moments later, and rejoiced upon seeing that the car was still there covered in camouflage.

They climbed inside, prayed for God's protection, and left for Kennett Square, to share the tragic news with everyone.

Lila kept entertaining the thought of how much better off she would be if one of the microfliers had caught them along the way, thus sparing her from the anguish of locking eyes with Jacquelyn.

They would soon discover that they wouldn't be the only ones with tragic news to share…

10

ELLIJAY, GEORGIA – THAT SAME DAY

A WEEK AFTER SALVADOR Romanero successfully executed his global blitzkrieg on Christian hideouts, Clayton Holmes, Travis Hartings, and Dr. Lee Kim had mutually decided that it was time to leave the tiny underground shelter, in which they had been holed up, and head north to Kennett Square, Pennsylvania.

This day couldn't come soon enough for Clayton. Just like all other past visits to this undesirable place, the tiny 10' by 12' parcel of dank living space was already too small for just one person, let alone three. He was grateful for God's protection. Other than that, he had never enjoyed a single moment spent there.

Travis and Lee often heard him mumbling the words, "There's no way I want to spend my last day on Earth at this place!"

Even Travis couldn't wait to leave. This property was purchased by the *End Times Salvation Movement* to be used as an emergency location only. This was their third time using it.

The first night spent there was before the global quake. Hartings had a rather vague dream, which ultimately led the two of them to travel from the safe houses at which they were staying, to Ellijay, before they left for the cabin in Oak Ridge, Tennessee.

That was when they were first introduced to Moishe. Once Travis and Clayton were satisfied that he was one of Yahweh's 144,000 sealed servants, the young man informed them that Yahweh had chosen their organization to house 5,000 of his sealed brothers.

After sharing this blessing of a lifetime with them, Moishe took the winds out of their sails by warning that many in their organization would soon perish. He didn't tell them *how* it would happen, or when, only that it would be soon. The very next day, they got their answer, when the global quake rocked the planet.

What took the two *ETSM* leaders 2.5 hours to drive to Oak Ridge, took three days to make it back. The destruction all around them was unspeakable. Many of the roadways were still undrivable.

What made it even worse for Travis that day, was that he dislocated his right shoulder trying to avoid one of the gaping holes created by the quake. He went airborne off his motorcycle and fell hard onto the road.

Clayton helped pop his shoulder back into place. Thankfully, his motorcycle had only sustained minimal damage. But it was difficult navigating it mostly with one hand. When they finally made it to Ellijay on that frigid night, they couldn't even access the shelter.

The hatch had bent and was stuck in such a way that they couldn't open it. They were forced to sleep aboveground in the frigid cold. Travis still remembered the excruciating pain he suffered that night. He thought he was going to die. He wanted to die.

When they arrived in Ellijay last week, it took two hours before they were finally able to make it below ground. Most of that time was spent opening the badly damaged hatch, then removing the mounds of dirt that had settled everywhere, then redepositing it above ground.

Even bundled up in thick coats, hoodies and ski masks, they feared being identified by one of those microfliers hovering above—armed with vocal and facial recognition technology—looking for dissidents like them.

With only two small beds between them, they agreed to take turns rotating each night. After just one night on the cot, Holmes offered to sleep on the floor every night, on a dusty throw blanket.

It was more comfortable on his back and knees than trying to squeeze his much thinner 6'5" frame onto the small cot.

To make room, the small wooden table in between the two beds had to be moved to the corner, next to the wooden ladder which led to the outside. But sleep still came hard for him. The loud snoring filling the small room didn't help.

Another challenge they had was, whenever they needed to relieve themselves, they had to put on the same coats, hoodies and ski masks, before climbing up to the surface, then praying every step of the way that the microfliers wouldn't identify them. They knew they were taking a huge risk each time.

When they heard Yahweh's angelic messengers making their dire warnings high above, tempted as they were to open the hatch to glance up at them, they feared Romanero was using these miniature spies hoping to identify more dissidents gazing at the angels in awe, which would lead to their detainment.

Everyone trapped underground heard them with the utmost clarity, whether they were saved or not, or whether they lived in a subterranean mansion or in a small dump, like the Ellijay safe house.

The unconverted in the world breathed a collective huge sigh of relief when the three angels stopped making their brilliant appearances a few hours after the global bombing campaign had ended. That is, until harmful and painful sores started breaking out on their bodies.

Another contributing factor to their wanting to leave Ellijay, as soon as possible, was out of necessity. The metal cabinet that was intended to prevent hungry mice and other rodents from gaining access to the contents stored inside, was also badly damaged in the global quake, a little more than two years ago.

Every MRE and plastic water bottle stored inside the cabinet, for future consumption, was consumed by the vermin. Had they not brought extra food supplies and water with them, they would have run out by now. What little supplies they had left needed to last until they arrived in Kennett Square.

Lee Kim's biggest reason for wanting to leave Ellijay was mostly due to utter boredom. With no electricity or Wi-Fi access, the IT man had no way of contacting anyone since the bombing.

Clayton and Travis caught him staring at the ceiling for hours on end, twiddling his fingers trying to bide his time.

Dr. Kim kept wondering if the satellite that Jefferson Danforth had sent into space, just for them, when he was still President, that had provided them with secure Wi-Fi all this time, was still operational.

Had it been discovered by Romanero's goons, then disconnected, among the mayhem? Then again, Lee didn't need Wi-Fi access to confirm that the vast majority of their safe houses were obliterated in Romanero's global attack on Christians last week.

Even though Holmes, Hartings and Kim had yet to communicate with anyone residing at the 5,000 remaining locations housing children, since they all had Yahweh's supernatural protection, they had every reason to believe they all survived.

This included the Kennett Square safe house. They just didn't know what to expect when they arrived there.

Before climbing out of the hole and leaving Ellijay for the last time, they huddled together and prayed for God's protection. No doubt it would be an intense, nerve-jarring trip to Pennsylvania.

Another thing they were running low on was fuel. Since they weren't in possession of one of the thousands of solar cars that Hartings had purchased by his now defunct auto company—which was under the *ETSM* umbrella—most of which they could only assume were destroyed last week—they prayed they would have enough fuel in the steel tank in the back of the van, to make it there.

Barring any traffic jams or any other unforeseen occurrences they might encounter along the way, Lee Kim estimated that they would have enough fuel to make it at least to the Maryland-Pennsylvania border. If not, they would have to venture the rest of the way on foot, which Kim estimated to be 25 miles.

In Clayton's opinion, even that would be better than spending one more night in Ellijay. He was the first one to climb up on the rickety old wooden ladder and race to the car, bundled up in everything he had brought with him last week.

Lee went next. He counted to 100 in his mind, nodded at Travis, then left the subterranean room as quickly, and as quietly, as he could.

Finally, Hartings counted to 100, then climbed up out of the hole. He raced to the vehicle, head down, practically diving into the passenger front seat. Before Travis could even fasten his seatbelt, Holmes put the car in drive and their journey to Pennsylvania was underway.

When they made it out of Georgia into the state of Tennessee, they silently rejoiced. The counter-measure detectors in their vehicle kept going off, like they were malfunctioning. There was so much activity in the atmosphere above that it rendered them practically worthless. It became so annoying that they ended up turning them off.

If the three *End Times Salvation Movement* leaders needed further confirmation that the majority of their locations didn't survive the attack, the faint, residual plumes of smoke they saw rising in the air, in various locations, removed all doubt.

Surely, every hideout on Romanero's dissident strike list, including their safe houses, were successfully targeted. And since they all took place simultaneously, millions of their residents went Home to be with Jesus, in the blink of an eye. They rejoiced for their brothers and sisters knowing they were in Glory now.

Upon reaching I-40, they headed east then merged onto I-81 north. When they were roughly 30 miles into Virginia, Clayton asked Travis to take over driving so he could record a message for all surviving *ETSM* members. It would be risky, he knew, but no one had heard anything from them since before the bombings.

Since they were headed to one of those properties, it would give those staying there plenty of time to prepare for their arrival…

With his right thumb, he pressed the record button and began, "Greetings, beloved. I hope this message finds each of you well among the mayhem. I just wanted you all to know we're still alive, but that's all I'll say for now." Holmes wasn't about to mention them by name.

"Even though we have no confirmation, as far as we can tell, roughly ninety percent of our safe houses were destroyed, leaving ten percent, or approximately five thousand remaining. We can rejoice knowing all locations housing children survived the attack. All were relocated to new safe houses.

"It's impossible to know for sure how many Christian hideouts, besides ours, were demolished last week, in Romanero's all-out attack on us. The only thing I know for sure is that five thousand of Yahweh's sealed servants reside at our places. The other one hundred and thirty nine thousand reside elsewhere. Wherever they are, we must assume that Yahweh also preserved those locations for His children, for the coming Millennial Kingdom. In time, we'll know."

Clayton said tenderheartedly, "To all you newcomers who received copies of the book we proudly produced, before being sent to our properties, let me remind you that this was all meant to happen. So, take heart knowing the Word of God is as accurate today as it was when it was recorded thousands of years ago.

"God's love for us far exceeds the chaos. So, hang in there a little longer. The reward you'll receive at the end of your suffering will be an eternity with Jesus. It won't be too much longer now. The future's bright for all of us!"

Everyone listening heard Travis Hartings and Lee Kim saying, "Amen."

Holmes continued, "All of us lost friends last week. It's okay to miss them and even feel sad. Let me comfort you all with the first four verses of Revelation fifteen: 'I saw in heaven another great and marvelous sign: seven angels with the seven last plagues—last, because with them God's wrath is completed. And I saw what looked like a sea of glass glowing with fire and, standing beside the sea, those who had been victorious over the beast and its image and over the number of its name.

"They held harps given them by God and sang the song of God's servant Moses and of the Lamb: 'Great and marvelous are your deeds, Lord God Almighty. Just and true are your ways, King of the nations, Who will not fear you, Lord, and bring glory to your name? For you alone are holy. All nations will come and worship before you, for your righteous acts have been revealed.'"

Clayton grinned at the marvelous vision in his head. "That's them, y'all! What could be more praiseworthy than that? So, as you do your best to adjust to the constant chaos, whenever you find yourself missing them, picture them holding harps that were given to them by God Almighty Himself, and singing that glorious song to King Jesus with multitudes of others, just like the scripture declares!

"Antichrist may have killed their bodies last week, but that monster is powerless from ever harming them again. They will never suffer or hurt or cry or feel pain ever again. So, let us rejoice knowing they're in the greatest Place ever, especially knowing we'll join them soon! Can I get an Amen?"

"Comforting as it is just thinking about where they are—I know I'd love to be with them now—let me remind you all that if you're still alive and hearing this message, it's because Yahweh has kept you alive for a reason. So, press on, faithful soldiers, it won't be too much longer before we'll see Jesus, face to face, and gaze into His holiness!"

The grin on Clayton's face vanished when he heard a noise out in the distance. He glanced over at Travis. "Do you hear something?"

Hartings silenced the radio. "Yes, but it's quite faint."

Holmes craned his head at Lee in the back seat. "Do you hear it, Lee?"

Lee rubbed his lower lip with two fingers, straining hard, trying to identify the pulse-pounding hissing sound that kept getting closer and louder.

Kim was the first one to confirm what Clayton and Travis had both feared. Panic rose in his voice. "I think we've been identified. Our voices must have been snatched out of the air by one of the microfliers!"

Before the three leaders could even brace themselves, the vehicle they were riding in was hit by a drone missile. Without the slightest regard for all other vehicles within close proximity of the target, it struck with deadly precision. The car was blown to smithereens, instantly snuffing out the lives of the three *ETSM* leaders.

The driver of the vehicle traveling three car lengths behind theirs suffered a heart attack and crashed into the back of another vehicle.

Clayton Holmes' final words on this side of eternity were, "Looks like we're going Home, fellas…" The instant his body became lifeless, his thumb lost grip of the cell phone screen, and the message was sent out to all still-alive *ETSM* leaders…

As it turned out, Clayton did spend his last night on Planet Earth in Ellijay, Georgia…

WHEN THE OWNERS OF the Great Smoky Mountain Lodge and Resort in Pigeon Forge, Tennessee, saw the images of the three men who were killed by drone strike, they instantly recognized them.

Even though the three kept their heads down the entire time, while staying in their hotel, one man was clearly Caucasian, one was black, and the other was Asian.

They felt betrayed by Dr. Shapiro for using their establishment to plot against their most high savior. They sent the surveillance video to local authorities, of the three men riding the elevator up to the top floor on which Shapiro had been staying.

They knew nothing would come of their inquiry, the damage had already been done, but it still made them feel like they were doing their duty by reporting it.

Their only wish was that they would have been killed in their home state of Tennessee instead of in Virginia.

11

KENNETT SQUARE, PENNSYLVANIA

HANA PATEL PEEKED IN on Tamika Moseley. She was resting on her assigned cot, eyes covered with a sleep mask, her Bible next to her.

Tamika always found it difficult to sleep with lights turned on, dim as they were. The constant noise and lack of privacy only made it worse. But now that the section reserved for married couples was available, at least she was able to sleep with her husband again, next to him rather.

With 3,000 children staying on the property, nurses, teachers, and daycare volunteers were in short supply, especially now that the global flu had spread to their underground safe house.

Even so, all expectant women were ordered to rest for a few days, before resuming their daily duties. This included nurses. The stress caused from being relocated one week early had caused two miscarriages already.

Those who weren't pregnant were being asked to pick up extra shifts. Hana Patel was among those now being trained as a nurse. Yasamin Dabiri-Uddin too. Since they both had small children, they wanted to teach children's classes. But since nurses were in greater demand, they went in that direction, at least until they got the flu under control.

On top of being pregnant, Tamika was severely depressed about leaving Brian and Tom behind in Chadds Ford. She was told to take all the time she needed. Much of her downtime was spent consoling Jacquelyn and Brian's parents. Her heart ached for them.

Hana nudged her softly on her upper back, then whispered in her ear, "Tamika, are you awake?"

Tamika recognized her Middle Eastern accent. "Yes," came the soft reply. "I wasn't really sleeping. Hard to at this place…"

Hana said, "Yeah, not too much privacy around here."

Tamika's brow furrowed. Hana's voice sounded a little too upbeat. "Do you need help with something?"

"No. I just wanted to introduce you to one of the nurses here. Her name is…"

When Hana paused for what seemed a little too long, Tamika rolled over and removed her sleep mask. The woman standing before her lowered her face mask, allowing her a better view of her face. Her mouth was agape.

Tamika sat up on the cot she was laying on, and blinked hard a few times, to make sure she wasn't imagining things. If this was who she thought it was, she wasn't as slender as she was a decade ago. And her long, black hair was much shorter now. Other than that, she looked the same. Her eyes popped. Chills raced up and down her spine. "No way! Nila Mirano? I can't believe it! My dream was true after all!"

Tamika's hands flailed wildly in front of her. Tears flooded her eyes. "Thank you, Lord!" she shouted, practically leaping off her cot. In a world so full of strange happenings, most of them horrific, it only figured. Thankfully, this one was blissful.

Nila couldn't erase the astonished expression from her face. She exclaimed, "Wow! It really is you, Tamika!" The two women embraced, shedding many tears.

Hana was emotional witnessing this surprise reunion between these two long lost friends. "Nila and I just met on this shift. When she told me she was having dreams about her former college friend being an ETSM nurse, I was intrigued. When she said your name, I couldn't believe what I was hearing!"

Just hearing Hana retelling the story as it happened, caused Nila to shake her head in astonishment. "Meera told us to take a short break so Yasamin could take me to you. We changed out of our hazmat suits and came straight here."

Hana added, "Meera wanted to join us but she's busy doing all she can to keep the global flu from further spreading underground. The quarantine area is filling up with patients."

Nila wiped her eyes with the sleeve of her shirt. "The first dream I had about you was that you were a Christian. What made it so strange was the last time I heard anything about you, it wasn't good."

Tamika asked, "In the news?"

Nila nodded, then placed her hands on her hips. "I'm dying to know, why did you dig up your grandfather's grave?"

Tamika wasn't surprised that her former college friend had heard about that insane time in her life. There wasn't a person of sound mind in New York City who hadn't heard about it. "What if I told you God used that incident to save my soul?"

"Naturally, I'd want to hear more."

"After I dropped out of college, I got married. We had a second son the following year..." Tamika took a deep breath and exhaled through her nose. "By this time, you and I already fell out of touch."

When she paused again, Nila probed, "Let me guess, your sons were taken in the Rapture."

Tamika's shoulders slumped. "Momma too. They were my whole world. I was angry, confused and frightened, not knowing what to expect from one day to the next. I couldn't think straight. All I knew was I was all alone and didn't want to live without my family."

Nila shook her head. "It was a difficult time for all of us..."

Tamika raised her hands. "You got that right! I knew nothing about the ETSM at that time, only about two of its members, Brian Mulrooney and Charles Calloway. Actually, they weren't members yet when I met them. Have you met Charles?"

Nila nodded yes. "Meera's husband?"

Tamika nodded. "God used him to win me to Christ."

Nila asked, "How so?"

"Ready for this? Charles was in my taxicab when the Rapture happened, and people suddenly disappeared all around us, including the man in the back seat with him! I can't recall his name. All I remember is they were business associates. I thought my eyes were playing tricks on me. After the initial shock wore off, I was terrified!"

Nila covered her mouth with her left hand. What blew her mind wasn't so much that the man in the backseat of her cab had vanished—he was one of many that day—but that Meera's husband was with her when it happened.

"Suddenly, a car slammed into us. The Plexiglas separating us broke off and tore into Charles' forehead, just above his right eye. He was desperate to get to his hotel so he could tend to his wound.

"I felt bad for him, I really did, but I told him I was going home to check on my sons and my Momma, before doing anything else. When they weren't there, I became even more panicked. I looked for them everywhere, hoping they didn't disappear too.

"Charles was gracious enough to let me keep searching for my children. Then again, he didn't have much choice. Anyway, when I finally dropped him off at his hotel, many hours later, I thought I'd never hear from him again.

"God had other plans. Turns out he was stranded in New York for quite some time. He called me on Thanksgiving Day, inviting me to have dinner with him at the Waldorf Astoria Hotel."

Tamika silently wondered if the Waldorf was still standing. She left it alone. "The only reason I finally decided to join him was that he kept insisting he knew why my family vanished. He tried convincing me over dinner that what happened was the Rapture. I was a hard sell though. I was still in deep mourning for my family. But I was also desperate for answers. I was determined to prove or disprove his theory, on my own, without his or anyone else's input.

"That's when I had a dream about my late grandfather. Strange thing was, I hadn't thought about him in many years. But I knew he was a believer. If the Rapture theory was true, it would mean Grandpa's body was raised first before everyone else still alive on Earth.

"After trying to talk myself out of it numerous times, I kept coming back to the same conclusion. I figured if his body wasn't there, I would embrace the Rapture theory. But if his body was still there, I would cross it off my list of possibilities. When Grandpa's bones weren't there, I received Christ as my Lord and Savior at the cemetery, on top of his damaged casket, if you can believe that."

Nila's face lit up. Hearing Tamika retelling the story fascinated her. "Amazing! It's nothing like how they portrayed it in the media."

"I'll say!" said Tamika, with a sigh.

Hana was equally fascinated hearing it. She was in India at that time, but she had heard bits and pieces of the story at safe house number one. Now that she was hearing about it in greater detail, she became breathless. But because Tamika was a fast talker, she had to strain hard at times, and had to listen very intently to keep up with her.

Tamika shook her head wearily. "Not sure if they reported this in the news, but when I made my escape from the cemetery, I was attacked by two guard dogs. One of 'em chewed on my leg pretty bad. I came this close," she said, using her two fingers as measuring sticks of sorts, "to coming to you for treatment. But I knew you'd be required by law to inform the police about my visit, friends or not."

Tamika stared at the wall opposite her, as she relived this traumatic time in her life. "I was forced to treat my injuries on my own. Things only went downhill from there, when they put a warrant out for my arrest…"

Nila shook her head in astonishment. "I confess I bought into all the hype."

"Can't say I blame you. I almost did myself," Tamika joked. "But, in truth, the only thing I was guilty of was damaging Grandpa's casket."

Nila asked, "Are Brian and Charles the ones who helped you escape from the city?"

"Yes."

"The media sure did a good job of demonizing them both."

Tamika frowned. "All because of me. Had it not been for the two of them, I probably wouldn't be alive. Life hasn't gotten any easier, but since I wasn't saved back then, that time in my life was more traumatic than everything that's happened since, including the global quake, and Romanero's recent bombing campaign. At least I know what's headed our way now. I also know I'll see my family again..."

"So, how did you meet Brian?"

Tamika glanced around the room to make sure Jacquelyn or Sarah weren't within listening range. "The same way I met Charles, in my cab, if you can believe that. But here's the kicker; before Charles and his business associate got into my cab, on the day of the Rapture, Brian's friend, Craig, just got out! They were my very next customers..."

Hana exclaimed, "Truly amazing!" Now 30, her eyes still sparkled when she smiled, but not nearly as much as they once did. But at least her hair had grown back. It was several inches below the shoulder now. She didn't miss the spiked haircut she had while making her escape from India to America one bit.

Tamika paused a moment to recall that traumatic time in her life—it felt like 50 years had passed—then continued, "Even more remarkable was, the reason Craig was going to the airport in the first place, was to go to Michigan where Brian had been living, to spend time with Brian and another friend they grew up with in New York City.

"Turns out their other friend was a born-again Christian. Brian and Justin were at a football game when Justin suddenly vanished into thin air. I can only imagine how freaked out Brian must've been when it happened. As freaked out as I was when that man vanished in my cab, I didn't know him. Brian and Justin were childhood friends."

Tamika looked down at her feet. "It got even stranger when Brian got back to his apartment, to find a Bible that Justin had left for him as a gift. Justin told Brian he was a born-again Christian the night before he disappeared. But Brian was only vaguely familiar with his brand of Christianity.

"First, Justin vanishes before his very eyes. Then, he leaves him a Bible, of all things, with a handwritten letter inside explaining the big changes in him. When Brian told his family what happened, they begged him to come back home to New York, for Thanksgiving.

"He started reading the Bible Justin gave him on the long train ride home. The day after Thanksgiving, who ends up in my cab? First it was Craig, then Charles, then Brian. I took him to Mitzi's deli."

"I used to go there for lunch," said Nila. "I loved that place."

"Craig's family used to own it." Tamika slapped her forehead. "How could I forget? One thing I didn't tell you was that He left his cell phone in my cab on the day of the Rapture. When I dropped it off to him, he paid me fifty bucks, and offered to buy me breakfast. I took a rain check.

"Even before Brian got in my cab, he knew Craig had lost his phone. When I told him he left it in my cab, his shock took on a whole new level. Of all the cabs in the city!"

Hana shook her head very slowly from side to side. "Simply remarkable!"

Tamika agreed, "It really was! I didn't know it at the time, but God was using my cab and Craig's phone to bring us all together. Brian got saved that day. Would you like to know where it happened?"

"Tell us!" said Hana.

"Get this, I drove him to the Waldorf-Astoria Hotel where Charles was staying. He shared the Gospel and Brian got saved in his hotel room, the same place Charles got saved a few nights before."

Nila remarked, "Only God could do something that amazing..."

"Craig and I became friends. But when the graveyard incident story broke on TV, he turned against me. He kept telling me to do the right thing and turn myself in. But why should I turn myself in when I was innocent of the charges? Had I gone to the police, who knows what would have happened to me!"

Sadness covered Tamika's face. "Turns out, Justin sent Craig a Bible too. But he made it clear that he wanted nothing to do with Jesus. When he heard Brian also became a born-again Christian, it was the end of their friendship."

Tamika shook her head sadly. "Tragically, Craig was killed when a Muslim terrorist stormed Mitzi's and opened fire on him. That was when Muslims declared war on Jews. I'm sure you remember..."

"I do...," said Nila. "That was around the time I got saved."

Tamika sat on her bed and placed her hands on her knees. "Of Brian's two childhood friends, one's in Glory, and the other's in Hades. We still don't know about Brian..."

Nila was confused. She asked, "What do you mean, Tamika?"

"He never left the safe house we vacated before it was bombed. He was very ill and didn't have the strength to make it to the van. He was taken to the underground fallout shelter with brother Tom." Tamika blinked a tear from her eye, then glanced around the room again, to make sure Jacquelyn or Sarah still weren't within listening range. "Brian's wife Jacquelyn, their daughter, and Brian's parents are all here. As you can imagine, they're still pretty shaken up over it..."

When Tamika became too choked up to continue, Hana took over, "Just to clarify, Brian's a believer. We just don't know if he's in Heaven yet or still here on earth."

"I see," said Nila.

Hana added, "Tom Dunleavey was a fellow resident who remained behind with Brian. Titus left early this morning to see if they survived. A few others went with him, including Lila, in case they survived and needed medical attention."

Nila said, "So, that's why she didn't show up for duty this morning."

"Yes. They would have gone sooner, but we needed to make sure local authorities wouldn't be there waiting for them. Like Tamika said, we should know soon enough."

Tamika stared blankly at the air. "They were two of the finest human beings I've ever known..."

Hana nudged Tamika. It was almost uttered in the past tense. "There's still hope. They may have survived..."

Tamika nodded at her friend. "You're right, Hana, sorry. But part of me hopes they're with Jesus now," she added, not knowing it had already happened.

Nila nodded at Hana, then asked Tamika, "You said you lost your two boys and your mother in the Rapture, but you didn't mention anything about your husband."

Tamika answered, "Why don't I let Isaac tell you himself..."

"Isaac's here?"

Tamika smiled wearily. "He sure is. Wanna meet him?"

"I'd love to."

"He's probably in the men's section having a group Bible study. We'll check there first. Follow me..."

The three nurses walked to the men's section looking for Isaac. Their minds were about to be blown again...

12

THE NEXT DAY

"WELL, HEY, NURSE, I wasn't sure if I'd ever see you again."

"Doctor Shapiro! Wow, what a surprise! So nice to see you!" said Nila. "How's the arm?"

Benjamin grinned at her. "GPS locator free, thanks to you."

Tamika's eyes bulged. She couldn't have been more shocked. "Wait, how do you two know each other?" Then it dawned on her. She put her hands on her hips. "Don't tell me, *you* removed his locator?!"

Nila chuckled at the way she had asked the question. "It was the first assignment I was given when I arrived in Kennett Square."

Tamika remarked, "I always assumed it was an ETSM nurse, Nila, but you? I never saw that in my dreams."

Benjamin was sitting on the edge of his cot, reading his Bible. He glanced up at Nila. *So, that's her name!* He knew not to ask for it at the house. "I haven't seen you in the hospital, Nila."

"I've been assigned to the quarantine area all week."

Benjamin's face lit up. He glanced at Tamika. "How ironic that the woman you went to college with, that we've been praying for all this time, is the same woman who removed my GPS locator! Only Yahweh could coordinate something this spectacular!"

Tamika told Nila, "When Doctor Shapiro left his house, he came to our safe house until we were relocated here…"

Nila replied, "I had no idea where he went. When I left his house, I went straight to the auto repair shop, then waited for Titus to bring me back here."

Benjamin said, "Can't say I'm surprised to see you here. In this strange new world, it only figures."

Hana's mind was already blown after hearing how God had brought Tamika together with Brian and Charles, followed by her former college friend. Now Nila and Doctor Shapiro? It truly was mind blowing.

Nila said, "I pray for you every day, Doctor Shapiro."

Benjamin nodded his thanks at her. "Speaking of prayer requests, do you remember the three men outside my house standing guard?"

"Yes, but not by their faces. I made sure not to make eye contact with them…"

"Understood. Well, the leader of the group is a man named Jack Nelson. I left the copy of *The Way* you placed inside in the bag for him. I believe Yahweh prompted me to do it. I even handwrote a personal inscription for him. Had I had more time, it would have been better, but I was up against the clock."

Nila asked, "Did he seem receptive to the Gospel message?"

Benjamin shook his head no. "But that doesn't mean Yahweh won't rescue him. I mean, look at me! I was Antichrist's personal physician, yet Yahweh saved me! If He uses my effort to save Jack Nelson, that's even better."

Nila shook her head in astonishment. "That will be my daily prayer for Mister Nelson from this day forward. You've prayed for me all this time, so it's the least I can do…"

"Thanks, Nila," said Benjamin in reply.

Tamika asked, "What safe house were you at, Nila?"

"In the Adirondack Mountains, in upstate New York, not too far from Lake Placid. I loved that place and never wanted to leave. It was so peaceful there."

Tamika glanced at Hana. "We can relate. How long did you stay there?"

"Nearly two years," came Nila's reply.

"Was your location also on the 'Montpelier' strike list?"

Nila nodded yes. "So, we knew our days were numbered. But when Romanero moved it up a week, it left us scrambling. The only good thing is that many of the toddlers I was caring for there, are now here.

"The rest relocated elsewhere. I've been caring for some of them since they were born. I never got married or had kids of my own. It's like they're my own children."

Benjamin said, "They're blessed to have you for a nurse."

Hana added, "I've seen her with them. They truly love her."

Nila blushed hearing this. "They give me strength each day to keep going." She said to Tamika, "By the way, congratulations on becoming a nurse! Did you go back to school after I graduated?"

A smile crossed Tamika's face, weary as it was. "No, but I never stopped reading my nursing books. Doctor Singh's been a wonderful teacher and mentor to me…"

Nila looked confused. "Singh?"

"Sorry, Calloway. She just got married when we relocated here. I can't get her maiden name out of my head. But I assure you the daily on-the-job training I got from her the past three years was better than anything our college professors ever taught me."

Tamika shook her head in amazement for the tenth time today. "Who would have thought in our college days that we'd end up living in hiding underground together, from the Antichrist of the Bible?"

Nila chuckled at the way Tamika had said it. She had really missed her sarcastic sense of humor. "When I heard on TV that you drove a cab for a living, I assumed you gave up on your dream."

Tamika grinned. "Thanks to the End Times Salvation Movement, my dream lives on. I realized after the Rapture that had I already been a nurse before then, I may have never met Brian and Charles."

Nila replied, "Once again, you've blown my mind, Tamika."

Tamika spotted Isaac and waved him over.

After introductions were made, Isaac said sheepishly to Nila, "I'm sure you don't have a very high opinion of me. If not, I don't blame you one bit."

Nila was confused by his remark. "Truth be told, the only thing I remember was Tamika getting pregnant and dropping out of college. But if my memory serves, everything she ever said about you was good."

Isaac ran his right hand across his forehead. "Phew!"

Nila chuckled, then said, "It doesn't matter what happened between the two of you after me and Tamika fell out of touch. The important thing is that you've remained together all this time, right?"

"Not hardly," said Isaac, in reply. "We just got back together a few months ago, after a very long separation."

Nila shot Tamika a sideways glance, clearly confused. "Really?"

"Yeah, it started long before the Rapture even…"

Isaac looked down at his threadbare sneakers. "Most of the damage was caused when I converted to Islam…"

Tamika shook her head, then shrugged. "Even after I got saved, I never thought I'd see the day when we would reconcile. Too much damage had been done, and we had zero communication for the longest time. When the kids disappeared, we no longer had that link between us.

"Then, much like I did with you, I started having dreams that me and Isaac would reconcile. But since he was so dedicated to his Islamic faith, I never expected it to come true. Part of me didn't want it to."

Isaac said, "But God had other plans."

Tamika grinned again. "We re-tied the knot shortly before we were relocated here. We're expecting our third child together."

Nila asked, "How many months?"

"I'm midway through my second trimester." Tamika kissed Isaac on the forehead, then said to Nila, "This sort of ties into the second dream I had, that you were an ETSM nurse. About that time, I also had a dream about John Reitz, a New York City police officer.

"I met him the day after the Rapture, when I went to the local police precinct to file a missing person's claim. When he heard me say it was for my two children, he all but shooed me away.

"I had totally forgotten about him until I started having dreams to contact him. But how could I contact him when there was a warrant for my arrest in his city? Long story short, Brian's father received a text message instructing him to go to this police precinct looking for Officer John Reitz, as a favor to his wife, Sarah, on behalf of me.

"Dick wasn't an ETSM member at that time, so we knew we were taking a huge risk. On top of that, he hated me, for what I did to his son. Needless to say, he only did it for his wife, not me.

"Officer Reitz wasn't working the day he went there. But when a fellow officer told him about Dick's visit, and that he only wanted to talk to him, plus he was Brian Mulrooney's father, he became curious.

"Turns out, he was a Christian. He went to Dick's house the next day after work. At first, Dick was hesitant to let him in. But after Officer Reitz said he believed Brian and Tamika were innocent, they spent a few hours together. Before he left that night, Dick asked him to go to Presbyterian Hospital looking for you."

Nila was blown away hearing this.

Tamika scratched the back of her neck. "My hopes were dashed when they informed him that you suddenly resigned your position, and no one on staff knew where you went. But here's the thing, God even used that failed mission to win Isaac to Christ."

"How?"

"It's quite a remarkable story. But to tell it, I must include another ETSM member, Amos Nyarwarta. Amos was a lifelong Muslim before his conversion. He came from Africa, in a country that was nearly one hundred percent Islamic. He converted to Christianity after the Rapture. Amos called me one day saying he was having dreams about Isaac."

Nila's eyes widened. "Seriously?"

"I know, you can't make this stuff up! It's not like they knew each other. Despite the danger he faced, Amos was determined to travel to New York City, to meet Isaac and share the Gospel with him. Brian's father drove from New York City to Chadds Ford, to take Amos back to New York with him.

"The next day, Dick introduced Amos to John Reitz. Amos shared his dream with John, about seeing Isaac pleading with a group of men to stop calling him by his Muslim name, because he no longer identified as a Muslim. As you can imagine, they felt completely betrayed by him.

"Before Dick went to Pennsylvania to get Amos, he asked Officer Reitz if he could locate my husband in the city. Dick handed him a piece of paper with a possible address for him. After confirming his address, John drove by Isaac's apartment building, to find a group of men loitering outside. Even though they were casually dressed, if they were trying to conceal their outlawed Islamic faith, they were doing a lousy job. They even had prayer rugs that faced the east.

"What really sparked John's suspicions about them was each time they finished praying, they would glance up at Isaac's apartment window on the eighth floor, as if waiting for him to leave or return home.

"When Amos confirmed that was precisely what he saw in his dream, it was enough for the three of them to drive there that day." Isaac took it from there, "By that time, I was already in a bad way. I knew they were out there waiting for me. But I also had to try to escape. Two of my former Muslim brothers tripped me when I left my apartment building. I ended up with a concussion. Just as they were about to kill me in the street for leaving the faith, Amos came to the rescue."

Isaac shook his head very slowly. "I'll never forget how he looked at me, and said, 'Greater love has no one than this, that a person will lay down his life for his friends.' At that time, I had no idea he was quoting John fifteen, thirteen.

"Amos pointed me in the direction of a car across the street, telling me to escape while I can. He told me not to fear for him. He said if I knew what he knew, I would be petrified for myself, not for him. He then said to me, 'The only hope you have is to believe in Jesus for your salvation! There's no other way to God but through Him!'

"This made the man with the knife in his hands even angrier. But the strangest thing Amos said to me that day was, 'You're still married! Go and have a child with your wife.' I couldn't believe my ears! I thought to myself, does this man know Tamika? If so, how?

"Amos then asked the man with the knife pointed at him, if he could pray for him. That's the kind of man he was. Instead of accepting his kind offer, the man growled angrily at Amos, shouted "Allahu Akbar!" then jammed the knife into his midsection, killing him."

Tears flooded Isaac's eyes. "Before I could reach the getaway car, two more men tackled me in the middle of the street. Since I already had a concussion, I posed no challenge to them.

"That's when Officer Reitz came to my rescue. He got out of the vehicle, opened the rear door for me, then started swinging at them with his walking cane. In his frail condition, he had no chance of overpowering them, but he did just enough for me to make my getaway. I watched them taking turns stabbing him to death. And to think his killers were my two former friends..."

Tears fell down Isaac's cheeks, but he didn't bother wiping them away. "I didn't know Amos or John. Yet, they both died for me. I didn't know the man in the car was Brian's father either. Then again, I didn't know Brian, or that he helped Tamika escape from New York City way back when."

Nila and Hana were spellbound hearing how it had all unfolded.

Isaac went on, "As we drove off to safety, Dick told me John's wish was that the huge sacrifice they were making for us would lead us both into the arms of Jesus. When we made it back to his house, we read the Word together day and night. That's when we both got saved for real."

Isaac looked at Nila. Even her eyes were moist with tears. "God used their deaths to save my soul. Brian's father, too. I still shake my head in awe whenever I think about that day. They were the bravest men I've ever met. And selfless."

Tamika rubbed her belly. "Had it not been for the two of them, Isaac wouldn't be here now, and I wouldn't be pregnant. We're praying for a son so we can name him after those two men. If it happens, his name will be Amos John. A.J. for short."

"Aww, so sweet," said Nila. "I'm amazed at how far God will go to rescue His children!"

"Thank you, Jesus!" Isaac asked, "Now you know our story, Nila. And the whole world knows about Hana's story. Why don't you tell us yours?"

"Ha! It can't compare to yours. I'm sure everyone here has a remarkable story to tell, of how God had brought them here. But I would be hard pressed to believe anyone topping the stories I've heard today. It's stranger than fiction. And who can top Hana's story!"

The reunion ended abruptly when Vishnu Uddin rushed into the men's section. "Charles would like to see us in the worship area."

"What for?" ask Isaac.

Vishnu shrugged. "He just heard from Clayton. That's all I know."

Isaac glanced over at Nila. "To be continued…"

MEANWHILE, YASAMIN DABIRI-UDDIN went to the women's area to inform them. Jacquelyn sat on a cot that wasn't even hers. It took much prodding from her sisters in Christ before she finally found the strength to lift herself up off the bed, and follow them down the long corridor leading to the worship area…

13

IT WAS EVIDENT TO everyone trickling into the worship room that Charles Calloway was deeply grieved. Now in possession of the only phone allowed at the safe house, he was the first to hear Holmes' final message to all surviving *ETSM* residents. The explosion at the end, followed by the deafening silence, had left him breathless.

He couldn't fathom how his two spiritual mentors were gone. After having a good cry, Calloway walked the long corridor leading to the hospital, so his wife Meera could listen to it, before summoning the adults into the worship room to share the tragic news with them.

Most of the equipment that was used at the safe house number one sanctuary, was brought to Kennett Square, including the sound system.

Calloway turned on a battery-operated microphone to address the hundreds gathered. "Since there's no way to sugarcoat it, I'll come straight to the point. It's with a heavy heart I inform you all that our leaders are dead..."

Loud gasping filled the room.

Jefferson asked, "How do you know, Charles?"

Calloway lowered his head, then spoke into the microphone so everyone would hear his reply. "I just listened to a recording from Clayton. They were on their way here, at least I think they were, when their car was hit by a drone strike. I heard Lee Kim say in a panic that a microflier detected their voices, just moments before impact."

He handed the phone and his earbuds to Jefferson. "Feel free to listen for yourself."

Jefferson pressed one of Calloway's earbuds in his ears, then offered the other one to Amy. She declined.

When he was finished, Tony Pearsall signaled that he wanted to hear it. When he was finished, Julio Gonzalez wanted to listen next.

Charles said, "I think it would be best if I played it so everyone can hear it. If you don't want to listen, cover your ears."

Jacquelyn did just that. What she saw on their faces offered her a grim precursor of things to come, regarding the fate of her husband. She was grateful to no longer be in possession of the phone. Had she been the first to hear it, it probably would have pushed her over the edge. Pain flooded her heart for her departed leaders.

Charles held the phone up to the microphone and pushed play. When it was finished, he said, "I can't tell you how many times I heard Clayton tell me he didn't want to be alive when the bowl judgments struck the planet. Looks like his prayer was answered. And the answer he received from God was, 'It's time to come Home, good and faithful servant.'"

"I couldn't be happier for our three leaders," remarked Julio Gonzalez. "How ironic that they joined our brothers and sisters in Heaven, mere moments after Clayton shared Revelation fifteen with us. I wonder, are they holding harps given to them by God, with the rest of the victorious, or do they have to be processed first?"

Charles shrugged. "Good question, Julio. All I know for sure is they're no longer carrying that massive weight on their shoulders from leading us all this time. We all saw it."

In a small way, it felt like that weight had just been transferred onto his shoulders. He kept that morbid thought to himself.

Calloway looked out at the gathering. He saw many new faces. They had all heard stories about the two leaders. It was time to broaden their perspectives a little more. "What can I say? Clayton and Travis were the two big brothers I never had. I loved them both dearly. For all you newcomers who may not know, I was first introduced to this organization through a website they created at the outset.

"Last Shot At Redemption took each visitor through the Book of Revelation, step by step, explaining in vivid detail what really happened on the day of the disappearances. It was an awesome site. It helped millions all over the globe, before Romanero shut it down.

"Clayton sure knew what he was talking about! I was struck by the conviction behind his words. Another thing I liked was his brute honesty. He confessed that his pride and ego had kept him from humbly seeking God all his life. He said he was so full of himself that he even had his own prophecy website that was named after himself—the 'Clayton Holmes' Ultimate Prophecy Site.'

"I was struck by the man's transparency. As a prideful false convert myself, raised in the church, but left behind like him, his words really resonated with me. I knew he and Travis were out to do big things for the Kingdom. I wanted in.

"It took several emails before Travis finally got back to me. He informed me to go online for a video chat. The instant I saw them on my laptop screen, I knew Clayton was the frontman of the organization, and Travis was the business mind and chief facilitator.

"This ultimately led to our first meeting. I was told to go to a Denny's restaurant just south of Atlanta, Georgia, of all places. After waiting for more than an hour, my waiter told me they weren't coming. I was shocked. How could he possibly know that? I thought I was being set up.

"Turns out Dylan was already a member of the organization I was hoping to join. He put my mind at ease a bit when he told me the meeting was still on. He then directed me to a hotel up the road where Clayton and Travis were staying. He told me to look for a woman working at the front desk, named Purnima, and ask for William Fuller.

"For the record, Dylan was the first person to say to me, 'Keep fighting the good fight. Pray for me as I pray for you. God is with us.' He was tall and skinny with tattoos all over his body. But, man, did he love Jesus! My shock knew no bounds when Purnima uttered the very same thing that Dylan had just told me at the restaurant. They later got married.

"Purnima directed me to the eighth floor. When I got off the elevator, William Fuller was waiting for me in the hallway. It was really Braxton Rice. If you don't know, he was the chief of security for our organization, until he was killed trying to help Yogesh Patel escape from Salvador Romanero."

All eyes shifted to Hana Patel. She lowered her head. She knew God had forgiven her, for the way she had treated her husband back then, but whenever his name was mentioned, the guilt still lingered. She still missed Yogesh every day.

Charles glanced at her as if to say, "It wasn't your fault," then continued, "Braxton was a no-nonsense type of person, and one of the bravest men I've ever met. He took me to Clayton and Travis. It was the start of a beautiful friendship and brotherhood between us.

"Once we started accumulating properties, I ended up staying at the safe house down south, with my Aunt Evelyn and her husband Ernest Stone. Dylan and Purnima also lived there. I got to know them both very well. We were there during the global quake. The four of them were killed. I was the only survivor…"

Charles took a few deep breaths to collect himself, then continued with his eulogy of sorts. "I was at my lowest point since losing my wife and five kids in the Rapture. And who found me there and helped me back to my feet? My two mentors, Travis and Clayton."

Calloway lost it. He hunched over and wept uncontrollably. It was a guttural sob that drowned out the room even without the use of a microphone. Everyone felt his pain.

Meera bent down next to her husband and kissed the top of his head. This tender action further justified to her that getting married at the most inopportune time in history was the right choice to make after all.

Meera took the microphone from her husband. She wiped her moist eyes with her right sleeve. "And we mustn't forget Lee Kim. Without his help, we wouldn't have been nearly as successful. His behind-the-scenes leadership was paramount to keeping us protected online.

"Since Doctor Kim was the only person to have access to the ETSM database, there's no way of knowing where the other surviving safe houses are located. We must also assume that the protection he provided for us as an IT expert is also gone."

Many heads nodded sadly in agreement.

"Some of the casualties suffered last week, were part of Jefferson Danforth's cabinet, when he was still President." Charles told her how broken he was when he first heard the news. Meera glanced at him. "Anything you'd like to say?"

Jefferson nodded yes, then cleared his throat. "It's true that some of my former cabinet members were also ETSM members. They were National Security Adviser, Nelson Casanieves, Chief of Staff, Aaron Gillespie, my military Joint Chief of Staff, William Messersmith, and one of my Secret Service agents, Anthony Galiano.

"When Braxton Rice was killed, these men took over the security for us. All were faithful servants, who ended up protecting us even more than we could ever imagine. For the record, Vice President Everett Ashford was also a believer. I can't wait to be reunited with them soon."

Jefferson stopped speaking when Titus entered the room and slowly made his way to the front. The four somber-faced individuals who went to Chadds Ford with him followed behind him. Their clothes were filthy and soaked all the way through with sweat. They all wondered in silence what had caused this gathering among them.

Titus ignored it for the time being. He whispered loud enough that Jefferson and Charles could both hear him, "They're gone. We buried their bodies in Chadds Ford before we left."

Lila looked down at her feet. "So sorry for your loss, Charles. I know how close you were to Brian and Tom."

Charles glanced at Jacquelyn. "Thanks Lila…"

Titus looked out at everyone. "What's going on?"

Calloway answered solemnly, "Clayton, Travis and Lee are dead."

"What?" The shock on Titus' face was evident. It was a gut-punch. Why did they survive their trip, short as it was, but their leaders didn't?

Calloway took a moment to explain to the five of them what had happened to their fearless leaders earlier in the day.

Lila wept silently as Charles recalled it in his mind. After a while, she dried her moist eyes and asked Charles, also in a whisper, "Did Brian and Tom have peanut butter crackers in their pods, before the strike?"

"Peanut butter crackers? I seriously doubt it. I remember seeing them on one of the tables, but not in their pods. Why do you ask?"

Lila glanced nervously at Dick and Sarah Mulrooney. "I found open wrappers in their pods."

Charles was astounded hearing this. "They survived the bombing?"

Lila nodded sadly. "It appears that way. But it's hard to tell for how long. I can't help but wonder if…" She paused, then pivoted. "I don't have the strength to tell Jacquelyn."

Charles sensed what she was thinking. Had only they gotten there sooner…"I don't think she needs to know," came his soft reply.

Jacquelyn watched the exchange between them. She was thankful she couldn't hear them. But just one glance at Lila was enough to confirm what she already knew—her husband was dead.

Charles took the microphone from Jefferson, then addressed the group again. "Sorry to be the bearer of even more sad news, but Brian and Tom didn't make it."

The room became even more still when Jacquelyn got up out of her seat and left, sobbing loudly.

Sarah Mulrooney let go of her husband's hand and followed her daughter-in-law out of the room. Mary Johnson then followed Sarah.

If anyone understood what Jacquelyn was going through it was Mary. But unlike Jacquelyn, even though Donald had been gone for many months, Mary still had hope, waning as it was.

If her husband was still at sea when the second bowl judgment struck the planet, how could he possibly survive? Deep down inside, she was resigned to the fact that Donald probably wasn't coming home.

Dick Mulrooney remained behind holding his granddaughter on his lap. As much as he wanted to console Jacquelyn and Sarah, he first wanted to hear what Charles would say about his son and Tom Dunleavey.

Dick went from hating Tom to becoming one of his closest friends, after he became a true believer and moved onto the Chadds Ford property. Now Tom was gone. Pain stabbed at Dick's heart from losing his only son and good friend at the same time.

Charles cleared his throat. "Clayton and Travis were my two spiritual mentors, but Brian and Tamika were my best friends." He sniffled into the microphone. "God brought us together in the most remarkable way. He blessed my life with two of the greatest friendships I could've ever asked for. What's best is I even got to share the Gospel with them."

Many who were relocated from safe house number one were familiar with how the three of them had met. Everyone else, the majority, listened with great interest.

Tamika's hormones were already out of whack due to her pregnancy. Tears streamed down her cheeks one after the next. She got up out of her seat and threw herself into her spiritual mentor's arms.

Isaac observed them clinging to each other, both shaking uncontrollably. He wasn't jealous. He knew how instrumental Brian and Charles had been in his absence. If anything, witnessing this Godly friendship they shared, caused him to respect Charles even more.

Tamika dried her moist eyes, then glanced at Nila and Hana, who had already heard about her soul-saving encounter up to this point. "Had it not been for Brian and Charles, I wouldn't be here now. Believe me when I say, I was so unhinged back then that I honestly thought I would commit suicide.

"Most of you don't know this, and I know Brian wouldn't want you to know, but when I was on the run from the cops, I was living in my car, in New Jersey, with my cat, Cocoa. I had no money, no gas in the tank, little food, and no place to go. I begged Brian to come to New York to help me, only I couldn't tell him about my problem online. Without demanding to know more, he agreed to come to New York."

Tamika fanned her face with her left hand, then took a few deep breaths, hoping to control herself. It didn't help. She exploded in tears. "And what did Brian do when we met? He let me stay with him in his hotel for two nights. Then, before he left for Michigan, to get married, he reserved a hotel room for me for two weeks, in his name.

"Had Brian not done that before Charles came to rescue me," she cried, "I would have surely been caught. Even though we only spent a few years together, it felt like a lifetime. Oh, how I'll miss him…"

Tamika looked at Dick Mulrooney. She still remembered how furious he was at Brian's wedding, upon realizing that one of his son's bridesmaids was a wanted criminal. And how could she forget the hate-filled glare on his face that was intended for her, before he stormed out of the church, mere moments before the wedding even started? Now they were the closest of friends. "So sorry for your loss."

Dick's lower lip quivered. Tears streamed down his cheeks one after the next. "I praise God for using my son back then to rescue you."

Tamika and Isaac went over to comfort Dick.

Calloway pounded his heart softly at Brian's father, expressing his love for him, as the three of them were engaged in a group hug.

Dick nodded back at him tearfully. He was just as shattered as they were.

After a while, Charles continued, "And let's not forget about Tom Dunleavey. He was a close second to Brian and Tamika. If you could have been a fly on the wall and heard what transpired in Brian's and Jacquelyn's bedroom, just before we were forced to evacuate safe house number one, you would have been moved to tears too.

"When it became apparent that Brian would never make it here, I offered to stay with him in the fallout shelter. Dick did, too. But Tom insisted that he be the one to do it. If going down to the bomb shelter with Brian meant death for him, he was fully resigned to it.

"Tom said it wasn't a suicide mission. He felt he was doing the will of God. He told me my leadership skills would surely be needed in Kennett Square. He then said he would never get married or have a child, but perhaps I might again someday."

Charles reached for Meera's hand. "That's when this beautiful woman answered the question for us, saying, 'Yes, he will.'" He glanced up at the ceiling, then took a moment to collect himself. "That's what I call a true hero in the faith. I was the last one to see Brian and Tom alive. I carried Brian down to the safe shelter. He was too sick to even walk.

"The last thing I told them was that I loved them. I can only imagine what they're experiencing right now. I'm sure they've already been reunited with Travis, Clayton, and Lee…"

Charles wiped his moist eyes with his shirt sleeve then added, "Without a doubt, the End Times Salvation Movement is the greatest organization I've ever been a part of. Since the good Lord has decided to take our faithful leaders from us, for all intents and purposes, the ETSM is no more. Well, at the very least, with no way of contacting the other five thousand locations, essentially, we're on our own...

"But this doesn't mean God has forsaken us or forgotten about us. Perhaps He's reminding us once again that Clayton and Travis were never in charge of this organization to begin with. It was always Him. In that light, we don't need to know where those other locations are.

"But don't think for a second that God has forgotten about us. He is as mindful of us now as he was when he knitted each one of us together in our mother's wombs. And we mustn't forget He chose this place to preserve our lives until Christ returns. So, let's all do our best to get along. Shall we?"

"In closing, while my heart aches over this latest round of casualties, I rejoice knowing they're in the best place ever. It's the very same place we'll all be going to soon enough. A place where we'll never sob or ache or feel anguished ever again. Amen?"

"Amen," came the soft reply of many.

Jakob was in the back of the room listening to everything being said. Before anyone could leave, he walked up front and took the microphone from Charles. It was time to clear up a few things for them...

14

"SHALOM!" JAKOB BEGAN, "I know you're all hurting over the loss of your leaders. Perhaps you're even confused about why they were killed, when all were faithful servants. This includes Brian and Tom."

Jakob let his words settle in their minds, then said, "As all of you know, the supernatural protection Yahweh provided when you were being transported here has since been lifted. What this means is, only those who still have missions to carry out, like those transporting expectant women to our safe houses, or those who will be caring for our children, will still have this supernatural protection, and will survive on the outside. All other believers will continue to be identified and martyred for their faith.

"Apparently, Clayton Holmes, Travis Hartings and Lee Kim were part of that equation. This could only mean the three of them had no further missions to carry out for Yahweh. Since their voices were already stored in the global database, from the website they launched at the outset, the instant Clayton's voice was snatched out of the air, the counter-measure detectors in their vehicle couldn't protect them from Antichrist's invisible forces."

The reason Jakob used the word "apparently" was, just like with his 143,999 sealed brothers, their knowledge was limited. By being Yahweh's sealed servants, they were fully protected from Antichrist, and their wisdom was unparalleled to anyone else's. Even so, they were still human, which meant their knowledge of the future was limited. This included not knowing who would be saved and who wouldn't be.

"Even though we mourn their losses, let me comfort you all with these words that are found in Revelation twenty, verses four through six. 'And *I saw* thrones, and they sat on them, and judgment was committed to them. Then *I saw* the souls of those who had been beheaded for their witness to Jesus and for the word of God, who had not worshiped the beast or his image, and had not received *his* mark on their foreheads or on their hands.

"'And they lived and reigned with Christ for a thousand years. But the rest of the dead did not live again until the thousand years were finished. This *is* the first resurrection. Blessed and holy *is* he who has part in the first resurrection. Over such the second death has no power, but they shall be priests of God and of Christ, and shall reign with Him a thousand years.'"

Daniel Sullivan shook his head in astonishment. But what he felt went beyond the beautiful scripture Jakob just read to them. He couldn't understand why he was still alive.

Now that his Secret Service skills were no longer needed, what other skills did he have to warrant his survival, other than transporting Tyler Stephenson to this place? What protection would he have when he left for Washington looking for Jefferson's children?

With billions of microfliers always out patrolling the planet, it was illogical to think that Christians could move about undetected. All Jakob did was further clarify what he felt all along—their technology could never outmaneuver Romanero's flying surveillance spies.

When Daniel carelessly called Jefferson on the way to this place, his voice had to have been recorded, like the three *ETSM* leaders. Not only that, but he was a government employee, which meant his entire DNA had long since been stored in the global database.

So, why was he still alive when they were dead? Clearly, they had so much more to offer the organization than he did.

Jakob went on, "I know some of you were shocked to discover that the safe houses you just evacuated were destroyed by Antichrist. Yahweh always has reasons for everything. With the second, third, and fourth bowl judgments looming, He repositioned His children to places that could still function into the future. I'll ask Eli to explain the two main reasons you were all relocated to Kennett Square."

Eli Yoder stood and took the microphone. "The first reason is that we have ample well water here, that's been completely sealed off to the outside world. So, we'll never have to worry about our water being turned into blood when the third bowl is poured out on the streams and rivers of the world.

"The second reason is solar power. Before the Rapture, our neighbors, the Millers, who went to be with the Lord at the Rapture, placed more than two thousand solar energy panels where their farmland used to be. They farmed most of that energy out, but they kept the rest for their own personal use.

"They invited us to tap into their personal usage whenever we wanted, in exchange for meat and produce. Now that we're housing so many Christians, and we're believers ourselves, with the sun soon to be dominating the skies above, we're blessed to be able to tap into this renewable energy, to help with the exponential growth.

"I'm certain they would be thrilled knowing they were helping us even in absentia." Eli sighed. "Just wished we would have believed like our children, grandchildren, and the Millers did before the Rapture…"

He handed the microphone back to Jakob. "Thanks Eli. All of you who were relocated from other safe houses to here, didn't have access to these things." He looked at Tamika and Nila, who were seated together. "Some of you could have been sent to safe houses that were closer than this place. But Yahweh, in His omniscience, brought you here to reunite with friends and family members who had all but lost contact.

"This is happening at all remaining safe houses, which, by the way, also have clean water and solar power. Since these will be our final residences before the Millennial Kingdom is ushered in, Yahweh wanted to bring those who were related together for comfort during the storm."

Nila reached for Tamika's hand and gave it a good squeeze. Both women were blown away hearing this.

Jakob glanced over at Jefferson Danforth. "Even the satellite you sent up in space, which provided us with safe communications all this time, has been compromised. Much like your departed leaders, Yahweh had protected it until it was no longer necessary."

A glow formed on Jakob's face. "Our remaining safe houses very much resemble what happened in Egypt, thousands of years ago, when the Most High passed through that wicked country, to strike down every firstborn of people and animals, to bring judgment on all the gods of Egypt. He passed over all houses with the blood covering the sides and tops of the doorframes of the houses where His chosen people, the Israelites, ate the lambs.

"Since Yeshua is the true Passover Lamb, all locations are covered by His blood. What this means is Antichrist has no power over this place or at any other location at which me and my sealed brothers are residing. To the enemy, our locations don't exist. They will remain supernaturally protected by Jehovah Jireh Himself.

"So, whenever you're here, you will be perfectly safe until Yeshua returns. Some of you may die here from disease or from old age. But the enemy will have nothing to do with it.

"Moving along, many of you newcomers still seem confused about the number six-six-six. Allow me to shed some light on it for you. Simply stated, six is man's number, as evidenced by the fact that man was created on the sixth day. With regard to the number six-six-six, one six represents Satan, or Lucifer, one six represents the Antichrist, and one six represents the False Prophet.

"Seven, on the other hand, is Yahweh's number. It is the number of both completion and perfection. We are reminded of this again in the Book of Revelation, which all of you know is the last book in the Bible. It's also known as the book of completion. Yahweh the Father represents the first seven, Yeshua represents the second seven, the Holy Spirit represents the third seven, thus making up the Holy Trinity, seven-seven-seven.

"Since the number seven-seven-seven reflects the perfect Trinity, six-six-six points to an unholy trinity, which will always fall short of the perfection of the Holy Trinity. It can never be complete, and it can never be divine. Now that this unholy Trinity has been firmly established, and all diabolical agents have been clearly identified, the system they are using to enslave the world is the internet."

Jakob further explained, "The first foundational clue Yahweh gave to humanity in these latter days, was the computer itself. The first one ever sold went for six hundred and sixty-six dollars. It was an Apple computer. It's no accident that the company logo was an apple, with a bite taken from it.

"This harkens back to the garden of Eden, when Satan tempted Eve with the forbidden fruit. The serpent told Eve that she would not die if she took a bite, but her eyes would be opened, and she would be like Yahweh, knowing good and evil. Eve took some and ate it, then gave some to Adam, who was with her. Then their eyes were opened, and they realized they were naked. This represented the fall of man.

"The final clue that this unholy trinity is using computer technology to ensnare the planet, is that the first income opportunity that Antichrist and the False Prophet offered to all mark takers, in this new global system, was capturing Christians. Now that those funds are being taxed, the False Prophet proudly declared that recipients would keep six hundred and sixty-six dollars for every thousand they would earn in that unholy endeavor.

"But just like everything else they link themselves to, it's not going according to plan. Antichrist warned in his speech, on the day Yahweh's angelic messenger interrupted him, that many who proclaimed to be his followers really weren't.

"He went so far as to say that not all heretics on the planet were Christ followers. He then added that in no way were they his true followers, including some he had elevated to such lofty heights."

Jakob glanced at his Uncle Benjamin. "I rejoice in saying that one of them was my uncle. My heart swells with joy every time I see you here. On behalf of everyone here, thanks for redirecting the many meds that are now being used to cure many who had caught the global flu."

His comment brought tears to Benjamin's eyes.

"And speaking about the global flu now running rampant on the planet, Yahweh sent it as a final act of mercy, for those receiving copies of *The Way* from His sealed servants. Instead of taking the mark, they are at home reading it, which will lead to their salvation."

Jakob went on, "In essence, Antichrist said the only way to eradicate this most grievous betrayal against him, and to know for sure who was truly with him, would be by implementing the mark. He said this would be the final proof of their allegiance to the new global economy, government, and religion that he and the False Prophet have put in place.

"Like everything else coming out of Antichrist's mouth, it was a lie. There are many mark takers who want the benefit of the mark and the chip, but who refuse to bow down in worship of him. These individuals have been placed on the False Prophet's new secular list.

"On the surface, it sounds confusing. They were all supposed to be on the same team. Essentially, they are. But the only reason they took the mark was so they could survive in the new global economy.

"This shouldn't come as a surprise to any of us. Listen carefully to Yahweh's third angelic messenger's warning against taking the mark. His last words were, 'There will be no rest day or night for those who worship the beast and its image, or for anyone who receives the mark of its name.'

"Did you get that? 'Those who worship the beast and its image, *or* for anyone who receives the mark of its name.' It's an either-or statement. This means there is a clear split between both the religious and secular sides. Most will do both, but many only want the mark so they can function in society.

"Antichrist's religious followers will be the most loyal. But his secular mark takers will not bow down to his statue in Jerusalem. In fact, this rogue faction will cause trouble for Antichrist and the False Prophet down the road. They will even try usurping their power.

"Even so, whether they bow down in worship to the statue or not, all who take the mark on their right hands, or on their foreheads will suffer the same eternal consequences. No one will take it accidentally. That's all I have to say for now. Yahweh's grace and peace be with you all."

At that, Jakob left them.

15

DICK MULROONEY WAS GLAD that he stuck around to hear the touching eulogy Charles gave for both his son and Tom Dunleavey. Even though he was too emotional to concentrate on his words at times, what he was able to absorb comforted him deeply.

He carried his granddaughter to the single women's section. He found his wife and daughter-in-law sitting on Jacquelyn's bed. Sarah was rubbing her shoulders.

Mary sat on her cot across from Jacquelyn's.

Jacquelyn wasn't crying because Brian was in Heaven. That was a cause for rejoicing. If anything, she was crying for herself.

Much like Mary and her mother-in-law, Jacquelyn had aspired to relocate to the married couples' section, once Brian returned to her.

Dick and Sarah transferred there two days ago, when it became available to them. Even then, Jacquelyn still held onto hope, slight as it was, that she would join them there. Now she knew it would never happen.

It was the worst kind of torture being crammed in a large room all week, with a bunch of women sleeping on small beds, all the while wondering if her husband was dead or alive.

Her gut kept telling her Brian didn't survive what hit him. Now that it had been confirmed, how much worse would it be from here on out?

Jacquelyn was grateful to be surrounded by so many women who truly loved her. On the other hand, she wanted to be alone so she could cry for hours on end, without being bothered by anyone.

She didn't have that luxury at this place.

But even that wasn't what tore her up the most. Had Brian only been able to hang in there a little longer, they could have remained married going into the Millennial Kingdom. That was the killer.

When they first got married, the one question no one could answer was, if married couples survived the seven-year tribulation, would they go into the Millennial Kingdom as husband and wife?

Jakob confirmed to everyone a few months ago that they would. He also confirmed that their children would get married and have children.

Jacquelyn was there when he said it. When Brian was sick with double pneumonia, just before they were relocated to this place, she pushed

Jakob's words back to the farthest recesses of her mind, in case her husband didn't get better. Now Brian was gone.

Mary was having similar thoughts herself. She hadn't totally given up on Donald just yet, but with the second bowl judgment looming, mindful that her husband was sailing on the oceans of the world, she wasn't confident that she would ever see him again.

With so many of their leaders gone, it further tilted her thinking that Donald might never return to her.

Dick handed baby Sarah to Jacquelyn, then sat next to Sarah. "You should have heard what was said about our son," he said tenderly.

Sarah wiped her nose with a tissue, then sniffled softly. "Why did we outlive our two children? We brought them into the world. They're supposed to be mourning for us, not the other way around."

Dick folded his hands on his lap. "I know. It tortures me too. I'm just grateful that God restored my relationship with Brian. If not, I'd be so much worse now. And we both know we'll see him again soon enough…"

"Of course, I rejoice knowing Brian is being comforted now. But how can I not think about Chelsea? I never thought I'd say this to you, but I hate thinking about her. Each time I do, pain stabs at my heart."

Dick was thinking similar thoughts himself. He held his wife in silence, as they both shed tears. "The price we're paying for being Christ followers is quite steep…," he mumbled more to himself than to Sarah.

He sighed, thinking, *Is this what you meant by carrying my cross daily and following you, Lord?*

Hana Patel's bed was situated on the opposite side of the massive room. But even from her vantage point, she saw Jacquelyn sitting on her bed, looking completely heartbroken.

She said to her daughter, "I think Jacquelyn needs lots of hugs."

Cristiana glanced up at her mother with those two beautiful brown eyes of hers. "Okay, Mama."

When they got there, without saying a word, Cristiana plucked baby Sarah off Jacquelyn's lap, plopped her down on her grandmother's lap, then hugged Jacquelyn as tightly as she could. It was a touching moment.

Hana said, "I'm so sorry for your loss, Jacquelyn. Brian was a dear friend and a true brother to me. If it weren't for the two of you, who knows where Cristiana and I would be now? Certainly not here.

"When Yasamin left for the married couple's section, it upset me very much. Of course, I'm happy for her. But this is the first time we've been separated since we met in Singapore.

"I know it isn't much, but I'd be honored if you took the bed she slept on before she left. It's right next to mine. Since we're both without our husbands, the least we can do is be there to comfort one another."

Mary looked down at her feet. She knew it was wrong to feel slightly jealous by the attention Jacquelyn was receiving. She wanted to scream, "What about me? Where's my hug? I'm also going through it…"

Hana sensed what she was thinking. "There's room over there for you too, Mary."

Mary looked at Hana sheepishly. "Are you sure?"

Hana shot her an assuring smile. "I'd love you to join us…"

Mary looked at Jacquelyn. She shrugged then nodded yes.

They followed Hana and Cristiana to the opposite side of the massive room. Jacquelyn knew where Hana's bed was, from the two wrinkled pieces of paper that were taped on the wall above it, with the scriptures Mark 8:36 and Romans 8:28 handwritten on them.

She remembered the story behind them. Hana had told her that Yogesh wrote Mark 8:36 on the one piece of paper, then hung it on the bedroom wall when they were still married. Whenever she would see it hanging there, it made her mad.

She confessed at that time she was enjoying gaining the whole world. But after her husband was killed, and she came to faith in Christ, she realized it was at the peril of her own soul, just like Mark 8:36 had warned. Hana wrote Romans 8:28 on the other piece of paper soon after that time.

Jacquelyn said, "I'm glad you didn't forget to bring them with you."

Hana followed her eyes upward. "I would never leave them behind. Those two pieces of paper traveled halfway around the world with me. They are precious to me. My only request upon being relocated here was that my bed was next to a wall, so I could hang them on it."

Mary started sniffling. Just hearing the words, "traveling halfway around the world" made her think of Donald. It triggered this next wave of depression inside her.

She dried her eyes with the sleeve from her sweater. "I understood Donald's reason for going, and I still don't blame him for it, but it seems like we got married and had a child in the blink of an eye. Suddenly, here I am all alone again without my husband.

"Ever since Jakob confirmed that husbands and wives would go into the Millennial Kingdom, much like Jacquelyn, I've been clinging to that hope. But with the second bowl judgment looming, I have serious doubts of ever seeing him again.

"You know how I've battled abandonment issues all my life. That's what it feels like now, like Donald left me all alone with Luke."

Hana said, "I can only imagine how difficult it must be for you. But it's because of your husband that me and Cristiana are even here in the first place. Brian and Jaquelyn got the process moving forward, but had Donald not made the long voyage, we may not even be alive. God used him to save four lives, the two of us, and Yasamin and Navid."

Mary felt like she had just been hit in the head with a frying pan. "You're right. Sorry. I need to do a better job of keeping things in perspective."

The three women were silent as they watched Cristiana playing with baby Sarah on the floor.

Finally, Mary said, "When me and Jacquelyn mailed that Bible to you, way back when, we met a young woman at a restaurant in New Jersey. Candace was our waitress. We later had dreams about her.

"When Clayton told us before we came here that if we had dreams about others, the time to contact them was now, suddenly, Candace came to mind again. But how could we possibly contact her when the only thing we knew about her was her first name? Even if she still works at that restaurant, how could we get to her?"

Mary looked at her badly chipped fingernails. She looked like she was a breath away from losing it again. "The worst part is that I became so depressed that I even stopped praying for her salvation."

"I'm sure God understands that, Mary."

"You're right, Hana. I'm sure He does. But you just told me God used my husband to rescue you. What if He was counting on me and Jacquelyn to rescue Candace?"

Jacquelyn lowered her head, among soft sniffling.

Mary wiped more tears from her eyes. "I became so self-absorbed with my own issues, that I stopped being obedient to what I feel was what He wanted me to do for His glory." She sat on Hana's bed and wept uncontrollably. "Forgive me, Lord, for making it all about me."

Cristiana was listening to the conversation. She got up off the floor and wrapped her arms around Mary, until she finished having a long cry.

Jacquelyn remained silent during the whole exchange. But she had listened to every spoken word very carefully. *Forgive me, Lord, for making it all about me...*

16

PROVIDENCE, RHODE ISLAND

"I LOVE YOU, RAUL," said Carmen Espinosa, to her husband, "and I can't imagine living the rest of my life without you. But please, for the love of God, would you at least reconsider taking the mark! How can we function without it?"

Raul's heart plummeted hearing this. "You already know my answer, Carmen. Nothing will stop me from refusing it, not even a six-month extension." His reply was soft, sad, and deeply pained.

Carmen's eyes bulged. She was relieved that the Pope had extended the deadline. But the fear of loss had weighed heavily on her, as the time slowly ticked off the clock. She didn't want to feel this way again six months from now.

Raul was grateful for the delay, too, but for different reasons than his wife of 17 years. It would give him more time to share the Gospel with his family.

Carmen was petite, with a curvy, voluptuous figure. Her hair was dark and curly. Before the Rapture, she was always smiling. Her mouth was large and full of bright, white teeth. She became emphatic with her husband, "Isn't life already difficult enough for us? Think about your health! You haven't been to your oncologist in many months.

"Now you're willing to put it off for another six months! You know you can't see him without the mark and chip. How do you know you'll still be alive by then?" She instantly regretted her remark. "Sorry. It got away from me."

Raul held up his hand as if to say, "It's okay, I understand," but he left it alone. Before his cancer prognosis, Raul was a tall strapping man with broad shoulders. The cancer was starting to take a heavy toll on him. He had already lost 80 pounds and it looked like he had shrunken three inches. He had a full head of dark brown hair, which matched the color of his eyes, which were large, dark and piercing.

What he didn't like about his wife's comment was their daughter was in the kitchen with them having spam, rice and beans for breakfast. It was apparent to him that Carmen was using Blanca as a pawn of sorts, hoping she would remain on her side, as she tried once again talking sense into her father.

Raul bit his lower lip and glanced over at their only child, seated across from him, trying to gauge her reaction. Unable to accurately pinpoint it, he said to his wife, "Like I've been telling you for a year and a half now, until you experience God's soul-saving power for yourself, you'll never know how transformed I feel."

"Are you trying to tell me I've never experienced it for myself?"

"Come on, Carmen, even when we had access to the word of God, how often did you read it? We've always proclaimed to be followers of Jesus, even though we really weren't."

Oh, no, you didn't just say that! Carmen shook her head from side to side, deeply offended by her husband's insensitive comment. It was one of many he'd made to her since his so-called spiritual conversion, 18 months ago.

A month or so into the five-month locust campaign, Raul drove to downtown Providence, to see his oncologist. He was diagnosed with stage two lung cancer, a year earlier, due to years of heavy smoking, plus from overexposure to asbestos on the job. Had the insurance company not gone bankrupt after the disappearances, he would have sued their socks off. That was the very last thing on his mind now...

It was the first appointment Carmen had missed. She wanted to go with Raul, to show her ongoing support, but she was too afraid to go outside.

The first time she was stung by one of those hideous demonic locusts, the pain was so excruciating that the thought of going outside for even a second terrified her.

Even indoors, they were constantly under attack. They did all they could to rid the household of those flying tormentors, but to no avail.

Raul wore every article of clothing he could fit on his body that day, to hopefully shield himself from their venomous stings.

Before he entered the medical center, he heard one of the 144,000 Jewish preachers boldly declaring the Word of God for all to hear, without the slightest fear of retribution. Raul was already in a foul mood. He had a foreboding that he would feel even worse after his checkup. The last thing he needed was this nonsense!

Just as he was about to give him a piece of his mind, the young man said to him, "'The days are coming,' declares the Sovereign LORD, 'when I will send a famine through the land—not a famine of food or a thirst for water, but a famine of hearing the words of the LORD. People will stagger from sea to sea and wander from north to east, searching for the word of the LORD, but they will not find it.'"

Raul knew he was quoting scripture, but he didn't know it was Amos 8:11-12. How could he possibly know when the Book from which he was preaching had been globally outlawed?

But what had really resonated with him, was when the young Jewish male added, "Antichrist may have succeeded in removing the Word of God from most places on the planet, but he cannot remove it from the hearts and minds of Yahweh's true children! If you're not trusting in Yahweh for your salvation, you're trusting in Satan, and Antichrist by extension, which will lead you straight into eternal damnation…"

After Raul's suspicion was confirmed by his oncologist that his lung cancer had been upgraded to stage three, he went home that day thinking more about the words the young man had spoken to him, than about his dire prognosis.

That was when he first started feeling the pull of the Holy Spirit on his soul. After being stung several times, he became so fueled by desperation that he drove to downtown Providence a month later, to hopefully glean something from the young Jewish preacher about why it was happening.

Raul wore several layers of clothing again, hoping to shield himself from their venomous stings. Paranoia poured out of him like sweat. But the locusts flitting this way and that, looking for humans to torment, had no effect on the preacher. They didn't bother the young man in the least. He kept preaching the Word of God as if they weren't even there.

As Raul had fully expected, his worst fear was confirmed when he was stung by one of them. He cried out in agony to Whoever was listening.

That was when the young man handed Raul a copy of *The Way*. He started reading it that night, when his wife and daughter were asleep. The instant he opened it, he knew he was reading the outlawed Word of God. But that didn't stop him from reading on. He couldn't stop!

Two days later, with his soul thirsting for the Word above all other things, Raul repented of his sins and trusted in Christ for his salvation, for real this time. He went from feeling utterly hopeless to suddenly hopeful. It was a remarkable transformation.

Even more miraculous, he suddenly stopped being stung by the locusts. They still hovered around him as if scanning him, but they never stung him. He knew it was a direct result of his spiritual conversion.

If he needed further proof of this, it was all recorded in the book he was reading. Plus, Carmen and Blanca remained under attack by them.

Raul confessed to his wife and daughter that he was reading the Word of God.

Carmen demanded to know where he got it. Raul told her the truth, that it was given to him by one of the 144,000 Jewish preachers, in downtown Providence.

Carmen went ballistic on him. "So, let me get this straight," she had said, "you went from detesting those young lunatics, to receiving that book from them? I want it out of this house!"

Instead of arguing this point with his wife—it would be pointless, really—he countered by saying, "You can't deny the locusts no longer have power over me. It has nothing to do with me and everything to do with my spiritual conversion, which came from reading the book and accepting the Gospel message.

"If only you'll read it for yourself, at the very least, you'll discover what I'm telling you is true. It's all there. But reading about it won't be enough to save your soul from hell. You need to repent of your sins and trust in Christ, and Christ alone, like I did, for your salvation."

Spiritually blinded to the Truth, Carmen refused to believe that was the real reason. One week later, however, she was so desperate to be free of their vicious stings, that she tearfully told Raul she would start praying the rosary with him again, and even to Mary, if that would put an end to it all.

Raul tried explaining that those things had nothing to do with his conversion. He stopped praying the rosary after he got saved. It had nothing to do with his no longer being stung by them. It all came down to being born again spiritually.

Despite his wife's constant threats to shred it into a million pieces, the more Raul kept growing in his faith, the more the arguing between the married couple intensified, especially since Carmen and Blanca kept being stung by the locusts, but not Raul.

Their marriage kept going downhill from there…

Raul reached for her hand. "I'm concerned for you, honey, deeply concerned…"

Carmen defiantly pulled her hand away and shot a condescending look at him. "No, Raul, I fear for you. You're the one who has stage three lung cancer! How can you ignore the many positive benefits the chip will offer to all who receive it? Evil as the Pope may be, and I'm not arguing against that point, but you heard what he said in Jerusalem. Only those who receive the mark can receive the chip. Even your oncologist is optimistic about it.

"The sooner we take the mark and the chip, the sooner the healing process can begin in your body." With as much empathy as she could muster in her voice, Carmen pleaded with her husband, "There's nothing I want more than to increase our years together. We're still young. We have our whole lives ahead of us. In less than three years, we'll celebrate our twentieth wedding anniversary. Don't you want to enjoy it in good health?"

Raul knew this was the strongest card she held in the argument deck. "Comforting as that all sounds, my love, now that I know the Truth, even if I ingested the chip and I got to enjoy good health, it wouldn't matter three years from now."

Here we go again! Carmen pointed her finger at him. "Don't you dare, Raul!"

"I can show you in the book where it says anyone who ingests the chip won't be around to enjoy it three years from now. That's why I'm no longer concerned about my recent cancer diagnosis. God will soon make all things new for all who belong to Him."

Raul went on, "The reason Christ followers are willing to suffer, even unto death, is our absolute belief that in a little more than three years, Christ will come back for us. The world as we know it will be forever changed, and all this craziness will finally come to an end."

Carmen remained unmoved by her husband's desperate pleas. "You seem so sure of yourself…"

Raul raised his hands in mock protest, palms out. "The only thing I'm sure of, honey, is what the Bible teaches. And what it teaches is anyone not belonging to Jesus will ultimately take the mark, which will result in eternal damnation for them."

Raul became teary eyed. "This includes you and Blanca. If you take it, there will be nothing you can do to change sides. This is my greatest fear for you, my love."

Carmen stared at him blankly. The way she kept posturing told Raul everything he needed to know. *He* was the problem, not *her*.

Raul went on, "But if you seek God with all your heart, mind and soul, and repent of your sinful ways, like I did last year, you'll discover everything I'm saying is true. But the instant you take the mark, your eyes will be forever blinded, and your heart will be forever darkened to the evil one's deceptive spirit, and there can be no turning back at that point.

"As difficult as it's been for us lately, the friction between us will be taken to a whole new level. It'll be impossible for us to live under the same roof as husband and wife. Not to further frighten you, but if you think the sting marks you suffered in the past were bad, once you take the mark of the Beast, painful sores will break out all over your body, which may never go away.

"The Bible makes it perfectly clear that it will be the first of the seven bowl judgments to be poured out on the planet. We may never read about it online or hear about it in the news, but it will surely happen. I'm sure it's already happening.

"But who will complain about it online? And what TV reporter would dare tell the story? Anyone foolish enough to do that would be put to death or in prison. Everything I'm telling you can be proven in the book I'm reading. Yet, you still refuse to read it."

Carmen gulped back fear. She was still mad at God for making her and Blanca suffer last year, after Raul stopped being stung by the locusts. When that dreadful time in her life had finally ended, instead of relief flooding her heart and soul, it was as if she was holding God in contempt for allowing it in the first place. He didn't protect her then, so why would He protect her in the future? According to Raul, He wouldn't.

"Stop it, you two! I can't take it anymore!" Blanca stormed out of the kitchen and raced up to her bedroom, not wishing to hear the next exchange between them. She had long since grown weary of her parents constant bickering, which started when her father switched from being a Catholic to a Christian. She could no longer tolerate it.

Raul's heart ached for his daughter. She was so young to have to endure all this. Even so, she needed to know.

"Now I know what Romanero meant when he called this particular brand of Christianity a mental illness! Just never thought it would happen to my own husband. Stop this craziness!" Carmen snapped.

I'm the crazy one? I'm not the one who's willing to trade my soul for three years of potentially good health! Raul took a deep breath, then tried reasoning with his wife again. His eyes projected a deep sorrow and sadness for his wife. "I can show you step by step what's still to come, and how much worse it will soon get for all who reject Christ, but my fear is that even then you won't believe me…"

Raul rubbed his throbbing forehead. "I don't have to remind you of how evil this Pope is. He's Romanero's partner in crime. So, by accepting Antichrist, you're also accepting the Pope, who is the False Prophet. I want nothing to do with either of them."

At first, Carmen was just as defiant against taking the mark as her husband. She was also disappointed with the Pope, for encouraging young girls to get pregnant.

Before cash became illegal, they stocked up on enough food to last a year, much like any preppers worth their salt would. But as the months kept passing, and their supplies kept dwindling, worry kept eating away at Carmen, and wearing down her defenses.

Now that the food and water were running out—not to mention that all households not taking the mark would soon lose water, electricity and Wi-Fi, she was at the end of her rope.

As important as those things were, her biggest reason for wanting to wave the white flag in surrender, and take the mark, was her husband's lung cancer prognosis. Now that there was hope for him, legitimate hope, he still wanted nothing to do with it.

Carmen rocked back on the heels of her feet. She was at the end of her rope. "I won't let you take Blanca with you!"

Raul lowered his head and slowly shook it from side to side. "That's not my decision, dear. Nor is it yours. It's a decision our daughter will have to make on her own."

"That's it!" Carmen stormed upstairs to her bedroom. It was time to get rid of the book that had brainwashed Raul, once and for all, before Blanca became curious about it.

When she opened the safe, it wasn't in there. She raced downstairs in a fit of rage, demanding to know where he was hiding it.

Enough was enough!

17

WHEN BLANCA HEARD HER mother storming up the stairs, she locked her bedroom door, hoping to barricade herself from her parents' constant quarreling. The last thing she wanted was for her mother to try putting her in the middle again.

If there was one thing she respected about her father, he never spoke badly about Mami, even if she spoke badly about him.

Blanca climbed back into bed and pulled the covers up over her head, without her smart phone. For someone who had been addicted to her phone all her life, she seldom used it now. It seemed whenever she did, depression always followed.

The only thing she found online was constant lies and deception. Nothing felt real to her anymore, or truthful. If the teen could access Truth on her phone, she would be on it day and night. But since she couldn't, she felt no need to turn it on most days.

Why bother, only to feel depressed and disillusioned again?

The gradual weaning off her cell phone addiction started during the locust invasion period. After she was stung the first time, she never wanted to be alone. She even slept in between her parents each night, hoping they could protect her from their vicious stings. It never worked. Being stung in the middle of the night, while she was sleeping, was the absolute worst experience for her. Even after all this time, just thinking about it forced shivers all throughout her body.

To help pass that dreadful time, Blanca played Uno, Monopoly, and did jigsaw puzzles with her parents, for many hours on end, to help fill the waking hours.

In the high-tech world in which she was raised, board games always seemed boring to her. Suddenly, playing these "offline" games with her parents had offered her a temporary calm in the storms of life.

But whenever they spotted another locust in the house, knowing they couldn't be swatted or sprayed away, the three of them would tense up and grip the kitchen table fearfully with all their might, hoping they wouldn't be stung again.

Everything changed for the worse after her father got saved. That was when family time turned into quarrel time…

After having a good cry, Blanca dried her eyes with the sleeve of her sweater and looked up at her bedroom ceiling. "I know You're up there, God. I know You exist. I believe Jesus is Your Son. I've believed this all my life. You know this already. So why does it feel like You're a million miles away from me? Why do I feel my life doesn't matter to You?"

Blanca started weeping again. But this was more of a wailing of the soul. It took a while before she was able to speak again. "At times, it feels as though You've left me all alone to fend for myself on this crazy planet. Can't you see I'm petrified?

"If Mami and Papi both believe in Jesus, why do they keep arguing over Him, as if He was two different Saviors? If what Papi keeps saying is true, reveal it to me, Lord. Please, I'm desperate. I can't take this life any longer. If You're listening, make Yourself known to me. Please, I'm begging You..."

The teenager never thought the day would come that her parents' marriage could possibly come to an end. They had endured so much tragedy over the years, yet they always found ways to stick together through it all. It was inconceivable to think that a difference of religion would be their downfall.

As much as she wanted to believe her father, that it all came down to his spiritual conversion, she had been deceived so many times since the disappearances, she didn't know what to think anymore.

Blanca rolled onto her side and thought about her best friend, Leticia Gonzalez. She hadn't heard a peep from her since she left Rhode Island more than three years ago, after getting pregnant by that 26-year-old monster who drove to Providence for that very purpose.

Soon after that, Leticia and her parents started believing the very same thing her father now believed. With little notice, they left Rhode Island for who knew where? At this point, Blanca just wanted to know if her former BFF was still alive, or was she one of the casualties from Salvador Romanero's recent dissident bombing campaign?

Deep down in her soul, she believed more and more that he was no man of peace, but a great deceiver of the masses. The man who helped reshape her impressionable mind and fill her young heart with hopes of a blissful future, no longer seemed like a knight in shining armor to her.

How could anyone still believe in him, when so many of his predictions never came true? Now he was destroying her parents' marriage.

On the other hand, it seemed everything her father kept saying always turned out to be right.

Blanca tossed and turned on her bed with one thought dominating her brain—should she take the mark with her mother, or refuse it like her father?

At 2 a.m., her eyes popped open with a single thought: *Could it be?* After not hearing a peep from Leticia Gonzalez for so long, was she reaching out to her in the real world, like she saw in her dream?

Blanca scratched her head in befuddlement, then powered on her smart phone after a two-day hiatus. She blinked hard a few times. After all this time, she finally had a message from Leticia: *This is your BFF! Sorry for not contacting you all this time, but I haven't had a phone. I want you to know I've had dreams about you. We need to talk ASAP.*

Blanca burst into tears. In normal times, she would have been relieved, but also hurt, angered even, that it took Leticia this long to finally contact her. BFFs weren't supposed to do that to each other. But since Christians were forced into hiding, it meant communicating with the outside world was virtually impossible.

Blanca took a moment to collect herself, then replied: *Thank God, you're still alive! I can't tell you how many times I tried texting you and leaving messages on your social media pages, without my parents knowing. They all went unread. When you left Providence, it was like you ghosted me.*

I constantly wondered where you were living, and whether you gave birth to a son or daughter...You may not believe this, but I had a dream about you too, just last night! Even more remarkable, before I went to sleep, I asked God to reveal to me whether you were dead or alive. Talk about perfect timing! It's a miracle!

Tears pressed through Leticia's closed eyes, as she praised God for the blessing. She typed onto her phone. *What a relief it is to hear back from you! I won't answer any personal questions by text message. Be careful with what you type. Never know who's listening. They can't locate me, but if they become interested in this chat it wouldn't be difficult to find you.*

Blanca replied: *Okay, I will...*

Leticia replied: *I need to ask; did you take the mark yet?*

No. Papi refuses to take it, but Mami's committed to taking it before the new deadline expires. As for me, I'm so confused.

Leticia replied: *I know I'm taking a huge risk by saying this, but if you take it, BFF, we can never be friends again. I pray you don't do that!*

*I understand...*Because of her parents, Blanca did understand.

Leticia replied: *I can only access this phone twice a week. So please be patient with me. I'll contact you when I can. For now, do your best to hang in there. Oh, and by the way, part of my dream was that you found a book under one of your pillows called The Way.*

Could it be? Blanca threw pillows off the bed, one after the next. Seeing it, her eyes widened in astonishment. Chills raced up and down her spine. The Book was staring back at her, begging her to open it and start reading it. *Now I know why Mami couldn't find it!*

Blanca went downstairs to find her father sitting in his favorite chair in the living room, praying. She stopped on the third step and waited for him to finish, before whispering to him, "When did you do it, Papi?"

Raul motioned for his daughter to come closer. When she sat next to him, he said, "After dinner last night, when you were in the shower, I felt something deep in my spirit urging me to do it. This was before Mami went looking for it."

Blanca blinked away a tear. Her heart was still pounding in her chest from what just took place in her bedroom. "I heard from Leticia, Papi..."

Raul's eyes popped. For the first time ever, the Lord had placed his daughter's former best friend on his heart. He had just been praying for her. "What? Really? What did she say?"

Blanca didn't know how to gauge her father's reaction. Before he became a believer, he forbade his daughter from contacting her. "This is gonna sound strange, but the reason I checked under my pillow in the first place was that Leticia told me to look for it there. She saw it in a dream. Only she never mentioned anything about you putting it there."

Raul became breathless. He inhaled deeply, filling his lungs with air, before collapsing again when he exhaled. "Really? She told you that! Hallelujah! What if I told you I was just praying for her, and it was the first time I ever did that?"

"That would be amazing!"

"Well, it's true! Do you think God's trying to get your attention?"

Blanca nodded yes. "How could I not, Papi, after finally hearing from my Christian best friend, after all this time, who then tells me I would find that Book under my pillow!" She sulked. "Curious as I am to read it, I'm also frightened, because of what it's doing to you and Mami. I don't want to have to choose between the two of you."

The room grew silent as Raul formulated what to say next to his daughter. As much as he wanted to comfort her, he refrained from hugging her. The last thing he wanted now was for Blanca to think he was trying to get him to choose him over her mother. God's salvation had nothing to do with favoritism.

He calmly said to his daughter, "I understand your concern, mija, but listen to me, you aren't choosing between me and Mami, you're choosing between God and Satan. When it comes to God's salvation, it's a personal thing. No one can decide for you. You must choose for yourself what to believe. It's vitally important that you understand this.

"I'm no better than Mami. The only difference between us is that I have God's eternal assurance and she doesn't. I don't deserve God's mercy or forgiveness. No one does! I'm just grateful to be saved.

"My prayer is that the two of you will get saved before it's too late. But like I keep telling you, if you take the mark, salvation can no longer be possible for you."

Raul saw his daughter flinch at his words. "How, Papi?"

"It's all there in that Book, mija." He added, "If you seek the Lord with all your mind, heart and soul, you will surely find Him, just like I did. I'll be happy to answer any questions you have…"

"Let's see what I can find on my own first, Papi…"

When Blanca stood, he added, "Oh, and one more thing…"

"Yes, Papi?"

"As much as I hope and pray that you'll read it, really read it, I'll need it back tomorrow. Like I've told you many times, it's the only Truth there is on this crazy planet. I can't exist without it. It's like oxygen to my soul. So, we need to share it, okay?"

Blanca nodded wearily at her father, then went back up to her room. The teenager stared at the Book that had radically transformed her father's and her best friend's lives.

She couldn't properly diagnose how she felt now. All she knew was she couldn't bear the thought of being let down and disappointed again. If it happened again, she would never recover from it.

Blanca took a moment to think about the many changes in her father since he started reading it. Before his conversion, no one had hated the 144,000 enemies of the planet any more than he did. His mindset toward them quickly changed, when one of them gave him the book that God used to rescue his soul from hell.

After his conversion, when the three flying angels started making their earth-shaking proclamations high above, he would often put his finger up to his lips, as if telling his wife and daughter to be quiet so he could focus on what they had to say.

Since nothing could stop anyone from hearing every word they uttered with exacting precision—including all deaf and special needs individuals—it was an unnecessary gesture on his part, especially since Blanca and her mother trembled in terror with each word they uttered.

And there could be no denying that her father stopped being stung by the locusts after he got saved. He even showed them in the book how it was prophesied more than 2,000 years ago, as one of God's judgments on humanity. Even more telling, he showed them both in black and white that it would end in five months, which it did.

He also warned them that those vicious sting marks were nothing, when compared to the outbreak of festering sores on the bodies for all who took the mark. This was already happening. *Worse than the locust stings? Could it be true?* This terrified her to no end.

But even more that all those things, was how her father kept insisting that he couldn't exist without that book, it was like oxygen to his soul, and the only Truth he knew of on this crazy planet.

Papi had always been a law-abiding citizen. He knew it was illegal to read, let alone possess that book. Yet it never stopped him.

Blanca took a deep breath, opened the Book to page one and started reading *The Way*, not knowing that many in the state of Pennsylvania were praying for her, and that God had already started softening her heart and opening her spiritual eyes and ears to His salvation message.

But Blanca Espinosa wasn't the only youngster on the planet stuck in the middle of a spiritual battle between her parents.

As part of Planet Earth's final harvest, before the unavoidable Battle of Armageddon, Yahweh was doing the same with millions of others from all nations, tribes, and tongues, and using His 144,000 sealed servants to spread the Gospel message for Him.

When the three flying angels started making their bold proclamations in the sky above, it created the first wave of youngsters fleeing their homes and going into hiding at numerous Christian hideouts.

Now that so many were faced with the possibility of losing internet service, not to mention water and electricity, God was using this to rescue the final wave of youngsters, by showing them how fleeting this life really was...

18

CEDAR RAPIDS, IOWA

THREE WEEKS AFTER THE Nelsons were scheduled to take the mark, it still hadn't happened. When Vicky woke up, on the morning of their first appointment, she was just as sick as everyone else in the household.

Like so many other families on the planet, the Nelsons were nearly out of food, water, fuel, medicine, and many other essentials. Until they took the mark, they wouldn't be able to replenish their supplies.

Which was why Vicky still wanted to go to her appointment. But with a quarantine now in effect for all who had the global flu, she had no choice but to cancel. Even though her household was in quarantine protocol, she could have made an appointment for her family to receive the mark at home, but the waiting list for that was long.

Vicky wasn't prepared for this. When Jack went to Pennsylvania, she made sure they had enough food, medicine, and other essentials to hold them over until he returned. When he was sent home earlier than anticipated, they still had enough food to last a few days.

But now that three weeks had passed, they were scraping rock bottom. Taking the mark would finally free up their finances, including the $10K bonus Jack had received for being selected to protect Benjamin Shapiro.

To have thousands of dollars in the bank, but not being able to access those funds, wore on a person after a while. That's where Vicky was now. Once the investigation process concluded and Jack was reinstated, everything would be fine again.

Now, on the eve of their second scheduled appointment, while the four of them were still experiencing mild symptoms of the global flu, they felt well enough to go in the morning.

As it turned out, Jack's biggest concern each day went far beyond the family's dwindling food supplies. After practically being bedridden for the past three weeks, he never burned the book in the fireplace that he had brought back with him from Pennsylvania. It was still in his briefcase.

He was still amazed at how authorities hadn't discovered it during his brief incarceration in Pennsylvania. It was a minor miracle, to be sure.

But if his wife ever found it inside his briefcase, it would be impossible to explain it away.

Jack was fully determined to stay awake all night, if need be, so he could finally burn the book, then take his secret to the grave with him. It needed to be done before he took the mark.

As the 11 p.m. hour approached, Vicky's mouth formed in a wide yawn. "Time for bed. Don't stay up too late. You need your rest."

"I won't." With his wife in bed for the night, and the kids in their rooms playing online games, Jack retrieved his briefcase from the closet.

Just as he was about to open it, he heard Liam and Laura yelling at their phones, no doubt complaining about the slower internet speed, he held off a little longer. Every few minutes, one of them would shout, "C'mon! Give me a break!" It was almost comical.

When it didn't stop, Jack decided to proceed. Just as he was about to set it ablaze, something deep inside urged him to read the inscription again that Dr. Shapiro had penned just for him.

It read: *The only secure future you can ever have can be found in the pages of this Book! I hope you'll read it, Jack!*

Try as he might, Nelson had no solid answer as to why the most famous physician on the planet had suddenly defected from Salvador Romanero. Even more confusing was why he had dedicated the book to him, without also including copies for Russell and Umberto.

It's not like he knew Dr. Shapiro any better than his two colleagues did. Aside from engaging in general chitchat each day when they saw each other, that was the extent of their relationship.

So, why did that man leave the book behind for him only, as if they had been friends forever? And why did he flee his prestigious life to go into hiding? Jack had no logical explanation for any of it.

He paused a moment to silently question his sanity, then sat back in his favorite chair. Perhaps the flu that had attacked his body the past three weeks had caused this irrational thinking in him, but it seemed like Dr. Shapiro's inscription had an endearing quality to it.

If, for only that reason, Nelson opened the book to Genesis, chapter one, and started reading. But he still was very much in favor of taking the mark in the morning. Bottom line: no mark, no job!

He didn't know God had other plans. Another thing he didn't know was, thanks to Dr. Shapiro, many Christians in Pennsylvania were praying for his salvation...

When Vicky woke up at 2 a.m. to use the restroom, Jack wasn't in bed beside her. She went downstairs to find him reading. What made this so peculiar was that her husband hated reading books. He preferred listening to audiobooks.

Vicky was the bookworm in the family, not Jack. Liam and Laura were also voracious readers at one point in their young lives. Now they couldn't pull their faces away from their cellphones long enough to read anything that wasn't online.

On that rare occasion when he was assigned specific books to read during his FBI days—mostly psychological profiling books—he always chose e-book format, so he could adjust the font size to his preferences.

The way he strained his eyes to adjust his vision in the darkness told her that whatever he was reading, it was very important to him.

As he flipped back and forth in the book, he noticed many key passages were highlighted. This helped speed up the learning process.

Vicky asked, "What are you reading?"

"Something I got at Dr. Shapiro's house…" He left it at that.

She shrugged it off and kissed him on the forehead. "Don't stay up too much later. Our appointment's at 10 a.m."

"Okay," he had answered half-heartedly, his mind a million miles away from the conversation. After jumping around in the Book, something went off inside that compelled him to want to read it from beginning to end. Being placed on temporary leave would give him plenty of time to do just that.

Vicky went back to sleep, not knowing that her family was on the verge of coming apart at the seams...

When she woke up again at 7 a.m., to find her husband still reading, she was quite shocked, but not overly suspicious. "Oh my! What could be so important that it kept you up all night?"

Jack looked at her over his reading glasses, then closed the book. "It's the most important thing I've ever read before."

Vicky asked, "What is it? Some old case you once worked on?"

Jack hesitated. Instead of answering the question, he handed the book to her. It would be so much easier than trying to explain himself.

Vicky opened it and fingered her way through the pages. Her eyes widened fearfully, seeing the Gospel of Matthew staring back at her. She knew it was the banned Word of God.

She dropped it on the floor, not wanting to touch it a second longer. "Where did you get this?!" she demanded to know. "And why did you bring it into our house?!"

Jack hesitated again. "I brought it back from Doctor Shapiro's house."

"I thought you told me you burned it in his backyard!"

Jack scratched his right leg. "That was a different book."

Vicky felt a full-blown panic attack brewing inside. "I don't understand. What's going on, Jack?"

"This is the book I told you I found in the food delivery bag. Doctor Shapiro left it for me, before he went on the run. He even personally inscribed it to me. Strangely enough, he didn't leave copies for Russell or Umberto. Only me."

Vicky flinched suspiciously. The fear stenciled on her face was unmistakable. "Why did he do that?"

Jack held out his hands. "I had no idea until I started reading it…"

Vicky put her hands on her hips. "And?"

Jack sighed. "He did it out of concern for my soul." He pointed to the book on the floor. "Reading that book made me realize I was a sinner who was headed straight to hell."

"Come on, Jack," snickered Vicky, "you don't really mean that. You're one of the good guys. You're a retired FBI agent."

Jack glared at his wife begging for her understanding. "I'm not a good guy, Vicky. I'm a sinner just like everyone else on the planet. When it comes to God's salvation, my profession means nothing. It's all in that book. I'll admit parts of it are frightening, but the more I read it, the more I realize how deceived I've been all my life."

"Okay, so, who deceived you, Jack?"

"Satan. He deceived you too! The world deceived us. Everything seems different to me now since I started reading that book." He sighed. "I now have serious concerns about taking the mark."

"What?! Don't be ridiculous," she snapped, now that she had finally pinpointed what had been bothering her husband all this time. "How can we function in the new global economy without it?"

"Sorry, but I'm not going. Anyone who takes the mark will be forever cut off from God's saving grace, which can only be found in Christ Jesus. I'm starting to understand why His followers aren't afraid to go into hiding. He is all they need. Well, He's all I need too…"

Vicky's eyes widened. Anything would have been better than hearing that. She scoffed, "Come again? I know you're tired, Jack. You haven't slept all night. We can be in and out in no time. When we get home, you can take a nap, and I'll do all the shopping…"

Jack shook his head sadly. "I'm not going…"

Vicky glared at her husband seated across from her. *Not a good guy?* Since the day she first met Jack, he was always clean cut. That clean-cut image was now hidden behind a three-week old beard and mustache. It was like he didn't care anymore.

"I can't believe you're being like this! I can't stand to look at you right now!" Vicky shot up off the couch and pointed at an unmarked car that was parked down the street. "Do you want me to tell them your secret? Don't push me, Jack. You know I'll do it!"

The vehicle first appeared on their block the day after the Nelsons missed their first appointment. It had remained parked there ever since. The only thing that changed was the drivers. Jack sensed they were there to monitor him because of his ties to Dr. Shapiro.

Jack buried his face in the palms of his hands and wept as quietly as he could. His family had never seen him like this. He went from being their rock and support system, to falling to pieces in front of them.

Finally, he said, through soft sniffling. "Think I need a nap…"

"I agree! Clearly, you're not thinking straight."

Now that Vicky was aware of the dangerous secret Jack was keeping from the family all this time, she was too angry to show him any level of compassion. And fearful! Hopefully that would come later, once he regained control of his mental faculties.

This went beyond being sick and being placed on administrative leave from work. *What happened to my superstar husband?*

What Vicky didn't realize, as Jack slowly climbed the steps, was that he was weeping for them, not himself, silently praying that they wouldn't take the mark.

Once they did, the family he had loved with all his heart would be eternally dissolved…

19

THE FOLLOWING MORNING

THE NAP THAT JACK Nelson desperately needed ended up being a fifteen-hour slumber. At least that's what his family thought. Most of that time was spent reading *The Way* in the spare bedroom, where he had slept each night since he returned from Pennsylvania. All that did was further reinforce the total transformation he felt taking place inside.

Vicky thought of waking him several times the day before, so they could take the mark, as scheduled. She finally decided to reschedule and let him sleep. Perhaps then he would come back to his senses.

She was about to see just how wrong she was…

Jack went downstairs carrying the Book their mother had told them he had brought into that house. Vicky was seated on the living room couch with Liam and Laura. They were good-looking teenagers.

Liam's hair was dark blond. It was long and wavy. He lived in Iowa, but he looked like a stereotypical California surfer boy.

Laura's hair was also dark blond. It went halfway down her back. She looked like the younger sister of a California surfer boy.

Jack hated to think that they might end up spending an eternity in hell. He took a seat on the chair opposite them. He didn't like what he saw on their faces. And for good reason.

When he was sleeping, Vicky informed the kids about what had transpired. What concerned the teenagers the most was the possibility of losing Wi-Fi. Even though the deadline wouldn't expire for another three months, it was dreadfully slow! All they had to do was take the mark and their internet connection would be back up to speed.

They were incensed that their father would have the audacity to bring that illegal book into their home. They did their best to bottle their emotions and remain calm, as their mother tried talking sense into him.

"Come on, Jack," she said, "burn that piece of garbage, and let's go take the mark, so we can function in the new global economy. Out of sight, out of mind, right? We should have just enough fuel in the car to get us there. We can fill up on the way back when our funds are freed up."

Jack gripped the book even more tightly and lowered his head. He could feel his wife and kids burning holes into him with their stares.

Liam grunted his frustration at him.

Vicky kept pleading with her husband, "Don't just sit there, Jack! Come on, do it! Let's get it over with."

A tear escaped Jack's left eye. This was, by far, the most difficult decision he ever had to make in life. He looked at his children, but he was unable to hold their gaze. "I'm sorry, but I can't…"

Vicky glared even more angrily at him. This went beyond depression. It had to be mental illness. What else could it be? Jack had always been a loving and caring husband and father. And a good provider. Now he was suddenly willing to throw it all away and become an enemy of the planet, possibly endangering them as well.

Vicky folded her arms across her waist, clearly fed up. "What is it with you and that book!" she snorted. "You know the danger you could bring upon us all by bringing it into our household! What if someone performs a spot search in our home and they find it? It's been happening with families with multiple cancellations."

Laura pleaded with him next, "We've already cancelled once, Dad. Twice, including yesterday. If we don't show up today, how do we know the authorities won't come knocking on our door!"

Dad? It didn't escape Jack's notice that up until now, his daughter had always addressed him as "Daddy".

Vicky became even more emphatic with her husband, "Do you want to see our children taken away in handcuffs?"

Jack looked up at her sheepishly. He didn't appreciate this mean-spirited jab from his wife. It was uncalled for. But mindful of her spiritual blindness, he remained silent. The more she kept pressuring him to take the mark, the more tightly he gripped the book in his hands.

Vicky grunted under her breath, then unleashed on her husband, "Can't you see everything's on hold because of you! In case you haven't noticed," she barked, sarcastically, "the cupboard's getting bare! Until we receive the mark, I can't even go food shopping!"

Jack wanted to reply by saying, "How could I forget? You remind me every day," but what would be the point? He just listened.

"Even our health insurance is on hold. My prescriptions alone cost nearly five hundred dollars a month without it! You know I can't function without them. How do you expect me to pay for them without the mark? We can't even access our savings, Jack!

"Have you forgotten when we were sick with the flu, that *you* brought back from Pennsylvania, I might add, I couldn't buy antibiotics for my family! That's why it took so long for us to recover. It's also why we had to cancel our first appointment.

"Do you want us to die, Jack? Is that your goal?" she asked angrily, throwing her hands up in frustration. "Now you want to cancel our next appointment! I don't know what's gotten into you! It's time to stop this foolishness and become a responsible husband and father again. Enough is enough!"

When Jack sighed, Vicky shot a desperate glance over at Liam and Laura, who were equally unnerved by their father's foolish actions.

Liam shook his head in disgust. *What happened to my father?*

Vicky's gaze returned to her husband. She took a few deep breaths to calm herself down, then tried reasoning with her confused husband again. "You have a great job, with full benefits. There's no way we can survive without it. The only way to fix this mess is by taking the mark. Once we do that, we can stop by the pharmacy for more medicine. When you get your job back, everything will be fine again."

Jack didn't need his wife to remind him that he hadn't been paid since he left Pennsylvania three weeks ago. Essentially, he had been paid, but until he received the mark, he couldn't access those funds. Even the $10K bonus he received for protecting the man who now was the most wanted man on Salvador Romanero's Top Ten list was on hold.

As the sole provider for the family, he was ever mindful that if he didn't take the mark, there would be no job to go back to. Not being able to provide for his family would eat away at him, each night, before he would finally drift off to sleep.

In short: without his income, they would have no chance of survival. They would be homeless in no time.

Another thing Jack knew was that his wife's desperation stretched beyond the dwindling food supplies. She didn't want to go back to work. Before the Rapture, Vicky was a kindergarten teacher. When she was informed that every child in her classroom had vanished on that fateful November day, nearly four years ago, she went into serious meltdown mode. It had been a steady stream of psychiatrists ever since.

The only good thing was that the disappearances happened on a Saturday. If it had happened on a weekday when she was teaching her class, who knew what would have followed?

The one thing her psychiatrist had never diagnosed her with was the one thing she suffered from more than anything else post-Rapture—demon possession.

The only thing her prescriptions did was temporarily tame the beast within her. Now that she hadn't been able to refill them, she wasn't in her right mind.

Jack knew it would only get worse after she took the mark. The closer he drew to his Savior, the more the demons inside her attacked him, using Vicky's mouth as his weapon.

Satan was also using Liam and Laura to do his bidding. This took the stress level at the Nelson residence to an all-time high.

Mindful that it was spiritual warfare at the highest level, Jack retreated to the spare bedroom.

Liam yelled at him on his way up the steps, "Come on, Dad, get your act together. Stop being so selfish!"

Jack took a few deep breaths to calm himself down. It wasn't what his son had just said to him, but *how* he said it that ruffled his feathers.

Vicky then shouted, "I'll reschedule this one last time, Jack! But if you don't come with us tomorrow, I wouldn't want to be you!"

After praying all night for God's direction and experiencing constant bouts of bawling his eyes out in his personal study, even though he was mentally, emotionally and physically drained, he had never thought so clearly in his life.

Since there wasn't a chance that he would ever take the mark, it would be too dangerous for him to remain in the house, not only for him, but also for his wife and kids. The more he kept putting off taking it, the more he knew he wouldn't be able to trust his desperate wife.

As it was, she had already threatened to call the police on him. This was the first time Jack had felt this level of distrust for his wife. He knew she felt the same about him.

In short, it was time to leave for good. Nelson prayed for God's protection, had another lamenting cry for his family, then tiptoed out of his study to the back door, hoping not to wake them.

He still had no idea where he would go. All he knew was that when he left his house; it would be for the last time. He couldn't take his vehicle. For one thing, the low fuel light was already flashing on his dashboard.

Even if he tried, he wouldn't make it off the block, without being pulled over by officers in the squad car constantly surveilling his house.

And without the mark, he couldn't access public transportation to take him wherever he might end up going. Wherever that place was, Nelson didn't know. All he knew was that it would be on foot.

The only things he brought with him were a sleeping bag, the clothes on his back and his copy of *The Way*. He wore jeans and a T-shirt, with a warm-up jacket tied around his waist, that he doubted he would ever need. Not in this heat!

Now homeless, the only place he could think to go was to downtown Cedar Rapids, where the young preacher shared the Word of God each day. Perhaps he could point him in the right direction.

When Yahweh's 144,000 sealed servants were first sent out on their global missions, Cedar Rapids wasn't one of those locations.

But with judgment after judgment constantly pounding the planet, all orchestrated by Yahweh Himself, and with sustainable living areas shrinking a little more after each new judgment, the young Jewish preachers kept being repositioned to the places at which they were most needed.

Jack walked the streets of his city, head down, still trying to process it all in his mind. When he went to Pennsylvania, to safeguard Salvador Romanero's personal physician, his star was on the rise. His resume was quite impressive, without a single infraction on it.

When the story appeared on the local news, Vicky was so proud of him. He quickly became the talk of the town. Whenever she would leave the house to see her psychiatrist or go food shopping, it was always with her head held high.

Nelson went from being a supernova to a fallen star, seemingly in the blink of an eye. None of this would have seemed thinkable a month ago. Had he only logged the book he was reading into evidence, he would still have his job, and his family would still be intact…

20

SIX WEEKS SINCE THE GLOBAL STRIKE

CHARLES AND MEERA CALLOWAY just finished giving another lengthy, detailed Bible study on the Book of Revelation. Their lesson today was on the seven seal judgments presently rocking Planet Earth.

The newlyweds started teaching this class three weeks ago. After successfully eradicating the flu from their subterranean dwelling space, and training more resident lay nurses to join her growing staff, Meera had a little more time to participate in other things.

Since there wasn't much husband-wife intimacy time between them, whenever Meera wasn't off seeing patients, and when Charles wasn't busy teaching other classes, they cherished this time together.

Charles ended by telling all new students, "Consider this the beginning of your three-year Bible college education."

At that, he prayed for everyone, and the room cleared so the next group of newcomers could occupy their seats.

Now that the massive property had been brought up to speed, with so little to do, aside from prayer time and doing their daily chores, most residents were eager to participate in the many classes being taught throughout the day and night.

The many newcomers, including scores of teenagers—sent there by Jakob—were still in the infancy stages regarding God's end times timetable. They were being taught daily what was going on in the world.

The main living area was crowded with younger residents, all there waiting for Joey's class to begin. He was among the first wave of youngsters, teens, and pregnant women to be moved to safe house number one, a little more than three years ago.

Joey was the youngest among them. He was only eight at the time. Mindful that he had been left behind, his nose was always buried in the Word of God. Now 11, he was a walking-talking Bible.

Joey started teaching classes to teens and pre-teens, two years ago, before they were all relocated to Kennett Square. What he liked most about this place was that his class size had doubled. He also liked that his students called him, "Pastor". But what he didn't like was that his classroom was underground, unlike in Chadds Ford.

Meera overheard a teenager she didn't know asking Joey, "Don't you feel sorry for the toddlers who never got to chew bubble gum, eat ice cream or cotton candy? They never even tried Coke or Pepsi!"

Meera answered for Joey, "Think of the bright side, our young ones don't have ADD or ADHD or weight and blood sugar issues. This pleases me very much!" That put an end to the conversation...

The Calloways went to the kitchen and spotted Benjamin Shapiro sitting with Bruce and Abigal Silver. The Silvers were sent to Kennett Square, two weeks after Jakob preached in their synagogue in Wilmington, Delaware.

Benjamin loved spending time with his fellow Messianic believers. Now that the Silvers were teaching him to read the Hebrew Bible, his love of the scriptures was taken to the next level. He wanted to learn everything he could about his Jewish lineage, a lineage he had totally disrespected until recently.

As grateful as he was when Jakob gave him a copy of *The Way*, it was a condensed version of the word of God. He ended up giving it to Jack Nelson. When he became a resident at safe house number one, he was handed a complete Bible with all 66-books inside. Reading it quickly became his favorite part of the day.

Elbows resting on his knees, palms cupping his cheeks, it became apparent to Charles that Benjamin was deep in thought. "Are you okay, Benjamin?" he asked. "It looks like you have a lot on your mind."

Shapiro glanced up at him, "I'm not doing all I can. I feel I need to do more."

Meera said, "You've done so much since joining the organization, Benjamin. We feel so blessed having one of the top physicians on the planet living among us. We've all learned so much from you."

Shapiro nodded his thanks to her. "It's not enough, Meera."

Charles added, "And let's not forget about the many life-saving medicines you sent our way. You heard what Jakob said, had we not had them, I'm convinced the quarantine section would still be full of patients. The timing couldn't have been more perfect!"

Benjamin answered, "Nothing gave me greater joy over the years than saving lives. But with the little time I have left, I want Yahweh to use me to save souls for Yeshua, starting with my brother, Seth."

Charles sensed where this conversation was headed. He spotted Dick and Sarah Mulrooney, Isaac and Tamika Moseley, Jefferson and Amy

Danforth, and Julio and Marta Gonzalez seated together at another table, and asked them to join them.

Once everyone was seated, Benjamin began, "With so many of our top leaders no longer with us, it's forced me to think about what I want to do with my remaining time on earth…"

Benjamin paused when Sarah Mulrooney lowered her head. He didn't have to ask why.

Dick mouthed the words, "It's okay," then motioned for him to continue.

Benjamin sighed. "I feel this deep burden in my spirit to go to Israel, to meet with my brother one last time, and plead with him not to take the mark."

Jefferson said, "Talk about a tall order!"

"I know it's absurd thinking on my part, but that's how I feel."

Tamika asked, "Have you had dreams about going there?"

"Yes, just last night, in fact. But it wasn't nearly as clear as the dreams I had about Jakob, before I joined this remarkable organization."

"What did you see?" asked Marta.

"I saw myself meeting with Seth at the Western Wall, in Jerusalem. Other than that, I can't remember anything else. I'm not quite sure what to make of it."

"Not to come across as pessimistic," said Jefferson, "but you have one of the most recognizable faces on the planet. Even walking the streets of Kennett Square would be a huge risk for you, me too, for that matter, especially with all those microfliers. How much worse if you attempt traveling to the Middle East as a wanted man?"

"You're right, Jefferson. But as burdened as you are about rescuing your children, that's how I feel about my brother."

Jefferson raised an eyebrow and nodded. "Fair enough."

Benjamin stretched his arms above his head. "I know what I'm suggesting would be difficult to pull off. It doesn't help that Seth wants nothing to do with me or Jakob. When Jakob challenged him spiritually, my brother felt so betrayed by his son."

Marta asked, "Why don't you text or email him?"

"I've already tried that approach. I even sent Seth a video explaining the dramatic turnaround in my life. He never even opened the email. And he never read my text messages. Even if he did watch it, who would he share it with, other than perhaps his wife, Naveh?"

Benjamin cleared his throat. "Our relationship has been strained for many years. Even when we talked on the phone, it never ended well. We're both prideful, stubborn men. The only common ground we have is our shared hatred for Salvador Romanero."

"That may be true," said Charles, "but it must baffle Seth's mind about how hard you worked to finally reach the top echelon in life, only to throw it all away so quickly. This should give you a voice with him."

"You would think so, Charles. But the instant I mention religion, all that'll do is arm us both for battle." Benjamin took a sip of milk, wishing it was coffee instead. How he missed his morning cup of joe! "There's another reason I want to go to Jerusalem..."

Meera asked, "And what might that be?"

Benjamin sat up a little straighter on his chair. "I don't want to leave this earth being known as the former physician of the Antichrist of the Bible. I feel like I have one big mission left in me."

Sarah asked, "And that is?"

"I'd love to be the first one to give an inside perspective on the inner workings of Antichrist. And I want the whole world to hear it. Imagine everyone hearing it from someone who was in his inner circle."

Jefferson said, "You already did that, Benjamin. I read the email you sent to your former colleagues warning to them about Romanero's true identity. Surely, God used it to open spiritual eyes..."

Shapiro slumped his shoulders. "It's not enough. I want to do more." He said to the Silvers, "Don't think it coincidental that the Pope wants everyone to address my former boss as 'Supreme See'—SS—like German Nazis. And why not? Those monsters both had the same objective—to exterminate the Jewish race."

Shapiro shook his head in anger. "And let's not kid ourselves, the Pope's just as vile as Romanero! All business must stop when he addresses the world? Seriously? What a megalomaniac!"

Dick Mulrooney said, "I still can't believe he prayed to Lucifer! I feel so ashamed for following that man up until my conversion."

"You and a billion others..." said Jefferson, empathetically.

Benjamin took a few deep breaths to calm himself down, then got back on track. "I really want to expose the two of them! And what better place to do it than in Jerusalem, at the Western Wall?"

"No doubt, that would be powerful," said Amy Danforth. "Was that also part of your dream?"

Benjamin twisted his lips from one side to the next. "No. The only thing I remember was meeting with my brother. Nothing more. I know my credibility is shot on the global stage. But I also know Yahweh uses His servants to accomplish His purposes. More than anything, I want Him to use my words to rescue more of His remnant.

"As an atheist American all my life, I never felt blessed to be part of Yahweh's chosen race. Now that I am part of His remnant, I'd love to walk the very same streets that Messiah Himself walked.

"Of course, if Antichrist becomes aware of my plan, there's a very good chance it will be my last day on Earth. But if multitudes hear about it, and get saved, what better way could there be to leave this earth!

"If Romanero doesn't catch on to my plan, I'll share the Gospel with Seth, then hopefully join my Hebrew brothers and sisters who are fleeing the country in droves, for Petra, or wherever they end up going.

"Talk about an honor! Don't get me wrong, you know how grateful I am to be here with all of you. I'm thrilled that we'll spend eternity together, but if given the chance, I'd love to go to Israel one last time, this time as a truly converted Jew."

Jefferson said, "If I were Jewish, I'd want to be there too."

"If I can find a way to get there, I'll do my best to share the Gospel with Seth. How much better if multitudes get to hear whatever the Lord puts on my heart to tell him. How can I accomplish that from here?"

"Good question..." came the reply from Dick Mulrooney.

"Talk about a challenge! A lifelong atheist trying to convert my lifelong rabbi brother to Christianity! Crazy, I know..."

Tamika rubbed her growing belly. "Sounds perfectly normal in these insane times."

Julio Gonzalez asked, "So, how do we smuggle you to Israel?"

"That's the million-dollar-question. After racking my brains the past few days, all I keep thinking is Yahweh safely delivered Hana and Yasamin halfway around the world, with two young children. If He did that for them, why can't He deliver me safely to Israel?"

Jefferson said, "True, but with the second and third bowl judgments imminent, I wouldn't recommend sailing on the Delaware River, let alone across an ocean to the Middle East..." He was glad Mary Johnson wasn't within earshot. Her husband might be doing that very thing, this very instant.

Benjamin let out a loud, prolonged sigh. Clearly, he was just as unsettled after the conversation as he was before it started...

Isaac asked Benjamin, "Have you told Jakob about your dream?"

"Not yet. I just had it last night. I'll tell him later when he gets back from doing his thing. In the meantime, I'd greatly appreciate your prayers in this matter."

Charles said, "Let's start now." Everyone held hands and Charles prayed for Benjamin...

21

TEN DAYS LATER – CEDAR RAPIDS, IOWA

VICKY NELSON HEARD A commotion outside that jolted her from her sleep. It was just after 7 a.m. More than a week had passed since Jack left the house. She heard him making his early-morning escape. She even watched him walking away. She had been a bundle of nerves ever since.

She kept hoping that a few days without a home to live in would do her husband some good. If that's what it would take to bring him back to his senses, so be it.

But after ten long, agonizing days, it still hadn't happened...

Without having access to her sleeping pills, which ran out weeks ago, Vicky couldn't sleep for more than an hour or two at a time, before being jolted awake again, fearing for her life. ???

The fan in her bedroom was always turned-on full blast. One reason for this was that the air conditioner could never keep the house cool in this blazing heat. The other reason was that the constant humming sound blocked out all outside noises. It didn't take much to rattle her nerves these days.

Since the Nelsons never showed up for their second appointment to receive the mark, Vicky kept waiting for the police to break down their front door, demanding to know why it happened again.

There wasn't a chance they could use the "flu" excuse again. More than anything, she kept waiting for her husband to walk through the door as a changed man.

Vicky went downstairs and glanced outside her living room window like she did each morning, looking for the government-issued vehicle she saw parked down the street every day.

Utter shock filled her face, upon seeing a SWAT team outside her house. She lost all her strength and collapsed to the floor on her knees. She shouted upstairs to her teenage children, "Come downstairs! They're here!"

Liam and Laura dashed down the stairs, mindful to whom their mother was referring. They followed their mother into the dining room, their bodies quaking every step of the way.

Without even knocking, law enforcement broke down the front door, to find the three of them huddled in a corner behind the massive dining room table, all in their pajamas, shaking uncontrollably.

Hearts melting inside them, they were handcuffed then taken to the prison camp closest to their house, for questioning. It was one of the newer barn-like structures with no heat, no air conditioning, or running water. It was surrounded by electrical fences to keep the animals caged in.

Authorities could have questioned them at home, but since the man of the house had received a book from the most wanted man on the planet, they wanted the Nelsons to catch a glimpse of what happened to dissidents at this place, in case they, too, were having second thoughts about taking the mark.

But the real reason Romanero had ordered their detainment was, after monitoring the Nelsons all this time, it was evident to those listening to their conversations that they were only interested in taking the mark and the chip, nothing more.

They wanted the benefits without worshiping him or addressing Salvador as "Supreme See" or "lord and savior". As potential secular followers, he wanted to humiliate them, by allowing their once envious neighbors to witness them being taken away in handcuffs.

But since the mark was voluntary, when they arrived at the prison, the handcuffs were removed. As of yet, they had done nothing wrong. All they could do was threaten them at this point.

Before being questioned, they were taken to where Christian dissidents were being beheaded. Even without handcuffs on, they felt like they were being perp walked.

They had occasionally watched beheadings on their phone screens, mostly out of curiosity. But seeing it up close and personal like this, with nothing distracting the view or muffling the unsettling sounds of humans being slaughtered, was nothing short of blood curdling.

After just one glance, Laura became so horrified that she looked away. She felt like vomiting.

From there, they were taken inside to separate interrogation rooms, to face similar questioning. Vicky saw her reflection in the dim mirror behind the woman questioning her. Her gray, frizzy hair was unkempt.

Before the walls of her family life came crashing down all around her, she applied hair dye once a month. The image staring back at her was yet another byproduct of not taking the mark.

It was basic mathematics—no money, no hair dye, no nothing!

She looked like an actress in a movie where makeup was applied to make her look many years older. Only there was no makeup to remove to make her look younger again.

The woman questioning Vicky wasted no time getting down to business. "Where did your husband go?"

Vicky's hands shook so severely, it looked like she was having an epileptic seizure. "I don't know. Honestly, I don't. All I can tell you is when Jack came back from Pennsylvania, everything changed. Soon after that, he became a Christian."

"How did it happen?" she asked, matter-of-factly.

Vicky's shoulders slumped, as she explained to the woman seated across from her, "Doctor Shapiro left him a copy of The Way, which Jack brought home with him. I didn't know anything about it until the day before he left. When I finally discovered what it was, I demanded that he get rid of it. That's when everything went downhill for us."

Without a shred of empathy, she pressed on, "What about the book your husband burned in Benjamin Shapiro's backyard?"

"It was the wrong one. He brought the real one home with him."

The female interrogator raised a suspicious eyebrow, then very calmly folded her hands on the table. "Why did he take it with him?"

"Doctor Shapiro personally inscribed it to him. It's the reason why he refuses to take the mark. But don't bother ransacking my house looking for the real book. When Jack fled the other day, he took it with him. Even if he hadn't, I would have burned it in the fireplace. Can you believe it? He's the last person I ever thought would lose his mind like everyone else reading that book. He was always so sharp."

The woman didn't care about Vicky's troubles. Showing empathy wasn't part of her job description. Her job was to find the truth. "I see you've had several appointments that you never showed up for. Is that your husband's fault too?"

Vicky may not have been under arrest, but it sure felt like she was. "I rescheduled it the first time. We were all sick with the global flu, and we couldn't leave the house because of the quarantine. But even when we started feeling better, Jack was dead set against taking it."

The woman glared at her skeptically. "But it's been ten days since your last cancellation. You could have gone with your two children by now. How can you explain this?"

Vicky was completely beside herself. "I kept hoping Jack would regain control of his senses, and come home, so we could take it together as a family. This way, when inspectors came knocking on our door checking to the mark, we would all be in compliance."

The woman glared at her skeptically. "How do we know the three of you will show up for your next scheduled appointments?"

Vicky held her hands out in protest. "We have no food or medicine! How can we possibly survive without it? Of course, we'll show up. We'll even take the mark here, if that's possible…"

"Wait here," the woman said nonchalantly.

She left the room to meet the two other interrogators. According to the truth scanners that were zeroed in on the three of them, it appeared they were being truthful. Satisfied that they had provided convincing answers to their many questions, the Nelsons were rejoined, then taken to another outside location where Christians were being beheaded for their faith in Jesus.

Their shock knew no bounds upon seeing a member of their own family strapped to a metal chair out in the blazing heat. They shared fearful glances seeing him naked. His face was bloodied, black and blue. As a believer, he wasn't being scorched by the sun, but with no comforting shade anywhere, his body was badly sunburned.

Vicky covered her mouth with her right hand. She was aghast by how thin her husband was. She couldn't believe someone could lose so much weight in so little time. "Where did you find him?"

Two guards stood on either side of Jack standing under SPF umbrellas. One was male. The other was female. They both had those painful sores on their cheeks and foreheads.

The buff man explained, "He was captured early this morning, in downtown Cedar Rapids, camped out behind a dumpster a few blocks away, in a sleeping bag, reading the book you said Shapiro gave to him. This gave us grounds to arrest him."

Vicky shook her head very slowly, unable to comprehend what she was hearing.

"We knew where he was all along. The only time he left there was to listen to that whacko preaching again. The reason we didn't arrest him ten days ago was our hope that he might lead us to Benjamin Shapiro. When it didn't happen, he was detained before he starved to death. He hasn't eaten much since he left the house, if anything at all."

Vicky snorted, realizing the questions they were being asked had nothing to do with Jack's whereabouts, and everything to do with probing to see if they had followed in his footsteps, spiritually speaking. She still couldn't believe what had become of her former FBI agent husband. Just a month ago, it would have been inconceivable.

The man glanced at Laura. "Despite being beaten for several hours, your father remains adamant that he won't take the mark, no matter what we do to him." Even he still wondered how these prisoners willingly subjected themselves to so much torture for a lie.

Laura lowered her head and started softly sniffling. Even though it was all her father's fault, the last thing she wanted was to see him in this terrifying predicament. She ached for him.

She tipped her eyes up and saw the mark proudly displayed on the guard's forehead for all to see. *Only a monster could work at this place!*

The guard shifted his gaze back to Vicky. "I'll leave you alone with him. It would be in your best interest to try one last time to speak some sense into your deranged husband. If not, you already know the outcome…"

Vicky gulped back a huge dose of fear, then nodded that she understood him perfectly clearly.

He went on, "Since the three of you are being truthful, once you take the mark, the thousand-dollar imbursement for his capture will be credited to your account immediately, so you can purchase the many things you need. If not," he added evenly, "I hope you enjoy this glimpse into the future for all who refuse to take it."

Vicky gulped hard again. None of them needed to be given this ultimatum either to take the mark or end up like Jack. "What about our bank accounts?"

The female guard looked at her notes. "Seventy-five percent of all your assets will be made available to you the instant you take the mark, to include the bonus your husband recently received. These funds won't be taxed.

"Since chances are good that he'll never be released from this place, you won't have to worry about not being in compliance. We'll leave you alone with him now."

When the two guards left them, Vicky whisper-shouted to her husband, "Have you completely lost your mind?"

Jack said in reply, "I understand how bizarre my actions must seem to you, foolish even. If only you could see through my eyes right now, you'd realize the stance I'm taking is the power of God living inside me."

Jack said to Laura, "I hate to tell you this, my sweet child, but with or without taking the mark, you'll never live to see twenty."

Vicky glared at her husband. "That's a horrible thing to say to our daughter, Jack!"

Laura turned her head away from her father. She couldn't look at him. The fact that this was the first time she ever saw her father without clothes on had little to do with it. What she saw in his eyes was the look of someone who was about to be killed. His eyes looked dead to her…

Vicky pleaded with her husband, "Jack, please listen to me, Russell and Umberto have already received the mark. And guess what, they both were reinstated with full pay. Isn't that wonderful news?"

There was just enough wiggle room for Jack to shake his head sadly for his two former colleagues. "No, it isn't good news. It's an eternal tragedy for them…" He paused then added, "And for you, too, if you follow their lead."

Vicky rolled her eyes and snorted anger. Her eyes recentered on her defiant husband. "I know it's been difficult lately. If you need some time to clear your mind, and pull yourself together, that's fine. I can always go back to teaching Pre-K, if that's what it will take to bring you back to your old self. But first you must take the mark."

Eyes darting from one family member to the next, Jack begged them. "Whatever you do, please don't take it. Everyone who does will surely end up in hell with Satan and his demons."

Vicky glanced up at the hot sky above. "Please, God, help my husband make the right decision…"

"I assure you, honey, God will never answer that prayer. Only Romanero would want that sort of prayer to be answered. So, shouldn't you say, so help me Antichrist?"

Vicky became furious hearing this. She slapped the table in front of her as hard as she could, then burst into tears. "You really are crazy, Jack! You're the one who should've been seeing a psychiatrist all this time, not me…"

"Enough!" Liam shouted as loudly as he could. He couldn't stand seeing his mother looking so anguished. He glared at his father. "I hope you burn in hell for this, *Dad*!"

If you only knew... Jack tried pleading with his son, "I understand why you're mad at me, Liam, but please don't take the mark. If you do, your eternal fate will be sealed, and nothing can change that..."

Liam growled at his father. "Don't tell me what to do! You're nothing to me now..."

At that, without even saying goodbye to his father, Liam got up out of his chair. "I'm ready to take it now," he told one of the guards.

Jack gasped loudly. His neck went limp. It was pointless.

Now that her husband was beyond hope, Vicky had to start thinking of herself and her two children. The first step to righting this ship was by taking the mark and freeing up their desperately needed finances. "Us too," Vicky said on behalf of herself, and Laura.

Jack was forced to witness his family, as they received the mark at the very station at which he kept refusing to take it. The two guards held his head up so he wouldn't miss anything.

When they were finished, the guard glared at Jack angrily. "You have one last chance to renounce your false God and take the mark!"

Jack was mindful of what Christ had said in Matthew 19:29, about anyone leaving houses or brothers or sisters or father or mother or wife or children or fields for His sake, would receive a hundred times as much and would inherit eternal life.

Right now, the only part of that promise that comforted him was the eternal life part. Everything else felt awfully dreadful to him...

Jack tipped his eyes up at the guard. "Jesus Christ is my Lord and Savior, and I am not ashamed. Nothing you will ever do to me will get me to take Antichrist's mark. The greatest joy I have is knowing my name is written in the Lamb's Book of Life."

Like everyone else being detained in Romanero's death camps, Jack couldn't wait for the blade to drop so he could close his eyes for the last time on this evil planet, then open them again in Heaven. Then he would finally be at rest...

Jack said to the guard, "If anything, I should be thanking you..."

The guard glared even more angrily at Jack. "Come again?!"

"Once you drop that blade on me, I'll be transferred from this hell hole and carried by angels straight to Paradise, in the blink of an eye."

Many of Jack's fellow prisoners shouted, "Amen!"

The guard snickered at them. "Your wish is my command, you lunatic!"

When the blade dropped, Vicky and Laura both refused to watch. Liam had one eye open and the other one closed. All three heard the sound the steel blade made when it chopped Jack's head off at the neck, followed by the dull thud it made hitting the concrete ground.

They started crying hysterically for their father. But had they known the repercussions of their own actions, they would be weeping for themselves.

Much like their father's death by guillotine couldn't be reversed, neither could their decisions to take the mark of the Beast.

All three willingly received the mark that day, so they would be without excuse...

Laura dried her eyes with a tissue. "What do we do now, Mom?"

Vicky sniffled a few times. "We go shopping. I desperately need my medication."

Instead of glaring at their mother for being insensitive, they both nodded in agreement with her. It was as if their hearts had become hardened against their late father...

THE INSTANT JACK NELSON stepped foot in Glory, he understood why his briefcase was never opened during his month-long detainment in Pennsylvania. It had been supernaturally protected by the one who saved his soul.

He also knew why God had sent the global flu. Had he not been sick, he wouldn't have read the book Benjamin Shapiro had given him, and he surely would have taken the mark with his family.

22

50 MILES OFF THE COAST OF BRAZIL

EIGHT WEEKS AFTER THE sailboat being captained by Sergei Ivanov left the Philippines, they finally reached the southern tip of South America, and they were now on their northbound part of the voyage, in the Atlantic Ocean.

With their fuel supplies down to one 300-gallon barrel, which was only half-full, they had to rely heavily on the wind to help navigate the vessel. Thankfully, God had blessed them with strong tail winds in the Pacific. So much so that the 17,000 miles (14,784 nautical miles), which normally took 62 days to sail, was shortened by five days.

But by having the sails raised for 57 days, like strutting peacocks, it made their vessel easier to spot. Whenever another boat or ship came into view, with no way of documenting their voyage in either direction, they held their collective breath until they knew for certain it wasn't a potential threat.

Another challenge they faced was the $14K Sergei spent on supplies, before his global monetary card was deactivated, was getting low. As it was, two-thirds of it had been spent on fuel. The fact that this trip was taking twice as long as originally anticipated was the reason.

They still had enough food to survive on. The problem was that they were running low on propane for the food items that needed to be cooked. But they had enough MREs, canned tuna, and various other canned good items, to last up to a year.

Other than that, for the most part, everything had gone relatively smoothly. The three sailors knew the peaceful calm wouldn't last.

What caused the most anxiety to swim through their bodies, the past eight weeks, was what they saw whenever they were able to look up into the heavenlies, without having a thick haze or cloud cover obstructing their view.

On those rare occasions when the sky was clear, some stars appeared brighter each time they gazed up. And larger! The three Christ followers knew they weren't stars, but meteors that were getting closer to the planet on which they felt desperately trapped!

They felt certain that even the unbelievers were mindful of it. How could they not be? All they had to do was look up! But what could they possibly do to stop this next imminent invasion of the planet? Much like the first time it happened, they would be completely powerless from stopping them. And there was only one of them last time...

What made it worse for Donald, Sergei, and Analyn was that a thick cloud cover had engulfed their part of the world for the past ten days, so they couldn't see beyond it. By having no access to the rest of the world, all they could do was wait, pray, and brace themselves for the second bowl judgment to be released.

The last place they wanted to be was on a boat out in the ocean. But what could they do about it now? They were mindful of the risk they were taking when they left Manila.

Still, it was the worst sensation. The trio found it impossible to relax.

Having already been through it once, Sergei wished it would happen soon, so it would be over and done with, regardless of the outcome.

Ivanov was an avid golfer before the disappearances. On the night of the Rapture—it happened at just after 1 a.m. in Thailand—he was scheduled for a golf outing with his buddies the next morning. Needless to say, it never happened. He hadn't been on a golf course since...

When Salvador Romanero rose to power, Ivanov became a big fan of the young Spaniard. He clung to his many promises that life would return to normal. He even held on to his golf clubs, hoping he would get to use them again at some point.

To help relieve the constant angst he felt, the past few weeks, he was finally able to put his golf equipment to good use. He would go to the top deck, usually as the sun was just setting, and pound ten golf balls a day on board the boat into the Pacific Ocean, using a 2 iron.

The last ball splashed into the ocean more than a week ago. He then hit their now worthless cellphones into the Pacific, using a 3 iron.

Finally, using the same 3-iron, he whacked the empty Anbesol liquid bottle Donald gave to Analyn in Manila, for her on and off again toothache. It shattered into many pieces before hitting the water.

With no more balls left to hit, Donald and Analyn frequently watched Sergei, at least his silhouette, practicing his swing on the top deck as if playing air golf. He would look up after each shot, squinting into the horizon, as though following the trajectory of the imaginary ball.

On day two of their northern part of the voyage, Sergei knew his air golfing days were over, when the second angel poured out his bowl on the sea. The three sailors trembled in stark terror, as the skies erupted with ear-splitting growling and rumbling noises coming in all directions.

The sonic blasts they made upon entering the Earth's atmosphere were so loud, it was a wonder they didn't lose their hearing, at least temporarily.

Had they been any closer, surely their eardrums would have been pierced all the way through. The heat radiating from the massive-sized fireballs was so intense, parts of their eyebrows and lashes were singed.

The global pulsation had caused every piece of glass on board the vessel to shatter. It was so hot that Sergei feared all things fiberglass on his sailboat would melt. This pulse was far worse than the pulse created by Romanero's manmade global bombing campaign, which the three of them still knew nothing about.

Suddenly, instead of seeing one singular meteor, numerous bits and pieces from multiple meteors slammed into the ocean all around them, at 500 miles per hour. It wasn't simultaneous, it was more like rapid fire.

They didn't need this front row seat to question what was happening. They knew they were smack dab in the middle of Bible prophecy coming to life before their very eyes.

They stared out at the horizon in all directions, totally breathless, as these alien objects of all shapes and sizes slammed into the ocean. They ranged in size from SUVs to massive buildings.

Regardless of size, each impact sent massive waves fanning out in all directions at 300 miles per hour, flash-boiling fish, and all other underwater sea life. Some waves rose hundreds of feet in the air.

Whatever the impact didn't kill within a 50-mile radius, the waves took care of. Even the smallest ones meant instant death for anyone and anything unfortunate enough to be in their pathways.

With so many strikes happening all at once, many waves kept colliding with each other.

Ivanov remembered hearing stories about it the first time around. Many who weren't incinerated by the impact drowned in the massive tsunami waves that followed, whether they were on a small fishing boat or on a massive container cargo ship. But this was far worse!

He shouted to Donald and Analyn, "Help me lower the sails, so we don't get blown over!" The fear in his voice sprung them both into action. It took a while, but they finally achieved that task.

With nothing left to do on the top deck, they retreated below and prayed for God's protection.

When Analyn's ears stopped buzzing, she said, "I'm scared, Ninong."

Sergei saw the fear in her eyes. He wrapped his arms around her trembling body, before Donald had a chance to.

As the initial warning waves started rocking the boat, Donald adjusted his scratched glasses on his nose, opened his Bible, and read Revelation 16:3 as loud as he could, so Sergei and Analyn could hear him, "'The second angel poured out his bowl on the sea, and it turned into blood like that of a dead person, and every living thing in the sea died.'"

Analyn gulped back fear. "Does that include us?"

Donald wiped his sweaty brow with the back of his right hand. "Guess we'll know soon enough." He read Revelation 16:4-7 aloud to them: "'The third angel poured out his bowl on the rivers and springs of water, and they became blood.

"'Then I heard the angel in charge of the waters declaring, 'You are just in these judgments, O Holy One, you who are and who were; for they have shed the blood of your holy people and your prophets, and you have given them blood to drink as they deserve.' And I heard the altar respond: 'Yes, Lord God Almighty, true and just are your judgments.'"

Donald looked up at the two of them. "I can almost hear them now."

The last time he experienced anything close to this, was when Tom Dunleavey was reading Revelation 6 at safe house number one, during their men's Bible study, just as the ground started quaking all around them, which turned out being the global quake.

But now that he was stuck on a boat, with no place to escape to, this was so much worse! The fear he felt couldn't be measured in human terms.

The three of them sat on the floor and held onto each other, eyes closed, praying for God's protection, not knowing what would soon become of them.

It took less than 15 minutes for the first waves to slam into their boat, carrying with them dead sea life of all varieties, and who knew what else?

The waves kept getting dangerously higher as the seconds passed by like hours. The vessel nearly tipped over sideways several times. It bent as far as it could without tipping over. Even the 100-foot sail poles were fully submerged beneath the water a few times, before finally resurfacing and pointing skyward again. But for how long?

Even though they all had God's eternal assurance, they felt utterly helpless. Massive as the first meteor strike was, this was so much worse. Whereas only a third of all ships and sea life were wiped out on that horrific day, this was a full assault on the planet.

To achieve His global objective, Yahweh sent multiple meteors to allow for an equal distribution on the seas. Bottom line: One meteor strike wouldn't have had the capacity to kill all living things in the sea. It took multiple strikes.

In that light, it didn't matter which body of water the three of them were sailing on—the Atlantic, the Pacific, the Indian, the Mediterranean, the Caribbean, or on any other large body of water—they were just as much in harm's way from the aftermath as everyone else unfortunate enough to be out on the open seas.

THE GLOBAL METEOR STRIKE quickly became breaking news.

One frightened female reporter bemoaned, "Just as we had feared, the multiple impacts have caused another round of volcanic eruptions planetwide. Many countries that were all but wiped out are once again being swamped by massive tsunami waves."

One geologist warned on live TV, "With countless meteor strikes happening all at once, not only will our oceans and rivers be polluted perhaps for as long as several decades, but the heat generated from the impact will surely melt all polar ice caps. This, in turn, will flood many coastal areas with millions of gallons of sea water and dead fish."

The man paused, not caring how completely disheveled he looked, or that he had festering boils on his face and body. He was one of the few brave news anchors to appear on camera with them.

He closed his eyes for a few seconds searching his mind for what to say next, knowing there was no way to sugarcoat it. He plucked his reading glasses off his face in frustration, and closed his eyes, still trying to absorb this latest tragic news.

Said he, "If you think obtaining clean drinking water was a challenge before today, it's only going to get worse. I cringe to think how many more countries will go to war now over this most precious resource."

Another expert said, "Our global security also took a huge hit, as hundreds of millions of microfliers were incinerated by the intense heat from the multiple meteors. Who knows how long it will take to replace them?"

Another top environmentalist took to the airwaves, still foolishly believing the planet could be saved, but only if drastic measures were taken immediately. It was nothing more than desperate, arrogant, wishful thinking on his part.

But most top minds now believed there could be no overturning the widespread devastation these judgments had caused to the ecosystem, that many had fought so hard to preserve before the Rapture.

They kept these personal thoughts to themselves…

What they all had in common, aside from the stark terror etched on their faces, was that each blamed the God of Israel for this heinous act against humanity.

They all had been ordered to call Him Israel's God, instead of Almighty God, hoping to minimize his Omnipresence and Omniscience. For most citizens on the planet, saved or unsaved, it wasn't working anymore…

The fact that the God of Israel's 144,000 servants kept proclaiming that the very One who had breathed it all into existence was now destroying it, caused the unconverted to hate them, and their God, even more.

As per Yahweh's eternal promise to all who loved Him, He would soon create a new heaven and earth that would be uncorrupted by sin.

Everything on this sin-stained planet would be made new again…

23

ONE WEEK AFTER THE METEOR STRIKE

TO SAY THAT IT had been a stressful week for Donald Johnson, Analyn Tibayan, and Sergei Ivanov, would be putting it mildly.

The first three days following impact were the most difficult for the three of them. Each time the bow of the boat dove into the oncoming waves, the cabin became flooded with more seawater.

Sergei tried ever so valiantly to steady himself up the stairs with buckets full of the blood red water, as Donald and Analyn mopped the floor. They also used beach towels to absorb as much of it as they could.

With the constant bobbing and swaying, more times than not, before Sergei could dump what was collected overboard, much of it had already spilled out of the buckets. He even slipped and fell a handful of times, forcing some of the polluted water to go back down into the cabin.

The fact that he had to do it each time the vessel took on more water was both demoralizing and painstaking. He had cuts and bruises on his body, and his arms felt like rubber. But he had no choice but to do all he could to keep the cabin as dry as possible.

After three straight days and nights, the three of them were bone weary, their bodies ached, and they all had queasy stomachs.

What made it even worse was, despite their best efforts, the cabin, while relatively dry, still reeked of dead fish and vomit. Even without the protective glass that was shattered upon impact, with no winds to filter the foul air out, they couldn't get rid of it.

But at least they were still alive. For that, they were grateful.

Finally, the waves had subsided enough for Ivanov to venture to the top deck for damage control, without fearing being plucked off the boat by a rogue wave. Dead sea life of all varieties littered the deck floor, including a small shark and even an octopus.

If they hadn't been flash-boiled, they might have been edible. But just one whiff was all it took to know they weren't consumable.

Even seven days later, the ocean was still dangerously choppy. Fifteen-foot swells slammed the boat coming from all directions, sending a blood red mist over the bow, constantly hitting Sergei in the face.

Even with a facemask on, the toxic stench was overpowering. It was like experiencing a red tide on steroids. And that was putting it mildly.

Now that Yahweh had turned the seas blood red, as far as the eye could see in any direction, they could no longer bathe in it or catch fresh fish to eat. A week ago, they had full access to the ocean any time they wanted. Even if it was too cold to stay in the water for too long, at least they had that option available to them.

Just like Sergei had feared, much of the sailboat that was molded together with fiberglass was warped in many areas from the intense heat.

Yet, not only had it survived in the most turbulent environment any sea vessel could survive, remarkably, it was still seaworthy.

Once again, God had placed him in the perfect position on the seas.

They may not have had access to GPS, but what they did have was an exact knowledge of the times in which they were living.

Had they not had access to the Word of God, they might have never filled all those steel barrels with sea water, before the second bowl judgment struck the planet. All of them were knocked over, but they remained sealed, thus safeguarding the precious resource inside them.

Sergei was grateful that the steel barrels had proven invaluable.

This was Ivanov's second time experiencing a meteor strike, while out on the open waters. It wasn't something one ever got used to.

Another thing that made it worse this time was that the sun kept heating the air and the blood red water to unhealthy levels. Not only had the stench reached critical levels, on top of that, the temperatures kept rising all week. They kept soaring to heights that had never been reached or felt before on the planet, without a cloud to be seen in the sky.

Sergei knew why. Revelation 16:8-9 had come to pass: *The fourth angel poured out his bowl on the sun, and the sun was allowed to scorch people with fire. They were seared by the intense heat and they cursed the name of God, who had control over these plagues, but they refused to repent and glorify him.*

When the trio left the Philippines, Analyn could never stay warm. She was always bundled up in whatever she could find for added warmth.

In the blink of an eye, the temperatures went from extremely chilly to sweltering hot. It was as if the meteors had cleared all cloud cover from the planet. The average temperature on the planet was 54 degrees Celsius (130 Fahrenheit). It was even hotter in the world's desert locations, but a little cooler in most mountainous places. Even the many sun worshippers on the planet writhed in agony, begging for cloud cover.

The ocean temperatures were even worse. Having absorbed the full brunt of the massive balls of fire striking them in rapid fire, some areas reached record levels topping 150 degrees Fahrenheit.

Had the atmosphere resembled anything like it was before the Rapture, it would have spawned numerous Category 5 hurricanes, which would have done catastrophic damage to every location on Planet Earth, destroying so many of the world's remaining islands, few as they were.

But with no clouds in the skies, and no moisture to tap into, it couldn't happen. Yahweh had supernaturally disrupted the entire global ecosystem. That was about the only good thing for those stranded on boats and ships.

It was quickly approaching the suffocating stage both above and below deck. And with no winds to propel them forward, and with extremely limited fuel, the sailboat often moved at a snail's pace.

Even at nighttime, it was so stifling hot inside the cabin that Donald and Sergei were always shirtless. Analyn wore shorts and a sports exercise bra that Hana Patel and Yasamin Dabiri had placed in the duffel bag for her.

Being surrounded by water, yet being restricted from accessing it, had created a new round of mental torture for the three of them.

The heat was so unbearable that Donald and Sergei shaved each other's heads, hoping to cool their body temperatures a bit.

When it was Sergei's turn, he frowned, upon seeing huge chunks of his long, straggly, bleached-blonde hair dropping onto the floor. Donald then applied shaving cream and ran the blade across his scalp, in steady up and down motions, marking the end of the hippie image Ivanov loved to project before his conversion. He thought this day would never come.

When they were finished, Analyn surprised Donald by asking him, "Can you cut my hair next, Ninong?" Her words were slurred because of her bad toothache. It was at full throttle now. Sergei had offered on several occasions to remove it with the use of pliers. She chickened out each time.

Donald flinched hearing this. "Are you sure that's what you want?"

Analyn took a deep breath, then nodded at him, ever so tentatively.

"Okay, then." He reached for the scissors and began the tedious task of cutting off huge chunks of her hair one clump after the next, then dropping them onto the floor. It was quite dry from overexposure to the salt water.

Donald vividly remembered how long and shiny her hair was the first time he was in her country. When they were reunited in Manila ten weeks ago, her hair was dirty, matted, and unevenly cut.

Just when it started to resemble how it looked before the Rapture, her hair was short again. Had she asked him to cut it off before the meteor strike, he would have tried talking her out of it.

Donald reached for the can of shaving cream, but Analyn put her hand up in refusal. A buzz cut was more than enough for her. Having already lost everything; her hair represented everything she had left in the world.

Now it was gone…Analyn had suffered her first bout with seasickness on the first few nights on the boat. Eventually, it went away, only to return after the meteor strikes. Just as she was starting to feel better, her stomach started churning violently again.

She looked out at the ocean through one of the ports with no protection glass. A steady flow of tears streamed down her cheeks, one after the next. Despite the joy she felt from growing closer to her Maker, it pained her too much to think about her parents' eternal conditions.

If they didn't renounce Mormonism and trust in Christ alone for their salvation, before they got swept away by the flood waters, it wasn't a cause for celebration for them. Analyn rejoiced, knowing she would see her daughter, Juliana, again. Had she not been swept away by the strong waters; she would be three years old now.

Just when she felt she couldn't look or feel any uglier, Sergei looked her square in the eyes, took an anxious breath, and said, "The reason I moved to Southeast Asia, aside from living the party life, was to find a nice Thai girl. But I found the woman of my dreams in the Philippines."

Analyn gulped hard, sensing where this conversation might be headed. The timing couldn't have been worse. She was depressed, baldheaded, and sticky from wearing clothes that were washed in salt water. Despite all that, her eyes widened in anticipation.

Sergei nervously rubbed his bald scalp. His tired, cobalt blue eyes became moist with tears, as he gazed into Analyn's dark brown eyes. "I know we just met three months ago, and we're still getting to know each other, but will you marry me?"

Analyn had developed strong feelings for Sergei too, but she wasn't prepared for this. She gasped.

Sergei looked deep into her eyes. "The instant I laid eyes on you in Manila, I felt something inside that I never felt for another woman. That feeling kept growing for you every day since."

Analyn shot an anxious glance at Donald. He shrugged his shoulders, equally surprised, sort of anyway.

Sergei took a moment to take a few steady breaths. "I love you, Analyn. If you feel the same about me, marry me. I don't want to be alone when we get to America. If, by chance, we don't make it there, I don't want to be alone out here on the open waters."

Analyn's lower lip quivered. "But look at me! I'm ugly!"

Sergei grinned at her, then assured her, "With or without long hair, you're still beautiful to me. Besides, it will grow back. Mine too."

Analyn's heart was pounding so fast, she could hardly hear anything else. She took a few deep breaths, then shook her head up and down. "Yes, I'll marry you!" More tears flooded her eyes. *Now someone can hold me at night.*

Sergei kissed his new fiancée on the lips, then glanced over at Donald. "Will you marry us, brother?"

Donald asked Analyn, "Are you doing it for love and not out of desperation only?"

She replied softly, affectionately, "Yes, Ninong, I love him too."

Donald beamed. "Well, then, it will be my honor. Truth be told, this will be the first time I've ever married anyone. I'll do my best."

Analyn hugged Donald. "Thanks, Ninong."

After pronouncing them husband and wife, Johnson said, "You may kiss the bride…"

Sergei kissed his wife, then said, "I never thought the day would come when I would kiss a woman with a buzz cut, let alone marry her!"

Donald burst out in laughter. "It must be true love! Now that you are bride and groom, you'll need plenty of privacy, in case you decide to bring a child into the world. That said, I'll remain here in the main living area. If I have to use the toilet, I'll knock first, just in case…"

The way he said it caused Analyn to look shyly at her husband. "Thanks again for everything, Ninong, I love you."

"I love you too, Analyn. Both of you."

Sergei smiled at the two people who had become his best friends in life. The former hippie who moved from Moscow to Bangkok, Thailand, hoping for a better life filled with booze, narcotics, sailing, surfing, golfing, and women, had found his true love in Christ Jesus.

Now his Savior had blessed him with a wonderful woman to love. It was a cause for rejoicing, despite their incredible situation.

Donald Johnson was happy for the newlyweds. But when Sergei told Analyn if they didn't make it to America, at least by having her by his side, he wouldn't feel alone, it pierced Donald deeply inside. It also made him long to be with his wife and son even more.

The last thing he wanted was to be stuck out on the open waters feeling terribly alone. *Who can I hold onto at night...*

Donald yearned for Mary every day. But now that he had just married this beautiful couple, he missed her even more. And since he hadn't communicated with his wife in many months, it was starting to feel like she was becoming a distant memory to him.

And that went double for his son, Luke.

24

LATER THAT EVENING, AFTER their nightly reading, Analyn asked Donald, "Ninong?"

"Yes, Analyn?"

She hesitated, knowing how lonely and homesick he was. Her hope was that her question would serve to reinvigorate him. She spoke through her facemask. "Can you tell us about the place we're going to?"

Donald scratched his chin. It was time to stop feeling sorry for himself. Now that they were out of danger for the time being, even though there would surely be more obstacles to overcome, having survived this most drastic of them, he could never lose hope of seeing his wife and son again. The thought that it might actually happen filled his heart with joy.

"Absolutely! Consider it your wedding gift! Let me begin by saying it was the very first *ETSM* safe house. It's also my favorite place on this God-forsaken planet. Brian and Jacquelyn Mulrooney discovered the property. Of course, you may know them as Brad and Joan Henriksen."

"That name sounds familiar," said Sergei, holding his wife's hand.

"They were the couple who sent the video to Yogesh Patel," said Donald, connecting the dots for them, "which led to his salvation."

Since the couple had made headline news long before the global quake and meteor strike, Analyn and Sergei were both mindful of them.

"Really? You live with them?" asked Analyn.

Donald nodded yes. "The nicest couple you'd ever want to meet. As the world vilified them, Yahweh used them to rescue Yogesh's soul from hell. Our organization was responsible for his escape from the Middle East. He never made it to our safe house, but what a legacy he left behind. I can only imagine how many got saved after he accused Romanero of being the Antichrist while in the man's presence."

Sergei had already met Hana in Singapore, and he was mindful of her husband's fate. "I hope Hana made it there safely…"

"Me too, brother. I can't wait to see Hana, Yasamin, and their children again. Luke and Mary too…," Donald uttered more softly. "Anyway, when they first laid eyes on the place, Brian called it a 'Pocket of Peace'. That's precisely what it is, a pocket of peace in a turbulent world."

"Really, Ninong?" *Pocket of Peace, wow*! *Exactly what I need now*!

"Yes, Analyn," came the reply with a smile. I feel so blessed to call it my home. Everyone is so nice. The best people you'd ever want to go into hiding with. The two of you will fit right in." Donald smiled at the vision in his head. "We even have a former U.S. President staying with us."

"Really?" asked Sergei. "Who?"

"Jefferson Danforth."

Sergei snorted in amazement. "President Osolovich never thought too highly of him."

Donald shook his head. "I'm sure the feeling's mutual. Only instead of wishing him dead, I wouldn't be surprised if Jefferson prays each day for the Russian president to be saved. But since Russia's a big player in these times, and he is Russia's leader, it seems unlikely."

Sergei replied, "Yeah, even before I left Mother Russia, I was always suspicious about Uri Osolovich. I always admired his strength and determination, but something about the man rubbed me the wrong way. He was creepy. My friends and I often joked that we'd hate to be his enemy. Now, I am his enemy, even though he doesn't know it."

Donald took a small sip of water, then redirected the conversation back onto safe house number one. "The property is full of quaint little cottages, a cafeteria, hospital, and several daycare locations. It was badly damaged in the global quake. Many of our residents died that night."

Even in the dim light, Donald saw fear creeping onto Analyn's face. "Don't worry, it may not be like it once was, but it's still inhabitable. I assure you it's nothing like what we left behind in the Philippines. That's because our safe house is being supernaturally protected."

Analyn sighed relief, then asked, "How can you know for sure?"

Donald grinned wearily at her. "One of Yahweh's sealed servants lives with us. His name is Jakob. All locations housing children have one of them assigned there. If my memory serves, five thousand were assigned to our organization. Since were one of those locations, praise God, Jakob assured us our safe house would survive the mayhem."

Sergei was mindful of the chilling message Donald had received from Clayton Holmes, in Singapore, warning about the microfliers spying on them. But since safe house number one was one of the protected properties, Donald took his words as precautionary.

Then again, he knew nothing about the "Montpelier List" being targeted, nor about Romanero's all-out attack on Christian hiding places the world over, including his beloved safe house in Chadds Ford. As the globe temporarily shook that day, the three of them felt nothing.

Totally oblivious to these harsh realities, he went on, "My favorite place on the thirty-seven-acre property, is the sanctuary. It's where Mary and I got married. On Christmas Eve, in fact. What a night it was!"

Analyn sat up straighter on the couch, her curiosity piqued. "Really?"

Donald nodded at her. "The property was covered in fourteen inches of snow. As snow lovers, it was like God had given us the perfect wedding gift! Sadly, it was the first and only time it snowed since we took possession of the land. It was bone-chilling cold outside!

"But talk about perfect timing. Our wedding night was on the same day that power was restored in America. Since the sanctuary didn't have a heating system in place, we took full advantage of the electricity by turning on every space heater we had. It helped, but still it was cold."

Sergei said, "In this heat, cold weather would be perfect now..."

Johnson smiled at the vision in his head. "You should've seen it! Handmade wreaths were hung about, and there were two lit trees on the stage flanking the pulpit. Acoustical Christmas music streamed through the speakers. The thousands watching online got to see and hear it all."

Donald stared at the wall opposite him. "It was spectacular! It was the first and only time it felt like Christmas to any of us, since before the Rapture. I can't wait to show you the sanctuary when we get there."

Analyn was greatly comforted by what she saw on Donald's face. The stress lines on his forehead weren't nearly as deep as they were a day or two ago. She wondered how long it would last...

Donald shooed away a pesky mosquito and went on, "At that time, we didn't have many residents, so we only anticipated a half-full sanctuary that night. We knew many would be watching online, including President Danforth. Other than that, we expected an intimate setting."

The hint of a smile on Donald's face vanished. "Needless to say, our wedding night didn't come without a few surprises."

Sergei asked, "What kind of surprises? Was your wedding as bizarre as ours?"

"After I tell you about it, you can answer your own question. But as you'll soon hear for yourselves, the emotional pendulum kept swinging back and forth that night, like a playground swing."

Sergei gave him a thumbs up. "Go on..."

"The first surprise was when another couple asked if they could get married alongside us. In normal times, the fact that Joaquim and Leticia Guzman were barely teenagers would have sounded ludicrous to us, especially since Leticia had just given birth to her son, who wasn't even Joaquim's. But in these crazy times, it seemed perfectly normal."

Analyn nodded in agreement, then got off the couch and sat on a throw-rug on top of the hard wooden floor, to stretch her legs.

Donald went on, "Another surprise was when Brian's mother suddenly showed up for the wedding. Sarah moved onto the property roughly four months before we got married, but she seldom left her bedroom. And since she didn't join us for Thanksgiving dinner that year, no one expected to see her that night, especially Brian. She was in deep mourning."

"Why was she in mourning, Ninong?"

Donald answered Analyn, "In order to move onto the property, Sarah had to leave her unbelieving husband after more than thirty years of marriage. As you might imagine, it was the most difficult decision she ever had to make. It got even worse when her husband sent her a video a few days later, of their daughter killing herself in the bathtub."

Analyn covered her mouth in surprise. "Oh my…"

"Yeah, Chelsea, her daughter, blamed Brian for brainwashing their mother into leaving her father. This pushed Sarah even deeper into her hole. In the four months leading up to our wedding, she very seldom left her room."

Sergei asked, "Her husband isn't saved?"

"At the time, he wasn't," said Donald, "but praise God he is now. Dick's one of our residents. The Mulrooneys are one of the few intact families on the property." Donald shook his head. "But even that wasn't the biggest surprise that night…"

"What was it then?" Analyn asked the question this time.

"Just as we were about to begin, one of our construction foremen, Tony Pearsall, burst through the door warning us that we had visitors at the front of the property. Instead of practicing our vows, four of us raced to the back of the church with night vision binoculars, to gain a better vantage point of the main entryway to the property.

"You can imagine how frightened we were seeing hundreds of bodies on the inside of the property, all headed in our direction. We had no clue who they were. We felt so powerless. It was an intense moment for us. Joaquim was with us. All this on our wedding night. And to think he was only fifteen at the time…"

Sergei was fully intrigued hearing this. "So, what happened next?"

"Just as we were about to race back to the church to warn everyone, the mob stopped in their tracks, lit candles, and started singing, 'O Come All Ye Faithful.'"

Donald saw the confused expressions on their faces, dim as they were. "The two of you look exactly how we did that night! Anyway, when they were finished singing, one of them said, 'Merry Christmas, Brian! Keep fighting the good fight. Pray for us as we pray for you. God is with us!' That just happens to be our organization's credo.

"Turns out it was Clayton Holmes, Travis Hartings, and hundreds of new ETSM members. Travis told us the fear and panic we felt was what Christians living on the outside faced every minute of every day, and that their surprise visit was intended to prepare us for when it happened for real." Donald could almost hear him speaking those words to him now.

He continued, "Two weddings turned into three when Clayton Holmes' aunt, Miss Evelyn, asked if she and her fiancé could join them. In normal times, no bride-to-be would dare share the altar with another couple, let alone two. But when Miss Evelyn told us marriage was the one thing in life she never got to do, and that it had been on her bucket list for more than forty years, how could we possibly say no to her?

"The original plan was that Brian would read Luke chapters one and two, before Tom Dunleavey performed the wedding ceremony. But Tom had a heart attack among all the commotion!

"Since he couldn't officiate the three marriages, Clayton Holmes agreed to do it. He felt honored to preside over his aunt's wedding. I can't wait until you meet the founders of our organization. They are true brothers in every sense of the word.

"Anyway, before we got to say our 'I do's', a choir of people, who were part of the mob, lined the stage in four rows, in single file. I still remember to this day how angelic they sounded."

Analyn and Sergei enjoyed watching Donald basking in the fond memory that they both wished they could have been a part of.

"Before marrying us, Clayton cautioned us that it very well might be the last time we would get to meet like that. How right he was!" Donald sighed. "I was still a new student of Bible prophecy at the time."

Sergei said, "You're a quick learner."

Donald shrugged his shoulders. "I had no choice! I still remember the aroma from the hams and turkeys in the cafeteria…"

Even in the near darkness, Donald saw Sergei licking his chops. "I would kill for turkey now!" Ivanov had long since grown tired of eating MREs and canned and boxed foods.

"You and me both. They were baked and deep-fried at the Kennett Square farm/safe house seven miles away, then delivered to our safe house for the wedding, with all the trimmings. It was the last time I had turkey. We didn't have pumpkin pie, but what I wouldn't do for it now, with lots of whipped cream and a scoop of vanilla ice cream."

Analyn said, "Please stop! You're making me crazy!"

"Are you saying you're tired of MREs, Analyn?"

Sergei laughed at Donald's joke, then asked, "Whatever happened to the man who had the heart attack?"

"Praise God, Tom survived. I was with him when he had a second heart attack after the global quake. Thankfully, he pulled through again."

Donald shook his head at the vision in his mind. "So, was my wedding as bizarre as yours, Sergei?"

"Absolutely!"

"Believe me, our weddings combined couldn't compare to Brian's and Jacquelyn's wedding night. But that's a story for another time. I really miss them. I can't wait to see them again."

Analyn rested her face in the palms of her hands. "I can't wait to meet everyone."

Donald smiled wearily. "When I left there to come get you, we had a stream of new residents coming in. Who knows how many will be there when we arrive. Now that you're married, if all cottages haven't been filled again, perhaps you can have one all to yourselves, until more newcomers arrive. But even if they are full, don't worry, we'll find some place for you. I just can't wait to sleep on my bed again…"

Analyn blushed in the darkness, then looked dreamily at her husband. This was the best she had felt in too long to remember. "It sounds like a wonderful place to live, Ninong."

"It truly is, Analyn," Donald said, not realizing his beloved safe house had been destroyed, and Clayton, Travis, Brian and Tom were dead. If he knew what had become of safe house number one, he wouldn't want to continue on…

25

LETICIA GUZMAN DROPPED J.J. off at his Pre-K class. By now, most Kennett Square residents had pretty much settled into their new lives.

The twelve separate areas were in full use, and all corridors connecting them had been fully reinforced.

Classes were being taught to children and teenagers around the clock. By being stuck underground with no television, radio, or social media, and with such limited space, time wasn't being kept the same way it was for those living above ground.

In that light, it mattered not what time the children went to school. The important thing was that they were being taught the Word of God.

With the Millennial Kingdom fast approaching, even the toddlers were being taught Bible prophecy, at least the soft version of it, if ever there was such a thing. It was time they knew what to expect, especially since it was incredibly good news for them.

They absorbed every word, as it pertained to the days in which they were living. The resiliency each had shown over the past few months was commendable. It was amazing how God's children clung to His Word during times of difficulty.

As the only demographic to not be saved at the Kennett Square subterranean safe house, they were also being taught the four Gospels daily. Bottom line: No one was born saved. Like everyone else on the planet, *ETSM* children were sinners in need of a Savior.

The proof was whenever the kids were left alone for even one minute, their selfish, sinful natures would often surface. Everyone stepping foot inside the Millennial Kingdom would be saved.

Being part of this protected organization couldn't save their souls. They needed to be born again! The only way that could happen for them was by placing their trust in Yeshua, for the forgiveness of their sins.

But by having no exposure to the outside world, and its constant evils, the seeds being planted in their young, impressionable minds each day, would never be exposed to those things. Add to that the childlike faith all children displayed, the very childlike faith all grown-ups displayed before being converted, and the only viewpoint they would develop would be the Christian one.

But unlike the belief many children had developed in Santa Claus, before the Rapture, their belief in Christ wouldn't fade in time. It would follow them into eternity. These toddlers had never even heard of Santa.

They were being taught the Word of God. Nothing more.

Much like the toddlers being inundated with Romanero's dangerous dogma, they had nothing else to compare the scriptures to.

Leticia overheard Amy Danforth saying to a parent of one of her students, "Imagine the sensation your daughter will experience when she sees God's creation for the very first time. Imagine going from never seeing the light of day, to seeing God's creation unfolding before their very eyes. It will be like they were released from prison and placed in the most glorious of earthly places."

Leticia smiled, knowing two of those children would be hers.

For most children born post Rapture, this was normal life for them. They never got to experience God's beautiful creation outdoors. Amy was right. They would be the most overwhelmed and overjoyed to step into the Millennial Kingdom.

What Leticia liked most about Amy's class was that she would set aside one hour a day for quiet time, for her students. During this time, they could read the Bible, write notes, poems or stories, even draw, but they weren't allowed to speak. Her hope was that it would help reduce all angst they were feeling from being in this enclosed environment.

Leticia kissed her son on the forehead. "See you later buddy."

"Bye, Mama!"

Leticia hugged J.J., then walked the long corridor to the dining area, looking for Charles Calloway. When he wasn't there, she walked down another long corridor to the play and exercise area.

Sure enough, the Calloways were walking on a crowded eight-foot-wide walking path, which took up the outer perimeter of the room. In between the lines, kids played, as teens and grownups did calisthenics.

Leticia waited patiently until they made it to where she was. "Sorry to disturb you, Charles. May I please use the phone?"

Calloway didn't need to ask her why she needed it. He knew. "Sure. But I'll need it back within thirty minutes."

"That won't be a problem. Will you still be here?"

"Probably not. I'll see you back at the married couple's room."

"Perfect."

Meera asked Leticia, "How are you feeling?"

"Fine. Won't be long now. Still walking every day. I must've walked a half mile already trying to find your husband."

Meera smiled at her patient. "I'm happy to hear that. It will make labor easier for you."

Leticia walked back to the married couples' section. She sat on her bed, took a deep breath, then read Blanca Espinosa's message. She shouted, "Hallelujah!" at the top of her lungs.

"What is it?" Joaquim was laying on the bed next to hers, his eyes closed, listening to music in his earbuds. The way his hands moved back and forth and up and down; he looked like he was leading an orchestra. He was startled by his wife's shout.

"Blanca's a believer now!" Seeing the name "Ticia" made her smile. It had been four years since she had heard that nickname, in this case, read it. Leticia turned the phone screen so her husband could read it. *I've been reading the book you told me about every day for the past few weeks. And guess what, Ticia? Jesus is my Lord and Savior!*

Joaquim sat up on his bed. "Praise God!" The joy on his face was evident.

Leticia kissed her husband twice on the lips, then typed onto the phone screen: *Thanks for sharing the marvelous news with me, BFF. Now we're eternal BFFs! How cool is that?*

Blanca replied: *I know you told me to be careful about what I type, but it's getting crazy here. Mami initially said she was willing to wait until the last minute to take the mark, for Papi's sake. But she's tired of waiting and feeling like she's in prison all the time. She wants to eat real food again and go to the hair salon.*

Leticia replied: *Sorry to hear that BFF. Is she aware that those taking the mark have painful sores on their bodies?*

Blanca replied: *Papi warned her about it many weeks ago. She doesn't seem too worried about it. Her appointment's for next week. She expects me to go with her, but I won't go. I know I'm asking a lot, Ticia, but is it possible to find a place for me and Papi to live?*

Leticia felt bad for Blanca. She was grateful that she never had to choose between her parents. She typed onto the phone: *Let me get busy clearing the way for you to join us here. Hang tight. It'll take some planning on my end.*

Blanca replied: *Please hurry. It's getting worse with my parents. All they do is argue.*

Leticia saw the Calloways entering the room: *I have to return the phone now. I'll get back to you as soon as I can. Until then, keep fighting the Good fight. Pray for me as I pray for you. God is with us...*

Leticia shared the good news about Blanca's salvation with them, and her dire situation at home. In short, she needed safe refuge.

Charles asked her, "Are you sure they're both saved?"

"Read it for yourself. Besides, we both had the same dream."

Charles and Meera both read the exchange. Charles said to Leticia, "This is a top priority. I'll be back at 8 p.m. after my class. Better yet, meet me there at 8 p.m. This way, we won't wake anyone here."

"Thanks Charles." At 7:55 p.m. that evening, Leticia was waiting for him outside his classroom.

When his students left, Calloway dictated as Leticia typed onto the phone: "Good news, BFF, we can offer you shelter. As much as we'd love to send someone to Rhode Island to get you, it's not possible. Since you and your father aren't on Romanero's dissident list yet, this gives you a slight advantage.

"But since neither of you have yet to receive the mark, it could be dangerous. So, please be careful. Many here will be praying that you don't get pulled over by the police. Just so you know, if either of you have the global flu, you'll be sent straight to quarantine when you arrive."

Blanca typed onto her phone screen: *Thanks so much, Ticia! We no longer have the global flu. But Papi has cancer. Can he still come?*

Leticia replied: *Aww, sorry to hear about your father. I really am. Of course he can come. We won't leave a brother behind.*

Blanca was teary eyed reading the reply. She typed onto her phone: *How will we know where to go?*

Leticia answered: *Once you agree to the terms, I'll text you the address. Someone will be waiting for you at the meeting location, before bringing you here. But don't search for it online or on GPS. All that will do is leave a digital footprint. I'm sure your father has an old roadmap laying around somewhere.*

Once you're here, you'll be safe. Getting here will be your biggest challenge. I've been told to advise you to leave your house when your mother goes to take the mark. I can't wait to hear about how God rescued you and your father.

Blanca replied: *Thanks again Ticia. I hope to see you soon. I'm so nervous, but I know it's what I gotta do. Papi too.*

Blanca waited until after her mother was sleeping, before sharing the update with her father. He was still reading the book he now shared with his daughter down in the living room.

Blanca tiptoed down the stairs with her finger up to her mouth.

Raul nodded that he understood. He placed the book on his lap and read Leticia's message. Whereas his daughter got choked up reading Leticia's words about not leaving a brother behind, Raul wept tears of joy. Blanca hugged her father tightly. Arguing with Carmen, day and night, while battling lung cancer had taken a toll on him.

"What next, Papi?"

Raul wiped his moist eyes, then whispered to his daughter, "What other choice do we have? Tell her we agree to the terms. I do have an old roadmap in the garage somewhere."

Blanca conveyed his message to Leticia, then added, *Thanks for doing this for us, Ticia...*

When they received the next message, the meeting location was a place called Kennett Square. *So, that's where she is!* Leticia thought.

"Never heard of that place," Raul said more to himself than to his daughter.

"Me neither, Papi." The only time Blanca had ever been in the state of Pennsylvania was when they drove to Florida for a summer vacation, four months before the Rapture.

It felt like several lifetimes ago.

A lump formed in Raul's throat. He was grateful that God was opening this door for them, but it caused his heart to ache for Carmen even more. Once they left the house next week, it would signify the dissolution of the family he had loved with all his heart and soul.

"What now, Papi?"

"Like Leticia said, we'll leave when Mami receives the mark next week. Until then, we need to act as normally as possible."

Blanca kissed her father on the forehead. "I'll do my best, Papi."

"I know you will, mija."

26

DANIEL SULLIVAN AND TYLER Stephenson were driving on U.S. 1 south, on their way to Georgetown, to hopefully rescue Jefferson's two children, and bring William and Janelle to Pennsylvania, but only if they were convinced that they were believers.

From a spiritual standpoint, the only thing they had to go on regarding Jefferson's two remaining children was something Jakob had told them about Janelle occasionally going to Washington D.C., to listen to one of his fellow sealed servants preach the Word.

Aside from this little tidbit from their most cherished resident, they had nothing else to go on. No dreams, no contact with Jefferson's kids, no nothing. Did William's wife, Christine, and Janelle's husband, Dr. Richard Benjamin, ever join her on those trips?

Before leaving the Kennett Square safe house, Tyler asked his brother-in-law, "If we find them, would you like me to tell them about you and Amy?"

Jefferson took a moment to mull it over in his mind. "No. I need to be the one to do it. I hope I get that opportunity."

Tyler nodded. He knew what his brother-in-law meant, if they were believers. "As you wish..."

Jefferson became teary-eyed. "Here you go risking your life for me again, Daniel. You have been my tried-and-true friend throughout it all. I don't know what I'd do without you."

"It's my pleasure, sir," he said, his eyes shooting downward, not knowing what else to say.

Jefferson placed one hand on Daniel's left shoulder, and the other on Tyler's right shoulder. "Be careful out there..."

"We'll do our best, sir," Sullivan said, on behalf of them both.

Amy said, "We'll be praying for your safe return." The way she had said it so tenderly, so sincerely, comforted the two men.

Titus drove them to the auto repair shop in the four-wheeler, in total silence. The solar-powered car Sullivan used to drive from Idaho to Pennsylvania, was fully charged, and waiting for them behind the shop, hidden beneath a military camouflage cover.

Daniel didn't mind doing this one last favor for his former boss, but with the odds stacked way against them, it felt more like a suicide mission than a rescue attempt. How could he think otherwise, when Jakob was explicit that the only lives that would be spared in their organization, were those transporting others to residences with specific assignments to carry out, before Christ's return?

As it was, Sullivan still couldn't comprehend how he had travelled cross country without getting caught, yet Clayton, Travis and Lee were killed on their way to Kennett Square. It's not like the two of them would be caring for the children.

Unless God had specific plans for William and Janelle to carry out, what assurance did they have of succeeding with this particular mission? That is, if they were located, and both were saved.

The only connection Daniel and Tyler had to the outside world was on the car radio. When they arrived in Kennett Square a few months back, their smartphones were destroyed.

The only disguises they had was that both men had grown full beards and mustaches. They also wore baseball caps and sunglasses.

Five minutes after they had crossed the Mason-Dixon line, and were in the state of Maryland, the announcement was made that the Supreme See, Salvador Romanero would address the world from his palace in New Babylon.

"This should be interesting," Sullivan said to Stephenson. "The Pope's been doing most of the speaking these days."

Tyler replied, "Yeah, I'm sure his many followers will be overjoyed to hear his voice again, instead of the statue only."

Daniel plucked the mini recorder he kept on the console next to his seat, so when he heard pertinent information, he could record it then share it with the others later, much like he did during the Pope's address the day after the global bombing campaign. He turned it on.

Romanero blessed his scores of worshippers, then came to the crux of his message. "Today marks a momentous occasion in our world. You will all get to witness the first child born after the disappearances to receive the mark. Now that so many of them have reached the age of three, some are old enough to reason, and, therefore, old enough to take it. Any child wishing to take the mark must first pass a battery of tests, including an aptitude test, to ensure they know what they are doing, and that they will take it willingly, not robotically.

"Naturally, our children do not have jobs to go to. But they will need to register for school, and they will have to see doctors, dentists, and orthodontists. In that light, upon receiving the mark for themselves, all children will receive a thousand-dollar credit in their virtual accounts.

"The fact that their little bodies are still growing, any mark or tattoo they receive now will surely be stretched to the limits by the time they reach adolescence, which means they may have to be reissued ten years from now."

Daniel looked at Tyler and mouthed the words, "Yeah, right!"

What had sparked Romanero's decision to walk back his original decree about children not taking the mark until they were better able to discern the magnitude of their decision, was the many children who were still fleeing underground to avoid taking it.

This incensed him more than anything else. For someone wanting to be called, "Supreme See" he still didn't have a crystal-clear vision of the future. But what he did know was that anyone taking the mark would be connected to him eternally. For better or for worse, he liked that.

"So, who is this blessed first child?" Romanero nodded for the young toddler to come to him. Placing his arm around him, he said, "As all of you know, former U.S. President, Lois Cipriano, was a good friend of mine. When she and her wife were sadly killed in the global quake, her son was the only survivor.

"Young Salvador has been living here in New Babylon ever since. He is a special child who is destined to do great things under my constant tutelage. If any child is ready to take the mark with the full knowledge of knowing what he is doing, it's him. He has become like a son to me. He will mark the first of many others to come."

Romanero kissed him on the forehead where the mark would soon be placed. The youngster genuflected before his lord and savior, then left the podium walking backwards without breaking eye contact.

Romanero became more stoic. "Speaking of former U.S. Presidents, Jefferson Danforth is still alive. I've always had my suspicions about his death. Those suspicions were confirmed when he appeared on our radar a few months ago. Turns out, he was never on-board Air Force One when it exploded in midair, three years ago. Even more ominous, he's been living in hiding as a Christian dissident all this time.

"By the time we had pinpointed the first location he was staying at, he had already left for another hideout in Coeur d'Alene, Idaho, which happened to be the nerve center for this particular outlaw organization. Danforth stayed there until he was relocated to Pennsylvania, along with many other Christian dissidents.

"The good news is that location was destroyed in the global bombing campaign. The bad news is, this was one of those locations the Holy See spoke of where everyone managed to escape beforehand, including Danforth himself, and a few other notables, namely Hana Patel, and my former personal physician, Benjamin Shapiro.

"Shortly before the bomb was dropped, a hundred guards stormed the property looking to rescue all children. They found no one there. But they couldn't have gotten too far. It's only a matter of time before we locate them again. Wherever they are, we believe Danforth's brother-in-law, Tyler Stephenson, recently went into hiding with them."

Fear snaked through Stephenson hearing his name being mentioned by the Antichrist of the Bible. He was terrified!

Daniel whispered to him, "I know you're frightened, but if we make it back to Kennett Square, they'll never find us there…"

Tyler brushed off a shiver. "If we make it back…"

"A month before the global bombing campaign, someone residing at the nerve center, in Idaho, found a way to tap into our global database. They gained knowledge of our plan, then tipped off all locations at which children were residing. As far as we could tell, everyone residing there were former members of Danforth's administration. They were all killed in the strike."

Romanero didn't say the satellite Jefferson Danforth had sent up into space for them had been located and compromised. "I'm happy to report that the founders of this organization, Clayton Holmes and Travis Hartings were killed a week after their locations were destroyed. Their voices were detected by a microflier in the state of Virginia, which led to their vehicle being hit by a drone strike.

"A third man was in the vehicle with them. Doctor Lee Kim was on our radar for quite some time. It is believed that he was the architect of a Christian website I took offline when I declared all things Christian illegal," Romanero said, regarding the www.LSARglobal.org site.

The Supreme See flinched angrily. "For the record, this group was also responsible for producing that Christian book that has been outlawed for more than three years now. Millions of children and teenagers have gone into hiding after being brainwashed by them.

"Mark my words, we will not rest until every stone has been overturned, and every child has been reacclimated into society, and ultimately deprogrammed by some of our top professionals in that field."

The glow returned to Romanero's face. "Thankfully, not everyone in the Danforth family has lost their minds. I'm proud to announce that Jefferson's son, William, and his son-in-law, Doctor Benjamin Richardson, will both receive the mark today, after young Salvador takes it. It will be my high honor to witness it being placed on their foreheads. I had them both flown to New Babylon for that very purpose. I even invited them to stay at my palace."

Daniel and Tyler stared blankly at one another. This marked the first time anyone from the Danforth clan had been seen or heard from in the media, since Melissa's death and Jefferson's disappearance.

Salvador glanced over at William Danforth. "Is there anything you'd like to say to your father, if he's listening?"

William said, "Dad, if you're listening, I want nothing to do with you! How could you do that to Mom? Faking your own death? Seriously? Do you know how long it took for me and Janelle to overcome that tragedy? We were still reeling after losing our kids in the disappearances.

"Now this? Instead of coming clean and informing us that you were still alive, you betrayed us. Whatever happened to protecting your family above all other things? I can't count how many times I've heard you say that to me! Yet, instead of doing that, you abandoned me and Janelle and went into hiding!

"Were you aware that Christine died in the global quake? I've been without my wife and children all this time! Where was the fatherly shoulder to lean on? I sure could have used it back then. Do you even care? Of course, you don't!"

Daniel and Tyler couldn't see William and Benjamin standing alongside the Antichrist of the Bible, but they heard every word and syllable coming through the car speakers perfectly clear.

"I can't believe you belong to the organization responsible for producing that illegal book! Really? I'm so disgusted with you! Your cruel and heartless actions clearly indicate that you are nothing but a coward! I don't know how I ever looked up to you in the first place.

"And to think you used to be the most powerful man on the planet. It blows my mind. You seem quite puny to me now. I'm proud to call Salvador Romanero my friend! He's twice the leader you ever were, and infinitely more authentic than you were even on your best day! The future's bright for everyone following his leadership.

"In fact, I've had the pleasure of meeting many of the leaders you've shunned and badmouthed throughout the years. Now that I've met them on my own, without your brainwashing me, all I can say is, they're nothing like how you made them out to be!

"Oh, and President Osolovich isn't a maniac. He's a kind and generous man. And very understanding. I've spent the past two days with him. One thing is painfully clear, your leadership skills pale in comparison to Uri's."

Daniel and Tyler couldn't see the "Proud Papa" smile plastered on Romanero's face, but they wouldn't be surprised by it if they could.

William shook his head in disgust. "I'm sure Erica and Christine are looking down on you, from wherever they are, and are sickened by your selfish actions. Your grandchildren, too, for that matter. I'll always be ashamed to call myself a Danforth. At least Janelle got to change her last name when she got married. Erica, too, before she vanished at Camp David. But I'm forever stuck with it. Even if I changed my last name legally, everyone would still know I'm your son.

"Since I no longer have family back home, I look forward to having a fresh start over here, as a new resident of this remarkable city. It truly is the greatest city in the history of civilization. The American patriotism you kept me trapped in all my life, has severely limited my overall approach to life. Salvador's globalism has really broadened my horizons. Think about that dad! Dad, what a joke!"

William paused, then addressed his sister, "Janelle, if you're listening, it looks like your dreams about Dad still being alive were true after all. I just hope you'll come to your senses soon, and lose all interest in his mythical Jesus, and turn to the only rightful savior, the Supreme See, Salvador Romanero. Now that you're with child again, I'm even more concerned about your overall safety."

Tyler glanced at Daniel again in total disbelief.

Daniel mouthed to Tyler, "Did you know she was pregnant?"

Tyler shook his head no.

William went on, "Stop your foolish running away from home trying to find them. Fall in line and take the mark, like me and Benjamin are about to. I can't tell you how honored I am to be taking it on the same day as young Salvador.

"It's time for you to come to your senses before it's too late, and you develop the same mental illness that Dad has. You know how much I love you, sis. There's still time to do the right thing…

"Uncle Tyler, if you're listening, what happened to you? It's like you vanished from the face of the earth eighteen months ago. Suddenly you resurface, only to end up with my father, Hana Patel, and Benjamin Shapiro? What a disappointment you turned out to be! You will surely come to regret it once you've been caught."

Dr. Benjamin Richardson was the next to speak. Sadness covered his face as he pleaded with his wife, "Janelle, I love you, and I can't imagine my life without you in it. I'm sorry for forcing myself on you and getting you pregnant against your wishes.

"My hope was that it might keep us together. I'm tired of the constant arguing between us. Remember how happy we used to be, sweetie? I want us to be that happy again."

Richardson wiped tears from his eyes with the sleeve of his shirt. "Please don't follow your father down into that rat hole. If you do, it will only be a matter of time before you get caught. You already know what that means. We're still young. We have our whole lives ahead of us. And we have another child on the way.

"My only hope is that you'll join me here in New Babylon. You should see the city our lord and savior has created over here! I can't put into words how mind-blowing it really is. No wonder why droves of global citizens are flocking here!"

Tyler glanced at Daniel in total disbelief. Both men understood what was happening and why they had uttered such atrocious words being strewn at Jefferson, still it was painful to listen to.

Ambiguous smile playing on his lips, Romanero pumped Benjamin's hand enthusiastically. His bright eyes blinked several times, before turning a shade or two darker, when he faced the camera again.

"It's no secret to any of you that I never got along with the former U.S. President. Our global views couldn't have been more polarizing. When I became the leader of the world, I knew he would eventually become a problem for me. I'm just glad his son and his son-in-law were able to see through it all and make the right choice!

"It's with that in mind that I wish to announce that these two fine men will serve key roles in my administration. William will serve as my personal assistant. Doctor Richardson will serve as my new personal physician. He will also be placed in charge of the chip presently being administered."

Devilish grin on his face, he added, "How ironic that I went from one Benjamin to another! What Benjamin Shapiro started with the chip before losing his mind, Benjamin Richardson will get to see come to fruition. I'll also be awarding the palace once occupied by Doctor Shapiro to Doctor Richardson."

Dr. Richardson's mouth was agape. "Thank you, Supreme See! I don't know wat to say. I'm speechless!"

"It's my pleasure, Benjamin. I'm sure you'll be comfortable in your new residence. Now, I invite you all to witness the first child on the planet receiving the mark. My grace and peace be with you all."

When the presser was finished, a female reporter said, "Can you believe the former American President had the audacity to send his wife to Colorado all by herself, on that fateful day, while he remained in hiding underground?"

She shook her head in disgust, clearly annoyed. "The nerve of him! He should be ashamed of himself! Even more cowardly was his own children had no idea he was still alive until now. I hope they catch him soon and he gets the justice he so richly deserves..."

Daniel could no longer listen. He turned the radio off...

27

"PULL TO THE SIDE of the road, Daniel, I think I'm going to vomit."

"Sorry," replied Sullivan, "but if local authorities spot us, we'll be sitting ducks. At least if we're moving, we might have a chance to escape, if we're ever pursued. If you gotta barf, do it out the window."

A few seconds later, Tyler did just that. Some of it ended up in the back seat. He wiped his mouth with a napkin. "Should we go back to Kennett Square where we'll be safe?"

Sullivan took a moment to rub his throbbing forehead and think things through. "No. Thanks to William, this mission suddenly makes a little more sense to me. Now we can narrow our search down to Janelle only. If we find her, and she's a believer, as William just alluded to, the fact that she's pregnant would explain the supernatural protection.

"Think about it. Her pregnancy just may be the reason we made it from Wisconsin to Pennsylvania in the first place. If we locate her, it will ensure our safe passage back to Kennett Square."

"Yeah, but we can't just knock on her front door urging her not to take the mark, then pleading with her to come with us. Now that William's crossed over, we could be walking into a trap."

Sullivan nodded in agreement. "One thing's for certain, the stakes have been raised to a whole new level." The former secret service agent silently wondered if there were microfliers up there listening to them now. If so, could they decipher whisper speak?

Ninety minutes later, Daniel Sullivan and Tyler Stephenson arrived in Georgetown. Originally established as a tobacco port town, in Maryland in 1751, it was no longer part of that state. It was part of the D.C. establishment before the Rapture.

Both men were quite familiar with this town, but as one of its former residents, Tyler knew it like the back of his hand. A bachelor all his life, when his brother-in-law became President, and his late sister became America's First Lady, he relocated from Wisconsin and rented a condo in Georgetown.

Even though he was significantly older than most other bar hoppers frequenting the many watering holes dotting the quaint college town, before the Rapture, Stephenson seemed to fit right in with everyone.

It wasn't uncommon to see him dining with young, attractive women at one of the live music lounges, or down on the riverside promenade having an intimate seafood dinner with whoever happened to be his date that night.

Tyler was even named "Georgetown's Most Eligible Bachelor" for two consecutive years, which had caused his popularity to soar to even higher levels than when he lived in Wisconsin, when Jefferson was the Governor. The fact that he was related to the most powerful couple on the planet back then had something to do with it.

Though he'd made a handful of good friends in his days living there, there wasn't a chance he would pay them a surprise visit, especially now that he had just been accused of being a Christian dissident by Antichrist himself. *Were they still alive?* He wasn't about to find out.

What had once been a charming area, with its cobblestone streets, upscale restaurants, and fashion and design shops, was anything but that now. Even local businesses that were slowly reopening had no choice but to conduct their business in dirty, grimy, unkempt buildings.

Tyler felt like he was in a time warp, only a post war one.

When they were a block away from the Richardson residence, they weren't surprised to see several unmarked cars parked outside.

Daniel tightly gripped the steering wheel, hoping law enforcement wouldn't notice them. Did the police presence outside the house mean that Janelle was under their protection? Or had she fled the residence?

With no way of contacting her, how could they possibly know? They couldn't just ring her doorbell. Nor could they honk the car horn to get her attention.

Both men exchanged nervous shrugs, before Sullivan made a right turn and fled the area as quickly and as unassumingly as he could.

They drove up and down the streets of Georgetown, for more than hour without seeing her. There wasn't a chance they would drive by William's house a few blocks away.

It was time to venture into D.C., to where one of Yahweh's sealed servants was preaching. Perhaps they might find her there.

Sullivan steadied the car across the Key Bridge—separating Northern Virginia from D.C.—and headed in the direction of where his former boss had lived, before Jefferson was forced into hiding.

It was eerie seeing the White House no longer standing there.

Since they didn't know the young preacher's exact location, they rolled down the car windows and listened intently for the voice that was always unafraid and supernaturally protected. If they drove within a quarter mile of where he was preaching, they would surely hear him.

Driving on 18th Street NW, Sullivan wondered again why they hadn't been caught yet! If they eventually found Janelle, it could only be Yahweh's supernatural protection. If they didn't find her, the only other logical conclusion Daniel could think of was that the blazing sun had scorched all or most of the microfliers in the area.

The way the sun was spitting fire down on all mark takers, this was a definite possibility. Even electric vehicles wouldn't start. The batteries were being fried in record numbers.

As believers, Daniel and Tyler weren't being scorched by the sun. But they sure felt its heat. Even with the air conditioner turned on full blast inside the car, both men were soaked with sweat.

It was infinitely worse for the unbelievers in the world. With what equated to first-degree burns on their bodies, each beam of sun on their skin must have felt like laser beams burning them. From the fairest to the darkest of skin tones, one's pigmentation mattered not.

And all of this on top of the festering sores covering their bodies. Still, they wouldn't repent. Now that they had the mark of the Beast, they had committed the one unpardonable sin, post Rapture, and there could be no turning back!

The streets were virtually empty from sunrise to sunset, so most people outdoors could get things done before sunrise. But when the sun was up, most pedestrians brave enough to venture outdoors made sure that their bodies were covered from head to toe, so they wouldn't be scorched by the unrelenting sun. Even that didn't help.

When they reached H Street NW, Sullivan made a right. Tyler spotted someone walking 50 yards ahead. The way the individual was dressed in baggy jeans and sneakers, not to mention that the head was covered with a hoodie, made it nearly impossible to discern whether it was a male or female.

But what made Tyler think this person could possibly be his niece, was the way the individual walked with such determined strides. The way the legs rotated in a circular motion, before flopping to the ground, only to repeat the process, was similar to the way he walked.

Melissa always told her daughter that she inherited her long, lanky legs from him. "Pull over, Daniel. That might be her."

Sullivan shot him a sideways look, and wanted to question him, but he did as he was asked.

"Janelle?" Tyler shouted it loud enough so the person of interest could hear him.

Whoever it was, he or she was clearly startled by his voice, and picked up the pace.

Sullivan followed closely behind her in the car. After driving a tenth of a mile or so, Tyler got out.

Here goes nothing! "Nellie, if it's you, it's Uncle Tyler. Please don't run away. I know you're frightened. But we need to talk…"

Nellie? Only her family and close friends had ever called her by her nickname. After watching the press conference from New Babylon, she slipped out the back door of her house, shortly before law enforcement arrived, fearful for her life, knowing she could never return.

Not knowing where else to go, she was determined to meet with the young preacher who had opened her eyes in so many ways. Perhaps he could point her in the right direction.

Janelle was surprised she had made it this far. The whole world had no doubt watched the press conference. They heard her brother and husband pleading with her from New Babylon to do the right thing, and not follow her father into spiritual oblivion.

She could almost feel millions of eyeballs on her this very instant. It creeped her out. She half expected someone to shoot her by now.

The voice sounded like her uncle. But with the vast increase of AI technology, could he have been cloned? Was he really the enemy in disguise? Could it be a trick? A thousand more shivers shot through her. She picked up the pace a little more, without bothering to glance back.

Tyler confessed to his niece, "It's true what Romanero said, Nellie, I'm living in hiding with your father. Jesus is our Lord and Savior! If He's yours too, I'm here to rescue you."

Daniel prayed that if the microfliers were up there, they wouldn't be recording his voice. If they did, it was game over for this rescue mission.

Janelle froze in her tracks. Those beautiful words washed over her like nothing else she had ever heard before. She turned to face him.

It took a few moments to adjust to her uncle's full facial hair. He was always clean shaven. Realizing it was him, she lost all strength and nearly fell onto the sidewalk.

Tyler ran over just in time to catch her. He held her in his arms the way he did when she was a child, only now she was with child. "Are you a Christ follower, Nellie?"

Janelle looked at him with tear-soaked eyes. She nodded yes.

"Get in the car now. We haven't a moment to waste."

Without asking a single question, Janelle lowered herself into the back seat of the vehicle. The only thing she had were the clothes on her back. Even if she didn't know it, by being pregnant, the three of them had Yahweh's supernatural protection covering them.

But Daniel and Tyler both knew. Sullivan sped off, no longer concerned about the possibility of being detected by those microfliers.

For the first time since he left Idaho, and drove thousands of miles in his vehicle, this was the only time he had ever felt safe behind the steering wheel. Now that one of his passengers was with child, he had every expectation of making it to the Kennett Square safe house.

He looked skyward. "Thank you, Lord!"

Tyler heard him. He smiled in agreement…

28

LATER THAT AFTERNOON

JEFFERSON DANFORTH SPOTTED DANIEL Sullivan and Tyler Stephenson entering the kitchen. Both men looked severely dehydrated, perhaps from heat stroke. They were soaked with sweat.

Ever since they left the safe house, for D.C., Jefferson was antsy, and full of nervous energy, as he and Amy kept praying for their protection. Relief flooded their souls seeing them again.

The Danforths had just finished having baked catfish, rice, a tomato and cucumber salad with oil and vinegar, and a slice of wheat bread each for lunch. Neither felt like eating, but they managed to finish their rationed meals. With so many residents, the kitchen was open around the clock. Everyone ate in shifts. The smell of food was always thick in the air.

Not seeing his son and daughter with them caused Jefferson's heart to sink deeper in his chest. *Had it been a failed mission*? "Well?"

Daniel motioned with his hands for his former boss and his wife to relax. "You may want to sit down again, sir."

Jefferson's brow furrowed. "What happened down there, Daniel?"

Daniel bit his lower lip. "Do you want the good news or the bad?"

Jefferson gulped hard. Usually, he would ask for the bad news first, to get it out of the way. But in a world flooded with nothing but tragic news, he was desperate to hear something good for a change. He glanced at Amy. She shrugged and left it at that. "The good news."

"We found Janelle. She's in the main gathering room."

Janelle only? Jefferson blinked hard, then decided to take it one step at a time, by focusing on this remarkable news before broaching the topic of his son. "Nellie's a believer?"

Tyler took another large gulp of water, then smiled wearily at his brother-in-law. "She certainly is!"

"Thank God!" exclaimed Jefferson.

Amy asked him, "Did you find her at home?"

"No. When we arrived, her place was surrounded by local authorities. If she was inside, there wasn't a chance we would have rescued her."

Amy pressed on, "So, where did you find her then?"

Daniel downed the rest of the water in his cup. "Walking on H street, of all places, not too far from where the White House used to be. She was clearly dazed, and frightened for her life, after the press conference."

Jefferson looked confused. "Press conference?"

"I'm coming to that, sir."

"What about William?" Jefferson braced himself.

Tyler answered the question for Daniel. "He's in New Babylon with Salvador Romanero…"

Danforth's eyes popped. He shot a nervous glance at Tyler, feeling totally deflated. "What?!"

Daniel shook his head sadly. "Your son-in-law Benjamin's there, too, I'm afraid. Apparently, Romanero flew them out there to receive the mark. He even invited them to stay at his palace. They both spoke at his morning press briefing."

Jefferson was exasperated. He asked, "Did you record it?"

Daniel nodded. "Not sure you'll want to listen, though. They didn't have anything kind to say about you. What's worse is they will remain in New Babylon. Both were given lofty positions in Salvador's cabinet. Your son-in-law just assumed Doctor Shapiro's former position."

Jefferson covered his face using both hands. "I want to hear it, Daniel, I need to!"

Sullivan took the mini recorder out of his pants pocket and played it for his former boss.

Jefferson listened to his son speaking so harshly about him in Romanero's presence. He couldn't see him standing alongside the Antichrist of the Bible, but he heard every angry word perfectly clear.

When Jeferson heard his son boasting about receiving the mark, so willingly, he started hyperventilating. He felt for certain that his heart would explode in his chest. He lost all strength and collapsed to the floor, wailing for his son, knowing what it meant for him.

Amy dropped to her knees and rubbed her husband's shoulders.

Tyler waited a few anxious moments before saying, "Janelle was a bundle of nerves on the drive here. You know how close she was to William, especially after Erica was taken in the Rapture. As a new

Christian, she's having difficulty processing it all. I'm sure being pregnant didn't help."

Jefferson found the strength to stand on his feet. "Take me to her!"

Clearly, this was a command. Sullivan said, "Follow me, sir…"

When Jefferson spotted his daughter in the main gathering room, he leaned against the wall so he wouldn't fall over.

Janelle got up out of her chair and threw herself into her father's arms, nearly knocking hm over. They embraced for the longest time. Just seeing him again after thinking he was dead, caused a deeper, more pronounced, emotion to well up within her, that she hadn't felt since his "alleged" funeral.

She pinched his cheeks, to make sure it really was him. She didn't care how much older he looked. She was just happy to see him again.

Jefferson gazed into his daughter's eyes. She looked as frightened now as she did as a little girl after having a nightmare.

Janelle was shocked to see Amy Wong. "Are you the chef here?"

"No. I teach children." Amy looked down at the floor. Ever since Daniel and Tyler left on their mission, she kept rehearsing in her mind the best way to explain to Janelle that she was married to her father.

Telling Tyler was one thing. Telling Janelle was altogether different. Instead of trying to explain herself, she reached for Jefferson's hand, unsure about whose was trembling more, hers or his.

The joyous smile on Janelle's face vanished. She shot an awkward sideways glance at her father.

Jefferson gulped hard. "It's true, Nellie, we're married." If there was one thing hearing the tragic news about his son did, it's that it made sharing this bit of news with his daughter slightly easier.

Silence filled the room, as Janelle tried processing this latest bizarre news to rock her world.

Tyler was the first to break the silence. "It blew my mind too, Nellie. Once you hear the story, you'll understand…"

Jefferson treaded carefully, "Like I told Tyler when we were reunited, there never was anything between me and Amy in my days as President. You know how much I loved your mother. We were college sweethearts. I was always faithful to her. Never in a million years did I think I'd ever remarry, let alone be in a relationship with anyone. It was the farthest thing from my mind.

"But since our final destinations are at the opposite ends of the eternal spectrum, I had to gradually remove your mother from my heart and mind, if I wanted to maintain my sanity. Just like we must now do with William, I'm afraid. I hope you can understand this…"

Janelle nodded that she did.

Eyes begging for understanding, he went on, "As the days passed, I didn't want to be alone in these crazy times."

Janelle hated seeing the painful expression on her father's face. It was a first for her. "How long?"

"Going on two years now." Jefferson sighed. "We got married on the same day I proposed to her. It was officiated on a video call no less. It wasn't a romantic wedding by any stretch of the imagination. To put it into perspective, our wedding supper consisted of peanut butter and jelly sandwiches."

Janelle was trying to piece it all together in her mind. All this time, she thought her father was dead. It was so much to take in all at once.

Amy sensed what she was thinking. Her line of vision dropped to the floor. "You know how much I loved and respected your mother, Janelle. I was devastated when she died. That's why I had serious reservations when your father proposed to me."

"I must say, Amy's a wonderful woman and a good and faithful wife." An awkward silence ensued. Jefferson broke it by saying, "None of this would have seemed thinkable before the Rapture."

Janelle was happy for them. But right now, she was too emotionally distraught to show it. It would take time to accept. She asked her father, "So, if you weren't on board with Mom, who was?"

Jefferson lowered his head. "One of my body doubles. His name was Harry Marshall." He shot an uneasy glance at Amy. "At that time, I was still trying to save America from Antichrist. Foolish, I know."

Janelle didn't need to hear this awkward confession of sorts coming from her father. When he placed his hand on the Bible and swore to protect the country he had just been elected to lead, she knew how firm his commitment was. But the way he said "your mother" sounded a bit strange. It was as if she had been completely removed from his life. "What about your funerals?"

Jefferson massaged his scalp using both hands. "When Romanero said he recently discovered I was still alive, he was lying. He knew it all along. He also knew it wasn't me in that casket. Instead of disclosing this vital information to everyone, he used it to his advantage by burying Marshall's mangled body next to your mother, in my stead. To this day, I regret sending your mother to Colorado without me." He was grateful he wouldn't have to explain himself to anyone else.

Janelle remembered that day as if it was yesterday. "That would explain the closed casket."

Jefferson nodded yes. "As I watched my funeral on TV, I kept shouting, 'I'm not dead! I'm still alive,' knowing you couldn't hear me. Marshall was given a full Presidential funeral for his service to his country. I didn't know him all that well. I just hope he was saved. If not, his current predicament is so much worse now than when his body was blown to pieces on Air Force One."

Jefferson shot another uneasy glance at his daughter. It was a poor choice of words since Melissa was also on board the aircraft when it happened. "Sorry for my insensitivity, Nellie."

Janelle waved off her father's apology. "What really happened to Everett after he was sworn in as President?"

Jefferson became teary eyed. He seldom thought about his former Vice President, or properly grieved his loss. He steepled his fingers.

Daniel Sullivan felt uneasy being part of this family conversation. But they didn't seem to mind. He weighed in. "May I, sir?"

Jefferson nodded to Daniel to answer the question for him.

Sullivan came straight to the point. "He was assassinated." He waited for a reaction from her. It never came. "Do you remember Secret Service Agent Anthony Galiano?"

Janelle nodded that she did. "I always liked Anthony."

"Me too. He was part of our group. He was killed in Romanero's bombing campaign. He believed after the old nuclear codes were changed, a secret service agent that neither of us knew inched up behind him and jammed a needle in the back of his neck, instantly paralyzing him. The poor guy never spent a single night at the White House, as America's new President.

"I confess I doubted his theory. What changed my thinking was when he told me Lois Cipriano was in the Oval Office during that time, already preparing to take over. That's when I became alarmed."

Jefferson added morbidly, "Since I was still alive, Everett had no legitimate claim to the White House. Lois Cipriano neither. Legally, I'm still the rightful President of the United States."

Sullivan then explained to Janelle, "The only reason Lois was in the picture to begin with, was because the Speaker of the House, Clarence Bannister, died suddenly of a massive heart attack. I never believed for a second that he died that way. They killed him too."

Sullivan could see that just reliving this tragic time in their lives had caused them both deep anguish. He once again took control of the conversation. "The reason Romanero had Bannister killed was so Cipriano could be quickly voted in as the new House Speaker.

"With Bannister out of the way, Antichrist kept waiting for his next big break, which came when Air Force One was shot down on his orders, no doubt. Then, when President Ashford chose to wait a while before choosing a new VP, the timing couldn't have been more perfect!

"When President Ashford was killed, it opened the door for Cipriano to become President. Acting as Romanero's puppet, they could easily control the government. It was a classic coup d'état."

Janelle gasped at this stark reality. The deception was mind numbing. "I always knew something was fishy about the way it all played out."

"Even if that position still existed, I wouldn't want it." Jefferson frowned, then glanced over at his daughter, still trying to let it sink in that she was there with him. "When did Christine die?"

Janelle replied, "Like William said, she was killed in the global quake. But what he didn't mention was that she had stage four breast cancer, so her days were already numbered."

"I see," came Jefferson's reply evenly. What else was there to say? He asked his daughter, "Did Benjamin really rape you?"

Janelle nodded affirmatively.

Amy asked her, "When did you get pregnant?"

"Four months ago. The last thing I wanted in these crazy times was to be expecting again. Even though it went against Romanero's decree that anyone performing or receiving abortions would be killed, I threatened to do just that.

"I was so mad at my husband. I ended up going for a very long walk that day to downtown D.C. When I walked past where the White House once stood, I had my first encounter with God. When I became a believer, my thinking about wanting an abortion quickly changed. Suddenly, I wanted to help populate the Millennial Kingdom."

"Are you familiar with Romans eight, twenty-eight?"

Janelle shook her head no.

Amy explained, "It says God works all things for good for those who love Him and are called according to His purpose. Think about it, had you not gotten pregnant, chances are good that you would have never gone for that long walk, which led you to one of Yahweh's sealed servants, which led to your salvation."

Eyes drinking in her new surroundings, Janelle asked, "So, where will I sleep?"

Amy answered, "Your cot awaits you. If you've never experienced underground living before, it'll take a little getting used to. It's new to us as well." She sighed. "Our last place was above ground. It was nearly perfect."

Janelle asked, "Was it bombed?"

Amy nodded sadly.

Janelle said, "I'm not thrilled about living underground with a bunch of strangers. On the other hand, I never want to leave this place."

"It may take a while, but you'll eventually adjust to subterranean living. But first, let's get you examined by one of our doctors. Don't worry, I won't leave your side."

Amy kissed Jefferson on the forehead, then walked her stepdaughter to the hospital section.

When they made it to the hospital area, before Tamika could even take Amy's vitals, her water broke. It was time for A.J. Moseley to make his earthly debut.

Two hours later, Leticia went into labor…

CHAOS IN THE BLINK OF AN EYE PART NINE: YAHWEH'S REMNANT

29

ONE WEEK LATER

"RISE AND SHINE, BLANCA, it's almost time to go…" Carmen said to her daughter, trying to sound cheerful.

Blanca hadn't slept a wink all night. She buried her face in a pillow. "I'm not going. I don't feel good. I got my period last night."

Carmen wasn't satisfied with her daughter's excuse. "This is important, honey. C'mon, get up."

Blanca rolled over on her bed to face her mother. She plucked the small pillow from between her knees, that she used to pad them when she was laying on her side. She covered her midsection with it. "I'm not nearly as concerned about going as you are, Mami."

Carmen flinched. "What's that supposed to mean?" She braced herself waiting for the answer.

Blanca rolled her eyes. "Duh! When was the last time I went shopping for anything, Mami? I don't even have a credit card!"

Carmen countered, "What about internet access? The only way we can keep it on is if everyone living here is in compliance."

Blanca grunted in frustration. "We still have time, Mami…"

Carmen was perturbed hearing this. "C'mon hija, this is your first step to becoming a responsible citizen. Once you start earning income in the new global economy, the mark will be your credit card. There are plenty of good jobs out there. Soon you can purchase your own tampons. How cool is that? I can't wait to go shopping with you again."

Blanca was tired of arguing with her mother. This was only one of the many quarrels that had recently transpired between them. Ever since her conversion last week, which her mother still knew nothing about, they could never find common ground on anything.

Carmen recently began noticing major changes in her teenage daughter, which went beyond battling adolescent hormones. Worse, her mannerisms were starting to resemble her father's. She was starting to have her suspicions. Was Blanca's reason for not wanting to go with her deeper than merely having her menstrual cycle?

Carmen glared at Raul. She rocked back on her feet, trying to gauge her husband's body language. "Did you get to her?!"

Raul shrugged. "It's her decision, Carmen."

Carmen snorted in anger. "She's still a teenager, Raul. As the only sane parent in this family, I'll decide what's best for her. If I were you, I would be more focused on thinking things through and making the choices. Don't you realize how impossible it'll be for you to avoid capture, with all those microflier thingies flying everywhere?"

Raul understood the anger in her voice, alarming as it was, and the fearful expression plastered on her face. She needed Jesus. "I certainly don't look forward to becoming a hunted man. But if I'm captured and beheaded for my faith in Christ, that would be better than taking the mark. Jesus said, if anyone wants to follow Him, we must deny self, carry our crosses and follow Him even unto death. I'm willing to follow His command."

He looked at his wife as lovingly as he could. "Please don't do this, my love. Don't go there. Believe me, you'll come to regret it."

"Don't tell me what to do, Raul!" she hissed, aiming her withering gaze at him. "This is all your fault!" She returned her gaze to Blanca. "Fine! I'll reschedule your appointment for later this week. By then, you should feel better. Just hope the compliance police don't come knocking on our door before then! Looks like I have to be the responsible one in the family who makes sure we don't lose power, water, and internet."

Blanca reburied her face in her pillow. Her mother's suggestion had sounded more like a command. *I thought it was my choice to receive or reject the mark!* She hated being dishonest like this, but now that she understood the gravity of the situation infinitely more than her mother did, it was something she had to do.

Carmen clenched her right hand into a fist and air-punched her husband. "I won't let you steal Blanca away from me!"

"Steal her from you?! Come on, Carmen, how can you say that?"

Carmen scowled at her husband, then stormed down the stairs and left the house, determined as ever to receive the mark. Her last words to Raul were, "Go ahead. Die from lung cancer! See if I care!"

It was like a knife in the heart. The hatred in her voice frightened him. The last thing on Raul's mind now was his failing health. He understood this was spiritual warfare. Still, it hurt. Carmen was the one true love of his life. It was like they no longer knew each other.

He glanced tearfully outside Blanca's bedroom window, as his wife walked to the car, in quick strides, like she couldn't wait to get to where she was going. The way she was dressed, one might think she was going to church. Her high heels echoed loudly, each time they struck the cement pavement. Raul was certain the neighbors also heard her.

Carmen angrily glanced up at her daughter's bedroom, then lowered herself into the car. The way she sped off, anyone watching would know she was agitated. Raul watched until her car was out of sight. He knew chances were good they would never see each other again.

In the 17 years in which he and Carmen were married, Raul had worked so hard to protect and provide for her. Just like that, their marriage was over. He dried his moist eyes, and said to his daughter, "Time to start packing! We don't have much time."

Blanca buried her face in the palms of her hands. She became frantic. "I can't think straight, Papi."

"I know this is difficult, sweetie, but when Mami comes home, we need to be as far away from this place as possible, in case she calls the cops on us, which I fully anticipate happening…"

The teenager lowered her head in defeat. "Okay, fine."

Raul placed a hand on her right shoulder. He felt her body trembling. This would be overwhelming for any teenager to cope with. "Everything will be fine. Just pack whatever you can as quickly as you can."

Blanca opened her closet door and removed a bunch of blankets. Beneath them were five hefty bags filled with the things she thought she would need to survive the next three years.

Raul's eyes widened. Anger crept onto his face. "Do you know how much trouble we'd be in if Mami ever saw this?"

Blanca looked down at the floor. "I started packing two nights ago, when you and Mami were asleep. Had I told you, Papi, you would've been mad."

"Not smart, Blanca!" he snapped.

Blanca wanted to say, "You're not a teenager, so you wouldn't understand!" She thought better of it. "Sorry, Papi. But how could I possibly pack the things I'll need for the rest of my life, in just a few moments? I can't borrow Leticia's clothes. I'm four inches taller than her. At least I was last time I saw her. I'm sure you still remember how scrawny she was, Papi. I'm sure nothing she has will fit me."

Blanca looked a lot like her mother, only she inherited her height and broad shoulders from her father. She liked her height, but she would have preferred her mother's smaller shoulders instead.

Raul sighed, then kissed his daughter on the forehead. "It's okay, mija. Just glad Mami didn't see it. If she did…"

He stopped when Blanca's lower lip started quivering. Now convinced that the parents she had loved equally could never be reconciled, the pain in her heart was so great, it was almost too much to absorb. She started sobbing uncontrollably.

Raul held his daughter until she stopped crying, before gently saying to her, "Get changed. I'll start taking your things down to the car."

Blanca stared at her father. He was no longer the tall strapping man he used to be. The cancer had really aged him. He looked a few inches smaller. He had to be down 80 pounds. She was sure the stress also had something to do with it. "Okay, Papi."

Raul kissed his daughter on the forehead again, then made the first trip down to the garage with her belongings. It took three trips just to load her things into the trunk of the car, before he finally had time to start packing his own belongings. He thought to disarm the cameras in the house, but if he did, Carmen would be notified on her cell phone.

He said to his daughter, "Give me ten minutes to pack my things. In the meantime, why don't you go to the kitchen and pack whatever snacks we may have left for the long drive? Mami can always get more. And bring a pen and paper so we can communicate along the way."

"Okay, Papi." Blanca also packed the board games and jigsaw puzzles she used to play with her parents.

Before closing his suitcase, Raul held his copy of *The Way* in his hands. As much as he wanted to leave it behind for Carmen to read, now that she was about to receive the mark, if he did, she would destroy it.

With that dreadfully sobering truth settled in his mind, he placed his daily source of strength and inspiration in his suitcase, beneath a pile of clothes, then carried it to the car.

Before leaving their home never to return, Raul said to his daughter, "Make sure you use the bathroom. Once we leave, I don't wanna stop until we reach Kennett Square."

"Okay, Papi..." There was no energy or emotion behind her words, only sadness.

With their bladders emptied, and the car packed with their belongings, they held hands and Raul prayed that they would make it to the meeting location 300 miles southwest of their home, without being pulled over by the local authorities.

The one thing they had going for them was Carmen had no idea where they were going. As far as Raul could tell, she would never suspect the state of Pennsylvania. That, plus they weren't on any dissident lists. This meant they were still free to travel.

But, like Leticia had warned, since neither had yet to receive the mark, if they were pulled over by law enforcement, they would be detained and questioned until a valid explanation could be given.

Raul gulped hard at the thought. *Please protect us, Lord...*

At that, he remotely opened the garage door, set the trip odometer at zero, something he did on all long drives, and they left the only house they had ever known as a family, without ever looking back...

30

WHEN CARMEN ESPINOSA ARRIVED at the location at which she would receive the mark, she spotted two of her neighbors waiting in line, twenty spots ahead of her.

When their eyes met, Roberto and Bonita Ortiz couldn't ignore the sadness they saw on Carmen's face. Or was it anger? Whatever it was, it wasn't good. There wasn't a trace of joy to be seen anywhere on her face.

The reason the seniors had waited so long to take the mark was that they both were asthmatics. They didn't want to catch the global flu again.

After Bonita received the mark, her husband checked their banking status online.

Bonita asked Carmen, "What's wrong? Why aren't Raul and Blanca here with you? Aren't you all supposed to take it together?"

Carmen's eyes flitted this way and that. "Not here," she said, clearly unnerved. "Tell you later…"

Bonita glanced at her husband. Roberto shrugged. A few seconds later, he clenched his right fist in the air. "Yes! Our funds are available!"

It was loud enough that everyone in line waiting to receive the mark heard him. They gawked at him expectantly. The proud glow on his face added to the elation he already felt. The way he stared so glowingly at the mark on his right hand, it was like a badge of honor. Now he and his wife would never be cut off from the life they had always known.

Roberto and Bonita never thought the day would come when the Catholic church would ever be part of a one world religion. As two of the final standouts at their parish, it left them feeling bitter and confused. They didn't trust the Pope. They knew he was evil. But when faced with the possibility of losing water and electricity, they finally caved in.

Bonita sighed relief, then asked Carmen, "Would you like to come over for lunch? I'm making seafood paella to celebrate taking the mark. It's been so long since I've prepared it."

Carmen shrugged. "Thanks, but I'm not hungry."

"Stop by, anyway. Who knows, you may be hungry by then."

The last thing Carmen wanted was to be home alone. She needed a break from it all. "Okay, sure. At the very least, I could use the company. But I may be here a while."

"Take your time, Carmen. I still need to go shopping for everything I need. The food should be ready in two hours, give or take. Do your best to enjoy the moment," bellowed Bonita joyfully.

Carmen's bloodshot eyes became flooded with tears. "I'm trying."

Bonita squeezed Carmen's left hand. "Everything will be fine. You're doing the right thing…"

Carmen sighed. "Thanks. I really needed to hear that."

"We'll see you soon…" At that, Roberto and Bonita left for home.

Thirty minutes later, with the mark of the Beast now tattooed on her right hand, the joy Carmen had fully expected to feel, before Blanca bailed on her, wasn't there. If anything, she felt worse. It was all Raul's fault.

At least she was able to reschedule her daughter's appointment.

Carmen updated the Wi-Fi access code, then checked the home security app on her phone. She didn't see Raul or Blanca in any of the common living sections, but she wasn't overly concerned by this. They were probably in their bedrooms as usual.

Satisfied that the house was safe, Carmen closed the app and left for her neighbor's house. When she walked through the front door, the aroma from the paella hung thick in the air. But even the tantalizing aroma couldn't snap her out of it.

Bonita beamed upon seeing her neighbor. "Your timing's perfect. The foods just about ready. I hope you're hungry now. I made plenty."

Carmen replied, "I'll try to eat. If not, I'll take some home with me."

"Why don't you try to do both? I mean, when was the last time you had my paella?"

"It's been a while," she said, dour expression on her face.

Bonita noticed and shot an assuring smile at her neighbor. "I can't tell you how good it felt to finally go food shopping again!"

Carmen couldn't deny that it felt good to have a normal conversation with her friend. "I'll go after lunch. I look forward to brewing fresh coffee in the morning again, with fresh milk instead of powdered milk, and cooking bacon and eggs for breakfast. Blanca's been missing that. We're tired of eating rice and beans every day. What I really miss is having ice cream in the fridge! The things I used to take for granted…"

Roberto nodded at her. "Let us pray…"

In the irony of all ironies, they held hands and thanked God for the meal. Roberto even ended by saying, "In Jesus' name we pray…"

Carmen took a deep breath, then explained to her friends how Raul had recently become a Christian, and that Blanca might also be one.

Roberto and Bonita were both stunned to hear their neighbor tell them this. They exchanged shocked glances.

Carmen put a shrimp on her fork and ate it. "I'm thrilled that I received the mark today. But the constant turmoil in my family has me stressed out of my mind. I can hardly think straight."

Bonita shook her head sadly. "Raul's the one with stage-three lung cancer. You'd think he'd be the first one in line to receive it, if only to qualify for the chip."

Carmen swallowed the food in her mouth. "I know, right? Yet, he's dead set against taking the mark. I don't know what's gotten into him, I really don't!"

"Mental illness, plain and simple!" Roberto shook his head in confusion. "Geez, just when you think you know someone…"

Carmen sighed. "I'm worried about Blanca. She's been acting strange lately, a lot like her father, in fact. What if she doesn't show up for her next appointment?"

Bonita reached across the table for Carmen's hand. "She'll be fine. Just give her time. She'll eventually come to her senses." *Thank you, Lord, that my three children all have the mark!*

Carmen's brow furrowed. "I'm not so sure. What happens if the authorities do a spot search on us, and Raul doesn't have the mark? I know he'll be arrested, but will they disconnect our power, water, and internet?"

Roberto became angry. "Would you like me to talk to Blanca?"

"That won't be necessary. The last thing you need, is to deal with a teenager just starting her monthly menstrual cycle. We're here to celebrate, right?"

Roberto raised his hands off the table, signifying that he understood. "Yes, we are, but if you need us for anything, we're here for you."

The way he said it forced tears into Carmen's eyes. Now that she had taken the mark, she felt completely cut off from her husband. She prayed it wouldn't be from her daughter as well.

Carmen finished her meal, then checked to see if her funds that were on hold had finally been freed up. She sighed in relief, seeing that they were. It had been six long months. *At least something went right today!*

She then checked the home security app on her phone again. Her eyes bulged. Her face became flush.

Bonita asked, "What's wrong, Carmen?"

"Raul's car is gone! He better not have taken Blanca with him!"

Roberto shook his head angrily. "What's gotten into him?"

"I was so flustered when I checked the app earlier that I can't remember if his car was there or not. I gotta go."

Carmen stormed out of the house. Even though her electric car was parked outside charging, she removed her heels and ran the short distance home in her stockings. She would come back for the car later.

She raced up the stairs as fast as she could and went straight to Blanca's bedroom. Seeing the many drawers pulled open and mostly empty, she screamed at the top of her lungs, "Noooo!"

Carmen raced down the stairs toward the garage. Her face burned with anger. She was already in a foul mood because of her defiant daughter. Now this? She shook her fists at the living room ceiling, and screamed at the top of her lungs, "I hate you, Raul!" Her voice was full of venom, unlike anything she had ever uttered in the past.

Just then, she felt a sharp pain in her right hand and on her forehead. She looked in the mirror and thought her eyes were playing tricks on her. They weren't. Visible sores started to appear in both places.

Carmen reached for her cell phone and called Bonita. "Blanca's gone too...," she said, through soft sniffling.

"Oh my...really? Where could they have gone?"

Carmen answered, "I don't know. But chances are good they went to one of those Christian hideouts."

Roberto barked into the receiver, "How could Raul do this to his own daughter? That's child abuse! I think you should call nine-one-one."

What made him even angrier was that he and his wife also had sores on their right hands and on their foreheads. They didn't tell Carmen. Why add to her troubles...

Bonita added, "My thoughts exactly..."

"Let me do that now. I'll get back to you."

The call ended. Carmen called 911. "Providence Police Department, what's your emergency?" asked the female officer.

"I'm calling to report a kidnapping," Carmen spoke into the phone angrily, fearfully.

This was the tenth call the female officer had received this week alone, from citizens making similar pleas for help. She knew it wouldn't be the last. "Who was kidnapped?"

"My daughter."

"Her name?"

"Blanca Espinosa."

"Do you know who kidnapped her?"

"My husband, Raul."

"I see," came the reply, clinically. "Do you know where they went?"

"No clue…"

"Did they leave a letter or text message?"

"Nothing." Carmen thought to herself, *You're too sick to get the mark, mija, but not too sick to run away from home*!

"How long has your daughter been missing?"

"Hard to say. All I know is when I went to receive the mark early this morning, they were at home. So, it could be anywhere from five minutes to five hours."

"That's potentially a huge escape window…"

"I know. I checked my home security cameras after I received the mark. But I can't remember if my husband's car was there or not. It's been a crazy day. Raul's dead set against taking it. I hope he hasn't brainwashed my daughter. I fear for her."

"I understand. What is the make and model of your husband's car?"

Carmen provided the information to her. In truth, the question was unnecessary. All she had to do was pull it up on her computer screen. It was all there.

"Got it," she said. "I'll put an APB out on them immediately. In the meantime, if you uncover anything on your end, give us a call back, so we can update the system."

"I will." The desperation in Carmen's voice was evident.

When the call ended, she couldn't control the uneasy energy racing through her. She didn't know it was partly demonic, which was a direct result of taking the mark of the Beast.

She hurried up the street and disconnected her electric car from the charger. Instead of going food shopping, she drove to downtown Providence, to pay a visit to the young man who was responsible for destroying her marriage. It didn't take long to find him.

"Where's my husband and daughter!" she demanded to know, when he was in mid-sentence. "Where did you send them?"

Instead of answering her questions, or empathizing with her, he ignored her like she wasn't even there. Now that she had received the mark, she was Yahweh's eternal enemy, and, therefore, his eternal enemy. There was nothing he could do for her now…

Carmen glared at him and gnashed her teeth as he resumed preaching his nonsensical message. The more he preached, the more her soul shrieked in terror.

When she could no longer tolerate being in his presence, she shouted a few obscenities at him, flipped him off, then left for home.

The peace she hoped to have from receiving the mark was nowhere to be found. She felt angry, incredibly angry, and deeply tormented in her soul. To make matters worse, the painful sores on her right hand and forehead were starting to look infected.

Remembering Raul's warning that this would happen, she screamed in agony at the top of her lungs. Even the thrill of going food shopping again was gone.

31

MEANWHILE, RAUL AND BLANCA Espinosa were well on their way to Pennsylvania, headed south in the state of New Jersey. They reached the 200-mile marker on Raul's trip odometer, just South of Newark Liberty International Airport.

The reason Raul knew this was because his eyes kept nervously shifting from the road ahead of him, to the rearview and side mirrors looking for flashing lights headed in their direction, then to the trip odometer. He was shocked they had made it this far.

To say that it had been an emotionally charged drive would be an understatement. When they left Rhode Island, a crushing depression fell upon their shoulders, knowing they could never return to the only state they had ever called home.

Carmen had to be home by now. Had she called the police on them? The anger in her voice earlier indicated that she probably had.

Blanca had never seen her father so jittery. The way he squirmed and shifted his weight in the driver's seat, every few minutes, made it impossible for her to relax.

She wrote on a piece of paper, "Are you okay?"

Raul shot his daughter a thumbs up gesture. But the expression on his face betrayed what he was hoping to project to her.

Each time they crossed into a new state, Blanca held up the same piece of paper. And each time, her father shot another thumbs up gesture at her. She knew he wasn't being truthful. His trembling hands on the steering wheel indicated that much. She didn't have to ask why.

Whatever she wrote down for her father to read, she made sure he could answer it either with a thumbs up or down.

They reached the 250-mile marker at the Pennsylvania border. Although they made sure to take small sips of water, they both needed to relieve themselves. Now that they were in the final stretch, they couldn't stop.

Raul mouthed to his daughter, "Can you wait?"

Blanca mouthed back her reply, "I'll try."

Raul's trembling increased. He had never driven in a communist country before. His grandfather often told him stories about his days living in communist Cuba, and how fearful he was most days even just walking down the street. That's precisely how it felt now.

If they were pulled over, Raul's biggest concern was that the police would find his copy of *The Way* in his suitcase, buried beneath a pile of clothes. That alone would be grounds to arrest them.

If they were incarcerated, they would never leave that place unless they took the mark of the Beast. The thought of his teenage daughter being tortured in one of Romanero's death camps, without being able to stop it, gave him the added motivation to remain vigilant.

Then again, with those miniature spies always out looking for people like them, vigilance only went so far. He kept praying that the intense heat from the sun would keep melting them, as it had been widely rumored.

Raul felt no need to communicate these morbid thoughts to Blanca. Why add to her worries? It was still difficult enough for her to wrap her confused mind around it all. She was still a teenager. He glanced over at her, just as new tears started falling out of her eyes.

What had caused this latest release was something her mother often did whenever she heard the third flying angel's stern warning against taking the mark of the Beast. She would cover her ears with both hands shouting, "Blah, blah, blah!" at the top of her lungs.

It had been a while, but since she had heard it so many times, Blanca had memorized it. Now that her mother had disobeyed the warning against taking the mark of the Beast, she would be subjected to that eternal Divine justice.

The teenager was already mourning her mother's spiritual death. Now, she had to do her best to stop thinking about her mother altogether. The very thought made Blanca burst out in tears again.

Raul didn't have to ask his daughter why she was wailing. He had also shed many tears for Carmen on this drive. He wanted to pull the car to the side of the road and comfort Blanca, but it would be too risky.

When they arrived in Kennett Square, both were still emotional wrecks. Raul pulled his vehicle into the agreed upon service station. The trip odometer was 316-miles.

It made him think of John 3:16: *For God so loved the world that He gave His only begotten Son that whoever will believe in Him shall not perish but have eternal life.* "I believe, Lord," Raul mumbled to himself, "I believe!" This comforted him, even if slightly.

Titus and Shamus Harmon were already there waiting for them, at the designated area that was texted to them.

"Raul?" asked Harmon.

The man who looked completely gutted nodded yes.

Titus fully expected to see him looking this way. Most newcomers he shuttled to the subterranean safe house resembled the way the two of them did now. He waved them over to the solar-powered four-wheeler.

The Espinosa's took a few moments to collect themselves, then got out of the vehicle for what they both knew would be for the last time.

Blanca asked her father, "What about my things?"

Raul eyeballed the two men. "Our things are in the trunk."

Shamus answered, "I'll come back for them later. Right now, we need to get you both to safety. I'll need your keys, all cell phones, smart watches, and all other mobile devices you brought with you."

This didn't come as a surprise. But it presented another layer of their lives being stripped away from them. The worst of which was Carmen's eternal condition.

Raul snapped out of it. "Everything we have is in the trunk, in bags and suitcases."

"Good. We'll take care of it then. Say goodbye to your car," came the cold, stern reply.

Shamus asked them. "Before we go, do either of you have any sickness that could be transmitted to others?"

Raul answered, "No, but I do have stage three lung cancer."

"Yeah, we were already informed of that. Sorry, to hear that." Harmon added, "Not to sound insensitive, but what you have isn't transmittable. So, you won't have to be quarantined when we get there."

Titus handed them camouflage bucket hats. They already had sunglasses on. "Put these on."

They left at once. They arrived at the safe house a few minutes later.

The four of them lowered themselves down the three sets of ladders leading to the bottom. Titus radioed his wife, Ingrid, on his walkie talkie.

"Tell Leticia it's time." He opened the steel door leading to the safe house and breathed a prolonged sigh of relief. They were safe...

Leticia met them in the main living shelter. She wore a face mask in case their new residents had the global flu. Just seeing her childhood friend forced a whole new round of emotions to well up inside.

But mostly, she was relieved. She grabbed Blanca's shoulders, to make sure she really was standing in front of her. Aside from her tear-swollen eyes, and the dark circles beneath them, she looked exactly the same.

Blanca couldn't say the same about Leticia. She wasn't that same scrawny, flat-chested young girl she was before they were separated a few years ago. She was still thin, but apparently giving birth had added more weight to her body. It looked good on her.

The teens clung to each other for dear life, nearly collapsing in each other's arms.

After a while, Blanca dried her tear-drenched eyes with the sleeve of her sweater. "You had me so worried about you, Ticia. I never thought I'd see you again. When news broke that Romanero destroyed tens of thousands of Christian hideouts, I feared you were dead."

"Sorry for making you worry about me." Leticia looked up at Raul. "Nice to see you again, Mister Espinosa."

"You too, Leticia," came the reply, sincerely. Raul had a whole new respect for her.

Blanca asked, "Did you give birth to a boy or a girl?"

A bigger smile crossed her face. "Both, actually."

Blanca covered her mouth with her left hand. "You had twins?"

Leticia chuckled. "I gave birth three weeks ago to a daughter. We named her Catalina after Joaquim's mother. My first child was a boy. His name's Julio junior, after Papa, J.J. for short. You'll meet them soon. You'll also meet my husband, Joaquim."

Blanca's eyes widened. "You're married?"

"Why do you seem so surprised?"

Blanca shook her head. "Most procreators aren't these days."

"They are with our organization." Leticia smiled brightly. "God has blessed me with a wonderful husband."

Blanca took a moment to process it all. "I'm excited to meet them."

As Raul observed this blissful reunion, he was amazed by how grown up they both sounded. The usual theatrics connected to teen girls reuniting was greatly tempered.

Lila Choharjo joined them. She lowered her face mask. "Doctor Calloway will examine you both, to make sure you're not bringing any sicknesses or illnesses down here. We have more than four thousand residents, so we need to be extra careful. I'm sure you understand…"

Raul nodded. "I already told Titus I have stage three lung cancer."

Lila nodded compassionately at him. "Leticia told me already. I was sorry to hear it."

Raul said, "It's okay. Soon, I'll have my new, eternal body."

"Indeed, you will, Raul. After the two of you are checked out, you'll be assigned beds to sleep on. Then you can meet the others living here."

Blanca asked Lila, "Why do you look so familiar to me?"

Lila looked down at her feet. "I used to be an actress…"

It dawned on Blanca. "Lila Choharjo?"

"In the flesh…"

"My mother was always a big fan of yours." Blanca lowered her head sadly. "I believe she watched every movie and soap opera you ever made…"

"I'm sure if she knew I became a Christian, she would hate me!"

Blanca's lips started quivering. *Oh, Mami!*

Lila reached for the teen's left hand. "I know how difficult this is for you. It may not always feel that way, and you'll always grieve for your mother, but in time, you'll come to grips with the fact that you both had a decision to make. Thankfully, you made the right one…"

Raul mouthed the words, "Thank you," to Lila.

Leticia broke the moment, "Lila isn't the only high-profile individual staying here. There are others."

Raul was intrigued hearing this. "Yeah, like who?"

Lila answered, "I'll give you the three biggest ones—President Danforth, Hana Patel, and Benjamin Shapiro."

"Hana Patel is here? Seriously?"

Leticia nodded with a weary smile. "Cristiana too."

Blanca was suddenly star struck. When Hana rose to prominence, like millions of young females, she followed her on all her social media platforms, until they were taken down. She liked and shared every post Hana made online, except for her last one, which was a live broadcast of Hana quoting Romans 1:16 to her millions of viewers.

What Blanca thought was mental illness at that time, she now wholeheartedly agreed with. She, too, was not ashamed of the Gospel. "I can't wait to meet them."

Raul was also impressed hearing that Hana was a resident, but he was more enamored with the former U.S. President. "I would love to meet President Danforth…"

Lila nodded yes. "You'll meet him after you've been examined. Don't worry it won't take long."

Blanca asked Lila in a soft whisper, "Do you have tampons…"

Lila smiled at her, "We sure do! Follow me."

32

AFTER RAUL AND BLANCA Espinosa were examined by Meera Calloway, and both were deemed flu and sore free, Titus walked Raul to the men's section to his assigned bed.

They all seemed happy to see him. Still, the way everyone stared at him made him feel like a prisoner being taken to his cell for the first time.

Leticia took Blanca to her assigned bed. With no closet space, she hoped her many belongings would fit beneath the rather small bed.

While they were being examined, Leticia spread the news that her BFF and her father had safely arrived. It was a cause for rejoicing.

Since there wasn't much for most residents to do these days, everyone wanted to meet them and be part of the conversation.

With limited space in the main living area, Leticia thought of moving it to the worship area, where there was so much more space. But she didn't want to overwhelm her BFF all at once. She invited only those who had been praying for this day to finally arrive.

When Raul and Blanca returned to the main gathering area, Leticia said to Blanca, "This is my husband, Joaquim, our son, J.J., and our newborn, Catalina."

"Congratulations, to you both! What beautiful kids you have!"

"Nice to finally meet you, Blanca," said Joaquim, holding his son, Julio Jr. in one arm, and his newborn daughter, Catalina, in the other. "I've heard so much about you."

"Until a few minutes ago, I didn't even know Ticia was married. But she had nice things to say about you. Let me help you."

Joaquim handed J.J. to Blanca. The toddler welcomed her with a warm smile and a hug. It felt good to feel the affection from someone else, even from a three-year-old. It was desperately needed.

Joaquim said to Blanca, "I can't tell you how thrilled I am that you and your father are believers! We prayed for your salvation every day. Leticia wanted to contact you for the longest time. But we were under strict orders not to attempt reaching out to anyone unless they had dreams. It seems that dreams are the only thing Satan can't monitor.

Leticia added, "Shortly before the global bombing, one of our founders, who, sadly, is no longer with us, urged anyone having dreams about unsaved friends and loved ones to contact them. We decided to wait until we were relocated to this place."

Joaquim added, "When she dreamt that you would find a copy of *The Way* underneath your pillow, we knew the time was now."

Blanca saw Leticia's parents, Julio and Marta. Marta was holding a female toddler in her arms. She asked Leticia, "Who's that cutie pie?"

"My sister, Ruth. Of course, she's a cutie pie! She resembles me, right?"

Blanca laughed, but then became puzzled. "Your sister?"

Marta answered it for her daughter. "A few weeks after we became grandparents, we became parents again! Now we're grandparents once again." Her eyes volleyed to Raul. "Crazy, I know?"

Raul said, "I thought life was already insane enough when you left Rhode Island. Man, oh man!"

"That's for sure!" replied Julio.

Blanca glanced at Leticia. "What hurt the most was that we never got to say bye to each other. I can't tell you how many times I cried myself to sleep over it."

Leticia replied, "Same here."

Julio and Marta had met Raul and Carmen on a few occasions before the Rapture, but they weren't close friends. When they forbade Blanca from seeing Leticia, after she got pregnant, they thought they would never see or hear from them again.

Blanca rubbed J.J.'s belly. "I still can't believe you're married."

Leticia smiled. "Even though she's our first child together, Joaquim treats J.J. like his own son."

Joaquim interjected, "He is my son. Right J.J.?"

J.J.'s face beamed. "Yes, Papa."

Joaquim fist bumped J.J. "Love you, buddy."

"Love you too, Daddy."

Blanca was deeply touched by the gesture. "I can see why you fell in love with him."

Leticia beamed. "I couldn't be blessed with a better husband. The first time I gave birth, I couldn't stop thinking about the man who raped me and got me pregnant. Thanks to him, I never think about that monster."

Julio patted Joaquim on the shoulder. "I couldn't ask for a better son in law."

Joaquim smiled his thanks to his father-in-law, then looked down at the ground, as his face took on a deeper shade of pink.

When Leticia announced she was also pregnant, at Tamika's 30th birthday party, Julio went off on Joaquim. Now they were like best friends.

"Let's not forget Leticia. She's a remarkable young woman!" Jefferson glanced at Raul. "If I was a prosecutor before the Rapture, I would have made sure that Julio and Marta were prosecuted to the fullest, for letting their daughter get married at such a young age.

"It took some getting used to, but I must say, they are a remarkable couple. You should see how they treat each other. They are mature beyond their years. They're teaching many of us older married folks a thing or two on how to treat our spouses.

"Now that we know for certain married couples will remain together in the Millennial Kingdom, my prayer is that God will bless the young couple with many more fruitful years as husband and wife."

"Amen to that!" came the reply of many.

Raul's mind was blown. The way the former U.S. President praised his daughter's best friend was mind blowing. It wasn't scripted. It was genuine and heartfelt.

If Leticia was overwhelmed by being in the presence of the former leader of the free world, it didn't show. Perhaps she did when she first met him, but not now. She felt perfectly comfortable being around him.

Hana asked Raul, "Who got saved first, you or your daughter?"

Raul answered, "I did. That's when life got very difficult in our household…"

Blanca interjected, "When Papi suddenly stopped being stung by those demonic locusts, Mami accused him of not being man enough to protect his family. I was happy for Papi, but I was also jealous. Believe me when I say, each new sting was more agonizing than the last one."

Benjamin Shapiro said, "You can say that again! I still have nightmares about them."

Leticia asked Blanca, "Do you still have sting marks?"

Blanca rolled up her sleeves and showed her scars to everyone. "Believe me, it hurt much worse than it looks!"

Raul sighed. "Each time they were stung, I wanted to ease their suffering, but what could I do? I kept insisting that I was just as much of a sinner as they were. The only difference was, after a lifetime of reckless living, I was finally forgiven by God.

"They knew the locusts no longer had power over me. They both saw it with their own two eyes. What more proof did they need? It all came down to trusting in Christ as Lord and Savior. It was a choice they had to make for themselves. All I could do was pray for them."

Blanca said, "When the attacks grew worse, I was so desperate that I went up to my room one night and begged God to make them stop. I promised that I would be a good girl if only He answered my prayer."

Her lower lip quivered. "The instant I blessed myself by performing the sign of the cross, I was stung again. I bawled my eyes out knowing God didn't answer my prayer."

Raul winced hearing his daughter retelling the story. "I told Blanca that night that her prayer must have been more out of desperation than from a repentant heart. This made Carmen even more angry with me..."

Blanca sighed. "Up until that time, my parents were always so happy together. Now look at them..."

Joaquim nodded at her. "There isn't a person living here who can't relate to that. We've all been through it."

Meera Calloway finished seeing her last patient, then joined them. She said to Blanca, "We already heard Leticia's account about the night the two of you met that creepy man who got her pregnant. Would you mind sharing your side with us?"

Hana Patel reached for Blanca's hand. "I'd love to hear it."

Hana Patel wants to hear about my life? Blanca gulped nervously at her. She couldn't help but feel like she was in the presence of royalty. She was even holding her hand!

She glanced over at her father. "Papi?"

Raul lowered his head, unsure if he wanted to hear it or not. Finally, he motioned with his hands that it was okay for her to go on.

Blanca took a deep breath and exhaled. Since that night represented the beginning of the end of her friendship with Leticia, she always tried blocking that difficult time out of her life. "When the Pope called on all young girls to get pregnant, it sounded exciting for two eleven-year-olds to meet with a twenty-six-year-old man for that reason. I saw nothing wrong with it at the time."

Blanca glanced uncomfortably at her father again, trying to discern the expression on his face. What she saw was a look of total resignation. She relaxed and continued, "I was only going along with her. I wasn't serious. I didn't think Ticia was either. But when he pulled into the service station down the block from her house, it no longer felt right.

"I grabbed Ticia's arm and begged her not to go with him. Not only was he old enough to be our father, but he was stoned on drugs or whatever. He shouldn't have even been driving."

Blanca twiddled her fingers. "The whole idea of the Pope encouraging young girls to get pregnant for the cause sounded exciting back then. Now it sounds so evil to me."

Leticia glanced over at Raul. "It wasn't your daughter's fault, Mister Espinosa. Your daughter tried stopping me many times. But I wanted to go with him…"

Blanca shook her head sadly. "When she got in his car and drove off, I ran home crying my eyes out. I wanted to call the police, but…" she glanced sheepishly over at Leticia's parents, "…if I did, the two of you would've been notified."

Julio waved off her apology using his left hand. "Leticia told us all about it."

His eyes were too intense for Blanca to hold his gaze for too long. "But it was my fault for lying to you in the first place, by saying she was sleeping at my house that night."

"All is forgiven," said Marta, meaning it.

Blanca sighed relief and went on, "Even if I called the police that night, what could they possibly do when what that jerk was doing was suddenly legal? That monster had no business meeting with us, especially for that reason."

She shook her head in disgust, then confessed to her father, "He offered to 'knock me up' too, Papi," using her fingers in quotations. "His words! What a pathetic man he turned out to be!"

Raul glanced around the room, still blown away that he was having this therapy session of sorts with his daughter, with the former U.S. President and Dr. Shapiro among them, of all people. It was surreal. In a way, he felt like his daughter had also been violated by that man.

This marked the first time Blanca was able to speak so candidly in front of her father. Now that they both were saved, it was like they were no longer father daughter, but brother and sister in Christ.

Raul draped his right arm across Blanca's shoulder, signifying that it was okay. "What's past is past," he said calmly, silently wishing he could put the past behind him as well. Perhaps in time he would. For now, it was still too fresh in his mind.

Blanca said to Marta, "When Leticia texted me the next morning, I was so relieved. But when she came to my house, I knew she had been sexually abused. When she told me what he said to her, that if she got pregnant, he wanted nothing to do with the child once it was born, because he was too immature to be a father, it made me furious."

Blanca flinched in anger. "He was twenty-six! We were eleven at the time! He was immature! I still think about that maniac every day."

Marta saw Julio stiffen. She said, "We pray for his soul every day."

Joaquim squeezed his wife's hand as a sort of reminder that she was safe now, at least when it came to her body.

Charles Calloway felt the tension in the room. He asked Blanca. "So, you found a copy of The Way under your pillow?"

Blanca nodded yes.

Charles grinned. "When I hear stories about the book we published winning new souls for Christ, it gives me added strength to continue on."

Raul gasped loudly. Everyone waited in silence not knowing what had caused his sudden outburst.

Finally, Jefferson Danforth asked, "Are you okay, Raul?"

"You printed those books?"

Calloway answered, "Yes, we did! We produced millions of copies with recycled paper from the many downed trees from the global quake. Yahweh's sealed servants have become our only source of distribution. Had it not been for them, we would have no other way. So, the harvest must be linked to them. But I feel blessed knowing our organization had a hand in it."

Raul wiped a tear from his eye. "I can't thank you enough for publishing it. I draw all my strength from that book. I met one of them in downtown Providence, on one of my oncology visits. He gave me the book. I never did get his name…"

Blanca said sadly, "Papi has stage-three lung cancer."

Sarah Mulrooney frowned. "Sorry to hear that, Raul."

Raul waved her off. "It's okay. My wife couldn't understand why I refused to take the mark and chip, if it would cure my lung cancer. That was her sticking point. Who knows, perhaps it would have. But at what cost? My soul? Anyway, the more I refused her constant urgings, the more convinced she was that I had become a lunatic like the rest of you."

The way he said it caused laughter to reverberate all throughout the room.

Raul also chuckled, before growing serious again. "Now that I'm saved, my life is in God's hands. I feel so blessed knowing if I don't survive until Christ returns, just knowing Blanca will be surrounded by believers gives me peace. This place really is a blessing."

Charles said, "Speaking of Yahweh's sealed servants, we have one of them living here with us. His name's Jakob. He's a remarkable man. He's the one who directed us to this location before our last safe house was bombed."

Benjamin Shapiro sat a little straighter on his chair. "He also happens to be my nephew."

Raul looked at Leticia and got choked up again. "And to think the person my wife and I forbade Blanca from seeing again, is part of the organization responsible for producing the book God used to save my soul. What can I say, my mind is blown!"

Even though Meera Calloway, Tamika Moseley, Lila Choharjo and Leticia's mother, Marta, had already heard Leticia recount the harrowing story, hearing Blanca's account of what happened that night, they were once again spellbound, as if they were hearing it for the first time.

Then again, they never grew weary of hearing stories of how God rescued His children out of the ashpits of life, before placing them straight into the arms of His Son, the Lord Jesus Christ…

Each new story was just as priceless as the last…

33

BENJAMIN SHAPIRO WAS STUFFED inside a wooden cargo crate, 40,000 feet above the Earth's surface, en route to Ben Gurion International Airport. Posted on all sides of the 10x5x5 crate was CAUTION: LIVE ANIMAL INSIDE!

Of the dozens of various sized wooden crates in the underbelly of the plane, all carrying animals, his crate was the only one with a black curtain on the inside. This was done to cover the many open slots in the crate that were intended to provide a steady airflow to the animals inside.

Shapiro was allergic to certain farm animals. Now that he was travelling to Israel with so many of them, he made sure to pack one of the portable oxygen concentrators that were recovered in Chadds Ford, that Brian and Tom hadn't used, in case he developed breathing issues from his fellow animal travelers.

The other reason he brought it with him was in case there was a delay. With the sun unceasingly scorching the earth, flight delays and cancellations were frequent. That, too, could have impacted his breathing.

Thankfully, his flight took off on time. The box was large enough for Benjamin to sit up and stretch his body. There was a throw mattress inside for him to lay on, and even a blanket and pillow.

To prepare for the trip, Shapiro slept in the wooden crate for three straight nights, as a trial run of sorts, so he wouldn't feel claustrophobic and freak out on the cargo plane, when it happened for real. So far, so good!

It took three months to finally set this plan in motion.

In the end, mindful that Yahweh used simple people and simple situations to carry out His earthly plans, they found a potential client on the shrinking black market, named Eugene.

Eugene had yet to take the mark. He was determined not to take it. His stance against taking it wasn't out of spiritual conviction, it was more out of self-righteousness.

He was offended at how the government was forcing tattoos onto their bodies, just so they could eat. It wasn't the tattoo itself; his body was covered with them. But it was his choice to put them there.

Who were *they* to pressure him to take *their* mark? It was beyond abusive in his opinion.

Crazily enough, although Eugene wasn't saved, when he met Shamus Harmon and Tony Pearsall for the first time, he made them show their right hands to make sure they didn't have the mark, before talking business with them.

Once they passed his inspection, not the other way around, Eugene told them he had a solid connection who might be able to deliver their client to Israel, no questions asked.

Harmon and Pearsall had offered Eugene a three-month supply of food, clean water, and medicines, for providing the service.

Without the mark, Eugene knew they couldn't pay him in monetary terms. He wanted a year's worth. Harmon and Pearsall knew these items were like gold in his hands. They ultimately decided on six months.

That was when Eugene revealed his source to them. His sister, Tanya, worked for a cargo shipping company, in Baltimore, Maryland.

Eugene had assured them that the only reason she took the mark was to keep her management job. She was a secular follower at best. The problem was, Tanya wasn't a risktaker, so he wasn't sure if she would be willing to do something that might cause her to lose her job.

Eugene told them he would talk to his sister, but he couldn't make any promises. Pearsall and Harmon sweetened the pot by offering another six months' worth of food, clean water, and medicine, for Tanya.

As an added bargaining chip, before parting company, they gave Eugene enough food and water to hold him over for a couple of days.

It was one of those, "There's plenty more where that came from, if your sister agrees to help us" maneuvers, that often worked in the movies. Eugene was grateful, especially for the fresh water.

It took another week before they met again. Eugene had told them, "I don't know how it happened, but my sister agreed to do it."

In the end, what pushed Tanya over the edge was the six-month water supply. She let Eugene keep the food for himself. She had a job and full access to her finances. Her brother didn't. But the fresh water was altogether different. Everyone needed that.

Eugene cautioned them that once they paid for the service, he could get them as far as the airport. His sister assured him that she would get the crate on the plane. After that, it would be out of her hands. She had zero contacts in Israel.

Harmon and Pearsall understood. As much as they wanted to share the Gospel with Eugene, it would be too risky. They did the next best thing by placing a copy of *The Way* inside one of the food boxes.

By the time he discovered it, they would already be gone.

The fact that Eugene was so determined not to take the mark was potentially a good thing. But it wouldn't get him into Heaven.

It took two months of planning, before Tanya finally decided on the best time to do it. The only shot they had would be when her company made the next shipment of animals to Israel, to help repopulate what was lost in the Jerusalem quake.

Among the mayhem earlier, from loading so many zoo animals onto the plane, in various sized wooden crates, that were all similar to Shapiro's, Tanya kept the loaders and handlers so busy that when his box was scanned through security, no one was there with her.

When the loaders questioned the black curtain, she lied by telling them the animal inside the crate was very ill and that she wouldn't recommend looking in it for any reason. It worked.

Tanya then manipulated the bill of lading to say paid in full, when it really wasn't. Miraculously, that, too, worked.

Tanya didn't know who was inside the box. She didn't want to know. Had she known it was Benjamin Shapiro, she would have washed her hands of it, and told Eugene to search elsewhere for help.

Even her brother didn't know who was inside...

In the end, while desperate for the clean water, more than anything, Tanya pitied her wayward brother, and didn't want him to starve to death. Another good thing was that he wouldn't have to constantly grub food and water from her, for at least six months.

Benjamin slept soundly for the first five hours of the flight. What woke him wasn't the frequent turbulence caused by the blazing heat. It was thoughts about his ex-wife and his three children.

He hadn't heard from them in many years. As far as he knew, they were living in California. But with the Golden State now in ruins, he didn't know if they were dead or alive?

As Romanero's former personal physician, he could have easily found their addresses if he really wanted to. He had full access to the global database back then. But he never did.

Then again, they never tried reaching out to him before he went into hiding. As hardcore atheists, partly thanks to him, now that he was a believer, if they were still alive, why would they want to hear from him now? If anything, his conversion would push them even farther away from him, if that was even possible!

One thing was certain, if they were still alive, if he got to meet with Seth, multitudes would hear about it, including them.

Benjamin was amazed at how much simpler making difficult decisions like these were, when he had Yahweh's eternal assurance.

As the plane started its initial descent, Benjamin changed into his disguise. It was the same one he had on when he first met Jakob on the park bench in Bucks County, Pennsylvania, a quarter mile down the road from where he used to live.

It looked just as ridiculous now as it did back then. When he packed his things before fleeing his former life, he figured he might need the disguise at some point in time. He just never thought it would be for something of this magnitude!

The last time he was in Israel, he had his own private plane and security team. Now he was all alone. He still had no idea how he would get from Ben Gurion Airport to the New Temple.

He was mindful of the foolishness of his actions, but he was determined to meet with his brother one last time.

Shapiro took a few deep breaths to calm himself down, then scanned the area through the box, looking for workers. Seeing none, he opened the latch from the inside and climbed out of the box as quickly as he could.

He took a moment to scan the room, made sure his disguise was properly on, then tiptoed toward the exit. He didn't make it too far.

"Hey, what are you doing here? This is a restricted area!"

Benjamin froze in his tracks. His body started trembling.

The man didn't see the mark on his forehead. And since he had both hands in his pockets, he didn't know if he had it on his right hand either. "Who are you?" he demanded to know.

When Shapiro remained silent, the man barked at him, "Show me your right hand. I want to see your mark!" Thoughts of a thousand-dollar payday danced in his head. "Now!" the man demanded again, reaching for his walkie talkie.

Benjamin ran his shirt sleeve across his sweaty brow, then lowered his head. "I don't have it, yet. I'm here to take advantage of the Pope's offer, before it expires."

"Oh, really! That would explain why you were smuggled inside a cargo box, instead of flying commercially. Tell me another one!"

"Okay, okay..." Shapiro rolled his shirt sleeve up, exposing a diamond-crusted Rolex watch. "It cost me twenty-five thousand dollars when I purchased it two decades ago. It may not be worth that much in today's economy, but I assure you it's worth much more than a thousand dollars. Would you like it?"

"What's the catch?" he asked, staring more at the watch than the man wearing it.

"Take me to the New Temple in Jerusalem. That's all I ask."

"Are you insane, mister!" he scoffed. "No chance! Besides, I'm working."

I must be insane to attempt doing this! Benjamin saw the mark on his right hand, plus the festering sores on the exposed parts of his body, which was a direct result of taking the mark of the Beast. He wondered how he could still perform his duties, especially with the sun spitting fire down on all mark takers. "How far can you take me?"

The man stared at the Rolex on his wrist, mulling it over, until his greed fully kicked in. He held up his hands. "To the main terminal only. After that, you're on your own."

Shapiro wanted to object, by telling him he could walk that distance and keep his watch. But if he did, what would his next move be? He held out his hands in surrender. "Okay, fine."

The man looked at him skeptically, still weighing his options, deciding if the risk-reward factor would be worth it. He glanced once more at the man's Rolex. "I'll need a few minutes first to clear the way."

"Thank you..."

The middle-aged burly man cleared his throat. "The watch?"

Benjamin shoved his hands in his pants pocket. "Once you drop me there, you'll get it..."

He snorted. "By the way, I don't know who or what you're hiding from, but your disguise looks ridiculous! It's so obvious..."

Shapiro shivered at his snide remark. He looked down at his feet and silently prayed again for Yahweh's protection.

Twenty minutes later, they were off to the main terminal arrivals section.

34

BEN GURION INTERNATIONAL AIRPORT

THE VEHICLE CAME TO a stop outside the main terminal at the arrivals area. The man nervously held out his right hand, not to shake Benjamin Shapiro's hand, but to receive the expensive watch he was promised for taking this massive risk for him.

Without making eye contact, Benjamin handed the Rolex to the man whose name he did not know. He thanked him in a whisper, then exited the vehicle.

The man behind the wheel wiped his sweaty brow with his free hand, then sped off, hoping this dangerous encounter wasn't recorded by one of the many security cameras, or captured by a microflier that wasn't fried or short circuited in the intense heat.

Benjamin was thinking similar thoughts. Even with a hat, facemask and sunglasses on, not to mention a disguise, he felt exposed.

Seeing the dozens of armed guards outside the terminal keeping the peace, and no doubt looking for people like him, his legs became wobbly. He didn't think he would have the strength to continue. It was a wonder he had made it this far. He blocked it all out and kept his body in motion. For the first time in his life, he actually felt his age.

With his soul eternally secure, he no longer feared death. But what he did fear was being taken to one of Romanero's prison camps, then being tortured for many days on end, until he was finally put out of his misery.

Shapiro had personally witnessed so many condemned souls suffering in Antichrist's diabolical torture camps, to know he wouldn't have the same level of strength his departed brothers and sisters in Christ had shown for their faith.

Benjamin took a few more heart-pounding steps, not quite sure where to go or what to do. He bent over and placed his hands on his knees. He felt so weak that he sat down to collect himself.

Eyes darting left and right, pulse racing in his ears, he silently prayed, "You have brought me all this way, Abba. How am I supposed to get to the Western wall? Give me the strength to do what I came here for." He was too afraid to close his eyes as he prayed, for fear of being ambushed by a gun wielding guard. The fact that he had made it this far was nothing short of a miracle!

If there was one thing Benjamin was thankful for, it was that his silent prayer was recorded in Heaven's memory, as if he was having a conversation with his Maker. Now that he better understood Yahweh's omnipotence, with all his sins forgiven—removed as far away as the east is from the west—he felt greatly comforted by it now.

The peace he felt quickly evaporated when he glanced back at the terminal door. Six guards were keeping a steady eye on him.

A shiver shot through him. *Are they on to me*? It was enough to almost stop his heart from beating. Not knowing what else to do, he nodded at the driver behind the wheel of a global community issued vehicle.

He rolled down his passenger front window. The blistering heat quickly invaded, slapping him in the face. Even with the AC turned on full blast, it did little to cool the inside of the car. "Where you headed?"

Benjamin said softly, nervously to the driver, whose face was both soaked with sweat and red from the blazing heat. "Are you offering free rides to the New Temple?"

Not seeing the mark on his forehead or right hand, the driver glared at him a little suspiciously. The white kippah he often wore on top of his head with the star of David on it, was replaced with a pea green colored beret to cover more of his head, in a desperate attempt to keep his scalp from being further scorched by the sun.

The other reason he no longer wore the kippah was that his religion was no longer legal. As a lapsed Jew, at best, he had no major issue with no longer wearing the head covering. But even saying the word, "Shalom" was frowned upon these days. It was a bit much.

Finally, he said, "It depends."

Benjamin took a few more panicked breaths to calm himself down. "On what?"

The driver eyeballed him. "On why you're going there…"

Eyes darting left to right again, Benjamin was starting to think his plan might not succeed after all. "Well, after hearing so many others who've received the mark in front of the statue call it a religious experience, I wanted to find out for myself."

The driver relaxed, then flashed the mark on his right hand for Benjamin to see. "Best decision I ever made! Get in. It's a little cooler in here, but not by much." If this man wasn't going there for that reason, he would have to turn him in to the local authorities.

Shapiro said another silent prayer, as his eyes nervously swept the area again. The six guards were still staring at him. With no other options to exercise, he reluctantly lowered himself into the vehicle.

He asked, "What took you so long to finally decide to get it?"

The proud expression Benjamin saw on his face from taking the mark frightened him. He didn't feel comfortable being in this man's vehicle. *If only you knew!* "With countless millions taking advantage of the offer, I was lucky to get a plane seat."

The driver nodded. "Ah, I can't tell you how many others I've already taken there for the same reason. This will be my fourth trip to the New Temple today, and it's just after seven a.m. And I'm only one of many drivers. Where did you fly in from?"

"America."

"I have family in Miami. They were forced to flee and relocate to Georgia after the global quake. They tell me the city's nothing like it used to be." The way he frequently spoke with his hands left Benjamin no choice but to constantly look at the mark on his right hand, and the sores. He also saw what looked like calamine lotion covering them. He doubted it would help. His heart ached for him.

Benjamin pointed at one of them. "Rumor has it those sores came after you took the mark. Is it true?" He already knew the answer.

The driver nodded ever so cautiously. "I can't speak for everyone else, but for me personally, it's true. Not gonna lie, it hasn't been pleasant. I've always been an easy-going guy. I never thought I could be so enraged. It's like it came out of nowhere. My girlfriend recently left me for having a hair trigger temper."

Benjamin frowned. This man didn't know the rage came not only from the painful sores on his body, but mostly because of the demons now controlling him. "I have to be honest, that's the real reason I waited until the last minute. Can't say I'm looking forward to having them on my body too."

"Yeah, part of me wishes I'd waited too. It hasn't been pretty. You should see my legs, back and chest. And the scorching sun only makes it worse. It feels like tiny laser beams burning my skin. The pain killers only do so much…

"Then again, I've never made this kind of money before. I barely survived the global recession. I never want to feel that level of destituteness ever again. What's most important is I went from being broke and jobless, to rolling in the dough in a matter of days! The sores on my body will go away, but my bank roll keeps increasing. It's like a tradeoff. All in all, it's been the only drawback so far."

Benjamin said, "Make it while you can, right?"

"Exactly!" The man broke eye contact in the rearview mirror and craned his neck back toward his passenger. "May I see your digital code please?"

Benjamin looked down at his lap. A shiver shot through him. He patted his shirt pocket. "Hmm, where's my phone?"

The driver held up his mobile device and aimed it at his passenger. "It's okay. Just remove your sunglasses, so I can take your picture."

Shapiro wanted to get out of the car and run as fast as he could. But the six-armed guards were still glaring at him. He wouldn't get too far.

He did as he was instructed. As soon as the driver took the picture, Benjamin covered his eyes again with his mirrored sunglasses. Not that it mattered much. His image would no doubt come back as a positive match in the global dissident database, which, in turn, would mean death for him, and a large reward for his driver.

The driver sensed his uneasiness, as he waited for the result to come back. Even if he didn't take his picture, the vehicle was armed with that technology, so it didn't matter. "Usually, it only takes a few seconds," he said to his passenger, getting agitated. *Time is money!*

Shapiro nodded that he understood. He gulped back another huge dose of fear and chided himself under his breath for his stupidity.

Finally, after waiting nearly five minutes, the driver received a message. It read: *Take passenger to the New Temple!*

The driver scratched his head in confusion. *That's strange*, he thought. *I never mentioned where I would be taking him! All I did was take his picture...* This was the first time he had ever received this type of message. Usually, it was a one word reply either, "proceed" or "detain", the latter meaning to contact local authorities immediately.

He glanced suspiciously at the man in the rearview mirror, then replied to the message: *Anything else I should know?*

He didn't have to wait long this time. It read: *Only that today is your lucky day! You will receive a generous reward for your service! Don't ask any more questions. Go now!*

A wry smile crossed the man's face. With a greedy glint in his eye, he put the car in drive. Without saying another word to his passenger, whoever he was, he began the 55-kilometer (35-mile) trip to the Western Wall. *That's why you waited until the last minute? Yeah right!*

When the vehicle pulled away, Benjamin glanced back at the terminal sliding doors. Sure enough, the six-armed guards were still staring at him. It seemed they were interested only in him.

Shapiro felt like he was riding in a casket instead of a car. *Is this man taking me to jail?* His body erupted in yet another volcano of fear.

Whenever this man drove passengers from A to B, which lately had been quite frequent, the instant the passenger's right hand or forehead was scanned and accepted, the fee went into his personal global account.

But for passengers who had yet to receive the mark, like the man in the backseat, if the search came back as a positive hit, he would receive a thousand dollars, for helping them catch another dissident.

As it was, he had already earned $16,000, from detaining 16 idiotic dissidents trying to take advantage of the free ride the Pope was offering to the New Temple. Not bad pay for just a few weeks!

Convinced his passenger was dissident #17, he wondered how hefty the imbursement added to his global account would be.

Could it be larger than all the others combined? He smiled at the thought, presently unaware that the passenger in the back of his vehicle was none other than Dr. Benjamin Shapiro, the most wanted dissident on the planet.

Benjamin tried blocking out the uneasy energy filling the car. It was impossible. The silence between them only made it worse.

Before leaving Kennett Square early this morning, many laid hands on him and prayed for God's protection. Everyone in the worship room knew he wouldn't be returning. Convinced they would see each other again; it made his departure a little easier, despite his tears.

Benjamin's parting words to them were, "If I'm meant to be there, Yahweh will deliver me. If I'm not meant to go there, it won't happen. It's that simple. My life is in His hands."

His last words to Jefferson Danforth were, "How ironic that my nephew is one of Yahweh's sealed servants, and your son-in-law now has my former job as Antichrist's personal physician."

He already missed everyone. When the New Temple and the Western Wall vicinity came into view, Benjamin silently thanked Yahweh. *I'm not going to jail after all...*

Still, he had a foreboding feeling that his cover had been blown. He squirmed in his seat and nervously said to the driver, "I'd give you a tip but until I receive the mark, how can I?"

The driver looked at him in the rearview mirror. "No worries. You're not the first one to tell me that, and I'm sure you won't be the last." *Besides, you just left me a huge tip, whoever you are*, he thought to himself. The expression on his face screamed, "We got you!"

Shapiro got out of the car and walked away from the vehicle as quickly as he could, without looking back, constantly reminding himself under his breath that he needed to remain focused until he succeeded with his mission. *Lord, help me...*

35

JERUSALEM

AS BENJAMIN SHAPIRO MADE his way to the Western Wall, more fear snaked through him with every step he took.

He kept looking over his shoulders waiting for someone to either shoot him in the back of the head or arrest him. The very thought sent chills up and down his spine.

Yet, despite all that, now that he had a whole new perspective and respect for his chosen Jewish race, he felt proud to be in the Holy Land.

For the first time ever, the sensation of walking on the very streets Yeshua Himself had traversed took his breath away. Only who could he share these awe-inspiring thoughts with?

The crowd size was massive. They all had UV-blocker umbrellas—which did very little to protect them—for when the sun rose. Benjamin heard on the car radio amid the silence between passenger and driver, due to the oppressive heat, the best times to worship the statue was from 7:00 pm to 9:00 am. From 9:00 am to 7:00 p.m., the entire Plaza cleared out, as mark takers did their best to stay out of the sun.

They already had those festering sores on their bodies. Having first and second degree burns on top of that was received by all of them, as even more intentional cruelty from the God of Israel.

The last time he was in Jerusalem, the Temple that his former boss promised to the Jews, for their sole use, still wasn't finished. On the day it was to be dedicated, Romanero broke his promise by entering inside it, and declaring himself to be God from that sacred location.

Instead of seeing people making pilgrimages to the Holy Land, to honor the religions they had once belonged to, all of which were now illegal, they were now there to receive the mark and bow down in worship to the new statue of his former boss.

Benjamin was still part of Romanero's evil alliance when it was still in the testing stages. Even before it was finished, it put all other AI technology advancements before it—impressive as they were—to shame, including those most thought would never be topped.

Now that it had been perfected, and it was doing what it had been demonically engineered to do, he wasn't the slightest bit surprised to see thousands mesmerized by it.

Watching them falling prostrate before the statue that was seemingly brought to life, sickened Benjamin. The way its eyes moved flawlessly up and down and back and forth, with such humanlike ease and motion, made it appear that it really was Romanero staring at him, following him even. And the way its mind could think, and reason, plus sound exactly like his former boss, as it spewed its nonsensical preaching for all to hear, was nothing short of mind blowing.

Having spent so much personal time with the man, his lifelike image was eerily spot on. Only the statue was much taller than his former boss.

Even a hundred yards away, it was easy to see why just one glance could cause most to become mesmerized by it. His likeness was so lifelike that it took every ounce of strength Benjamin possessed to pry his eyes away from it. And he was among the converted!

It was frightening. Had it not been for his soul-saving encounter with his nephew, Jakob, he too would have bowed down to it in worship by now.

When Benjamin heard his former boss declare, "I am the Way, the Truth, and the Life," he nearly vomited, especially when many gathered uttered the reply, "Yes, you are, lord! We praise your holy name!" It very much resembled the way it was done in most Catholic churches.

The statue then said, "I am the bread of life. Whoever comes to me will never go hungry, and whoever believes in me will never be thirsty."

Once again, the written response from the masses was, "Yes, you are, lord! We praise your holy name!"

Romanero then declared, his statue anyway, "I am the light of the world. Whoever follows me will never walk in darkness, but will have the light of life."

Again, the collective response was, "Yes, you are, lord! We praise your holy name!"

The statue went on, "I am the resurrection and the life. The one who believes in me will live, even though they die; and whoever lives by believing in me will never die." Without a trace of robotics, the statue pointed at the crowd in such a way that everyone thought he was pointing directly at them. "Do you believe this?"

The response this time was, "We believe you are the messiah, who came into the world to save us."

It went on, "I am the vine; you are the branches. If you remain in me and I in you, you will bear much fruit; apart from me you can do nothing."

"Yes, lord, Amen!" came the collective reply.

Then, "'For God so loved the world that he gave his one and only Son, that whoever believes in *me*, shall not perish but have eternal life.'" The way the statue pointed at itself was flawless, human-like.

He went on, "In this world you will have trouble." Pointing at the wound on his head that was healed, he added, "But take heart! I have overcome the world. You have seen this with your own eyes!"

The fact that the head wound was already on the statue, before their lord and savior was assassinated, and before the Holy See resurrected him, as the whole world watched, was truly prophetic, and reason enough to fall prostrate before him in praise and worship.

The Pope, who narrated all texts, recited a rewritten version of John 20:24-29, when some of Christ's disciples told Thomas, who was one of the Twelve, that they had seen the Lord! Thomas didn't believe them. He said to them, "Unless I see the nail marks in his hands and put my finger where the nails were, and put my hand into his side, I will not believe."

His wish came true a week later, when he was with the disciples, and Jesus showed up. He said to Thomas, "Put your finger here; see my hands. Reach out your hand and put it into my side. Stop doubting and believe." Thomas said to him, "My Lord and my God!"

Then Jesus told him, "Because you have seen me, you have believed; blessed are those who have not seen and yet have believed."

The statue then declared, "'The harvest is plentiful, but the workers are few.'" This wasn't intended for those refusing the mark, but for all secular partakers who wanted to function in society, but without bowing down to the statue in worship. Their numbers kept increasing as the days passed.

Everyone bowing down to the statue felt the spiritual high they already had being taken to the next level. As the many worshippers prayed to the statue, they also pleaded with the Holy See to heal their sores. He had healed their lord and savior of his fatal headwound, so this should be easy for him. Only, it hadn't happened yet...

At any rate, they were eager to get back home so they could share the message with all secular mark takers. They needed to know what they were missing out on by not taking the next step in faith.

Essentially, by so doing, the religious condemned would be preaching their false gospel to the secular condemned.

Benjamin couldn't remember exactly where those quotes were recorded in the Gospels, all he knew was that they were there, and Antichrist and the False Prophet had stolen them. But by parroting the words of Jesus, the diabolical duo weren't only guilty of plagiarism, but they were also guilty of blasphemy at the very highest level.

Contrasting the great evil taking place, Yahweh's sealed servants who were positioned at the Western Wall vicinity kept preaching and quoting scriptures, without fear, or without missing a beat.

This started on the day the Pope seemingly resurrected Romanero. They kept repeating the same scriptures, numerous times throughout the day, as the massive crowds kept changing.

Truly, there never had been street preachers like them…

Benjamin was comforted by the conviction the four young men exuded while they were preaching. Even among the constant horror, to have the unspeakable privilege of watching the word of God coming to life before his very eyes, was too wonderful to put into words.

The one who was positioned closest to the statue, shouted 2 Thessalonians 3-4, to the multitudes bowing down in worship of it, "'Don't let anyone deceive you in any way, for that day will not come until the rebellion occurs and the man of lawlessness is revealed, the man doomed to destruction. He will oppose and will exalt himself over everything that is called Yahweh or worshiped, so that he sets himself up in Yahweh's temple, proclaiming himself to be Yahweh.'"

"Shut up, you!" yelled an elderly woman who'd travelled all the way from Australia to be there. "You're ruining my religious experience!"

Totally undeterred by the threat, he declared Revelation 13:16-17 next, "He, Antichrist, causes all, both small and great, rich and poor, free and slave, to receive a mark on their right hand or on their foreheads, and that no one may buy or sell except one who has the mark or the name of the Beast, or the number of his name."

"Go away! You're not wanted here," shouted someone else.

He then declared Daniel 9:27 aloud, "He will confirm a covenant with many for one 'seven.' In the middle of the 'seven' he will put an end to sacrifice and offering. And at the temple he will set up an abomination that causes desolation, until the end that is decreed is poured out on him.'"

"Leave us alone!" shouted another pilgrim.

He then declared Daniel 11:31 aloud, "His armed forces will rise up to desecrate the temple fortress and will abolish the daily sacrifice. Then they will set up the abomination that causes desolation.'"

"How dare you threaten us like that!" yelled someone else.

Finally, he declared Matthew 24:15-21 aloud, "So when you see standing in the holy place 'the abomination that causes desolation,' spoken of through the prophet Daniel—let the reader understand—then let those who are in Judea flee to the mountains. Let no one on the housetop go down to take anything out of the house. Let no one in the field go back to get their cloak. How dreadful it will be in those days for pregnant women and nursing mothers! Pray that your flight will not take place in winter or on the Sabbath. For then there will be great distress, unequaled from the beginning of the world until now—and never to be equaled again."

Yet, despite these eternal warnings, multitudes ignored him, cursed him, or simply blinked him away. Their sole purpose for being there had nothing to do with this detractor, and everything to do with bowing down to the statue in praise and worship.

Benjamin lamented in his spirit for the countless doomed souls praying to the statue. But praying for their salvation now would be fruitless.

At any rate, the fact that he was still walking the streets, and not in handcuffs, forced even more questions to the forefront of his mind.

Even if the microfliers kept melting in the unrelenting heat, as it had been widely rumored, all it would take would be for one phone with the facial recognition app on it to record his voice or capture his image, and he would be identified.

Then there were the six armed guards staring at him outside the airport terminal, the suspicious looks he received from the man who drove him there, and the scores of security cameras at the airport.

With all these factors working against him, it seemed implausible that he hadn't been spotted by one of them by now, impossible really. So, why hadn't it happened?

For someone who was the most wanted human being on the planet, everything was going too smoothly. What were the odds?

It very much reminded him of Vishnu Uddin's experience, when the cargo container ship worker from Bangladesh, smuggled Hana Patel,

Yasamin Dabiri, and their two children all the way from Singapore to the United States, seemingly with the slightest of ease.

After Uddin shared his harrowing account with him, Benjamin knew his assumptions were spot on. He assured Vishu that day that Romanero no doubt gave the order to let the four of them travel safely to the States, hoping to catch many other big fish in the process, himself included.

That's precisely how it felt for Benjamin now, like his former boss knew he was in Jerusalem. He knew someone was watching him. He could feel it. Senses on full alert, if this ended up being his final mission on Earth, he didn't want to fail. He couldn't fail!

36

IT DIDN'T TAKE BENJAMIN long to find his brother a short distance away from the Western Wall area, fiercely debating one of Yahweh's sealed servants, with his two best friends, and fellow rabbis, Yosef and Tobias. All three had full beards, and they wore traditional clerical robes.

Benjamin frowned, listening to his brother berate the young man, "You say Yahweh's supernaturally protecting you. Ha! Whatever protection you have, I assure you it doesn't come from the God we serve. Your Two predecessors made that very same claim before they were slain! Why don't you come out from underneath this so-called shield of protection you appear to have, and speak to us man to man, where we can all be on a level playing field?!"

The young preacher named Jeroham replied, "You are right to say we don't serve the same God. If you *were* being protected by Yahweh, that would put us on the same playing field. But clearly, we're not."

"Blasphemy!" Yosef shouted at the top of his lungs. His face was already red from the sweltering heat, now it burned with a deeper shade of anger. As a lifelong student of the Torah and the Book of the Prophets, he couldn't handle being disrespected from someone a third his age.

Seth barked furiously at him, "Whatever shield of protection you have comes from the darkest and most evil of places. You're being demonically protected, just like they were!"

Benjamin was deeply troubled by the hatred his brother had just spewed at the young man. Finally, he said, "Shalom, Seth!"

Benjamin? Seth's eyes bulged seeing it was his brother. Was the heat causing him to hallucinate? He surveyed the area hoping they weren't being monitored by global community officials. "What are you doing here? If someone spots you, or scans you with their mobile devices, they'll kill you! You shouldn't have come here."

Benjamin shrugged. "True, but if my being here leads to the conversion of your soul, whatever happens to me will be well worth it."

Seth flinched hearing this. He gritted his teeth. "Please don't insult me in front of my friends!"

"I'm not here to insult or embarrass you, Seth. I came all this way hoping that you'll escape Yahweh's coming judgment!"

Seth flinched at his brother's arrogance, then glanced at his fellow rabbis, who were equally perturbed, incensed was more like it. They were also fearful of possibly being linked to Salvador Romanero's former physician, before he lost his mind. The more he spoke, the more convinced they became that the rumors were true after all.

Jeroham listened to the exchange in silence.

Seth grabbed Benjamin's right arm and practically dragged him away from Yosef and Tobias. Once they were alone, he said in a whisper shout, "Imagine that, my younger brother, a staunch atheist all his life, wants to redirect my spiritual compass!"

"I know how crazy it sounds. A few months ago, I would have laughed at the notion of trying to teach you anything religious. You know how vehemently I rejected it in the past. But now that I've been awakened spiritually, mostly thanks to Jakob, the changes you see in me are real."

Seth grimaced at the mention of his son's name, then glared more angrily at Benjamin. The disguise he wore did little to cover up his recognizable facial features. At least he wasn't wearing that pathetic toupee now. *See, we're both bald after all!*

Another major change Seth noticed in his wayward brother was, whereas Benjamin had always exuded a strong, even arrogant, character, he looked weak now, passive, indecisive, surely someone lacking the leadership qualities he once possessed in mass quantities.

Then again, the same could be said about Seth himself. The only difference was that he kept trying to project those characteristics when out in public, by remaining defiantly vocal against Romanero.

But his body quaked most nights as he tried sleeping. Not even his wife could calm the deep stirring in his soul.

Seth surveyed the area again. "Why would you come here and add more trouble to my life? Don't you realize what they'll do to me, if they see us together? I'm already on thin ice. I don't deserve this!"

Benjamin's eyes remained focused on his spiritually lost brother. He repivoted, "You know how greedy and tight fisted I was. You also know how much I loved my position and status in life. This includes my castle in New Babylon. If you're wondering if I'm jealous or envious that the other Benjamin now occupies it, I'm not.

"I didn't lose those things, Seth, I walked away from them. When I was finally awakened spiritually, the many material things I'd accumulated over the years suddenly meant nothing to me. Those temporal things can never come close to the satisfaction and contentment I feel just knowing I belong to Yahweh."

Seth nervously surveyed the area again, then demanded to know, "What's your point with all of this, Benjamin?"

"Look at me now! I have nothing! I'm an international fugitive, number one on Romanero's Top Ten Most Wanted list, in fact. That's how convinced I am that my former boss is the Antichrist of the Bible.

"When I went into hiding, I sent an urgent e-mail to everyone on his staff, who survived the Jerusalem quake, hoping to reveal Romanero's true identity to them.

"Don't you find it a little strange that Yahweh sent the quake three and a half days after the Two Witnesses were assassinated, which delayed the New Temple dedication?"

When Seth didn't answer the question, he couldn't, Benjamin went on, "Yahweh was shaking the city to wake His chosen people. The fact that so many Jews are going into hiding is proof of this.

"For the record, all of this was prophesied more than two thousand years ago. I'm sure you know on the day he was assassinated, then resurrected, I was supposed to join them and give a speech detailing the countless benefits the microchip will offer to all who take it into their bodies."

Benjamin glanced over at Yosef and Tobias. The scowls on their faces were aimed at him.

He blinked them both away, and continued, "As the chief engineer, I can state with certainty that everyone who has it injected will surely experience multiple health benefits. But those benefits will be extremely short-lived. Three years from now, no one who takes it will be alive to enjoy whatever health benefits they receive."

Benjamin slumped. "Romanero and the Pope may not force anyone to take it, but he's made it impossible to function in his New World System without it. Even so, regardless of what benefit those taking it wish to receive, whether it be wanting better health, putting food on the table, or anything in between, it will be a willful decision on their part."

Seth was annoyed hearing this. He shook his head incredulously. "Duh!"

Benjamin thought to himself, *When the dust of your spiritual ignorance settles...if it settles!* He searched the area again for anything out of the ordinary, and went on, "I know you already know this. But what you may not know is that the Word of God describes it as the Mark of the Beast, in the New Testament."

Seth shook his head defiantly, then gritted his teeth in anger. *New Testament, Ha!* "So, let me get this straight. You traveled all the way from America, as the planet's most wanted fugitive, to tell me that I had it wrong all along and the Christians had it right. And you expect me to think you're in your right mind, Benjamin?"

The way he said it was almost comical. "I don't blame you for thinking that way, Seth. While it's true that we Jews are Yahweh's chosen people, only those who come to Him in faith and repentance will be saved. What I'm trying to say, brother, is being a Jew isn't enough to save you! You must be born again! Until you experience true conversion for yourself, it's unexplainable."

Seth had proudly and joyfully converted a handful of Gentiles to Judaism in the past. But he couldn't fathom the notion of Jews ever converting to Christianity.

Benjamin once again surveyed the area, hoping no one was on to them, but always sensing that they were. "I've had the great privilege of living with many Gentile believers. The love they have for the Jews is real and genuine. That's because we serve the same God. They are dear friends and wonderful people.

"My only hope is that you won't let your pride be your downfall. Open your heart to the scriptures, all of them, including what's written in the New Testament. If you'll only do that, you'll come to see that Jakob was right all along."

Seth flinched again at the mention of his son's name.

Benjamin noticed, and kept going, "You'll also discover that Jakob really is one of Yahweh's one hundred and forty four thousand sealed servants. The protection they have, that you just called evil to the young man over there, really does come from above.

"Have you ever wondered how your son can materialize from A to B, in the blink of an eye? I experienced it firsthand when we first met on a park bench not too far from my house, which led to my spiritual conversion. One moment he was there, then poof, he was gone. Who else on the planet can do that? I assure you it's not from his own power. Only Yahweh can orchestrate something so remarkable.

"Whether you choose to believe it or not, as one of Yahweh's sealed servants, Jakob is fully protected from Antichrist and the False Prophet, just like his Two predecessors were, before they were slain. This was also recorded in the book of Revelation, two thousand years ago."

Seth raised his hands in objection. He wanted to say something, but it was like his tongue was tied.

Benjamin went on, "You know how defiant I was to all of this, before I started having dreams about your son. But the more Jakob spoke to me, the more the scales kept falling from my eyes."

Finally, Seth found his voice. He asked, "Is Jakob in America now?"

Benjamin nodded yes. "When he handed me a copy of Yahweh's Word, to back up everything he was saying, I went from being spiritually blinded to suddenly understanding what was written in those divinely inspired pages."

A glow formed on his face. "It was a remarkable transformation. One thing I realized by reading it was that I was gaining the whole world, at the peril of my soul. After repenting of my sinful lifestyle, and trusting in Yeshua as Lord and Messiah, my life has never been the same."

Seth glared at his brother. "Duh!"

Benjamin brushed aside his brother's sarcasm. "I meant it in a good way." He pointed at the scar on Seth's left forearm. "I also have scars on my body from the locust attack nearly two years ago. But I can honestly say that once I was converted, they stopped stinging me.

"Truth be told, the only reason you don't have those hideous sores that so many in the world now have covering their bodies, is because you haven't taken the mark yet. You may not hear about it in the news, but only those taking the mark have them."

Seth scoffed at his brother, "Yet?! Believe me, Benjamin, I'll never take it! With or without the sores, I'd rather starve to death!"

"That may be so, but even if you reject it, and you're forced into hiding as a result, you'll be doing it for all the wrong reasons. You may overcome the mark, but unless you repent of your sins and trust in Yeshua alone for your salvation, you won't escape Yahweh's coming judgment! You will be eternally doomed just like the others."

Even though it was uttered softly, and lovingly, Seth's face became full of rage. He raised his left fist in the air to rebuke his fugitive brother. "I know what the Torah teaches, Benjamin, I've studied it all my life. I know it far better than you could ever hope to…"

"That may be true, but Yahweh's salvation has nothing to do with your belief that you're in good standing with your Maker. I assure you

you're not! Please don't think I'm being arrogant like I was in the past regarding this topic. I was blind back then, but now I see. So, I say it out of pure concern for your spiritual well-being.

"The book of the Law, the book of Prophets, and the book of Psalms and Proverbs, comprise only a small portion of the Word of God. Yet, every prophecy you've studied in those Books all your life, pertaining to the future Messiah, all point to Yeshua, and only to Him! Yes, Yeshua is Israel's Messiah, even though our people rejected Him and killed Him."

Seth barked at Benjamin, "How dare you! I've dedicated my whole life to serving Yahweh!"

"Yes, you have, but Yeshua said that those who don't know Him do not know the Father who sent Him. So, by rejecting Yeshua, it means you don't really know the One you serve."

Benjamin paused, then said, "I must say, your life reminds me a lot of the life of Saul of…"

Seth's face reddened hearing this. "I remind you of King Saul?!"

"Not King Saul. Saul of Tarsus."

Oh, no, you didn't just go there! Seth couldn't comprehend that his brother would make such a harsh accusation. He was deeply offended by it. He glanced over at Yosef to Tobias. Had they heard it, Yosef, especially, would already be in Benjamin's face.

In many Jewish circles, Saul of Tarsus was hated even more than Yeshua, for creating a new religion that worshipped Yeshua not only as Messiah, but also as God Himself. He was yet another reason most Jews were forbidden from reading the New Testament.

Benjamin noticed the angry glare on his brother's face, but it didn't deter him. "Saul was one of the greatest Messianic believers to ever roam the earth. He wrote most of the New Testament, in fact."

When Seth opened his mouth to protest, Benjamin held up his pointer finger, signifying that he wasn't finished making his point. "Before Saul's conversion, his life very much resembled yours. The reason you've never heard about him is that you've never read the complete Word of God, including the New Testament."

"Believe me, Benjamin, I've heard of him…"

"Are you even aware that Yahweh's using this time of tribulation to gather His remnant? Surely, you must be familiar with Isaiah ten, verses twenty through twenty-three, and with Zechariah thirteen, verses eight and nine. These prophecies are being fulfilled before our very eyes, along with many others."

Seth was astounded. It was the first time Benjamin had ever quoted scripture to him. It freaked him out. It was time to put this mostly one-sided conversation to an end. He took an anxious breath, cleared his throat, then asked his brother, "When do you plan on going back to the States, and how will you get there?"

"I'm not going back. When I left there, I knew it was for good."

Seth shot a sideways look at Benjamin. "Where will you stay? Sorry, but you can't stay with us!" He waited to see if anger would surface on his brother's face, like it always did when they had disagreements in the past. But it didn't happen. He added, "Besides, we have no food or water."

Benjamin nodded that he understood. "I had no intention of staying with you. I wouldn't last a single day at your residence. If I survive the day, I'll figure it out. Just knowing I'm part of Yahweh's remnant tells me that I'll be fine no matter what happens." He sighed. "I just pray that you are, too."

"That I'm what?" asked Seth angrily.

"One of Yahweh's remnant. It would be in your best interest to carefully search everything I'm telling you in the Scriptures. If only you'll do that, you'll come to realize everything Jakob tried telling you before you disowned him, was one hundred percent true."

Seth remained defiant. "And you risked your life to travel all this way to tell me this!"

Benjamin lowered his head and started weeping. "I know we never got along. We're always at each other's throats. We're both stubborn and opinionated. I'm no longer interested in winning arguments with you, Seth. All I care about winning is your soul to Yeshua."

He stared at his brother affectionately. "I love you, and I don't want your soul to end up in Hades, separated from Yahweh. You've dedicated your whole life to the service of the Lord. Unfortunately, you weren't plugged in to the proper Source. Which is why I plead with you to check what I'm telling you, because it's all true."

He loves me? Seth blinked hard a few times. He hadn't heard those three words coming from his brother in decades. He was shocked to say the least! Either Benjamin had turned into a very good actor, or he really was a changed man. But was it for the better? Or was he among the masses having serious mental illness issues.

Seth was suddenly unsure…

37

AS IT TURNED OUT, Benjamin Shapiro's suspicion that Salvador Romanero was on to him was spot on. Not only was his former boss mindful of his present whereabouts, he was listening very intently to the conversation between them.

He also heard the recorded conversation between the man who drove Shapiro from the cargo area to the ARRIVALS area, and about the Rolex watch he received for giving him a ride. And every word spoken with the driver who took him to the New Temple was also recorded.

To observe this level of disloyalty coming from his former physician sickened him to no end. But knowing what would soon become of him, as eager as the six guards at the airport were to detain him, the order was given to stand down and observe only.

Romanero wanted to let it play out and see where it all might lead. In short, it was only because of him that Benjamin Shapiro was still alive. There wasn't a chance that he would hand this assignment off to anyone else. It was too personal.

The Supreme See didn't know whether Seth Shapiro would eventually cross over and take the mark, or if he would remain defiant like the numerous rabbis who had fully supported him and the Pope, before the Temple was completed. The fact that he didn't know should have nullified his new title as the supreme seer of all things.

With dozens of armed guards monitoring them both very closely, if either brother aspired to join the millions of Jews fleeing the area, it would never happen. Any chance of escape would be quickly squashed.

Once all global networks were alerted about what was about to happen at the Western Wall, the caption, BIG NEWS COMING SOON FROM JERUSALEM flooded every phone screen on the planet.

In truth, Romanero didn't need to alert the media. Once he gave the signal, everyone would receive push alerts. He did it to further sensationalize the story.

It was then that Romanero gave the order for Benjamin Shapiro to be detained at gunpoint. "Place your hands above your head, Doctor Shapiro, you're under arrest!"

Benjamin did as he was told without putting up a fight. He knew if he went quietly, he would be taken to one of Romanero's death camps, in Jerusalem, then tortured mercilessly.

With that sobering truth settled in his mind, he slowly removed his mirrored sunglasses, followed by his disguise, but without ever taking his eyes off the two armed guards with their automatic weapons pointed at him. The reason he did it was that he wanted everyone to know it really was him, thus preventing conspiracy theories from surfacing.

Now that his former boss was on to him, the media had no doubt been alerted. Benjamin needed to take full advantage of the situation. He thought about when Hans Greinhold stripped down to his underwear, to show his brothers and sisters in chains, and the millions of viewers streaming online, that he hadn't been stung by the demonic locusts.

Before Greinhold's hands and neck were tightly secured in the stocks, he explained to everyone the reason he hadn't been stung by them was because of his faith in Jesus.

Moments before the guillotine blade separated his head from the rest of his body, he got to share the Gospel with everyone. The result of his stark bravery was that God had used his testimony to win multitudes of souls. That's what Benjamin hoped to achieve now.

What made this opportunity potentially better was, whereas Greinhold had millions of viewers watching it live on their phones, the new global push system would ensure that more than a billion would get to watch what he would say, whether they wanted to or not.

With his disguise completely removed, Seth's fear was taken to a whole new level when his brother started shouting at the top of his lungs, "Salvador Romanero isn't a savior! He represents Satan himself! He doesn't love the Jewish people. His promise of peace and protection is nothing but a lie.

"When he first came to power, he told us the reason he exterminated the Muslims was so we Jews could once again sacrifice to our God, without persecution. Like every other promise he made to the Jews, it was pure deception on his part. I was part of his cabinet back then, so I should know."

Seth became increasingly fearful for his safety. He glared at one of the guards and opened his mouth to speak, but no words came out.

Benjamin went on, "After that, as part of a three-pronged approach, Romanero went after Christians next. I don't need to remind any of you about the atrocities that were committed against them. But don't be deceived, even while he worked tirelessly to silence those two religions, his eye was always on destroying Israel and everything we Jews hold so dearly. Man of peace? Seriously?

"My nephew, Jakob, who is one of His sealed servants, told me it was a systematic approach. The only way Antichrist can be wholly worshiped in Jerusalem, as Israel's true king, would be for those three religions to be forever silenced.

"Now that two of them have essentially been wiped out, his focus now is to exterminate the Jews next. For the first three and a half years since he came to power, Romanero was the clear leader of the world. But he was never recognized as the ruler of Israel until now...

"The fact that the Antichrist of the Bible has defiled the very Temple he promised would be for the Jews, should confirm to you that he doesn't care about our religion. The only thing he wants is to be worshiped, nothing else!

"Make no mistake: the only Jews who will survive in Romanero's system, are those who take his mark and worship him. Those who do that must also forsake Judaism in favor of his global religion. The rest will be put to death, just like the countless Muslims and Christians.

"The hundreds of thousands of Jews who are fleeing their homes are part of Yahweh's remnant. He's using this time to pull them away from Antichrist, as was recorded in His Holy Word thousands of years ago..."

Shapiro pleaded with everyone watching and listening, which he hoped was in the tens of millions. "I can't stress this point enough, Jew or Gentile, if you take the mark, you will surely perish within the next three years. Not only does the Word of God definitively prove that Yeshua was Who He said He was, the Savior of the World, but it equally proves that Romanero is the Antichrist. Believe me, I know."

Seth trembled in fear, as his brother kept ranting against his former boss. His features became more subdued, more unreadable, as he tried piecing this unbelievable situation together in his already blown mind.

He was surprised that the two soldiers pointing their automatic weapons at his brother—one at his head, the other at his heart—hadn't shot him dead yet. But since he was a high-profile dissident, they were merely waiting for further orders to be given, on what to do with him.

Benjamin glanced at his brother. "Since you don't have access to a Bible, you have no way of confirming for yourself that Romanero really is the Antichrist of that blessed Book. That's why he outlawed the Word of God in the first place."

Benjamin knew his time was growing short. It was time to make one final plea. "To my ex-wife and children. If you're watching, and I pray you are, as far-fetched as this may sound to you, it would be in your best interest to obtain a copy of The Way from one of Yahweh's one hundred and forty four thousand sealed servants, in your area, then carefully search everything I'm saying in the Scriptures.

"Did you know our nephew Jakob is one of them? It's true. So, even if you still hate me, don't do it for me, do it for yourselves. By so doing, you'll discover for yourselves that Salvador Romanero really is the great deceiver of souls…"

That was the final straw. Romanero could no longer take it.

Benjamin noticed one of the gunmen straining hard to hear the order being given in his earpiece. "Arrest him now and have him brought here to New Babylon, so I can deal with him personally. But leave his brother alone for now."

The order couldn't have come at a better time. With the sun slowly rising, it would soon resume spitting its fire down on all mark takers.

Benjamin heard him relay the order to his counterpart. Visions of what Salvador did to Prince Javier from Spain, when he first came to power, invaded his brain. He was there when the order was given for his execution, by way of guillotine, in front of a full capacity crowd at a colosseum in Spain, as the whole world watched. *No doubt he'll want to publicly humiliate me too!*

Benjamin pleaded with the guard, "Please let my brother go. I'm the one you want. He had no idea that I was coming here to meet him. It was all my idea."

The other guard growled, "Your brother has yet to take the mark."

Benjamin replied, "Just because he hasn't received it doesn't mean he won't. I just pray for his sake that he doesn't." Benjamin glanced at Seth compassionately, then added, "If he does, his soul will be sent to Hades for all eternity, just like the two of you. But if you kill me, I'll go to be with Yeshua, in Paradise, to be forever comforted. It's a promise to all His dying saints! It's a Place where Salvador Romanero and his millions of followers will never step foot.

"Romanero is no giver of life, only a taker of it! Even his claim that he was responsible for children repopulating the planet was a lie. Just so everyone knows, Hana Patel was already expecting before the contest was announced. Many women were, in fact. This is yet another proof that my former boss is a counterfeit savior, a fake.

"I do wish to thank him, however, for the many medicines I was able to redirect in the global database, to locations he will never find no matter how many troops he sends out searching for them. The medicine was greatly needed during the global flu outbreak. Many who will never bow down to you in worship were cured as a result.

"Quoting from Genesis chapter fifty, verse twenty, in the Book he banned the whole world from reading, it states, 'As for you, you meant evil against me, but God meant it for good, to bring it about that many people should be kept alive, as they are today.' Apparently, this even applies to the Antichrist of the Bible..."

Romanero seethed betrayal by his former doctor. His words burned his soul as if being seared by a hot iron. He barked out new orders, "Don't bring him to New Babylon! Kill him now!"

Ah, the command they had hoped for all along. With the green light officially given, they nodded at each other, then squeezed on the triggers, firing several shots into Shapiro's head and chest.

There was no flailing of the arms. It happened too quickly for that reaction. Benjamin fell hard to the surface, in a pool of blood that kept expanding with each passing second.

Seth's eyes widened with fear. "No!"

The man glared angrily at the rabbi. His gaze drilled into him. His expression was hard, unrelenting, dangerous. "You should be thanking us! Your brother no longer suffers from mental illness. At least he's out of his misery now."

Without a shred of compassion, the other soldier pointed to the slain body on the cement. "Don't end up like him. Take the mark!"

At that, the two soldiers left him there to mourn the loss of his slain brother. They left with their heads held high. Nothing on the planet came close to giving them the feeling of taking the lives of others, without repercussions. The fact that they would both be celebrated for killing Romanero's top dissident made it even better.

THE APOSTLE PAUL WROTE in 2 Corinthians 5:8, about being absent from the body and present with the Lord.

Benjamin Shapiro was living proof of this most blessed assurance. Because of what Yeshua did for him on the cross, his ascension to Heaven happened in the twinkling of an eye.

The former personal physician for the Antichrist of the Bible, left Planet Earth with a full expectation of going to Paradise.

For that reason alone, he wasn't afraid of dying. Before the gunmen pulled the trigger, he wholeheartedly believed that when he closed his eyes for the last time in Israel, the next time they would open, he would be with the Lord. That's precisely what happened.

Nothing on the Planet from which he had just been evacuated, could compare to the perfect peace he felt being in the presence of his glorious Savior. The intense pain he would have felt had he survived the shooting back on Earth, was not allowed where he was.

To feel the embrace of the One who died for his sins was too wonderful to tell. After being perfectly welcomed Home by the King of kings and Lord of lords, Benjamin was reunited with his brothers in the faith, who left the planet before he did—Clayton Holmes, Travis Hartings, Lee Kim, Brian Mulrooney, and Tom Dunleavey.

But that reunion couldn't compare to seeing Jack Nelson there. They instantly recognized each other. It was a glorious reunion.

The expression on Jack's face conveyed to him just how grateful he was that God had used the man he was hired to protect to save his soul.

When Benjamin left his former security guard a copy of *The Way*, before fleeing his prestigious life and going into hiding, he wasn't sure at the time as to why he had personally inscribed the book to a man he didn't even know.

The joy he felt knowing Yahweh had used him to win Jack Nelson to Him, could never be properly conveyed to anyone back on Planet Earth. He wanted to shout at the top of his lungs to all of Heaven's blessed inhabitants, "I won this man to Yeshua!" not out of pride or arrogance, but because he now understood the magnitude of the value of his soul.

Had he been able to shed tears, he would have. But there were no tears in Glory.

But Benjamin didn't have to utter a single word. It was already recorded in heaven's memory, where nothing would be overlooked or forgotten, including the numerous salvations that would soon come from his efforts in Jerusalem, leading up to his death as a martyr.

While his Redeemer would receive all the praise, honor and glory, each new convert would be eternally cherished like a personal treasure to him.

Jack Nelson had just offered him a precursor of what was still to come. Even better, both would return to Planet Earth to be priests of God and of Christ, and would reign with Him a thousand years.

And what could be better than that?

38

SETH SHAPIRO LEFT THE Western Wall with a deep sadness in his heart. The place he loved going to more than any other in Jerusalem, since relocating his family to Israel, nearly two decades ago, had just become a Wailing Wall to him, like it had for so many Jews over the past 2,000 years.

The shock and pain in his heart from witnessing his younger brother being assassinated was so strong, he was surprised he could walk at all. He practically dragged himself home, crying most of the way.

Before the whole world went crazy, Seth enjoyed walking to the Western Wall each day, to meet with Yosef and Tobias, and engaging in fierce debates with the Two deranged Witnesses, before they were killed.

Once those Two were out of the way, their wrath was then directed at the young Jewish preachers. He thought it slightly ironic that his only brother was shot dead not too far away from where they were slain.

Walking there each day was part of Seth's daily exercise. By not having the mark displayed on his right hand or forehead, even if he wanted to drive there, he had no choice but to walk.

The only thing that changed in his daily ritual was that he usually met Yosef and Tobias in the afternoon. It was too hot for that now.

Seth arrived home deeply grieved, and with a splitting headache.

Naveh was waiting for him at the front door. What he saw on his wife's face told him she knew what happened. Apparently, she took advantage of the final day of free Wi-Fi, before it was shut down again and made available only to mark takers.

Seth collapsed on the living room sofa. "Benjamin told me he loved me. I should have lowered my guard and told him I loved him too. Now I can't. He's gone. He was delusional, but he was my only brother."

Naveh held her husband as he wept uncontrollably. This time he didn't stop. He couldn't. Part of her dress became soaked with his tears.

After a while, Seth went to his study to read the two scriptures that Benjamin had mentioned to him.

He read Isaiah 10:20-23 first. "In that day the remnant of Israel, the survivors of Jacob, will no longer rely on him who struck them down but will truly rely on the LORD, the Holy One of Israel. A remnant will return, a remnant of Jacob will return to the Mighty God.

"Though your people be like the sand by the sea, Israel, only a remnant will return. Destruction has been decreed, overwhelming and righteous. The Lord, the LORD Almighty, will carry out the destruction decreed upon the whole land."

Seth took a moment to meditate on this familiar verse, then flipped to Zechariah chapter 13, and read verses 8 and 9. "'In the whole land,' declares the LORD, 'two-thirds will be struck down and perish; yet one-third will be left in it. This third I will put into the fire; I will refine them like silver and test them like gold. They will call on my name and I will answer them; I will say, 'They are my people,' and they will say, 'The LORD is our God.'"

Seth scratched his throbbing head in confusion. He was more blown away by his brother's spiritual transformation than he was with his own son's. Jakob already had a spiritual foundation in place. Benjamin didn't. *Suddenly, he's quoting the scriptures to me?*

Seth thought about his late father, Chaim, and his grandfather, Ehud. Both were solid religious leaders who had dedicated their whole lives in the service of the Lord. Were they in Heaven now?

Had he posed this question to Yosef and Tobias, both would have answered him with a resounding yes.

But had he asked the same question about Benjamin, they would have laughed in his face, and told him to get serious. On the surface, they would be right. Whereas Seth proudly fell in line and became a rabbi himself, to keep the familial lineage in check, Benjamin chose the field of medicine. He also chose atheism.

Yet, the confidence he had in his own salvation wasn't prideful or arrogant. Those character traits never surfaced. If anything, he was genuine and sincere. These were emotions Benjamin never had the capacity to display toward anyone in the past. *He told me he loved me...*

Seth thought about what the Lord said, in 1 Samuel 16:7, "For *the LORD does* not *see* as man sees; for man looks at the outward appearance, but the LORD looks at the heart."

To see his brother's life so radically transformed was nothing short of astounding. Was he in Heaven now? Had Seth just witnessed the Lord's salvation in his brother, like he kept insisting? Or had he been brainwashed like everyone else belonging to that religious cult?

Seth didn't know how to answer these questions. But Benjamin was right on one thing. He didn't lose the many material things he had worked so hard to obtain. He really did walk away from it all, just like he had said. *That had to count for something, right?*

CARMEN ESPINOSA WATCHED IT all unfolding at the Ortiz residence, with Roberto and Bonita. She spent most days with them, not wanting to be alone. She even slept there on occasion.

When Benjamin Shapiro repeated what Raul had told her, about anyone taking the mark not being around three years from now to enjoy its benefits, she screamed at the top of her lungs, then tossed her half empty teacup against one of the living room walls, shattering it into many pieces. She wanted to throw it at the television, but it wasn't hers to break. "Sorry for that."

Roberto waved off her apology. If anything, she beat him to it. Just hearing that deranged man telling his brother Seth the only reason he didn't have those hideous sores on his body, was because he hadn't taken the mark yet, felt like acid being poured on his body.

It confirmed what Roberto had suspected all along. Even his three children had sores covering their bodies. He silently wished they could all un-take the mark he was so proud of at the outset. But it was irreversible.

"What kind of a life is this?" Carmen bellowed. "How can it be that Raul has lung cancer, yet we're suffering more than he is?" Much of the pain and anger she felt in her heart, from being separated from her husband and daughter, was replaced with an emotion she never thought she could have the capacity to show toward them—sheer hatred.

Roberto and Bonita lowered their heads remorsefully.

When they were notified on their cell phones to expect big news coming from Israel, their hope was that a new breakthrough drug or vaccine would soon be available, to help reduce the pain everyone felt from these lingering sores. That news never came...

The pain they felt from the locust stings, two years ago, while excruciating, eventually went away. Only the scars remained.

These sores weren't going away. And the pain kept worsening. Only mark takers couldn't express their anger online, or in the news, even though they were suffering in constant agony. In the medical profession, pain management was at an all-time high!

Many who couldn't gain access to morphine, were now jabbing needles full of heroin into their veins, hoping to take away the pain, including those who had never used drugs before.

The one thing Roberto and Bonita had always enjoyed doing, in their more than five decades of marriage, was to sit on the front porch together, before lunch and after dinner.

Now they wouldn't dare expose themselves to the sun for even a second. The shades were always drawn during daylight hours, so they wouldn't be scorched by the sun's dangerous rays, like ants being burned alive beneath huge magnifying glasses, from even inside the house!

This was yet another freedom that was stripped away from the couple in these bizarre times. It caused them both to hate the God of Israel and the Jewish race even more. Like all others taking the mark of the Beast, it was as if their bodies and minds had been supernaturally rewired.

One of the biggest changes in them was that they now hated the nation of Israel. Both had always been staunch supporters of the tiny nation. Now it was if they had been transformed into anti-Semites.

Yet, Roberto still ended every prayer in Jesus' name. They didn't know it yet, but praying in that Name wasn't doing them any good on this side of the grave. Nor would it do them an ounce of good on the other side...

VICKY NELSON WATCHED EVERYTHING unfolding in Israel, with her two children, Liam and Laura.

Like all other mark takers on the planet, the three of them were in agony. Just hearing the man her husband was hired to protect spewing his nonsensical preaching for all to hear, sickened her even more.

The hatred she felt for Benjamin Shapiro couldn't be measured in human terms. She screamed at the TV, "I'm glad they killed you! You brainwashed my husband and ruined my marriage! You destroyed my family! If I had a gun, I would've done it myself! You're nothing but a worthless piece of garbage! I hope you rot in hell for what you did!"

As the days passed, Vicky was slowly but surely losing control of her mental faculties. The psychiatric meds she was taking stopped working on the day she refilled her prescriptions, after receiving the mark. The constant pain from the sores on her body caused too much anguish for the meds to work effectively.

Liam and Laura weren't doing much better themselves. Like everyone else on the planet, whose bodies were covered with sores, they were hoping to hear that a remedy had been discovered. It never came.

With the internet deadline now upon them, the two no longer resembled the attractive teenagers they had always been. Nor did they look healthy. They looked like zombies.

Liam and Laura were in no danger of losing their internet service at the end of the day. But the way they both felt now, they would gladly trade it just to rid their bodies of the painful sores on their bodies.

Tragically for them, their condition would never improve. Even if they didn't know it yet, they had traded their souls for what they were now suffering…

THE MAN WHO DROVE Benjamin Shapiro from Ben Gurion International Airport to the new Temple, watched it all unfolding on his mobile phone screen.

Like everyone else on the planet, he received an urgent push alert on his mobile phone mere seconds before it happened.

He couldn't believe what his eyes were seeing. *Benjamin Shapiro?* "How fortunate for me that that traitor was in my vehicle!"

Nor could he believe his sudden good fortune when he was notified that his global account had just been credited with one million dollars!

He pounded the steering wheel excitedly. "Just like that, I'm a millionaire! This really is my lucky day!" In his wildest dreams, he figured his reward might be in the $50K range at most.

It didn't take long before his mobile device started blowing up with text messages, from news outlets eager to interview him.

He ultimately chose a young woman from Greece for the phone interview, because of how hot she was. If he could see the same Herpes-like sores on her body that he had, he might think otherwise.

Had it not been for their repulsive skin conditions, he would have been flown to Greece and interviewed in front of a live audience. But with no way of covering them up, it had to be done over the phone.

Before the interview began, her producer cautioned him not to mention anything about the sores. Said he, "It needs to be positive and upbeat at all times."

When the driver agreed to the terms, the interview began.

"How does it feel to suddenly being celebrated as an international hero?" asked the female journalist, enthusiastically.

"Like I'm living the dream…" He looked in the rearview mirror, as another sore appeared on his left cheek. He winced in pain, thankful that no one listening to the live interview could see him. He gripped the steering wheel so tightly his knuckles were bone white.

The woman giggled into the receiver. "So, what are your thoughts on the mark?"

The man smiled into the phone, despite the pain. "Let me put it this way, before I received it, I was jobless and penniless. Now I'm a millionaire! How do you think I feel about it? Take it from me, the future's bright for all who take the mark and become part of the new global system. I see nothing but prosperity from here on out!"

The woman smiled glowingly in return. "I know what you mean. Why would anyone not want it? What sense does that make?"

"Two words—mental illness. I didn't know the man in my car was Benjamin Shapiro. All I knew was that he wasn't well. He told me the reason why he waited so long to take the mark was…" He stopped. He wasn't allowed to mention anything about the sores. "Anyway, serves that lunatic right!

"You did a good thing today," the Greek journalist declared. "Enjoy your newfound success."

"Thanks," came the reply. At that, the phone interview ended. He glanced in the rearview mirror. The new lesion on his left cheek kept growing. He went into another rage, hissing at the image staring back at him. *Now that I'm a millionaire, I'll find a way to get rid of this pain!*

AFTER WATCHING THE INTERVIEW, the man who drove Benjamin Shapiro from the cargo area to the ARRIVALS area at Ben Gurion Airport, contacted the media, hoping it would lead to a huge payoff for him as well. Maybe not a million dollars, but even a hundred thousand would be welcomed. After all, he was part of the equation.

He thought wrong. As it turned out, his exchange with the disguise-wearing man who turned out to be none other than Benjamin Shapiro, was captured on three different security cameras surveilling the outside of the airport. Much like the six guards stationed there, authorities were told not to arrest him until the order was given.

He was sentenced to six months in prison for his vile crimes. He was also fired from his job, for transporting a dissident in a company vehicle. Even the Rolex he received from Shapiro was confiscated.

He wasn't the only one…

Tanya, the woman who worked for the cargo shipping company, in Baltimore, Maryland was also arrested, for her part in the diabolical scheme to smuggle the planet's most wanted dissident to Jerusalem.

She was likewise terminated from her job and sentenced to six months in jail. Had it been anyone other than Benjamin Shapiro inside that crate, she surely would have gotten away with it.

Tanya called her brother, Eugene, on the phone, and went off on him. "You're responsible for all this! I can't believe I let you talk me into it. I never want to speak to you again! We're no longer siblings!"

Eugene had never heard this level of venomous anger in his sister's voice before. But Tanya was right. He was responsible for losing her job, and for her incarceration, for working out the deal with Shamus Harmon and Tony Pearsall.

This devastated him. But seeing how radically changed his sister was, it further cemented his decision never to take the mark. Suddenly, something went off inside his heart, that kept pushing him toward the book that was given to him by Tony Pearsall and Shamus Harmon…

TITUS RETURNED TO THE Kennett Square safe house with a recording of everything that had transpired in Jerusalem. He hung out at the auto repair shop all day waiting for something to happen.

When the announcement was made that big news was coming out of Jerusalem, all radio stations went live.

Titus turned on the mini recorder that Daniel Sullivan gave to him. He listened to Benjamin with a huge smile on his face, punching the air excitedly, as his brother in Christ accused Salvador Romanero of being the Antichrist of the Bible, with more than a billion other listeners.

After Benjamin was gunned down in cold blood, the radio station then played the conversation between Benjamin and his brother Seth, before he was arrested. Titus made sure to record it too.

After playing it for everyone gathered in the church area, Jefferson Danforth said, "Benjamin recently shared with some of us his yearning to go back to Israel. He told a few of us that he had one last big mission left in him. Did he ever! Looks like God has answered his prayer.

"He got to share the Gospel with his brother, accuse Salvador Romanero of being the Antichrist of the Bible, with the whole world watching and listening, then go to Heaven. Now, that's what I call an extremely productive day! Let's pray that Yahweh will use his valiant effort to draw many Jews to Him."

The expression on Jefferson's face conveyed to everyone that he couldn't have been any prouder of Benjamin. "In the brief time I knew him, we became close friends. I can't wait to see him again, when he returns with Christ to reign with our Lord a thousand years! It won't be too much longer now.

"Until that glorious day comes, we must now pray for the salvation of Seth and Naveh Shapiro, Benjamin's ex-wife and their three children, and of course, we must keep praying for Jack Nelson."

They didn't know Nelson was already in Paradise, or that he arrived there even before Benjamin. In that light, their former resident had already stored up treasures in Heaven, before he even made his bold declaration in Jerusalem.

And for mass producing the book that Benjamin had used to win Nelson to Christ, they, too, had stored up treasures, by extension, which would never be lost or stolen...never!

39

CHESAPEAKE BAY, VIRGINIA

DONALD JOHNSON AND SERGEI and Analyn Ivanov were presently unaware of what had transpired in Jerusalem. Then again, by being out on the open sea during the second, third, and fourth bowl judgments, they already had more than enough to worry about.

The three *ETSM* members were amazed, and relieved, that they had survived the long and turbulent voyage from the Philippines to America, while enduring the second, third, and fourth bowl judgments.

There were no high fives or "God Bless America" utterances among them, only silent rejoicing. They weren't home yet.

They wouldn't rejoice until they made it to safe house number one, hopefully within a week.

Donald cautioned them both in a soft whisper, "Now that we're inland, we need to be even more careful. Those microfliers never sleep or take breaks. They're always watching and listening! Even if most of them may have melted in the heat, all it would take is for one of them to detect us, and we'd be in a world of trouble."

The Ivanovs nodded that they both understood.

What should have taken them three weeks to make the 5,850-mile trip (5,075 nautical miles) from the southern tip of South America to the Chesapeake Bay, ended up taking three grueling months.

The reason for this massive inconvenience was, once the hurricane-force waves and winds created by the multiple meteors had subsided, there were hardly any winds at all.

The sailing pendulum had swung both ways, only in this case, both ends presented unfavorable boating conditions. It went from furnace-hot winds howling so hard, it was a wonder the boat had remained upright, to total calmness. They still had the movement of the ocean, but without the wind to guide them, it made for slow, misdirected sailing at times.

Sergei wished he could have bottled up some of the winds they had in full abundance, on the way from the Philippines to the tip of South America and used them now.

On a planet that rotated every 24 hours, at the speed of one thousand miles per hour, it was a wonder how any location on the globe could ever be wind free for even a second, at any given time.

Yet, that's what they were faced with over the past few weeks. This wasn't good when stuck on a sailboat with very little fuel left in the tank.

With no winds to help propel them through the smelly pollution encapsulating them from all angles, there were several times throughout the day when Sergei had no choice but to power on the engines, to give the sailboat a little boost in speed, and point it in the right direction when they started sailing sideways, before shutting them down again.

Even with very few boats and ships out on the water, navigating through scores of dead sea life—whales, dolphins, shark, marlin, tuna, sea turtles, and everything in between—was reminiscent of being stuck in traffic in downtown Bangkok or Manila.

Only instead of automobile fumes invading their lungs and nostrils, it was the overpowering stench of death from trudging through blood red waters every nautical mile of the way.

Even with facemasks on, it wasn't something they ever got used to. Since they didn't have access to inhalers or nebulizers, to help them breathe a little more easily, all three of them had developed chronic wheezing issues.

And the chemicals in the facemask had caused Analyn's chin to break out with pimples, from wearing it day and night.

Throw in her buzz cut hairstyle and she looked nothing like her former self. She tried her hardest not to look in any of the mirrors on the boat. Yet, Sergei was still willing to marry her.

If he was willing to love her at her worst, she would dedicate herself to loving him to the best of her ability, for the remainder of her days.

Because the Atlantic Ocean was so vast in dimension, as the weeks slowly passed, it gradually started losing its blood red color, eventually turning more of a rusty brown.

The Chesapeake Bay, however, being nowhere near as vast as the Atlantic, had retained more of its crimson color. With scores of dead fish still floating on top, they were forced once again to battle the same unhealthy pungent odors attacking their nostrils.

To make things even worse, the Chesapeake was much more placid than the Atlantic, making sailing even more difficult with little wind to guide them.

They were also still dealing with the fourth bowl, which was poured out onto the earth soon after the meteor strikes, which gave permission for the sun to scorch people with fire.

As believers, the three voyagers weren't being scorched by the sun, but they definitely felt its heat. It felt like God had turned a giant size hairdryer on maximum heat, then pointed it at the planet.

What came as no big surprise to Sergei, was that the portable desalinization system stopped working soon after the meteor strikes. And the three replacement filters became clogged from overuse.

It was then that Sergei put the solar desalination system to good use. Unlike the reverse osmosis system they had been using, the hydrophobic membranes on this system propelled the salt water, leaving only water vapor to pass through them.

Directly powered by the sun's radiation, when the salt water was heated up, it evaporated and turned into vapor. That vapor then passed through the membranes, turning the vapor back into water on the other side, leaving the salt behind.

The device could produce up to six liters per hour. But since they didn't have extra bottles or containers to hold the filtered water, they produced two liters each, per day.

As the solar desalination system provided them with their daily water consumption, they continued to bathe and wash their clothes with the salty seawater in the 300-gallon barrels.

It kept their bodies relatively free from body odor, but it was so hot, it felt like they were washing their bodies in jacuzzi water. It also made them feel sticky. And their clothing became uncomfortably hardened by the salt water.

Even the drinking water was too warm to quench their thirsts. Regardless, they thanked God for sending them this lifeline. Once again, He had proven faithful by meeting their daily needs, even if it kept evaporating a little more each day in the blazing heat...

Analyn never thought the day would come when she would see the Land of Opportunity, as a married woman, no less.

She had family in New York. They stopped talking when Analyn's parents tried force feeding Mormonism down their throats, with Donald Johnson leading the way. It nearly split the family in half.

Analyn thought back to when her cousin would post selfies in front of some of Manhattan's finest hotspots on social media. She would sometimes feel envious, thinking she would never get to see those places up close and in person.

She hadn't heard from her cousin since before the global quake. They used to be so close. She wondered if she was still alive.

With no way of knowing, for all intents and purposes, the only people she knew in America were on this boat with her. She looked forward to meeting her brothers and sisters at safe house number one.

Before the Rapture, she thought she would spend the rest of her life in Australia with her former fiancé, just like he kept promising her. Then he got her pregnant and dumped her.

When that dream died, Analyn never thought she would step foot outside of the Philippines. With her country totally obliterated, had she not left there, chances were good she would be dead, or she would have taken the mark by now.

Unlike so many immigrants before her, she would never get to see the Statue of Liberty standing in New York City harbor, as a proud beacon of hope for anyone seeking safe refuge.

Then again, she seriously doubted if it was still standing...

It took another week for Sergei to navigate his sailboat safely to Wilmington, Delaware. He used the Chesapeake and Delaware (C&D) Canal, which connected the Chesapeake Bay to the Delaware River. This route took them through the Ports of Baltimore and Wilmington.

Since there weren't many other boats out on the water, they sailed only at night with all navigation lights turned off. As they had fully come to expect, the long and winding Delaware River was even more blood red in color than the two other bodies of water they had sailed on.

The blood had thickened the river to the extent that it felt like they were sailing on quicksand at times. The stench was ungodly. They battled similar conditions on the C&D Canal as well.

It offered the three sailors yet another example that the planet on which they lived was indeed disposable.

Finally, after eight long, uncertain months of sailing, Sergei docked what had always been his most prized possession in a desolate area, in southern Wilmington, for what he knew would be the last time. He would have loved to dock his boat in northern Wilmington, which, according to Donald, would have been closer to the safe house.

When Johnson first arrived at safe house number one, way back when, he flew into Baltimore, Maryland. The only thing he remembered about Wilmington was driving north on I-95, through downtown, and exiting at U.S. 202, then taking it north. Other than that, this city was as foreign to him as it was to Sergei and Analyn.

Even though this would add a few miles to their walking part of the trip, Donald didn't want to chance sailing past downtown.

Ivanov gave a tearful salute to the vessel that took them halfway around the world. His bruised and battered sea vessel had once again proven trustworthy. When he purchased the boat with winnings from a fishing contest he had entered in Thailand, Sergei wasn't saved.

Back then, he didn't want to hear anything about Jesus. He was enjoying living a life full of debauchery too much.

Now he was saved, married, and thankful to the very One he once hated for helping them survive the long and turbulent voyage from the Philippines to America, amidst His unrelenting bowl judgments.

Before getting off the 30-foot sailboat that had been their home the past eight months, Analyn shaved their heads again.

Sergei offered to shave her head next, but she declined. Once was enough for her. Soon to be meeting with members of her eternal family, she wanted her hair to grow back. She had already surpassed the buzzcut stage and her hair was now in between lengths.

Besides, it did little to cool her off the first time.

They filled three backpacks with whatever they would need for the last part of the journey home, including binoculars. Donald prayed for God's protection, then they set out for safe house number one, on wobbly sea legs. Without even taking the first step, the three of them were already exhausted from the long voyage, and discombobulated.

Even at 5 a.m., the heat was sweltering. They covered their bodies with as much clothing as they could tolerate, covered their heads with bucket hats, covered their eyes behind sunglasses, and began the tedious twelve mile walk to Chadds Ford, Pennsylvania, mostly in silence.

With the sun still scorching all of earth's inhabitants not belonging to Jesus, everyone wore extra layers of clothing when they were outdoors, as if it was the dead of winter.

So, in that regard, they didn't stand out too much.

The next challenge they faced was that Donald didn't know where they were going. With this being the newlyweds' first time in America, the Ivanov's couldn't offer him any assistance.

Johnson wasn't interested in getting to know Wilmington. He just wanted to get home, so he could see his wife and son again.

Without the use of GPS, they headed north away from the river, mostly on badly damaged side streets, looking for still-standing street signs with I-95 or U.S. 202 posted on them.

The three were soaked with sweat from the stifling heat. They each consumed one bottle of water. It did little to quench their thirsts.

At 3 p.m. that day, Analyn's feet were swollen and full of blisters from the long walk. The strap on her left flip flop looked like it was a step or two away from breaking off.

She also had another bad toothache. It was time to call it a day.

The three refugees camped out behind a dilapidated building on U.S. 202, on the northbound side.

As Analyn slept, Sergei searched the grounds looking for anything he could find to tighten his wife's flip flop. Finding an old solar swimming pool covering, he retrieved a camping knife from his backpack, then cut dozens of stringlike slices in the plastic.

Come daybreak, before they set out on foot again, he would tie them around his wife's footwear, and then around her ankle.

Hopefully, it would hold until they made it to their cottage at safe house number one. Barring any unforeseen trouble, they would be in Chadds Ford come daybreak.

As they settled in for the night, if there was one good thing, they were far enough away from the river that they no longer had to breathe in the toxicity created from the many dead fish.

But Donald couldn't hide his frustration. He had fully expected to make it all the way to safe house number one by now. The thought of being so close to his wife and son, yet not being able to see them, was quite deflating.

Johnson was tempted to leave the newlyweds there for the night, then come back in the morning with food and water, before taking them to the safe house.

But if something happened to them in his absence, he would regret it for the rest of his life.

40

AT 5 A.M., THE next morning, Donald was eager to get moving before the sun rose. The problem was that Analyn felt sick again. Even being on dry land for 24 hours, she still battled motion sickness.

The long walk in the blazing heat, the day before, only made it worse. And her mouth still throbbed from the toothache. It ached a little more with each step she took. She dreaded the thought of having a repeat performance later.

On top of that, when all hell broke loose in the Philippines, the constant stress she was subjected to had completely thrown off her menstrual cycle. The new bride hadn't had a regular period since the floodwaters plucked her daughter out of her arms, sweeping her away with the rest of her family.

Juliana was only three years old when her life was taken from her. Analyn felt like she also died that day, until God brought her back to life spiritually. Now here she was in a new country, halfway around the world, as a married woman no less. She felt totally out of sorts.

Donald had no choice but to remain patient, until she felt well enough to walk again.

An hour later, Analyn signaled that she was ready to make the final leg of this tumultuous journey. Sergei took a few minutes wrapping the plastic stringlike strips he had cut out of the tarp, under her left flipflop, then around her ankle and foot. He repeated the process three times, hoping his "makeshift shoelaces" contraption would hold.

When they were a mile away from safe house number one, the terrain became more familiar to Donald. The sun hadn't yet risen, but as sure as the sky above kept getting brighter, it would soon follow.

As much as he would have loved to walk them through the front property entryway, then give them the grand tour of his beloved safe house, damaged as it was, all comings and goings were made through the rear entrance. He was moments away from seeing just how irreparably damaged it really was.

Donald made sure to steer clear away from the property, hiking through the woods a quarter mile away from the fence line until they reached the back entrance. He didn't want to startle his brothers and sisters on the inside. Nor did he want to ruin the surprise.

A surge of enthusiasm shot through him. His energy level increased. He was so close now to being reunited with his wife and his son.

The last thing he wanted was to be caught by the enemy. He picked up the pace a bit. Analyn and Sergei did the same, as thoughts of quaint little cottages danced in their heads.

Even if they had to share a cottage with others, Analyn was perfectly fine with it. It would beat what she had left behind in the Philippines by a longshot. What she wanted more than anything now was medicine for her throbbing toothache, and a bed to sleep on for the rest of the day.

When they were a hundred yards away from the back entrance, the anticipatory expression on Donald's face evaporated.

Something wasn't right. Why were only parts of the fence still standing? And what had caused the remaining trees to be charred?

Donald blinked hard a few times, seeing the destruction in all directions, wondering if his bleary eyes were playing tricks on him.

Realizing they weren't, he lost all strength and reached for Sergei's shoulder so he wouldn't collapse to the surface. "How could this be?" he cried, not caring that he had practically shouted out his question. He could care less about the microfliers at this point...

The slight sense of triumph he felt for surviving the 25,000-mile trip, from start to finish, in the worst possible conditions, was gone, seeing safe house number one reduced to ashes.

Since so many months had passed, there were no plumes of smoke or fiery smell in the air to warn them of what they would soon encounter.

Analyn and Sergei felt equally deflated. The place that Donald had done a fabulous job of describing to them, that they couldn't wait to see with their own eyes, was gone.

Sergei said softly to his wife, "There goes our pocket of peace..."

Donald's shoulders slumped; his heart melted deep within him. He gasped. *Did I make the wrong decision by leaving my family behind to rescue Analyn and bring her to safety*? he thought selfishly to himself.

"Jakob assured us all safe houses raising children would be spared God's judgments," he bemoaned. "That's one of the reasons I decided to take this trip. So, where is everyone?"

Donald collapsed onto the dirt surface and wept uncontrollably. At this point, he didn't care if someone heard him. Having his head chopped off suddenly seemed pleasant. At least then his suffering would be over.

The newlyweds watched in silence, not knowing what to do or say to possibly console him.

Donald thought back to when he drove to Florida with Manuel Jiminez, before setting sail for Singapore. He clearly remembered thinking back then that the only way he would consider it a successful mission, would be for four things to happen. 1) the small fishing vessel that Manuel boarded in Tampa, would arrive safely in Brownsville, Texas, and he would be safely smuggled to the safe house in Guadalajara, Mexico, 2) Donald would arrive safely in Singapore and help smuggle Hana and Yasamin on board the container ship back to the States, 3) when he arrived in the Philippines, Analyn wouldn't have the mark of the Beast on her right hand or forehead, and she would convert to Christianity, 4) everyone involved would ultimately end up where they were going, unimpeded.

Aside from the fact that he made it to Singapore, and Analyn never took the mark of the Beast, he had no way of confirming anything else.

He didn't know if Manuel Jiminez made it to Mexico, or if Vishnu Uddin was successful in smuggling Hana, Yasamin, and their two children to America. If they did make it to safe house number one, he unknowingly sent them to their deaths, but at least they were with Jesus now.

Donald leaned against a charred rock, weeping for the longest time. Apparently, Clayton's dire warning about the microfliers was more dire than he had thought.

He cupped his shaved head with both hands. "I'm sorry, Mary. I should have never left you and Luke alone. You were right. When I left safe house number one, it really was for the very last time…"

Tears streamed down Analyn's cheeks, as guilt snaked through her. This was all her fault. She rubbed Donald's shoulders. The pain behind his words was so intense, all she could do was weep herself.

Sergei remained patient, giving his friend all the time he needed to grieve, before asking, "What do we do now? Is there a Plan B?"

Donald sniffled a few times as he tried regaining his composure. Hair sticky with sweat, he answered, "The only other safe house I know of is in Kennett Square," he said softly, sadly.

Analyn asked, "Is it far from here, Ninong?" Going on another long-distance walk was the last thing she wanted. But with wave upon wave of guilt snaking through her tired and weakened body, for doing this to the man who sailed halfway around the world just for her, she kept this unnerving thought to herself.

"It's about half the distance of what we walked to get here."

"Do you know how to get there?"

Donald heard the sheer exhaustion in her voice. His legs and feet hurt just as much as hers did. He sniffled a few more times. "Yeah. I spent a lot of time there when I first came to Pennsylvania. Let's just pray it's still standing when we get there. Perhaps some of the residents here managed to escape whatever hit this place and relocated to Kennett Square. But if Plan B fails, there is no Plan C…"

Sergei asked, "What then?"

"We wait for the enemy to capture us. I already let my wife down. My son too. If we get caught, we get caught. The way I feel now, I wish the sailboat would have capsized in the Atlantic, so I wouldn't have to see this now. At least then, my suffering would finally be over…"

41

KENNETT SQUARE, PENNSYLVANIA

TWO DAYS AFTER DONALD Johnson and Sergei and Analyn Ivanov left Chadds Ford, they arrived in Kennett Square.

It was a difficult night for the three of them, as they slept in the woods. Donald kept weeping and sniffling all through the night. He was racked by a crippling depression.

Analyn held on to him as tightly as she could, heart breaking inside her chest, as her husband held them both.

It felt awkward for Sergei to be spooning in threes, especially since one of them was a man, but they were so close together that he couldn't hold his wife, without holding Donald too. Even with a body in between them, he felt Donald's body trembling.

The Ivanov's were doing their best to remain strong for him. But Donald sounded defeated. Clearly, he couldn't be alone now. To make matters worse, ants and other insects kept feasting on them all night.

When they woke in the morning, Donald uttered softly to them, "Thanks for always doing your best to make me feel like I'm not alone. I appreciate it more than I can ever say..."

Analyn hugged him. "We need each other, Ninong."

The walk to Kennett Square seemed so much longer than the tedious trek from Wilmington to Chadds Ford, and this was nearly half the distance. What they thought would be a one-day walk, when they got off the sailboat in Wilmington, had turned into four grueling days.

What made it even worse for Analyn, aside from her ongoing motion sickness, and aching tooth, was that the plastic strap on her left flip flop finally broke off, an hour outside of Chadds Ford. Her husband's attempt at jerry rigging it didn't work. And one of the rashes on her left foot, caused by the plastic straps, looked infected. She thought to herself, *If this is the American dream, I'd rather be back in the Philippines...*

Since U.S. 1 was hilly in so many areas, it made traversing it more difficult. Still, Sergei carried his wife for a quarter mile at a time, until he could no longer manage. Their water supply was just about gone. They were forced to take smaller sips of hot water throughout the day, which, at this point, was barely even enough to whet their whistles.

As much as Johnson wanted to go to the auto repair shop first, then wait for someone to hopefully show up—as was the protocol—he couldn't remember where it was located. His mind was too flustered.

When the safe house came into view, what little expectations Donald had of finding anyone alive quickly dissipated upon seeing the many buildings that were there last time, reduced to piles of rubble.

Only the main barn was still standing. He knew the Yoders stopped producing food and dairy for the unconverted after the global quake.

Donald asked himself, "Are Eli and Susanna still alive?"

"Who, Ninong?"

"The farm owners." Donald pushed that thought from his mind. At least there was no crater at this place, like at safe house number one. The fact that this hideout was underground was a good thing.

He saw a rusty backhoe resting beneath a dead, leafless oak tree, a mile away from the barn. It probably hadn't tasted water in years. He pointed in that direction. "Follow me."

The soil was riddled with rotten corn stalks, small pebbles and thorns. Combined, they wreaked even more havoc on their feet.

Sergei knew there wasn't a chance Analyn could traverse this rough surface on only one flip flop. As bone tired as he was, he hoisted his wife on his back and carried her there.

He placed her gently on the ground and wiped his sweaty brow. "What do we do now?" he asked Donald, through heavy breathing.

Johnson pulled binoculars out of his backpack and stared out in the distance. "The only thing we can do, we wait and hope someone emerges, before making our move."

Analyn asked, "Why can't we just take our chances and run inside the farm?"

Donald answered, "It's too soon for that. If we don't see anyone by sundown, that's what we'll do. The last thing we need now is to walk into a trap."

As the day dragged on, they kept repositioning themselves to remain in the shade. The tree was massive, but with no leaves on it, it offered little help. Once the sun reached its zenith, they had no choice but to position themselves directly beneath the farming equipment.

After waiting in the blazing heat for nearly six hours, with no food or water, all three were malnourished, and suffering from heatstroke.

Donald thought his eyes might be playing tricks on him, when he saw a body emerge from the barn. Realizing they weren't, he tightened his grip on the binoculars, hoping whoever it was, he was on their side.

Was this man an *ETSM* guard, or the enemy? With his hands trembling, he whispered to Sergei, "Are you able to run over to him?"

Sergei's eyes volleyed from Donald to the man out in the distance, then back to Donald. "I think so..."

"I'd do it myself, but I don't have the strength. Do you remember our organization credo?"

Sergei heard Donald recite it once or twice, but he never memorized it.

"Say these exact words to him, 'Keep fighting the Good fight. Pray for me as I pray for you. God is with us.' It's important that you say it right. Let me hear you say it."

Sergei cleared his throat then repeated it back to Donald, word for word in his thick, Russian accent.

Donald nodded wearily. "Perfect. Go now, before he heads back underground. Don't worry, if he's part of the End Times Salvation Movement, he won't have a gun. Jesus was committed to a ministry of non-violence, so they're not allowed on the property."

"And if he's the enemy?"

Donald looked away from Sergei. "It is what it is, right?"

Ivanov nodded his reply, then kissed Analyn hard on the lips. "I'll be back, my love." He picked himself up off the dirt surface, and sprinted toward the man he didn't know, hoping he wasn't the enemy.

When he was 20 yards away, Titus saw him coming. He braced himself for who knew what.

Sergei flailed his arms over his head shouting, "I come in peace! I come in peace!" His accent was thick and clearly Eastern European.

Donald saw Sergei's mouth moving in his binoculars, but he couldn't hear what he was saying from this distance.

Titus gulped fearfully, his line of vision swinging back and forth, praying this man wasn't the enemy. He looked skyward hoping those miniature microdevices weren't hovering above recording them.

Titus knew this location was being supernaturally protected by Yahweh. Jakob had assured them of it. But what about aboveground? If not, could this man bring trouble to their hideout?

Sergei stopped five feet away from the man, raised his hands above his head and did a 360, so he would know he wasn't armed.

Whoever this intruder was, his face was red, his skin was dry, his lips were blistered from overexposure to the sun, and he was drenched with sweat. Even his dirt-stained clothing was soaked all the way through. He was so thin that his cheek bones protruded through his skin.

Titus took a few deep breaths to calm himself. Jaw jutting in that certain way he was known for at moments like this, he scrutinized the man's face with intense concentration. "Who are you?!" he whisper-shouted, trying to sound forceful, "And what are you doing here?"

Sergei paused to take a much-needed breath, then said, "Keep fighting the Good fight. Pray for me as I pray for you. God is with us."

Titus placed his hands on his knees to stop them from shaking so much. It didn't work. "Who are you?"

"My name is Sergei Ivanov. I'm here with my wife, Analyn. We sailed all the way from the Philippines with Donald Johnson. Do you know him?"

Titus couldn't believe what he was hearing. He knew Analyn was the name of the woman that Donald set out to rescue in the Philippines. "Donald's still alive?"

Sergei nodded yes.

"Where are they?"

Sergei craned his neck and pointed in their direction. "Hiding behind that farm equipment. We went to the other safe house, but it was destroyed. So, we walked here."

"From Chadds Ford?"

Sergei nodded yes.

Senses on full alert, Titus said, "Follow me…"

Sergei did as he was told and followed the man inside the barn. "There's no way my wife can walk from there to here."

Titus mounted a four-wheeler. "I'm one step ahead of you. Wait here. Be right back." He raced off in the direction of the rusty backhoe.

Sergei sat on the ground, wiped sweat from his forehead, and prayed they wouldn't be spotted by one of those microfliers.

Titus circled the oak tree, came to a stop, and waved Donald and Analyn over. Once the two of them were safely on the four-wheeler, he sped back toward the barn.

Analyn was grateful for the ride. Without it, the only way she could have made it to the barn on her own would have been by crawling on her hands and knees. Her feet hurt. Her legs hurt. Her back hurt. Her head hurt. Everything hurt at this point. She didn't feel 24.

Less than a minute later, they were back. "Thank you, Jesus!" said Sergei.

Titus turned off the engine and removed his face covering.

Donald's eyes bulged. "Titus!" he said, hope rising in his voice. "You're here!"

"So good to see you again. What can I say, I'm shocked! Welcome back, brother!" The two men exchanged a hot, sweaty hug.

Donald asked him, "What happened to safe house number one? We just came from there."

Titus lowered his head. "It was on Romanero's strike list."

"Strike list?" Donald looked at Analyn and Sergei. They looked as confused as he was. "What strike list?"

"Seriously? You don't know?"

Donald put his hands out. "Before we left Singapore, I heard Clayton's warning about the microfliers. But that's all I heard. Been on a boat ever since. It's a miracle we made it this far."

Titus was astounded. "You may be the only people on earth to not know. Most of our safe houses are gone. Thankfully, we received advance warning, and we were relocated here before it happened. Everyone but two, that is…"

Donald took a deep breath and braced himself.

Analyn squeezed Donald's hand.

Titus realized what he was thinking. He held his hands out. "Relax. Your wife and son are both fine. They're down below."

Donald sighed relief, then asked, "Who didn't make it then?"

Titus answered, "Let's get you down below first, and get you some water to drink. It's much cooler down there."

"Cooler sounds perfect to me," said Sergei.

"Follow me." Titus climbed down the ladder first. When the three of them joined him, he said, "One down, two to go."

Sergei saw his wife grimacing. "Get on my back. We can climb down together."

"I wouldn't have the strength to hold on to you, baby." Analyn summoned another burst of strength, then gingerly lowered herself down the next two ladders, wincing in pain with each step downward. The blisters on her feet were no match for the hard aluminum ladders.

The lower they submerged themselves into the bowels of the earth, the cooler the ladders felt. They reached the bottom and followed Titus through the 100-yard tunnel, before reaching the steel door leading to the main gathering room.

"Just so you know," said Titus, "it's overflowing with people, mostly children. More than three thousand little ones, in fact. Since we're all stuck underground together, all newcomers need to be examined, to make sure they're not carrying any transferable flus or diseases, before joining the general population."

"I want to see Mary. Besides, it's only been the three of us the past eight months. To the best of my knowledge, none of us have the flu. We all had motion sickness, and for good reason, but not the flu."

Titus asked, "Wouldn't you at least like to get cleaned up first?"

Donald reiterated, "It's been many months, Titus. It can't wait."

"After what the three of you survived, I'm sure we can make an exception. You can't blame Mary for thinking you were dead. Even before the second and third bowl judgments struck the planet, she believed that. The meteor strikes sealed it for her. Will she be shocked to see you again!"

Titus radioed his wife, Ingrid, on his walkie talkie. "Yes, sweetie?"

"Can you bring Mary Johnson to the steel door please?"

"New arrivals?"

"You'll see when you get here…"

"I just finished feeding Max," she said, regarding their 4-month-old son. "Be there as soon as I can…"

"Copy that…" Titus holstered his walkie talkie onto his belt. *I can't wait to see this reunion!*

Ingrid asked Yasamin to watch her child, then went in search of Mary. "Do you have a minute?"

Mary glanced up at Ingrid. "Sure. What's up?"

Not sure, exactly." Ever since the second bowl judgment struck the planet, everyone tried keeping Mary's mind occupied, so she wouldn't think too much about her husband. "Follow me…"

"Did something happen to Jake?"

"It's nothing like that…"

"Where are you taking me then, Ingrid?"

"To the steel door."

"The steel door? What for?"

"Guess we'll both find out soon enough…"

42

ONCE THEY WERE SAFELY on the other side of the steel door, Titus poured them each a measured cup of cool water. They were so parched they emptied them in just a few gulps.

Titus looked at the newlyweds. "Welcome home…"

Sergei said, "Thanks. It's not what we expected. Our hearts were set on living in one of the cottages Donald told us about in Chadds Ford."

"I know what you mean. I miss my cottage too," Titus said. "But at least you'll be safe here. Jakob assured us this'll be our final hiding place, so consider it your last residence before Christ returns."

Analyn sighed relief. "Thank you, Lord!"

Titus gave them more water to drink, then said to Donald, "This place is a lot different than the last time you were here. The twelve holes that were dug back then, are all being used now."

Donald took another large gulp of water. It could wait no longer. "Which two didn't make it here, Titus?"

"Brian Mulrooney and Tom Dunleavey…"

Donald nearly spit the water out of his mouth. "What happened to them?"

"Brian had double pneumonia. He didn't have the strength to make it here. Tom volunteered to stay with him in the fallout shelter. They didn't survive…"

Donald couldn't contain his shock. "Are you saying they were there when the bomb struck?"

Titus rubbed his sweaty brow. "I'm afraid so. A handful of us went there a week later and found their bodies. Before leaving Chadds Ford, we buried them there. I can only imagine how shocked you were seeing the place destroyed. At least we knew what to expect. You didn't."

"Was I ever!" said Donald. "My first thought was, why? Jakob promised us we would be fine there, right?"

Analyn and Sergei listened with heavy hearts. They knew Brian and Tom were two of Donald's closest friends. After hearing so much about them, they were eager to meet them. Now it wouldn't happen.

Titus twisted his lips. "That's not all. Travis and Clayton are dead."

Donald shot a sideways look at Titus. "What?!"

"Lee Kim, too, I'm afraid. We think they were on their way here when their car was destroyed by a drone blast. Clayton was leaving a message for all survivors when it happened. They were identified by a microflier, which led to their car being targeted. We all heard it."

Johnson took a moment to process what he was hearing. "How could we travel halfway around the world on a sailboat, in the midst of the second, third, and fourth bowl judgments, yet our leaders, who were the true driving forces of the organization, couldn't make it from Georgia to Pennsylvania?"

Titus answered, "Our minds were blown too. According to Jakob, they no longer had God's supernatural protection. Only those who still have missions to carry out still have it, those reuniting family members and friends, for example, or transporting pregnant women. All others have been identified and taken out."

Donald replied, "Did all five thousand safe houses with Yahweh's sealed servants staying there survive, Titus?"

"Based on Clayton's final address, it appears that way. But with no way of contacting anyone, for all intents and purposes, we're all alone. The reason we were transferred here was that we have clean well water and solar power, things we didn't have in Chadds Ford."

Titus' walkie talkie crackled. Ingrid said, "Be there in five…"

"Copy that, my love." Titus said to Donald, "She'll be here soon."

Perhaps it was because of how bad he looked and smelled, but Donald was nervous. "Did Hana and Yasamin make it here?"

"Yes, praise God! Vishnu and David Wilcox are here too. They were with us in Chadds Ford before we were transferred here."

"That's a relief!" *Guess I didn't send them to their deaths after all!*

"Vishnu and Yasamin recently got married."

"I'm happy for them. I spent time with Vishnu on the way to Singapore. He's a good man. What about Manuel Jiminez?"

Titus shook his head sadly. "He never made it to Guadalajara. He was arrested at the border and ultimately beheaded. I'm guessing you didn't hear about what happened to Benjamin Shapiro…"

"Don't tell me…He's gone too?"

"Yes. Do you remember the prison guard, Hans Greinhold?"

"Of course! The man from Europe. How could I forget him?"

Titus nodded in agreement. "Benjamin had a similar experience, only with more people watching. We have a recording of it. After you get situated, you can listen to what he did before he was taken to Glory. All I'll say for now is it happened in Israel…"

There was a loud scream. It was Mary. Donald turned and saw his wife fainting, twenty feet away from him. She fell hard to the ground.

He ran over to his wife and tapped her face a few times to revive her, but it was soft enough that it wouldn't hurt her or leave a mark.

When Mary came to, Donald sat her up, as Ingrid filled a cup with water for her to drink. She took a small sip, then started sobbing.

Donald held her, as she rested her head on his shoulder.

When her sobs were reduced to soft sniffling, she asked him, "Is this really happening? I thought I'd never see you again."

Donald kissed his wife on the right cheek. "Yes, my love, it is…"

Relief flooded Mary's soul. She looked up at the ceiling. "Thank you, Jesus!" She cupped Donald's face with her hands. "You've lost a lot of weight. And hair!"

Donald chuckled nervously. "It's unbelievably hot out there. Pardon the unpleasant odor. I haven't showered in a while."

"I don't care. All that matters is you're home and we're back together." She glanced up at the ceiling again. "Thank you, Lord! Sorry for my unbelief…"

"Yes, Amen!" said Donald.

Mary asked, "How did you get here?"

"We walked."

"No, what I mean is, how did you know where to find us?"

"When we found safe house number one destroyed, this was the only other place I knew to go."

Mary glanced up at Analyn. She looked nothing like the young girl she saw on video chat, roughly a year ago. "It's nice to finally meet you in person. I can't tell you how many times I've prayed for this day to come. Welcome home!"

Analyn's lips started quivering. Without uttering a word, she sat on the floor next to Mary and threw herself into her arms.

Mary rubbed the top of her head, as Analyn wept uncontrollably. Now that her husband had miraculously returned, the anger she had harbored toward the young woman was gone.

Mary didn't know who smelled worse, Analyn or her husband.

Finally, through soft sniffling, Analyn said, "I'm so sorry for putting you through all this. But had you not let your husband come to rescue me, I would have surely taken the mark. I didn't see any other way out."

"I understand, Analyn. What's most important is that you're part of God's family! It makes all the suffering worthwhile…"

"I'm a married woman now." Analyn glanced up at Sergei. "That's my husband, Sergei."

Mary raised a confused eyebrow. "Husband?" She still remembered how lonely and distraught she was, before Donald left to rescue her halfway around the world. And heartbroken. *Now she's married?*

Donald said, "I married them on Sergei's boat…"

"Congratulations to you both," Mary said, as warmly as she could.

Sergei said, "Thanks. For our honeymoon, we got to take a cruise to America."

"Not hardly," said Analyn, with a snicker.

Mary said, "I can only imagine how horrific it must have been out on the water, when the second bowl judgment was unleashed."

Donald said, "You have no idea. It's only by God's grace that we're here now."

"Amen to that," said Sergei. He helped Analyn to her feet. "There were times I thought we would surely die. The heat was unbearable. Even at night, it was too much. What made it worse was the constant smell of dead fish in the air. It never went away."

Donald got up off the floor then helped Mary to her feet. "I'll say! I had such a hard time breathing most days. It made my lungs hurt. I still have that foul stench in my nostrils. I'm happy to be done with boats for the rest of this life! And the heat! Man, was it stifling!"

Analyn added, "Thankfully, we were never scorched by the sun. But it was so hot on the boat I thought I would pass out at times."

Mary said, "The last thing any of us heard, Vishnu boarded the cargo ship for the States, with Hana and Yasamin, and the two of you left for Manila on Sergei's boat. Vishnu told us how bad it was in Singapore, so I figured it was just as bad in the Philippines."

Sergei offered, "I think Manila was even worse."

Mary said to Donald, "Not sure if you know, but the boat you slept on in Singapore was destroyed. It happened on the same day you left for the Philippines."

After just hearing about the deaths of so many of his brothers in Christ, Donald wasn't surprised hearing this. "I'm just glad they made it here. If it wasn't for Sergei, we wouldn't have. What a sailor he is! And thanks to him, we had just enough food to eat and water to drink."

"Thanks for bringing my husband back to me," Mary said to Sergei, tenderly, sincerely.

"You're welcome. But believe me, it was a team effort. I couldn't have done it alone."

Mary squeezed Donald's left arm with her left hand. "I'll never let you out of my sight again!"

Donald kissed her on the lips. "I won't let you let me out of your sight again! Where's Luke?"

"In class. Would you like to see him now?"

"Yes, but I'd like to shower first. Exposing one family member to the unpleasant smell is already bad enough…"

"As you wish…"

Analyn cupped her chin with her right hand.

Ingrid asked, "Are you okay, Analyn?"

Analyn shook her head no. "I have a bad toothache. I've had it for a long time. And I think my left foot is infected."

Ingrid saw the numerous insect bites on her arms and legs. "You poor thing. One of the nurses here does basic dental procedures. She can remove it for you. I think she's Filipino too. I'm sure she'll be thrilled to have someone to talk to in her native language again. Come with me. Let's get you checked out…"

"Can I shower first?"

Ingrid smiled warmly at her. "Absolutely! Follow me…"

Analyn was relieved. This would mark the first time she would be seen by a doctor since she gave birth to her daughter, four years ago.

Sarah Mulrooney watched it all unfolding. When Mary didn't come back, Sarah became curious and went to the main gathering area searching for her best friend.

To see God reuniting the married couple, after all this time, was a cause for rejoicing. Sarah couldn't be happier for Mary.

But she felt even worse for Jacquelyn. How much worse would she be when she hears the news? It would only be a matter of time before she found out about it. *It might as well come from me*, Sarah thought, leaving the main gathering area for the single women's section.

43

AFTER SHOWERING AND CHANGING into clean clothes, as Analyn was being examined, Donald Johnson and Sergei Ivanov were taken to the men's section of the hospital. They were assigned beds.

Donald said to Lila Choharjo, "I'd like to see Luke before you stick that needle in my vein."

"Sorry, Donald," Lila said, preparing the intravenous needle for his left arm, "but you're severely dehydrated. We need to get some fluids in you. Luke will just have to see you here in a hospital bed. But I'm sure he won't mind."

Word had quickly spread that Donald had made it back from the Philippines. In no time, the hospital was full of non-patients all there to welcome him back. Eli and Susanna Yoder were the first ones to see him. Both were shocked that their good friend was still alive.

Susanna exclaimed, "Thank God, you made it back! When we heard about your mission, we had all but given up hope. You've been missed."

Eli clasped Donald's free hand. "It must feel good to be back on dry land."

Donald said, "For sure. But I'm still trying to catch up. The whole time we were out at sea, we had no clue what was happening on dry land. We knew God's judgments were being executed, but we knew nothing about Romanero's attack on our safe houses, and no idea that Clayton, Travis, Lee, Brian and Tom were dead.

"I keep wondering how we made it this far without being discovered by those microfliers. Not only that, but we were stranded on a sailboat for eight months, with the sails up. Then, when we docked it in Wilmington, we walked all the way to Chadds Ford, then on to Kennett Square! Four days out in the open without being spotted! Seriously?"

Eli shook his head in amazement. "No doubt God was protecting the three of you..."

Donald was equally amazed. It was still so hard to comprehend. "Then, when I saw only the farmhouse left standing, I thought something bad happened here too."

Eli explained, "We tore everything down so we could remain on the property without coming under suspicion by the enemy."

Donald glanced around at the massive subterranean hospital space. "It seems like forever ago when we preserved all those fruits and vegetables. Look at the place now. You've come so far."

Susanna replied, "Those were the days. There haven't been too many easy days since. Yet here we all are…"

Mary sat with her husband. "You can say that again, Susanna!"

Meanwhile, when Meera was finished with her examination, she said to her patient. "Now that your sailing days are over, thank God, and your feet are on solid ground again, the motion sickness should go away soon. But the morning sickness…"

Analyn's eyes grew wide as silver dollar pancakes.

Meera grinned at her. "You're pregnant. I'm guessing two months."

Analyn said, "I should have known. I never went three months without having my monthly cycle until now. I can't wait to tell Sergei."

"I'm sure he'll be thrilled with the news," said Tamika. "Do you want to tell him first, or have your tooth pulled?"

"Let's tell him first…"

"You got it! But first let me put some aloe on your left foot, and wrap it in gauze, so it can heal more quickly."

"Thanks for your kindness, Tamika…"

Tamika smiled at her patient. "I recently gave birth again, so my goal is to minimize your pain wherever I can. Can you walk to the men's section, or would you like a wheelchair?"

"Wheelchair please."

"Hop on. Fasten your seatbelt…"

Analyn grinned at Tamika's joke. Her mouth hurt too much for a full smile.

When they arrived at the men's section of the hospital, Isaac joined Eli and Susanna Yoder. He was carrying A.J. "Well, bless my soul! Donald Johnson! When I heard you were here, I had to see for myself."

Donald's face lit up. "Isaac! Long time no see! Who's this cute little fella?"

Isaac smiled. "My son A.J."

"Our son!"

"Yes, our son," he corrected himself, glancing at his wife.

"Congratulations, to you both! I'm happy for you both."

"You must be Sergei." Isaac said to the man on the bed next to Donald's.

Sergei nodded his reply.

"Thanks for bringing our friend back to us. How do you feel?"

"My lips are severely blistered. Other than that, I feel fine."

Tamika interjected, "Happy to hear that, Daddy."

Sergei assumed she was talking to her husband. Realizing she was staring at him, not Isaac, he flinched. "Daddy?"

Analyn smiled at her husband. "I'm pregnant, sweetie! We're going to be parents…"

Sergei closed his eyes, and he praised God for yet another miracle. Now that they were safe, it really was wonderful news. He got out of bed, careful not to dislodge the IV needle in his arm. He kissed his wife hard on the lips. "Wow! We're going to be parents! Unbelievable!"

Tamika said, "You better believe it, Sergei, because it's happening!" The way she said it made him laugh. "I'm taking Analyn to have her tooth pulled. We'll be back soon."

Tamika pushed her pregnant patient to the other side of the hospital. "Nila, I have a new patient who needs to have a tooth pulled."

Nila was washing her hands. "Be right with you…" When she turned to face them, Analyn's eyes widened in disbelief. She straightened up on the wheelchair. "Nila?"

Nila didn't recognize her at first with her short hair, but there was no mistaking the voice. "Analyn?"

Analyn nodded yes.

Nila screamed loudly. "No way!? What are you doing here? How did you get here?"

Analyn shot out of the wheelchair and threw herself into her cousin's arms. They held each other sobbing for the longest time, both praising God for this miracle. For Nila, being reunited with Tamika was already miraculous enough. Now this?

Tamika couldn't believe it. *Wait till everyone hears this!*

Nila sat down. "I thought I was the only one still alive in the family. If you think my father was upset when your father tried converting us to Mormonism, it was nothing compared to how furious he was, when I got saved, and I told him I no longer wanted to be a part of the Catholic church. I never saw him so angry."

Nila sighed. "I haven't spoken to them in quite some time, but I'm sure they both received the mark by now." Not wanting to relive it in her mind again, it would only depress her, she said to her cousin, "Let's pull that tooth. I know you're in agony."

Nila pulled the tooth, then helped Tamika push the wheelchair back to the men's section. The room was full of non-patients.

This wasn't the ideal place to have a gathering of this size. It would have been better in the church area. But since their three newest residents would be spending the night there, under observation, it would have to do.

Tamika wasted no time. "Listen up y'all, 'cause I'm about to blow your minds! I'm so excited I can barely stand it! First, can we praise God for bringing our dear brother, Donald, back to us? And can we give a warm welcome to our two new residents, Sergei and Analyn? Talk about a miracle!"

Loud cheering filled the hospital area, along with many "Amens" and "Thank You, Lords."

Tamika looked up at the ceiling, "God you are so good! Okay, I'm sure you all heard by now when Hana, Yasamin and Vishu set sail for America, Sergei offered to sail Donald to the Philippines, to rescue Analyn."

Yasamin said, "Don't forget about Cristiana and Navid."

"Oops, sorry!" said Tamika in reply. "Here's the kicker: When they found Analyn in Manila, she wasn't saved. Talk about taking a huge risk! With all those mark takers out there looking for people like us with their cellphones, just meeting with her was dangerous.

"Until recently, meeting with unbelievers was a no-no in our organization. But praise God, Analyn got saved before they left the Philippines! Otherwise, they would have had no choice but to leave her behind. Welcome to God's family, girlfriend! You too, Sergei!"

Many started clapping their hands.

Tamika went on, "Since they didn't have the mark, it took them twice as long to get here. They had to sail all the way down past the tip of South America, before coming here. And all this during the second, third and fourth bowl judgments! I know we prayed for their safety every day, but c'mon let's be honest, how many of you thought they were in Glory now? I know I did!"

A bunch of hands went up.

Tamika shook her head. "I mean, how could anyone possibly survive that! But God had other plans. And we just had another miracle."

"We already know Analyn's pregnant!" said Lila Choharjo.

"No! God just performed another miracle." Tamika paused for effect, then added, "You all know how God brought me and Nila back together. Well, it was just topped. Ready for this? Turns out Nila and Analyn are cousins!"

A loud gasp filled the hospital area. All eyes shifted from Tamika to the two women with tears of joy running down their faces. They felt shy from the rush of attention they received.

Nila squeezed Analyn's hand. "We haven't seen each other in many years. I can't fully express how grateful I am to God for bringing us together. As many of you know, I was raised a Catholic. Analyn was raised a Mormon. Yet here we both are. I still can't believe it."

Charles shook his head in astonishment. He said to Donald, "How cool is that? Even before Analyn got pregnant, you had God's supernatural covering all along. Even though you didn't know she would bring a child into the New Millennial Kingdom, Yahweh knew."

Donald shook his head in awe. Titus had already explained it to him, but it hadn't fully sunk in until now. The reason was that he didn't know Analyn was pregnant when they first arrived. "So, basically, when I left Chadds Ford more than a year ago, God's hand was on me, from start to finish, despite the constant danger I faced?"

"That would be correct, brother," said Charles.

Donald rubbed his wife's left shoulder. "Now it all makes sense!"

Mary thought to herself, *All that worrying for nothing!*

Daniel Sullivan said to Donald, "I was sort of in the same boat, if you'll pardon the pun. I drove thousands of miles cross country hoping not to be identified by the microfliers."

Sullivan nodded at Tyler Stephenson. "Tyler too. But on our final trip back here, we transported an expectant mother, who just happened to be Jefferson Danforth's daughter, Janelle, and Tyler's niece!

"By this time, Jakob had already told us that those who would be transporting pregnant women would have Yahweh's supernatural covering. So, when she got in the car, I knew we were safe. But before then, I was convinced that me and Tyler were always a breath away from being caught, especially after our leaders were killed..."

"You can say that again!" Tyler replied, standing next to his niece.

Sullivan nodded at him. "Yet, we had His supernatural protection all along."

The room grew quiet as everyone let it all settle into their minds.

Luke Johnson broke the silence. "Daddy!" He darted across the room and jumped onto his father's bed. He wrapped his little arms around his father's neck, not wanting to let go.

Jacquelyn Mulrooney watched and listened to it all. The last time she had experienced God's peace that surpassed all understanding, it was on the night before they were evacuated from safe house number one.

Brian suddenly showed up at the sanctuary with double pneumonia and stared out the window behind the pulpit. He asked everyone to look at the dim sunlight on the trees, before saying, "Doesn't it blow your mind how that beam of light came from more than ninety million miles away? With a constant haze hovering above the planet, we can't see a mile away in any direction. Yet, dim and faded as it is, it still found a way to penetrate through it all, by traveling millions of miles, even as the sun is setting, no less. It's mind-boggling!"

Jacquelyn shook her head. It was still vivid in her mind. But what she just witnessed was right up there with it. Yahweh had just provided them with yet another miracle, by reuniting Nila and Analyn, not to mention Donald and Mary.

The fact that He had guided the sailboat they were on halfway around the world, among His unrelenting judgments, to reunite them was quite remarkable. How could it not be considered a miracle?

If this reunion did anything, it caused Jacquelyn to understand that a believer could be completely miserable in their present situation, yet still have the joy of the Lord in their hearts.

That's precisely how she felt now. It was God's will to take Brian, just like He did with hundreds of millions of other Christians around the world. It was also His will that she was still alive. It was time to accept it for what it was and move on.

For the first time since being relocated to Kennett Square, Jacquelyn found her smile again, brief and weary as it was. It was time to embrace the joy of her salvation again. That could never happen until she stopped feeling sorry for herself.

Now that her Maker had given her a spiritual attitude adjustment, by once again shifting her heart fully toward her Savior, ever so gently, everything was starting to make sense again. It felt good...

SIMILAR SCENES LIKE THIS were taking place at all remaining Christian dissident and Jewish hiding places. Yahweh had reunited family members and friends, from every nation, tribe and tongue. It was an amazing thing to behold.

As life had very quickly become a lying-in-wait in dingy, dusty underground dwellings for all Christians who had survived Antichrist's fierce bombing campaign, Yahweh had once again blown their minds, by safely bringing family members and friends to their final locations until His Son, and their Redeemer returned for them. Who else could do it? The answer was both obvious and comforting—no one!

With the Church safe and secure, and everyone being where they needed to be, Yahweh could now focus His full attention on His beloved wife, Israel...

44

SETH SHAPIRO WOKE FROM a troubling dream he had about his son, Jakob. Three months had passed since his brother was assassinated in the streets of Jerusalem. Having been an eyewitness to it all, he was still emotionally and psychologically out of sorts.

The biggest change in his daily ritual, since his brother's assassination, was that he stopped going to the Western Wall altogether. This was partly because Jews who hadn't taken the mark were being rounded up and put in prison, until they did. It was reminiscent of what Hitler did to their people in the 20th Century.

The other reason was that he chose to remain at home and study the Book of the Law and the Prophets, day and night. This time, not as a teacher but as a student.

Since the Shapiros were desperately low on food, and they had no running water, Seth certainly felt like a student again, a very poor one.

They were thankful for the solar power they had access to. At least they could keep the fans turned on. Not that they helped much though. The air flowing through them was too hot for comfort. To say they were in dire straits would be putting it mildly.

On top of all that, Seth was still wrestling with many of the things Benjamin had told him before he was gunned down, especially about his son disappearing and reappearing elsewhere, seemingly in the blink of an eye. Jakob did appear in his dream, last night, but anything could happen in dreams.

Seth couldn't remember how the dream started. All he remembered was that Jakob picked up where his brother left off, before he was killed at the Western Wall. "Your life reminds me a lot of the life of Saul of Tarsus, Father."

Again?! Saul winced. As much as he wanted to scowl at Jakob, like he did to Benjamin, it was a dream, so he couldn't control his reactions like he could in real life. He had no choice but to listen.

"When Uncle Benjamin compared you to the Apostle Paul, I can only imagine how offended you were hearing it. I still remember what you told me about Saul of Tarsus, when I was a child.

"But what you need to know, father, was that it was said to you under the influence of the Holy Spirit. Despite what you believe, Saul was a well-respected Pharisee among the Jewish people in the days of old. Before his conversion, Saul was known by everyone in the land as a man among men, as a Jew among Jews, a Pharisee among Pharisees.

"He was a descendant from the tribe of Benjamin, and he was well versed in the scriptures. Everything changed for Saul one day on the road to Damascus. Before I share his life-altering experience with you, allow me to begin where he was first mentioned in scripture, in the book of Acts, chapter seven, in the New Testament."

Usually, just hearing anyone joining the words "New" and "Testament" together would force Seth's guard way up. When uttered separately, it was fine, but hearing them combined caused his skin to crawl, especially from his own son.

Instead of chastising Jakob, like he'd done on numerous occasions when he first converted to faith in Yeshua, Seth cautiously nodded for his son to continue. Even if he wanted to argue the point, again, it was a dream.

Jakob explained to his father, "After Messiah was raised from the dead three days after being crucified for the sins of many, and seated at the right hand of Yahweh, the Church grew exponentially. At that time, it was called, 'The Way'. But it didn't come without stiff opposition from Jewish leaders. Believers faced fierce persecution for their faith in Yeshua. Many were killed for it.

"The first martyr was a man named Stephen. A Jew himself, he was a faithful servant. He was full of Yahweh's grace and power, he even performed great wonders and signs among the people. Yet, he was stoned to death for his faith in Messiah.

"His opposers couldn't stand up against the wisdom the Spirit gave Stephen as he spoke. So, they stirred up the people and the elders and the teachers of the law, and secretly persuaded some men to lie about him."

Jakob stared at his father, "Does that sound like truth to you?"

"They seized Stephen and brought him before the Sanhedrin. The false witnesses testified against him saying, 'This fellow never stops speaking against this holy place and against the law. For we have heard this man speaking blasphemous words against Moses and against Yahweh. We also heard him say this Yeshua of Nazareth will destroy this place and change the customs Moses handed down to us.'

"The high priest asked him, 'Are these charges true?' To this Steven gave a brief dissertation of Jewish history. He was well versed in the five books of the Torah and in the Books of the Prophets. He proved it by walking them through Genesis, Exodus, Leviticus, Numbers and Deuteronomy, with perfect clarity.

"When he finished giving his lengthy dissertation of their nation's long and turbulent history, he became indignant with the Sanhedrin. He called them a bunch of stiff-necked people whose hearts and ears were still uncircumcised. He accused them of being just like their ancestors, who always resisted the Holy Spirit.

"Steven asked them, 'Was there ever a prophet your ancestors did not persecute? They even killed those who predicted the coming of the Righteous One.' He then accused the men in his presence saying, 'Now you have betrayed and murdered Him—you who have received the law that was given through angels but have not obeyed it.'

"When the members of the Sanhedrin heard this, they were furious and gnashed their teeth at him. They covered their ears and shouted at the top of their voices, as they dragged him out of the city and began to stone him. This is where Saul was first mentioned in the Bible, Father. The witnesses laid their coats at his feet, and Saul nodded his approval for the stoning to continue.

"Steven's death caused a great persecution to break out against the church in Jerusalem. Saul's goal was nothing short of destroying the Church. Fully convinced that he was on Yahweh's good side, he went from house to house, breathing out murderous threats against the Lord's disciples, dragging off men and women who were followers of Messiah, and putting them in prison.

"When Saul got word that many believers were scattered throughout Judea and Samaria, he went to the high priest and asked him for letters to the synagogues in Damascus, so that if he found any there who belonged to the Way, whether men or women, he might take them as prisoners to Jerusalem.

"It was on the road to Damascus that Saul had his encounter with Yeshua. Suddenly a light from Heaven flashed around him. He fell to the ground and heard a voice say to him, 'Saul, Saul, why do you persecute me?' Saul replied by asking, 'Who are you, Lord?' Yeshua replied saying, 'I am Yeshua, whom you are persecuting. Now get up and go into the city, and you will be told what you must do.'

"The men traveling with Saul stood there speechless; they heard the sound but did not see anyone. Saul got up from the ground, but when he opened his eyes, he could see nothing. So, they led him by hand into Damascus. For three days he was blind and didn't eat or drink anything.

"Meanwhile, the Lord had also called upon one of His Disciples in a vision, a man named Ananias, and commanded him to go to the house of Judas, in Damascus, and ask for a man from Tarsus named Saul.

"Ananias became fearful. He answered, 'Lord, I have heard many reports about this man and all the harm he has done to your holy people in Jerusalem. He has come here with authority from the chief priests to arrest all who call on your name.'

"But the Lord said to him, 'Go! This man is my chosen instrument to proclaim my name to the Gentiles and their kings, and to the people of Israel.' Then Ananias went to the house and entered it.

"Placing his hands on Saul, he said, 'Brother Saul, the Lord—Yeshua, who appeared to you on the road as you were coming here—has sent me so that you may see again and be filled with the Holy Spirit.'

"Immediately, something like scales fell from Saul's eyes, and he could see again. He got up and was baptized, and after taking some food, he regained his strength."

Seth remembered his brother uttering those very words about scales falling from his own eyes. It was like having a dream within a dream.

"Saul spent several days with the disciples in Damascus. At once he began to preach in the synagogues that Yeshua was the Son of Yahweh. Imagine that, Father, going to Damascus to persecute those who preached those words, to suddenly becoming one of them? He went from hunter to hunted just like that!"

Before Seth could answer, Jakob further explained, "All those who heard him were astonished and asked, 'Isn't he the man who raised havoc in Jerusalem among those who call on this name? And hasn't he come here to take them as prisoners to the chief priests?'

"Yet Saul grew more and more powerful and baffled the Jews living in Damascus, by proving that Yeshua was the Messiah. When he went to Jerusalem, to join the disciples, they, too, were afraid of him. They didn't believe that he really was a disciple.

"But Barnabas told them about what had happened to Saul on his journey to Damascus, and how he had seen the Lord and that the Lord had spoken to him, and how he had preached so fearlessly in the name of Yeshua. So, they accepted him with great joy.

"Saul stayed with them and moved about freely in Jerusalem, speaking boldly in the name of the Lord. He talked and debated with the Hellenistic Jews, but they tried to kill him. When the believers learned of this, they took him down to Caesarea and sent him off to Tarsus.

"Under the influence of the Holy Spirit, Saul, now Paul, went on to lead many Gentiles and Jews to Yeshua. He also authored many of the Books in the New Testament. From the time of his conversion to the time of his death, Paul was an awesome soldier in God's army."

Finally, Seth asked his son, "Is there a point for all of this, Jakob?"

"My point, Father, is that Saul, a well-respected Pharisee before his life transforming incident with Yeshua, didn't even know to Whom he was speaking. When the Lord asked him, 'Saul, Saul, why do you persecute me?' he replied by asking, 'Who are you, Lord?'

"Saul knew he was speaking to the Lord, he even addressed Him as Lord, only he didn't know who He was, until the Lord replied, 'I am Yeshua, whom you are persecuting.' Doesn't it strike you as odd, Father, that someone who studied under Gamaliel and was thoroughly trained in the law of our ancestors didn't even know Who he was serving?"

Seth didn't answer his son. He couldn't. But he knew Gamaliel was a leading authority in the Sanhedrin in the early first century CE.

"Sadly, tragically, with regard to the Jews, nothing has changed in two thousand years. But for Saul, this divine appointment in his life had caused a radical change in him. Instead of blaspheming Yeshua for being a fraud, Saul obeyed His command and went on to Damascus, even temporarily blinded. From that day forward, Yahweh used him mightily to spread the Gospel to both the Jews and the Gentiles."

Jakob stared at his father. "I know you think Uncle Benjamin had a mental illness. But nothing could be farther from the truth. What he experienced was the same sensation of crossing over from spiritual death to life that Saul of Tarsus had so many centuries ago. This is something you have never experienced in your many years as a rabbi, Father."

Jakob's words felt like a hammer blow to his chest.

He went on, "Uncle Benjamin challenged you to read the New Testament for yourself. What you must understand, Father, is in the Old Testament, we get the facts. In the New Testament, we get the explanation and the fulfillment of them.

"If you'll only put your defenses down, and seek Yahweh's wisdom with all your heart, mind and soul, you'll come to see for yourself that

Yeshua really is Israel's Messiah. If not, you will remain that same spiritually blinded religious man that Saul was before his conversion.

"Even if you keep refusing to believe it, it doesn't make it any less true. Only by trusting in Yeshua will you ever get to see Heaven. You must be born again!"

That was when Seth woke up in a cold sweat. He could feel his heart pounding in his chest like a drum. For someone who had been a fierce debater all his life, usually, he could win any argument by simply quoting straight from the Torah. But in his dream, he could do nothing to challenge his son. It was as if his tongue was suddenly tied.

Even though it was only a dream, he felt this emptiness inside as if his life's work and service for Yahweh hadn't mattered. It was like the spiritual carpet upon which he had built his foundation had just been pulled out from under his feet. It was the worst sensation.

Could it really be true?

45

THREE DAYS LATER, SETH Shapiro became so desperate for answers to the many questions swirling in his head, that he risked his freedom by leaving the house to meet with his two fellow rabbis, Yosef and Tobias.

His hope was that they might help break him out of his spiritual stupor. If he didn't find them at the Western Wall, he would go to their homes next. There wasn't a chance he would share his dream with them.

How could he possibly explain how he was visited by his son, in la la land of all places, only to be told how off track his life was spiritually?

At least Jakob didn't mention the passage to him that had caused great separation among so many Jewish families, including his own, before the Two Witnesses were assassinated at the Western Wall, just like his brother three months ago. That passage was Isaiah 53.

When Seth arrived, it was just after 6 am. It was all abuzz with tens of thousands of pilgrims, all in line to bow down in worship of the ridiculous statue. They all had UV-blocker umbrellas for when the sun rose, which did very little to protect them. The nasty-looking burn marks on their bodies which were already covered in sores, indicated that much. It was so much worse than what he witnessed three months ago.

Seth didn't bring his umbrella this time. He didn't expect to stay very long. Unlike all other past visits to this place, he wore plain clothes this time. He could no longer wear the clerical robe he usually had on.

The blistering heat had nothing to do with it. If he was seen wearing it, it would surely lead to his arrest. But there wasn't a chance that he would cut off his beard. *Some savior of the Jews!* Seth never believed Romanero was a savior anyway.

He walked to their usual meeting place, but Yosef and Tobias weren't there. He searched the entire area looking for them, but he didn't see them anywhere. Perhaps they were just as fearful of being arrested as he was.

Seth saw Jeroham. Without a trace of anger in his voice, Seth asked the young man he had heckled every day, "Have you seen my friends?"

The 21-year-old with dark brown, curly hair that reached down to his shoulders, answered, "They haven't been here in many weeks."

Seth became fearful hearing this. He looked lost, directionless. "Were they arrested?"

"I don't know. All I can say is they haven't been here in a while."

The young preacher broke eye contact with Seth and shouted 2 Thessalonians 2-9:12 at the top of his lungs, for everyone within the sound of his voice to hear. "'The coming of the lawless one will be in accordance with how Satan works. He will use all sorts of displays of power through signs and wonders that serve the lie, and all the ways that wickedness deceives those who are perishing.

"'They perish because they refused to love the truth and so be saved. For this reason, God sends them a powerful delusion so that they will believe the lie and so that all will be condemned who have not believed the truth but have delighted in wickedness.'"

Jeroham refocused his attention on Seth. Now that Antichrist and the False Prophet were detaining all defiant Jews who hadn't yet taken the mark, the only person foolish enough to be in the vicinity without it, was the man standing in front of him. He handed Seth a copy of *The Way*. "Your son asked me to give this to you…"

When Seth saw the title of the Book, chills shot up and down his spine. He remembered Jakob telling him in his dream that the early church was called *The Way*. Without saying another word, he gulped hard, shoved the book in his shirt and hurried home, hoping and praying every step of the way that no one would stop him.

He had witnessed many Jews of all ages asking the four young men for copies of the book he now had tucked in his shirt. It happened so many times he stopped counting long ago. Now *he* was the recipient!

If Yosef and Tobias could see me now…

Seth didn't know that whenever one of the 144,000 handed out copies of the book, all recipients had Yahweh's supernatural covering. This meant the enemy had no way to capture the exchange in any capacity.

With the two arch enemies of the God of Israel tightening the screws all throughout the land, if Seth didn't have this supernatural protection, he surely would have been arrested by now.

When Seth arrived home, breakfast was waiting.

For the third day in a row, their neighbors had provided food for them—a half a loaf of barley bread, two hard boiled eggs each, and two measured cups of water. Even though Seth was their beloved rabbi, they knew feeding anyone who refused the mark was illegal.

They also knew the danger they faced if they got caught…

They kept pleading with the Shapiros to take the mark, so they could function in society again. "If we get caught," they had warned, "they'll arrest us too!" But the Shapiros remained defiant.

The garden that Naveh had worked so hard growing fresh fruits and vegetables stopped producing crops when the water turned blood red.

Without the mark, they couldn't wait in line, in the middle of the night, when it was noticeably cooler, for their daily rations of fresh water. Then again, even with water, the sun's rays were too strong and damaging to grow vegetables in what once was her garden.

Seth pulled the book out from underneath his shirt and placed it on the small coffee table. He waited for his wife's reaction.

Naveh glanced at it and almost looked relieved. Now 60, she didn't know how much more she could take. Their lives had come to a standstill. At the very least, it would break the stagnation in their lives.

Naveh didn't need her husband to remind her that for all who believed the Message it told, Jew and Gentile alike, the book on the table was an extension of the Torah, the Book of the Prophets, and Psalms and Proverbs, which made up the Old Testament.

What followed in the New Testament was what had caused so much separation among the Jews, since Yeshua's crucifixion.

When this book was first being mass produced, it was a condensed version of both the Old and New Testaments. Now that Yahweh was gathering his remnant, they were being given the complete Word of God, not the condensed version of it.

Now that his parents had received a copy of *The Way*, Yahweh sent Jakob to visit his parents in person.

Just when they finished eating, he suddenly materialized in their living room. "Shalom, Mother, Father! It's nice to see you both again."

Naveh screamed so loud that Seth nearly jumped off the sofa. She clutched at her chest thinking she might have a heart attack. This marked the first time she had seen her son since Seth disowned him. She had suffered mightily since that time. But nothing could compare to how she felt on that day. It was the worst day of her life.

The Shapiros had heard about their son's ability to materialize, but they had never witnessed it with their own two eyes. All skepticism had just been removed, in the blink of an eye.

Jakob sat next to his mother and rubbed her back, until he knew she was okay. The longing in her eyes was evident. She missed him. The son she gave birth to in her late 30s looked different. But beneath the surface, she still saw her little boy.

Naveh adjusted her weight on the couch, dried her moist eyes, and kissed her son on the forehead many times.

Jakob said, "Whatever conversation we have is being supernaturally protected from the outside world. So, speak freely."

Before Naveh could ask her son how he was doing, where he lived, or if he had a girlfriend, Seth spoke first. "You told me in the dream the Old Testament provided the facts, and the New Testament provided the explanation of them."

"That would be correct, Father. And the fulfillment of them."

Naveh asked her son, "Care to elaborate?"

"Sure. The reason so many prophecies recorded in the Book of the Prophets are still a mystery to you both, is that they were all answered in the New Testament, save for the handful that are still to come. There are more than three hundred prophecies in the Old Testament which point to Yeshua, as being Israel's long-awaited Savior."

Seth became fidgety on the couch. He looked nervously at Naveh, then motioned with his hand for his son to continue.

"In the interest of time I'll give you a few of them for now, beginning with Isaiah seven-fourteen: 'Therefore the Lord himself will give you a sign: 'The virgin will conceive and give birth to a son, and will call him Immanuel.'"

Jakob couldn't ignore what he saw on his parents' faces. They knew where he was going with this prophecy. Like most Jews, Seth and Naveh were both mindful of bits and pieces of the life of Yeshua, and with Miriam's so-called virgin birth. They just never believed it.

Jakob saw his father shifting uncomfortably on the couch. Even his mother was fidgety. "This was fulfilled in the New Testament, in the Gospel of Luke, chapter one, when Yahweh sent the angel Gabriel to Nazareth, a town in Galilee, to a virgin pledged to be married to a man named Joseph, a descendant of David.

"The angel told Miriam she had found favor with Yahweh, and she would conceive and give birth to a son, whose name would be Yeshua. He would be called the Son of the Most High, and would be given the throne of His father David. He would reign over Jacob's descendants forever; His kingdom will never end.'

"Miriam was greatly troubled and asked the angel, 'How will this be, since I am a virgin?' Gabriel told her the power of the Most High would overshadow her. Miriam accepted the message in faith, saying, 'I am the Lord's servant, may your word to me be fulfilled.' Then the angel left her."

Jakob looked at his father. "I know you disregard this as a nonsensical fairytale that was created by the Christians. You even taught me that in my childhood! But it really happened, thus fulfilling Isaiah seven, fourteen. Even Yeshua's birth was prophesied in Micah, five-two. I know you're familiar with it, Father."

Seth straightened up on the couch and recited it to his son, "'But you, Bethlehem Ephrathah, though you are small among the clans of Judah, out of you will come for me one who will be ruler over Israel, whose origins are from of old, from ancient times.'"

Jakob nodded, then looked at the book on the small coffee table. "While it's true that the angel Gabriel visited Miriam in Nazareth, she gave birth to Yeshua in Bethlehem. Feel free to check it for yourself later in Luke, chapter two." Jakob stared at his father. "Those are just two prophecies about the birth of Messiah. But they are the two most substantial, because they pinpoint His virgin birth and the exact location.

"Let's fast forward to just before Yeshua was crucified. I'll give you two from Zechariah. They're rather simple, mundane even, yet they both point to Yeshua, and only to Him. The first one is chapter nine, verse nine: 'Rejoice greatly, Daughter Zion! Shout, Daughter Jerusalem! See, your king comes to you, righteous and victorious, lowly and riding on a donkey, on a colt, the foal of a donkey.'

"This, too, was fulfilled in the life of Yeshua, as recorded in the four Gospels. Matthew wrote, "As they approached Jerusalem and came to Bethphage on the Mount of Olives, Yeshua sent two disciples, saying to them, 'Go to the village ahead of you, and at once you will find a donkey tied there, with her colt by her. Untie them and bring them to me. If anyone says anything to you, say that the Lord needs them, and he will send them right away.

"The disciples went and did as Yeshua had instructed them. They brought the donkey and the colt and placed their cloaks on them for Yeshua to sit on. As our Lord made His triumphant entry into Jerusalem, a very large crowd shouted, 'Hosanna to the Son of David! Blessed is he who comes in the name of the Lord! Hosanna in the highest heaven!'"

Naveh was mildly impressed that her son had memorized those passages. Whether or not she believed him was altogether different.

Jakob sighed, "One week later, they crucified Him. I know you're familiar with the scripture, Father. You're also familiar with Zechariah eleven, verses twelve and thirteen, which prophesied about the thirty pieces of silver that was paid to the one who would betray Messiah.

"I don't need to tell you who fulfilled this tragic prophecy. You both know it was Judas Iscariot. It was fulfilled in the Gospel of Matthew, chapter twenty-six, among other places. You both know Yeshua was betrayed for 30 pieces of silver. You also know He rode into Jerusalem on a donkey. Only you still refuse to believe He was Israel's Messiah.

"No one knows better than you, Father, that Zechariah represents a chronology of events for Israel and the end times. But it can only be understood by those who have all the facts in front of them. The only way for that to happen is by reading and studying the complete word of God, from Genesis to Revelation."

It was stifling hot inside the house. The air being pushed through the fans offered very little relief. Seth and Naveh fanned themselves with fans made from palm branches, hoping to cool themselves. It wasn't working. The conversation wasn't helping.

The heat didn't seem to bother Jakob in the least. "As you know, Father, Yahweh had decreed four hundred and ninety years of judgment on Messiah rejecting Israel."

Seth squirmed on the sofa. *Messiah rejecting Israel?*

Jakob noticed, but he kept going, "Until recently, only four hundred and eighty three of those years had come to pass. The Prophet Daniel said the final week or seven years wouldn't be fulfilled until after Israel's Savior was cut off. While it's true that more than two thousand years have passed since Yeshua's crucifixion, the final week of judgment toward Israel couldn't commence until after the church was removed.

"What happened nearly five years ago really was the Rapture of Yeshua's Church. It had to happen so Yahweh could once again focus on His chosen people. What you need to understand, Father, is while the Jews are the wife of Jehovah, Christians are the bride of Christ.

"When Antichrist signed the peace treaty with Israel, the final seven years were ushered in. And this means, what was put on hold for more than two thousand years, is once again being fulfilled. This was what the

Prophet Jeremiah called, 'The time of Jacob's trouble'. We are more than halfway through this final week of judgment.

"The problem for most Jews, is that they have been waiting for a conquering Messiah to come, who will vindicate the Jewish people, liberate the nation from their earthly oppressors, and elevate Israel to world dominance economically, politically, and militarily.

"That's why they never recognized Yeshua as Israel's Messiah. It's hard to profess faith in a Savior who was born in a manger, only to die on a tree." Jakob paused. "The Jews are right to say Messiah is coming. But what they don't realize is He will be coming for the second time.

"Only those who have a true understanding of the times in which we're living know what's going on. Now that the Church age has passed, these final seven years are the final years of Israel's punishment."

Jakob's face became radiant. "But among the constant persecution, it's also the time of Israel's redemption. Yahweh is now gathering His remnant, which as you know will be one-third of the Jewish race. The other two-thirds who reject Yeshua will perish."

Jakob pointed at the book on the coffee table. "Without comparing the many prophecies you've studied over the years, in the New Testament, Father, it will be impossible for either of you to gain a clear understanding of Yahweh's final timeline.

"Check the facts for yourself. If you do, you'll discover for yourselves that everything I'm saying is recorded in the divine pages of scripture. My prayer is that the two of you will read it and come to believe it for yourselves…"

Naveh smiled to herself. *The student is teaching the teacher!*

Jakob paused and glanced around the house. They had no food on the shelves, no running water, only solar electricity. "The course of human history as we know it will soon come to an end. As bad as things are now, it's only going to get worse. The only way out is by trusting in Yeshua as Lord and Messiah. But if you keep rejecting Him, I assure you this will be as good as it gets."

Naveh's face quaked in anguish.

Jakob looked at his parents tenderly, compassionately. "As one of His sealed servants, you can't deny I'm being supernaturally protected. All of us are." He pointed to the copy of *The Way* on the coffee table again. "You can read all about us in the Book of Revelation, in chapters seven and fourteen. But hurry! What Uncle Benjamin told you about everything ending for all mark takers is one hundred percent accurate.

"The many Jews who are fleeing their homes and going into hiding, are the remnant. They will remain supernaturally protected, until our Redeemer returns for us. I sincerely hope the two of you will join them. But this can only happen by trusting in Yeshua for your salvation. You must be spiritually born again, both of you."

Seth and Naveh shared more astonished glances. When their eyes resettled on their son—Jakob was gone—poof—leaving them as mysteriously as when he arrived. Both were rendered speechless.

The Shapiros weren't the only Jewish family being visited by the 144,000. All of Yahweh's sealed servants had been sent out on similar missions, as their Maker kept adding to His remnant...

46

AFTER TAKING A FEW moments to absorb what had just transpired in their living room, and still wondering if it really happened, Seth plucked the book off the coffee table. If the things Jakob had said really were true, all prophecy really did point to Yeshua as being Israel's Messiah.

Since they couldn't further question their son—he left them before they could even say goodbye to him—they had no other choice but to check things for themselves in the New Testament.

Seth wanted to begin in the book of Acts. But Naveh was insistent that they start in Revelation 7, so they could read about their son, if, indeed, he really was one of them.

Prior to this unusual meeting with their son, the only way Seth would dare read the New Testament would be more from a "Know Thy Enemy" standpoint.

Chapter 7 confirmed what Jakob had told them about the 144,000 that Yahweh had sealed. Since their lineage was destroyed thousands of years ago, the fact that He had sealed 12,000 from each of the Twelve Tribes of Israel was quite miraculous.

Was Jakob really one of them? Neither of them could deny how he materialized before their very eyes, before leaving them the very same way. Verse 3 said that Yahweh had put a seal on their foreheads. They didn't see it on their son's face, but did that mean it wasn't there?

The next few verses also confirmed what Jakob had told them, about a great multitude which no one could number, of all nations, tribes, peoples, and tongues, standing before the throne and before the Lamb, clothed with white robes, who would come out of the great tribulation, having been washed in the blood of the Lamb. All because of them…

Naveh turned the pages to chapter 14. When she read verses 4 and 5 aloud, "'These are those who did not defile themselves with women, for they remained virgins. They follow the Lamb wherever he goes. They were purchased from among mankind and offered as firstfruits to God and the Lamb. No lie was found in their mouths; they are blameless.'"

At least now I know Jakob never had a girlfriend, thought Naveh.

Seth, on the other hand, was more focused on verse 5, about no lie being found in their mouths, that they were blameless. If Jakob really was one of them, hmm…

The couple exchanged shocked glances seeing the section heading before verse 6—*the Three Angels*. The Shapiros couldn't deny this, too, had come to pass. They heard their stern messages with their own ears.

Seth flipped back to chapter 11 and read verse 3 aloud, "'And I will appoint my two witnesses, and they will prophesy for 1,260 days, clothed in sackcloth. They are 'the two olive trees' and the two lampstands, and they stand before the Lord of the earth. If anyone tries to harm them...,'" Seth locked eyes with Naveh, "'...fire comes from their mouths and devours their enemies. This is how anyone who wants to harm them must die.'"

Seth wasn't devoured by fire coming from their mouths, but for the first time, he realized they had devoured him with the Word of God. Ever mindful of what Jeremiah 5:14 said, "I will make my words in your mouth a fire and these people the wood it consumes," that's precisely how Seth felt now, consumed by the words they once spoke to him.

Seth read on, "'They have power to shut up the heavens so that it will not rain during the time they are prophesying; and they have power to turn the waters into blood and to strike the earth with every kind of plague as often as they want.'" He couldn't deny this happened too.

When Seth came to verses 7 and 8, he paused, "'Now when they have finished their testimony, the beast that comes up from the Abyss will attack them, and overpower and kill them. Their bodies will lie in the public square of the great city—which is figuratively called Sodom and Egypt—where also their Lord was crucified.'"

Seth grimaced. This happened in front of his very eyes. He was an active participant and one of their chief agitators. Overcome by guilt, his eyes became soaked with tears.

Naveh read verses 9 and 10 to Seth, "'For three and a half days some from every people, tribe, language and nation will gaze on their bodies and refuse them burial. The inhabitants of the earth will gloat over them and will celebrate by sending each other gifts, because these two prophets had tormented those who live on the earth.'"

Naveh paused, and waited for Seth to nod that he was okay, before continuing with verses 11-13, "'But after the three and a half days the breath of life from God entered them, and they stood on their feet, and terror struck those who saw them. Then they heard a loud voice from heaven saying to them, 'Come up here.' And they went up to heaven in a cloud, while their enemies looked on.'"

They went to Heaven? Seth wept like a baby in his wife's arms. "I was one of their mockers, and fiercest critics. I was all for denying them proper burial. I even said it publicly for all to hear…"

Naveh kissed her husband's hand, then read the next verse, "At that very hour there was a severe earthquake and a tenth of the city collapsed. Seven thousand people were killed in the earthquake, and the survivors were terrified and gave glory to the God of heaven."

Her mouth was agape. Everyone knew 7,000 people were killed in the Jerusalem earthquake. Romanero tried taking credit for it. But how could he take credit for something that was written so long ago?

Naveh turned to Revelation chapter 1. It was time to start at the beginning and see what else they might discover that had come to pass in these crazy times. After reading the Book of Revelation all the way through twice, the Shapiros took a break. Naveh slept, but not Seth.

Lying next to his wife, he kept thinking, if this really was written 2,000 years ago, the fact that it had all come to pass in their lifetime proved what Jakob had said about the facts being presented in the Old Testament, but being fulfilled in the New Testament…

When Naveh woke from her nap, they ate the leftover bread their neighbors gave them earlier, then resumed their reading, this time in the Book of Acts. For the first time in many years, the married couple read the scriptures together, like two students.

Then again, since this was Seth's first time through the New Testament, he had no choice but to read it as a student, and not as a learned rabbi. The good thing was the many years he spent studying the scriptures helped him piece things together more quickly.

Seth was fascinated by the book of Acts. Thanks to Jakob, he knew what to expect in chapters 7 through 9, with Steven and Saul.

When they got to chapter 13, his curiosity became quite piqued, as Naveh read verses 26-31, "'Fellow children of Abraham and you God-fearing Gentiles, it is to us that this message of salvation has been sent. The people of Jerusalem and their rulers did not recognize Yeshua, yet in condemning him they fulfilled the words of the prophets that are read every Sabbath. Though they found no proper ground for a death sentence, they asked Pilate to have him executed…"

Seth's face became flush, as he thought about when Jakob told him how the chief priests had produced false witnesses against Steven in his dream. His son asked him, "Does this sound like truth to you, Father?"

Naveh read on, "When they had carried out all that was written about him, they took him down from the cross and laid him in a tomb. But God raised him from the dead, and for many days he was seen by those who had traveled with him from Galilee to Jerusalem. They are now his witnesses to our people.'"

Seth then read verses 38-40, "Therefore, my friends, I want you to know that through Yeshua the forgiveness of sins is proclaimed to you. Through Him everyone who believes is set free from every sin, a justification you were not able to obtain under the law of Moses.'"

He skipped a few verses, reading 44-47 aloud, "'On the next Sabbath almost the whole city gathered to hear the word of the Lord. When the Jews saw the crowds, they were filled with jealousy. They began to contradict what Paul was saying and heaped abuse on him.

"'Then Paul and Barnabas answered them boldly: "We had to speak the word of God to you first. Since you reject it and do not consider yourselves worthy of eternal life, we now turn to the Gentiles.

"'For this is what the Lord has commanded of us in Isaiah 49:6, "'I have made you a light for the Gentiles, that you may bring salvation to the ends of the earth.'"

Seth shook his head in astonishment. He couldn't ignore what he felt inside. It was the Holy Spirit convicting him.

When Seth read what Paul had said to the people of Athens, in Acts 17:22-23, he became short of breath. Said he, "'I see that in every way you are very religious. For as I walked around and looked carefully at your objects of worship, I even found an altar with this inscription: TO AN UNKNOWN GOD. So you are ignorant of the very thing you worship—and this is what I am going to proclaim to you.'"

Seth stared at a painting on the living room wall opposite him. *Am I ignorant of the very thing I've worshiped all my life, like Saul before his conversion?* He felt this pit deep in his stomach. It was that same overwhelming sensation coursing through his body he had at the end of his dream with Jakob.

Seth fingered his way down to verse 30-31, and read it to Naveh, "'In the past God overlooked such ignorance, but now he commands all people everywhere to repent. For he has set a day when he will judge the world with justice by the man he has appointed. He has given proof of this to everyone by raising him from the dead.'"

The more he read about the life of Saul, the more he felt like him. His life transformation couldn't be denied. And the humility he exuded was remarkable.

Instead of reading Romans next, Seth flipped back to the Gospel of Matthew. He was struck by the fact that the New Testament began with the genealogy of Yeshua. Even more peculiar was that from Abraham to David *were* fourteen generations, from David until the captivity in Babylon *were* fourteen generations, and from the captivity in Babylon until the Christ *were* fourteen generations.

Much like how the Old Testament was perfectly chronicled, apparently, this was the case with the New Testament as well...

The Shapiros read through the four Gospels with open minds and hearts, which, in and of itself, was quite miraculous. The Gospel of John had a seismic impact on Seth, especially chapter 8.

"When the Pharisees told Yeshua the only Father they had was Yahweh, He said in reply, 'You belong to your father, the devil, and you want to carry out your father's desires. He was a murderer from the beginning, not holding to the truth, for there is no truth in him. When he lies, he speaks his native language, for he is a liar and the father of lies.

"'Whoever belongs to Yahweh hears My words. The reason you do not hear is that you do not belong to Him. Very truly I tell you, whoever obeys my word will never see death."

"They accused Yeshua of being demon-possessed, then exclaimed, 'Abraham died and so did the prophets, yet you say that whoever obeys your word will never taste death. Are you greater than our father Abraham? He died, and so did the prophets. Who do you think you are?'"

"Yeshua replied, 'Your father Abraham rejoiced at the thought of seeing my day; he saw it and was glad.'"

"'You are not yet fifty years old,' they said to him, 'and you have seen Abraham!'" Jesus answered, 'Very truly I tell you, before Abraham was born, I am!'" At this, they picked up stones to stone him, but Jesus hid himself, slipping away from the temple grounds."

Seth sniffled a few times. The way he felt now, he wanted to stone himself for his unbelief all his life. *All roads truly do lead to Yeshua...*

Naveh's shock knew no bounds when her husband flipped back to the one section that had caused him to disown his son, the Prophet Isaiah, chapters 52 and 53. Seth read the section heading before verse 13—*The Suffering and Glory of the Servant.*

His body started trembling as he read the last three verses of chapter 52 aloud, "'See, my servant will act wisely; he will be raised and lifted up and highly exalted. Just as there were many who were appalled at him—his appearance was so disfigured beyond that of any human being and his form marred beyond human likeness—so he will sprinkle many nations, and kings will shut their mouths because of him. For what they were not told, they will see, and what they have not heard, they will understand.'"

Seth wiped his moist eyes. Having just gone through Matthew, Mark, Luke and John, Yeshua's crucifixion was still vivid in his mind.

He turned the page to chapter 53. "Verse one, 'Who has believed our message and to whom has the arm of the LORD been revealed?'

"Verse two, 'He grew up before him like a tender shoot, and like a root out of dry ground. He had no beauty or majesty to attract us to him, nothing in his appearance that we should desire him.'

"Verse three, 'He was despised and rejected by mankind, a man of suffering, and familiar with pain. Like one from whom people hide their faces he was despised, and we held him in low esteem.'

"Verse four, 'Surely he took up our pain and bore our suffering, yet we considered him punished by God, stricken by him, and afflicted.'

"Verse five, 'But he was pierced for our transgressions, he was crushed for our iniquities; the punishment that brought us peace was on him, and by his wounds we are healed.'"

Seth could no longer read. He wept hysterically again.

Naveh wiped her eyes with a tissue and took over. "Verse six, 'We all, like sheep, have gone astray, each of us has turned to our own way; and the LORD has laid on him the iniquity of us all.'

"Verse seven, 'He was oppressed and afflicted, yet he did not open his mouth; he was led like a lamb to the slaughter, and as a sheep before its shearers is silent, so he did not open his mouth.'

"Verse eight, 'By oppression and judgment he was taken away. Yet who of his generation protested? For he was cut off from the land of the living; for the transgression of my people he was punished.'

"Verse nine, 'He was assigned a grave with the wicked, and with the rich in his death, though he had done no violence, nor was any deceit in his mouth.'

"'Verse ten, 'Yet it was the LORD's will to crush him and cause him to suffer, and though the LORD makes his life an offering for sin, he will see his offspring and prolong his days, and the will of the LORD will prosper in his hand.'

"Verse eleven, 'After he has suffered, he will see the light of life and be satisfied; by his knowledge my righteous servant will justify many, and he will bear their iniquities.'

"Verse twelve, 'Therefore I will give him a portion among the great, and he will divide the spoils with the strong, because he poured out his life unto death, and was numbered with the transgressors. For he bore the sin of many, and made intercession for the transgressors.'"

For the first time ever, Seth felt the Spirit of the living God changing his heart. Each verse shot straight into his heart of stone, softening it a little more. "Jakob was right. It really could be the fifth Gospel. Then again, since it was written hundreds of years before the four Gospels were recorded, it should be called the first Gospel."

Naveh nodded in agreement. She was experiencing the very same sensation. The scripture that was widely rejected and removed from the annual reading of the Torah and the Prophets, truly did point to none other than Yeshua Himself. The parallels were unmistakable.

Now that Yahweh was focused again on His chosen race, He was changing the direction of the preaching of the 144,000 away from those forbidden scriptures, by having them focus on the Book of Acts.

Yahweh was using the life and ministry of Saul of Tarsus to turn many stone hearts to flesh, thus fulfilling Ezekiel 36:26: *I will give you a new heart and put a new spirit within you; I will take the heart of stone out of your flesh and give you a heart of flesh.*

That's precisely how it felt now. Through soft sniffling, Seth asked his wife, read Zechariah twelve, verse ten. "And I will pour out on the house of David and the inhabitants of Jerusalem a spirit of grace and supplication. They will look on me, the one they have pierced," Naveh paused, then sniffled a few times before finishing the verse, "and they will mourn for him as one mourns for an only child, and grieve bitterly for him as one grieves for a firstborn son.'"

Unaware that thousands of believers were praying for them in America, the couple knelt on the living room floor, held hands, and repented before Yahweh, declaring Yeshua as Lord and Savior. They sobbed uncontrollably, feeling His grace flood their hearts and souls.

When the sun rose the next morning, they both knew what they had to do. It was time to meet with Jeroham, so he could advise them on how to flee Jerusalem and head south with the rest of the remnant...

Seth said to Naveh, "Before we go, I need to meet with Yosef and Tobias one last time. I owe it to them to share the Gospel with them. But I'll need a day or two to read it so I can better understand it myself."

"I agree with you on both counts. Let's pray for them now."

Seth smiled wearily at his wife, lowered his head, and prayed for Yahweh's guidance regarding these all-important matters...

47

48 HOURS LATER

AT 6 A.M., SETH Shapiro went in search of Yosef and Tobias.

The fact that there had been no communication between them, over the past three months, he didn't know if they were still alive or even in prison. There wasn't a chance he would go looking for his two rabbi friends at the Western Wall, or even at their homes.

It would be too dangerous. The only other place he could think to go, was the place they had all agreed to meet when the time came to flee.

That location was in the basement of an abandoned building that was destroyed in the Jerusalem quake.

Thankfully, Seth found his two friends at the agreed-upon hiding spot, fearing for their lives. When they saw him, they rejoiced.

Yosef asked, "Where's Naveh?"

"At home."

"It's not safe for her to be there."

Seth nodded that he understood. "We're leaving today…"

Tobias said, "There's plenty of room here. But bring whatever food and water you have. We barely have enough to feed ourselves."

"We're not staying in Jerusalem," Seth replied. "We're leaving with the remnant."

Tobias glanced confusedly at Yosef, then asked, "Are you okay, Seth? You don't look okay."

Seth looked down at his feet. "I haven't been the same since Benjamin was killed."

"That's understandable. It's only a matter of time before Yahweh restores all things, and blesses our obedience to Him…"

Seth was anguished. Not for himself, but for his two friends. "I believe that with all my heart, Tobias. Only I no longer believe it the way the two of you do."

"Oh?" asked Tobias, shooting a quick glance at Yosef. He shook his head and shrugged.

Seth waited until he had their full attention. "The two of you were eyewitnesses to what happened to my brother, three months ago. You heard the entire exchange before they killed him. But you didn't hear the conversation we had before his arrest."

Yosef exclaimed, "Thank Yahweh for that!"

Seth paused a moment, then asked Yosef, "What if I told you Yahweh Himself had ordained it?"

Yosef snickered, then said, "Go on…"

Seth broke eye contact with him, and looked down at his feet. "The long and short of it is that Benjamin told me the only chance I have of escaping Yahweh's coming judgment, was by repenting of my sins and trusting in Yeshua alone for my salvation."

"Yeshu! Ha!" barked Yosef.

Sadness covered Seth's face. Many Jewish scholars called Him "Yeshu", instead of "Yeshua". In many circles in Judaism, "Yeshu" stood for "May his name and memory be blotted out".

What Seth saw on Yosef's face was how he himself had always looked, when someone mentioned the name of Yeshua to him in a positive light. "Naturally, I rebuked my fugitive brother, by reminding him that I had studied the Torah all my life and I knew what it taught. I was the one who had dedicated my whole life to serving Yahweh, not him!

"Despite all that, Benjamin was emphatic that Yahweh's salvation had nothing to do with being Jewish, or with memorizing scriptures, or even performing good works. He told me those things could never put me in good standing with my Maker. It all came down to Yahweh's saving grace."

Both men rolled their eyes. They were stunned hearing this.

"He also believes Christians are right in saying the book of the Law, the book of Prophets, and the book of Psalms and Proverbs, comprised only a small portion of the Word of God. He was convinced that all prophecy in those Books we've studied all our lives, pertaining to the future Messiah, pointed to Yeshua, and only to Him!"

Yosef shook his head in disgust. This wasn't exactly newsworthy. Before Benjamin was murdered, he had made sure to say that publicly for all to hear. The rabbi gritted his teeth at the memory in his head.

"Yeshu! Ha!" barked Yosef again. "Stop with this nonsense, Seth."

Seth held out his hands. "You certainly won't like what he told me next. He said my life reminded him of the life of Saul of Tarsus. Talk about the ultimate insult! I couldn't believe my ears."

Tobias snapped, "How dare he say that to you!"

Seth lowered his head sadly. "Yeah, that's what I thought too. Turns out, he was right. My life really was a lot like Saul's. The same can be said of the two of you as well."

"This is preposterous!" scoffed Yosef.

Seth replied, "Indeed! But we all know Yahweh works in mysterious ways. He used my brother, who you both know was Antichrist's personal physician, and my defiant son, to rescue me from Yahweh's coming judgment."

Tobias asked Seth, "What possessed you to say this to us?"

"I'm coming to that." Seth paused to catch his breath. "Five nights ago, Jakob visited me in a dream. He basically picked up where Benjamin left off, saying my life reminded him of Saul of Tarsus.

"Jakob told me Saul, who later was known as Paul, was born in Tarsus, but he was brought up in Jerusalem. I was surprised to discover he studied under Gamaliel, and he was thoroughly trained in the law."

They both knew Gamaliel was a leading authority in the Sanhedrin way back when. They were impressed hearing this, but the expressions on their faces covered it up.

"Three days after my dream, I was still shaken. I went to the Western Wall looking for you both. I was confused and was hoping for spiritual guidance from the two of you. But you weren't there.

"I asked Jeroham if he had seen either of you. He said no, then handed me a copy of *The Way*. He told me Jakob had asked him to do it. Instead of throwing it back at him, like we demanded so many others to, when they took it from him in the past, I tucked it into my shirt and went home. I knew it was illegal, but I confess I was curious to read it.

"After Naveh and I had finished eating lunch, things got even stranger when Jakob suddenly materialized in our living room."

Tobias asked him, "Are you sure you're okay, Seth?"

"I assure you I'm not out of my mind. It really happened. Much like Jakob, the reason Jeroham can't be harmed at the Western Wall, or at any other place on the planet, is that he truly has Yahweh's supernatural protection, just like all His sealed servants."

A glow formed on Seth's face. "I'm proud to say my son Jakob is one of them. None of them have the mark, yet they are free to do whatever they want with no repercussions. If we dare go there without it, we'll be arrested on the spot. You know it's true."

Seth grimaced. "After studying the New Testament the past two days, I've come to learn that the power they have isn't Satanic, like I had openly accused them of having. It really does come from the very One we're supposed to be serving, the One I recently discovered I never really knew at all."

Seth took another deep breath and went on, "Another thing I discovered was that Saul was even more zealous for the traditions of our fathers than us! He took it to the next level, by persecuting the followers of this Way to their death, arresting both men and women and throwing them into prison.

"When he got word that many from the Way had fled Jerusalem to spread what he thought was a new and false religion, Saul obtained letters from the chief priests to their associates in Damascus, then went there to bring these people back to Jerusalem, as prisoners, to be punished.

"That was where Saul had his encounter with Yeshua. Suddenly a bright light from heaven flashed around him. He fell to the ground and heard a voice say to him, 'Saul! Saul! Why do you persecute me?' Saul asked, 'Who are you, Lord?'" Seth stopped for a moment. "I know you're wondering where I'm going with all this."

The look on their faces confirmed his statement.

"The point I'm making is the same one Jakob made to me in my dream. Saul addressed Him as Lord, even though he didn't know to Whom he was speaking. I confess this blew my mind. The Lord said to him, 'I am Yeshua of Nazareth, the One you are persecuting…'"

"Yeshu! Ha!" said Yosef again. "Stop saying that name!"

"I can't. Not until I finish with everything the Lord has put on my heart to tell you. After Saul's conversion, no one worked harder to spread the gospel he received from the Lord than him. No one went to prison more than him, had been flogged more severely, or exposed to death again and again. Five times he received from the Jews the forty lashes minus one. Three times he was beaten with rods, once he was pelted with stones, three times he was shipwrecked.

"Imagine that, so much suffering for someone who studied under Gamaliel? One thing Jakob told me that had a major impact on me was that the Old Testament gave the facts, but the New Testament explained and fulfilled them."

Yosef and Tobias exchanged more anguished glances. Just hearing Seth calling the book they had studied all their lives the Old Testament, like the Christians did, bothered them both to no end.

Seth noticed but kept going, "When I asked him to further explain it to us, he walked me and Naveh through parts of the New Testament."

Seth paused. "He was right. Every Old Testament prophecy truly does point to Yeshua…"

Yosef growled at Seth in anger. "You're hurting my ears! I've been a rabbi all my life! Are you now condemning our religion to hell? How dare you!" He pulled at his long gray beard. If he had sackcloth on, he would have torn it by now.

Seth blocked it out and went on, "Please hear me out, I'm only a messenger. Yeshua Himself said that those who don't know Him do not know the Father who sent Him. So, despite a lifetime of faithful dedication to Yahweh, by rejecting His Son all my life, it meant I didn't really know the One I served, just like Saul before his conversion.

"I can emphatically state that he wasn't starting a new religion! He was merely being obedient to Yahweh's calling on his life. The Gospel Saul preached wasn't of human origin. He didn't receive it from any man; rather, he received it by revelation from Yeshua Himself.

"When our ancestors rejected Yeshua, Yahweh grafted in the Gentiles, until the full number of the Gentiles came in. Saul, who later was known as Paul, wrote to the Romans, saying, 'What the people of Israel sought so earnestly they did not obtain. The elect among them did, but the others were hardened, as it is written: 'God gave them a spirit of stupor, eyes that could not see and ears that could not hear, to this very day…"

Seth paused, then said, "Saul called Christians ingrafted branches, saying because of our transgression, salvation came to the Gentiles to make Israel envious. Saul said Israel would experience a hardening until the full number of the Gentiles has come in. The Rapture of Yeshua's Church nearly five years ago started the process of Yahweh gathering His remnant.

"It had to happen before Yahweh could focus on His chosen people again. You know, us! Now that the Church Age has ended, He has been using His sealed servants, His three flying angels, even the Two Witnesses that we saw murdered up close and personal, to gather His remnant. Nothing even remotely like this had ever happened during the Church age period. Yahweh sent them to grab our attention!

"I know neither of you will take the mark, but like Benjamin told me, by rejecting Yeshua, it means you don't really know the One you serve. He really is Israel's Messiah. I know how much it stings hearing this. It's like acid being poured on the soul. But it's true, even if you choose not to believe it."

Tobias became angry. "I never thought the day would come when I would hear these words come out of your mouth, Seth."

Seth held out his hands again, palms out. "Hear me out, Tobias, you know me. I was where you are all my life. I'm sure that had my son not materialized before my very eyes, in my living room, I never would have opened that book, let alone allow it in my house. Yahweh knew it would take something so bizarre like that to shift my thinking."

Tobias glanced over at Yosef. He shook his head incredulously. They knew Seth was still in mourning, but this was over the top.

Tobias wanted to say to him, "I know you've been through a lot but, clearly, you're not thinking straight. Life hasn't been easy for me either. Have you forgotten that I lost my wife in the quake?" Instead, he offered, "I must ask again, are you sure you're okay, Seth?"

"I'm fine, Tobias."

Yosef rolled his eyes defiantly. "If you say so!" he snapped.

Seth ignored the rant and went on, "If you'll only read the New Testament for yourself, you'll see everything I'm telling you is one hundred percent true. Once the timeline comes into full view, it all starts to make perfect sense. But without accessing the New Testament, it will continue to be a blur to you…

"I still have so much to learn. So many dots still need to be connected. But I know enough to tell you it'll be impossible for anyone to comprehend what's happening without it, including the two of you.

"Like Jakob rightly said, the Old Testament gives the facts, and the New Testament gives the explanation of them. As much as I don't want to part with it, I'm willing to give you my copy of the book Jeroham gave to me, so you can check it for yourselves. Then you will see…"

Yosef's face burned with anger. "Stop this blasphemy, Seth! I can't take it any longer." He covered his ears and walked away from the conversation…

48

TOBIAS SAID TO SETH, "Perhaps you should go…"

Seth pleaded with his friend, "This very well may be the last time we see each other, so please let me finish. Then, if you still choose not to believe me, I'll go."

Tobias motioned ever so cautiously with his hands for him to continue.

"One thing that further cemented my belief that Yeshua truly is our long-awaited Messiah, was how many times the Sadducees and Pharisees produced false witnesses not only against Him, but against all His followers, hoping to preserve what they believed was the Truth.

"Naturally, I understood their anger. They thought Saul was starting a new religious cult. Until just recently, I thought that too. But you know this already."

Seth shook his head. "When Jakob visited me in my dream, he told me about a man named Steven, a well-respected Jew who was learned in the scriptures. But when he started following Yeshua, the Sanhedrin did the same to him, by producing false witnesses to testify against him, so they could have him put to death. Steven was the first martyr in the New Testament for Yeshua."

Tobias glared at him signifying that he had no idea what he was getting at.

Seth proceeded, "My son asked me, 'Does that sound like truth to you, Father?' Think about it, Tobias, if our side was right, why would we ever feel the need to lie or produce false witnesses, to preserve what we believed was the truth? If the truth was on our side, there would be no need to do such things. All we'd have to do is stand on Yahweh's eternal truths, without compromise, right?"

Tobias remained silent.

Seth knew his comment had landed hard. He went on, "Over the past two days, I've read the New Testament all the way through. I can't tell you how many times our side produced false witnesses against Saul to discredit him. At one point, they were so desperate to kill him, more than forty Jews bound themselves under an oath to the chief priests and elders, saying that they wouldn't eat or drink until they had killed him. I must say, this grieved my spirit when I read it.

"Of course, the One they plotted against the most was Yeshua Himself. When He was condemned to death, even Judas, who we all know betrayed Him, was seized with remorse and tried returning the thirty pieces of silver to the chief priests and the elders. He told them he had sinned, by betraying innocent blood.

"Instead of taking it back, the chief priests told him it was his problem. Judas threw the coins back at them, then went and hanged himself. Since it was blood money, the chief priests knew it was against the law to put them into the treasury. So, they used it to buy the potter's field as a burial place for foreigners. You know it's still called the Field of Blood to this day.

"If they really were men of truth, wouldn't they have done all they could to make things right? But they didn't. In case you're wondering, this fulfilled Zechariah's prophecy. This was only one of the hundreds of prophecies we've read to our congregations all our lives which pointed to Messiah. All were fulfilled by Yeshua, save for the few that are yet to come. But I assure you He will fulfill them too!

"It didn't end there. Before Yeshua was crucified, the chief priests furthered their lie by encouraging Pontius Pilate to hand a condemned killer named Barabbas over to them instead, and order the death of an innocent Man.

"And here's something significant we were never taught in Hebrew school. After Yeshua was crucified, there was an earthquake. The earth shook, the rocks split, and the tombs broke open.

"The bodies of many holy people who had died were raised to life. They came out of the tombs after Jesus' resurrection and went into the holy city and even appeared to many people.

"Even more significant, the veil of the temple was torn in two from top to bottom, separating the holy of holies. I now believe that the veil was symbolic of Yeshua Himself as the only way to the Father.

"Yeshua's death and resurrection removed the barriers between Yahweh and man. Now we can approach Him with confidence and boldness, both Jew and Gentile alike. Don't you find this significant? For me, it was a real game changer!"

Tobias wouldn't look Seth in the eyes, but Seth knew his friend enough to know he was listening. But was he hearing?

"The next day, after Yeshua was taken off the cross, you'd think the chief priests and the Pharisees would have finally been satisfied. They weren't. They went to Pilate and told him that before His death, that deceiver told His followers that after three days He would rise again.

"They asked Pilate to give the order for the tomb to be made secure until the third day, in case His disciples stole the body and told the people that He was raised from the dead. They convinced Pilate that this last deception would be worse than the first one.

"Pilate agreed to their desperate wishes. He ordered the guards to make the tomb as secure as they knew how. They even put a seal on the stone. I can't help but wonder, if they really believed Yeshua was a false prophet, or from the devil, as they had often accused Him, why worry about His body if He was slain.

"It didn't stop there. Three days after His crucifixion, there was another violent earthquake. That's right, two of them in three days. This time, an angel of the Lord came down from heaven and rolled back the stone in front of the tomb. His appearance was like lightning, and his clothes were white as snow. The guards were so afraid of him that they shook and became like dead men.

"The angel told the women who went there to check on their Savior, to not be afraid, for the One they were looking for, who was crucified, was no longer there; He had risen, just as He had said. He even let them go inside the tomb. Sure enough, it was empty.

"The angel told the women to go quickly and tell His disciples: 'He has risen from the dead and is going ahead of you into Galilee. There you will see Him.' They hurried away from the tomb, afraid yet filled with joy.

"Suddenly Yeshua greeted them. They clasped his feet and worshipped Him. Then He said to them, 'Do not be afraid. Go and tell my brothers to go to Galilee; there they will see me.'

"As all that was happening, some of the guards went into the city and reported to the chief priests everything that had happened. And what did the chief priests do? Instead of checking the facts for themselves, they chose again to cover it up.

"They devised a plan, and gave the soldiers a large sum of money, telling them to spread their lie by saying, 'His disciples came during the night and stole him away while we were asleep.' They assured the soldiers if word ever got back to the governor, they would keep them out of trouble, by confirming the lie. So the soldiers took the money and did as they were instructed."

Seth shook his head, clearly ashamed of what his fathers had done. He glanced over and saw Yosef straining hard to hear him. "As you know, this story has been widely circulated among the Jews to this very day. We even helped spread it ourselves!

"Talk about fraught with corruption! Just like the Roman officer found nothing warranting death or imprisonment for Saul, Pilate found no fault in Yeshua. And yet the chief priests bribed them to cover it all up, eventually killing them both. This dark, ugly part of our nation's history cannot be blotted out. The three of us know what happened."

Yosef and Tobias looked at Seth. Both men were clearly perturbed. They couldn't fathom how he, of all people, could have been deceived like his brother and son had been.

Seth tried pleading with his two friends one last time. "The two of you have dedicated your whole lives to the service of the Lord. Unfortunately, like me, you weren't plugged in to the proper Source. If our side is right, if we represent the Truth, there would be no need to ever cover anything up. And what we've been covering up for more than two thousand years is that Yeshua truly is our risen Messiah."

Yosef shouted across the room, "Blasphemy!"

Seth went on, "Until the other day, as Yahweh's servants, I was convinced that the three of us were guaranteed Heaven at the end of our lives. I no longer believe that. I assure you that being a rabbi won't be enough to save you. Only the remnant will escape what's coming.

"What links the remnant is that we all believe Yeshua is Israel's Messiah. We represent the true Israel. I just pray that the two of you become part of the remnant too. I don't want either of you to end up in Hades, along with everyone else who dies still in their sins. I don't need to remind you what scripture has to say about the other two-thirds."

Yosef and Tobias shared awkward glances. Since there were three of them there, and he had already proclaimed to be part of the remnant, was he insinuating...

Yosef asked, "Are you subliminally telling us that we represent the two-thirds who aren't part of the remnant?"

Seth stared at them both and said as compassionately and as tenderly as he could, "For your sakes, I hope not. But like I already told you, what links the remnant is our belief that Yeshua is Israel's Messiah. So, the question begs, do you believe that?"

Instead of answering the question, Yosef barked, "We can't even walk down the street, yet you say you will flee Jerusalem with your wife, with no money in your pockets and no food or water to take with you, and head south with the others who now trust in Yeshua. I thought your brother was insane!"

Seth grinned wearily. "That's correct. We will abide in the shadow of the Almighty, and nothing or no one will be able to touch us, not even Antichrist and the False Prophet. I plead with you both to repent of your sins, and trust in Yeshua, before it's too late."

At that, Seth left them for home. His heart ached for his two spiritually blinded rabbi friends.

49

THE SUPREME SEE, SALVADOR Romanero, summoned all his global and military leaders to New Babylon, for an emergency meeting.

This gathering had nothing to do with finding solutions to the massive water shortage that humanity was faced with, stemming from the second, third, and fourth bowl judgments to strike the planet.

Nor was it to announce a breakthrough drug that mark takers the world over had been screaming for, to alleviate the agony they felt each day from those painful, festering, malignant sores covering their bodies, which they all knew was a direct result of taking the mark.

Even after all this time, they were nowhere near finding a cure. The new utopia that their lord and savior was creating, had quickly turned into being morphined up day and night, or having their veins full of heroin, until a cure was finally discovered.

Without these strong narcotics in their systems, most found it impossible to sleep at night. Utopia? This was nothing but a cruel, heartless joke that was being played on everyone!

This gathering of the minds had been in the making for quite some time. It was focused on a tiny parcel of land situated 500 miles northwest of New Babylon. Dozens of nuclear tipped missiles were already pointed in that direction, with the goal being the utter destruction of Israel.

Everyone knew the constant judgments pounding the planet were being sent by Israel's God. As always, the Most High took full responsibility for what He was doing, without apology.

The more they tried one-upping Him, the more ridiculous He made them look. The only way they could achieve peace and harmony on earth, would be by destroying Israel.

Only then could their new utopia finally be realized...

After exhausting the full repertoire of ideas looking for solutions, with absolutely no success, they believed the only way they could ease their suffering, and silence Him, would be to destroy His chosen people.

The logic among them was, "No worshipers, no God!" Yes, by destroying Israel, and taking His true followers away from Him, at the very least, it would render Israel's God powerless.

Only then would the judgments stop, and the painful sores on their bodies disappear. Then they could finally live in peace!

This meeting was already being labeled by the press as the cure of all cures for what kept paralyzing them from achieving their global objectives. But as Antichrist was preparing his global armies for battle, against Israel, he was totally unaware that a rogue military faction was preparing to attack his headquarters in New Babylon.

Missiles would soon be pointed at the remarkable city he had built, by some of his mark takers, no less.

When leaders of this aptly named "secular" group—which now numbered in the millions—became aware of the meeting, the green light was given to dig up their nuclear weapons, dust them off, and prepare for battle. This, too, had been in the works for quite some time.

Most of these hell-bent warriors were raised in Islamic or atheist countries. The northern coalition were led mostly by Russian, Chinese, Turkish, Afghani, and Lebanese citizens. Citizens from Iran, Syria, Saudi Arabia, and Ethiopia would also collaborate on the mission.

They were all for the world coming together as one. They had no problem with taking the mark and ingesting the chip, but only from a health and economic standpoint, not a religious one.

The Muslims representing this secular faction had never adhered to the tenants of Islam. They merely went through the motions, nothing more.

Conversely, the only religion the atheists in this group ever knew was government. They believed religion was the chief cause of much of the bloodshed and hatred in the world, over the centuries.

Because of this, they had always yearned for a one world system, without religion. How could anyone, including Salvador Romanero and the Pope, create a new utopia with scores of religious zealots roaming the planet, preaching their hate speech? They couldn't.

One thing was certain, if they seized global control, they would never order anyone to worship them.

This rogue faction refused to address Romanero as "Supreme See", let alone as "lord and savior". Many of his prophecies had never come to fruition. Had he been effective against the God of Israel, many from this group might have bowed down to him in worship by now.

It was commendable how Romanero had succeeded in building his global kingdom, in the face of constant calamity. But as the days kept passing, it became more evident to them that the God of Israel was all powerful, and the two global leaders weren't. If anything, they were just as flawed as they themselves were.

Now they were trying to force them to bow down in worship of a man who had signed the seven-year peace treaty with Israel. In fact, it was the first thing the Spaniard had done when he first came to power.

In the first three and a half years, Romanero made sure that the Zionists were the most protected people on the planet.

And if that wasn't enough, when all Islamic religious strongholds were destroyed in the failed sneak attack on Israel, on the original peace treaty signing date—by Muslim pilots no less—Romanero vowed not to let them rebuild. But he gave permission for the Zionists to build their Temple where the Dome of the Rock had stood!

Then, there was the first earthquake that Romanero proclaimed to send, targeting all countries responsible for the failed sneak attack. Their countries were among those targeted on that dreadful day.

As many of their Muslim friends, family members and neighbors were killed, many of the survivors lost their homes. Then, as they were slowly rebuilding their lives, the global quake destroyed what they were rebuilding. Many had been living in tents and trailers ever since.

The only nation that wasn't affected by the quakes was Israel. Romanero proclaimed to the whole world that he had spared them both times. It was yet another knife being twisted in the backs of all who wanted Israel wiped off the face of the earth.

They rejoiced when the Jerusalem quake rocked the tiny nation, until it became evident to them that the God of Israel had sent it to punish Romanero, not the Zionists. They even had to reschedule the Temple dedication, as a result.

It was as if the God of Israel knew the true intentions of his heart, which caused Him to preemptively send the Jerusalem quake.

Now, on top of all that, their bodies were covered in these painful, festering sores. This had nothing to do with their unwillingness to bow down to Salvador Romanero in worship.

It all came down to taking the mark. They were assured that once they did that, they would be protected. This was yet another lie they were fed all along. To add insult to injury, the two leaders didn't have these sores on their bodies. The reason for this was painfully obvious: neither man had taken the mark. This was an unforgiveable act!

But without fail, whenever one of their followers took it, the Supreme See and Holy See both felt it deep in their souls. They never discussed it among themselves. What would be the point? They kept it a private matter.

Now, all of a sudden, they want to destroy Israel. Why the about face? They were acting like politicians who had failed their constituents and were now promising to turn things around before the election, hoping to win them over again.

Even most Buddhists and Confucianists who had faithfully supported Romanero all this time, were suddenly fearful of him. And angered! How could they not be after he took their peaceful religion away from them?

That's precisely how this group of more than a million determined members of this military group felt about the two world leaders.

This sudden reversal on their stance on Israel was too little too late. What if they threw their support behind Romanero and the Pope, only to be lied to and let down again?

Even if the penalty for refusing to worship him was death, they would never do that. That was where they drew the line.

If there was one thing for which they were thankful, it's that Romanero had already taken out most Muslims and Christians.

Two disruptive religious groups down, one to go—two actually. Now that the Pope had started his new global religion, once the Jews and the two leaders were taken out, it would mark the removal of all "disruptive" organized religions.

Then, and only then, could there be peace on earth…

As much as they hated the two world leaders, they hated the Jews even more. This hatred toward the Zionists soared to even greater heights after taking the mark. They were consumed by revenge—first on the two global leaders, then on the Jews themselves.

They were all for them plotting against Israel, only they wanted to strip the power away from them, beforehand, so when Israel was attacked, they would lead the way. The only thing they wanted from the two global leaders was the limitless power they harnessed, nothing more.

Their plan for taking them out was to detonate an electromagnetic pulse (EMP) over New Babylon, 36 hours from now, just before global leaders gathered there, and thrust the city into total darkness.

With more than a dozen warheads at their disposal, for this particular mission alone, all they would need was for one of them to successfully detonate twenty miles above New Babylon, and the effects of the electromagnetic discharge would be irreversible, permanently crippling their power grid, until it could be rebuilt.

This would clear the way for an invasion. Although invasion was too strong a word, since their only goal was to take out the two men who wanted to be worshipped.

But since the diabolical duo had the full support of all global leaders, they couldn't seek the advice or assistance from leaders of their own countries. Nor could they compete with Romanero's armies, which outnumbered them by at least a thousand to one.

Which was why it needed to be a sneak attack...

Once they achieved their objective, their hope was that the rest of the global leaders would fall in line. If not, they would be crushed before they even got started.

But at least they would leave this planet having done something good for humanity.

Since they were in good standing in the global community, they could still move freely about the planet. They also had internet access, which they used to communicate with their brothers in arms. But it was very slow at times, due to their low social scoring ratings.

But before a single warhead could be discharged, their plan was suddenly disrupted when the fifth angel poured out his bowl on the throne of the beast, and its kingdom was plunged into darkness...

As the sun kept scorching all mark takers with fire and searing them with mind-numbing heat, extremely dangerous amounts of gamma rays had also been emitted all this time. What had started with car batteries and cell phones being fried had just been taken to an extraordinary level.

These intense wavelengths of light disrupted, and in many areas, fried all power grids, simultaneously. Even their solar panels were overwhelmed, rendering them worthless, thrusting New Babylon, and the entire planet, into darkness.

It was as if Yahweh Himself had turned off Planet Earth's power switch, using the sun to do His bidding. It was executed without firing a single nuclear warhead, once again showing that Yahweh didn't need humanity to carry out His judgments...

50

WITH PLANET EARTH SUDDENLY plunged into a thick, suffocating, fog-like darkness, the spiritual darkness all mark takers felt was infinitely weightier than the physical darkness pressing in all around them.

Regardless of geography, by being full-fledged members of Antichrist's kingdom, they all felt it seeping into their souls like an overpowering evil. This judgment was the exact opposite of the fourth bowl, that exposed them all to the blistering sun. Now it was as if the sun had been completely extinguished. For how long, no one knew.

This sudden, seismic shift in the atmosphere had completely thrown them off. Everyone was forced to either sit or lay down in the pitch blackness. No one dared walk anywhere, let alone ride bicycles or drive vehicles.

Most were too afraid to even turn on flashlights. Just feeling the darkness pressing in on them was already terrifying enough. If something was lurking out there, they didn't want to see it coming for them.

They covered themselves with blankets, hoping to hide from the One who had sent the darkness. But instead of being comforted, they felt more terrified as the seconds passed.

Combined, the fourth and fifth bowl judgments offered them a foretaste of the fiery torment and the outer blackness of hell. The Bible described hell as an eternal lake of fire, and as an outer darkness.

In the fourth bowl judgment, they were scorched by the sun. Hell was often described as a fiery torment. Jesus described it as "the eternal fire prepared for the devil and his angels."

In that light, the scorching heat everyone felt from the fourth judgment, only to be plunged into darkness, gave them a foretaste of what hell would be like for them, even if they didn't know it yet.

God is light and in Him no darkness is found. But He did show up as darkness whenever He executed His judgments during the most heinous atrocities perpetrated by sinful humanity.

One instance of Yahweh showing up as darkness, was when Moses confronted Pharaoh, demanding that he let Yahweh's people go. When Pharaoh refused again, Yahweh sent the ninth plague to Egypt.

In Exodus 10:21-23, "The LORD said to Moses, 'Stretch out your hand toward heaven, that there may be darkness over the land of Egypt, darkness *which* may even be felt.' So Moses stretched out his hand toward heaven, and there was thick darkness in all the land of Egypt three days. They did not see one another; nor did anyone rise from his place for three days. But all the children of Israel had light in their dwellings."

The next time Yahweh showed up as darkness was when His Son was crucified. As it was recorded in Mark 15, for three hours, when the sun was at its zenith, a suffocating darkness fell over Jerusalem. So much so that no one spoke during those three hours. Not even Christ Himself.

Messiah spoke before the darkness appeared and after it was lifted, but not during. He couldn't speak, because that was when His Father laid the full fierceness of His wrath on His Son, as punishment for the sins for all who would believe in Him.

The condemning weight of Yahweh's judgment was so terrifying, the first words Christ spoke after the darkness was lifted were, "My God, my God, why have You forsaken Me?"

This was the first and only time that Christ had ever addressed His Father as "God", instead of as "Father".

Just like Pharaoh's regime was founded on a deep rebellion against the Most High God, the same could be said about this global regime being led by the Antichrist and False Prophet of the Bible.

Since darkness was a symbol of sin and judgment, Yahweh once again sent that very same darkness "to be felt" to impact all who were part of Antichrist's kingdom.

It was so terrifying that it rendered everyone spitless. They couldn't see two inches in front of their faces. It was painfully clear to them at this point that the God of Israel really was the one true God.

The proof was, when the fourth angel poured out his bowl on the sun, and the sun was allowed to scorch people with fire, *they cursed the name of God, who had control over these plagues*, but they refused to repent and glorify him.

Now that the fifth bowl judgment had been poured out on them, they gnawed their tongues in agony and once again *cursed the God of heaven because of their pains and their sores*, but they refused to repent of what they had done.

Nothing had changed in that regard, except that they were tired of hearing that Israel's God was limited in His power.

The whole world was slowly coming to grips with the fact that their God was the most powerful, Omnipotent, in fact.

With everything that kept happening to them, how could they possibly believe otherwise? He had proven to humanity time and again that He was the Creator of Heaven and earth, and everything in them…

What they didn't know was the reason Yahweh had sent the seven trumpet and seven seal judgments, in the first place, was to bring them to repentance. The first five bowl judgments were also sent for that very same reason.

Up until now, it was their unwillingness to repent. Now they sensed deep down in their spirit that they couldn't repent.

They would rather sever their tongues with their own teeth, than to acknowledge their sin and embrace the only One who could save them out of it all. Their refusal to repent demonstrated the total depravity of their hearts and souls. They were now reaping the anguish they had sown in rebellion.

With total darkness enveloping them, just when they couldn't feel any more terrified, when they felt incredibly alone and helpless, begging to be comforted, every mark taker on the planet—religious or secular—heard it loud and unmistakably clear, "If anyone worships the beast and his image and receives a mark on his forehead or upon his hand, they, too, will drink the wine of God's fury, which has been poured full strength into the cup of his wrath.

"'They will be tormented with burning sulfur in the presence of the holy angels and of the Lamb. And the smoke of their torment will rise for ever and ever. There will be no rest day or night for those who worship the beast and its image, or for anyone who receives the mark of its name.'"

They all heard the soul-condemning message, only it wasn't the voice of Yahweh's third angelic messenger this time. Their aerial ministries had concluded long ago.

This was infinitely worse. It erupted in their hearts, minds, and souls, like volcanic lava exploding in their chests, with nothing to drown it out—no phones, no TVs, no light, no one, nothing.

Just like it had pleased Yahweh to crush His Son, who became a sin offering for all who would believe in Him, that's precisely how all mark takers felt now—completely crushed in their spirits.

Dreadfully alone with their thoughts, their sin, and their guilt, with no one there to rescue them, they felt the full weight of their decision to take the mark of the Beast.

It was so evilly intense, it literally felt like Satan had taken up residence in their hearts and minds. None of them had ever experienced a feeling quite like it. Fear coiled its ugly hand around their throats.

The worse part was that they couldn't switch sides now. Their decision to take the mark of the Beast was an eternal one...

WHEN YAHWEH SENT DARKNESS to descend upon Egypt, He made a clear distinction between the Egyptians and the Jews. One group was being protected; the other group was experiencing the Most High's judgment upon them.

Exodus 10:23 made it crystal clear that when Egypt was plunged into darkness, they did not see one another; nor did anyone rise from his place for three days. But all the children of Israel had light in their dwellings...

The same was true now, not only for the remnant, but for all of God's children. Not a single solar panel being used by any of His children anywhere on the planet was damaged or destroyed. They all had full power and plenty of clean water to drink.

It was as if their Father in Heaven had performed another Passover miracle for them. Only this time it was a power Passover.

And for His beloved remnant, with Antichrist's Kingdom now steeped in darkness, the light of the Lord led the way, lighting a pathway south of Jerusalem for them to travel safely on, among the chaos.

The wings carrying the remnant to safety wasn't the United States of America, nor the Israeli government, but Yahweh Himself. They were resting under the shadow of the Almighty, and nothing or no one could touch them, not even the Antichrist and the False Prophet.

Among this protected massive sized group, heading south, were Seth and Naveh Shapiro...

*The sixth angel poured out his bowl
on the great river Euphrates,
and its water was dried up
to prepare the way for the kings from the East.*

*Then I saw three impure spirits that looked like
frogs; they came out of the mouth of the dragon,
out of the mouth of the beast and out of the mouth of
the false prophet.*

*They are demonic spirits that perform signs,
and they go out to the kings of the whole world,
to gather them for the battle on the great day of God
Almighty. "Look, I come like a thief!
Blessed is the one who stays awake and remains
clothed, so as not to go naked and be shamefully
exposed."*

*Then they gathered the kings together to the place that
in Hebrew is called Armageddon. (Revelation 16:12-15).*

Epilogue

When will power be restored to Planet Earth?
Now that Yahweh's remnant is heading South, where will they settle?
Will Seth's Shapiro's rabbi friends, Yosef and Tobias repent of their way and trust in Yahweh, through Yeshua?
What will become of this rogue faction of seculars? Will they get their chance to take out Salvador Romanero and the Pope?
Who will represent the 200,000,000 person military that will cross the Tigris and Euphrates Rivers for the Battle of Armageddon?
How many believers will enter into Yeshua's Millennial Kingdom?

Find answers to these questions and so much more as you continue in this prophetic series...

Thanks for taking the time to read the ninth installment of the CHAOS series. I would be most grateful if you shared your thoughts on Amazon. Even a short review would be appreciated. May God continue to bless and keep you.

Once completed, there will be 10 installments...

To contact author for book signings, speaking engagements,
or for bulk discounts, email @ patrick12272003@gmail.com.

PATRICK HIGGINS
About the author

Patrick Higgins is an Amazon bestseller and award-winning author of the end times prophetic series, *Chaos in The Blink of an Eye*. The "CHAOS" in our world is well documented in this series, which won the Radiqx Press Spirit-Filled Fiction Award of Excellence, after the first installment was published.

The latest recognition for the CHAOS series was winning the 2024 International Impact Book Award (Best Fiction - Christian Fiction).

To date, more than 15,000 positive ratings/reviews have been posted on Amazon and Goodreads, on the first 9 installments...and counting!

Once completed, there will be 10 installments. Look for the final installment to be released in 2025.

He also wrote *I Never Knew You,* winner of the 2021 Readers' Favorite Gold Medal in Christian fiction, 2021 Independent Author Network (IAN) book of the year winner in Christian fiction, and Finalist in both the 2022 American Best Book Awards, and the 2021 International Book Awards, *The Unannounced Christmas Visitor,* which won both the International Publishers Awards (IPA) and the 2018 Readers' Favorite Gold Medal Awards in Christian fiction, *The Pelican Trees,* and *Coffee In Manila.*

While the stories he writes all have different themes and take place in different settings, the one thread that links them all together is his heart for Jesus and his yearning for the lost. With that in mind, it is his wish that the message his stories convey will greatly impact each reader, by challenging you not only to contemplate life on this side of the grave, but on the other side as well.

After all, each of us will spend eternity at one of two places, based solely upon a single decision which must be made on this side of the grave. That decision will be made crystal clear to each reader of his books.

Higgins is currently writing many other books, both fiction and non-fiction, including a sequel to *Coffee in Manila,* which will shine a bright, sobering light on the diabolical human trafficking industry.

Thanks for taking the time to read the eighth installment of the CHAOS series. I would be most grateful if you shared your thoughts about this story on Amazon. Even a short review would be appreciated. God bless and keep you always.

To order more paperback copies at discounted prices:
www.patrickhigginsbooks.com
To contact author: patrick12272003@gmail.com
Like on Facebook: https://www.facebook.com/patrick12272003
X: https://x.com/patrick12272003
Instagram: https://www.instagram.com/patrick12272003
Amazon: https://www.amazon.com/Patrick-Higgins/e/B005ANHSU2
Goodreads: https://www.goodreads.com/author/show/10796904.Patrick_Higgins
Looking for an editor? Contact Susan Axel Bedsaul – complete-editor@outlook.com

Made in the USA
Columbia, SC
28 April 2025